BONDED BY FRIENDSHIP AND FATE

BONDED BY FRIENDSHIP AND FATE

THE HOUSE OF WARD BOOK TWO

A.R. ABBOTT

Lost Warren Books

First paperback edition October 2025

ISBN 978-1-967520-05-3

Published by Lost Warren Books LLC.

www.arabbott.com

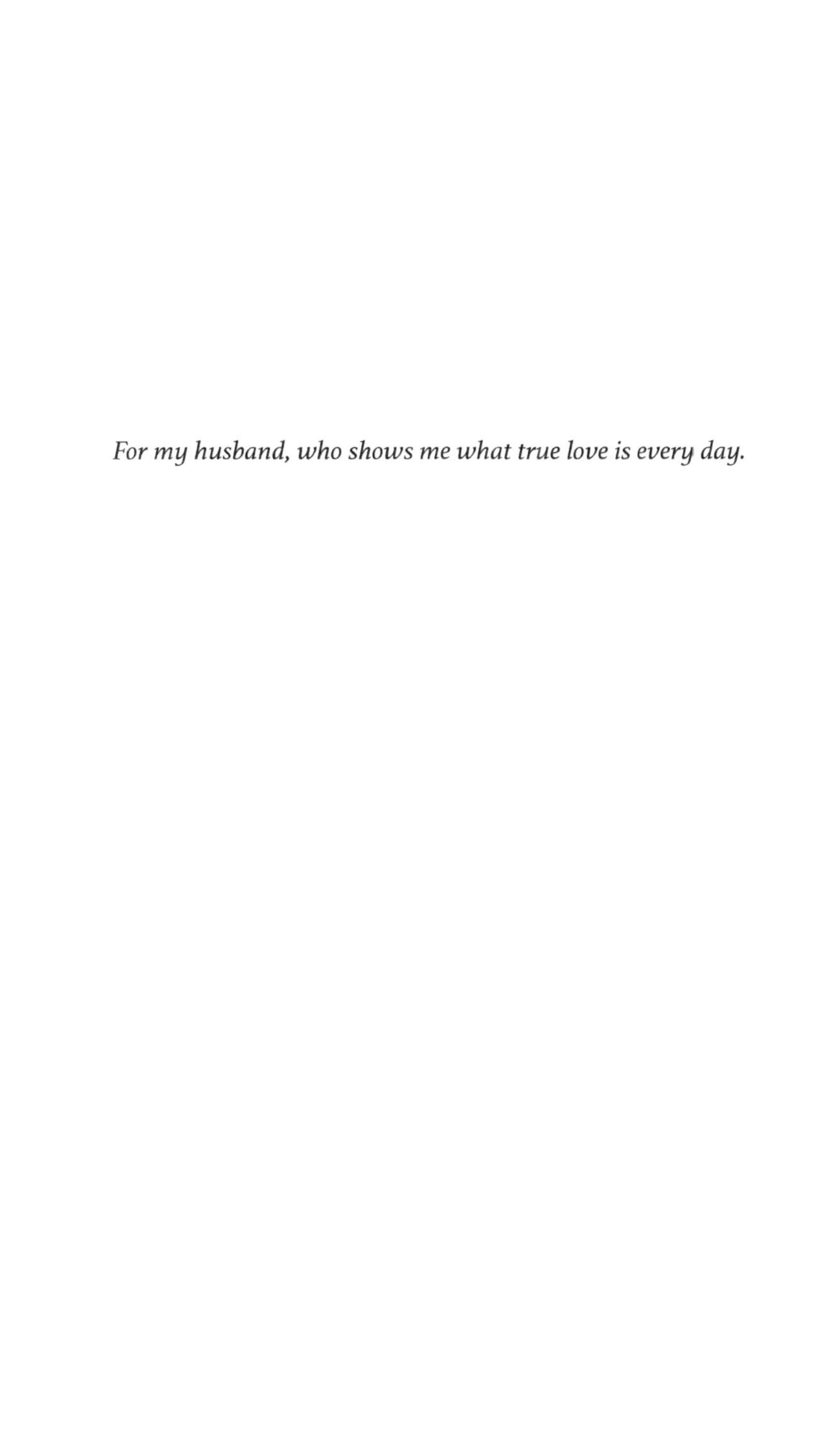

For my husband, who shows me what true love is every day.

1

BRUCE

I walked along the sidewalk on my way to work, thinking, *My life is pretty solid.* My job paid well, I owned my apartment in the city, and I lived in Seattle, where I could comfortably walk outside even in January. My medium-weight jacket, worn over my uniform of a black shirt and black slacks, was enough to keep me warm in the wet, chilly winter weather.

I felt happy as I traveled the familiar pavement. The choices I'd made hadn't always landed me where I'd expected, but I'd always landed on my feet. I was in control of my life, and that was more than most people could say.

My apartment was several blocks from the bar where I worked, and it was nice to walk each day, regardless of the season. I appreciated that my commute didn't involve sitting in traffic. Additionally, after work, I sometimes found myself in no shape to drive. Not because I drank on the job—although I occasionally did—but because the job took a toll on me physically.

I turned the corner and caught sight of the wooden sign that advertised the bookstore directly above my place of work. It was a functioning bookshop, but also served as the main entrance for the patrons visiting the bar below. The bar itself was styled as an old-fashioned speakeasy, with a hidden passage behind a bookshelf in the shop that added to the ambiance while providing an extra layer of security.

Before I reached the heavy brass and wood of the bookshop door, I turned left down a narrow alley situated between the bookshop and a hardware store. Partway down the alley stood a heavy metal door, monitored by a security camera. The employee entrance was far less dramatic than the one used by patrons. I rapped my knuckles against the door and stepped back, tilting my head up to show my face to the camera above. After a few seconds, I heard the familiar electric buzz and pulled the door open. I stepped inside, only to be met with another door. This one featured a keypad, and I entered my code before descending the stairs.

It was a significant amount of security, but the clientele of this particular bar was very exclusive. They demanded stringent safeguards and anonymity, and the Tap House was more than happy to provide them. Each employee underwent rigorous vetting, was registered, and monitored for potential breaches of contract. I was aware of all this before I started working there, and it didn't bother me at all. I enjoyed being part of this exclusive world and was content with the job security it offered. A person could keep a job here or with an affiliated establishment for as long as they wished. It wasn't that no one was ever terminated, but it was never without cause. It was a lifelong contract, and the pay was excellent.

Employees arrived one hour before their shifts. I, however, typically showed up at least two hours early. As a shift supervisor, I hoped to one day become the general manager's assistant. I had put in the years and was reasonably sure that the position would be mine when the current assistant moved on. Despite the promise of lifelong employment, at thirty-three, I was one of the longest-serving workers at the bar.

While the job security and pay were excellent, most employees were in it for the connections they made. They did their best to become a favorite of one of the patrons, hoping to be hired away or to become friendly—or more than friendly—with someone in a position of power. However, that was not my aim. I was just as captivated by the customers as the other employees, but I liked my life just the way it was.

I walked through the staff hallway, passing a locker room, several storage rooms, a sizable staff dining area, and the kitchens. For a bar, the Tap House boasted one of the best kitchens in the entire city. The chefs and kitchen staff would arrive shortly to start preparing meals ahead of opening. However, the food wasn't for the diners. When the workers arrived, they were each served a Michelin-quality meal tailored to their preferences, which had been well arranged in advance. It was one of the perks—and requirements—of the job.

I continued to my office at the back, passing the kitchens and the in-house clinic, but just before the security office, which occupied a sizable portion of the establishment and operated twenty-four hours a day. I stared at the heavy security doors at the end of the hall, thankful that I'd rarely had to interact with those who worked behind them. I had never given security a reason to mistrust me, and I never would. The individuals who worked at the end of the hall were intimidating, and the consequences for breaching the contract were ... severe.

The offices for the shift supervisors were small but pleasant. I shared the space with three other people, but we all worked different shifts. My replacement would arrive about an hour before I was scheduled to be on the floor. I worked most days; however, like all the other employees, I only worked the floor two times a month. This was non-negotiable, meaning we maintained a large staff at all times. Given the turnover, recruiting, vetting, and hiring were a full-time job that I was thankful the security team mostly handled. My role was to train the new staff and ensure the floor ran smoothly during my shift. And I was very good at my job.

I stowed my backpack and took a seat at my desk. I scanned the documents that had been left out from the previous evening. I usually worked the first shift. The Tap House was open from sundown to sunup. In the middle of winter, it made for long work hours. We added an extra shift on those nights. The evening before, I had left around midnight, and by the looks of it, the rest of the night had gone without incident. That was a good night. It wasn't unusual to have an emergency or two over the course of an evening. It was rarely the employees who caused the trouble; it was the clients. They were powerful, wealthy, and accustomed to getting their way, especially from those who served their needs.

As I reviewed the schedules for the evening, I noticed that I had been removed from the floor for the night. I double-checked and found my name on the roster for an earlier shift. This was more than unusual, and it raised immediate alarm bells. I was now scheduled to be on the floor at nine, which would effectively end my shift three hours early and require another shift supervisor to cover.

And sure enough, Tamera was set to arrive by eight. *What the hell,* I thought.

I rose from my desk and went in search of the only other person in the building, besides security, the general manager's assistant, Michael. He worked in the GM's office above the staff rooms. I walked back down the hall toward the exit and took a right up a separate flight of stairs to reach the office. I rapped twice and waited for Michael to answer, knowing he would be in. The GM, Anthony, wouldn't arrive until after the patrons started showing up, but he liked his assistant to get there before all the other staff.

I didn't have to wait long. Michael opened the door and let me in. The office was large and richly appointed, mirroring the turn-of-the-century style of the main floor, full of plush velvets and shiny brass fixtures.

Michael glanced at my expression. "Bruce, I take it you saw the schedule," he said. It was not a question.

Alarm bells rang louder. This better not be what I feared. "Yeah, are you giving me half the night off?" I asked, trying to lighten the mood in hopes that my gut feeling was wrong. I didn't want to start with accusations, not if this was something different.

Michael grimaced. "I wish that were the case. But no. A private party has booked you," he said.

"Private party," I repeated. "Anyone I've served before?"

"Yeah. It's Margaux."

I swore under my breath, my body feeling numb as the words sank in. This was bad. This was bad for a whole host of reasons. "I know you are aware that I have requested not to serve her table anymore," I said. It wasn't a question.

"Yes, I know. Anthony and I discussed it at some length. However, calls were made, and threats were issued. Your request was denied."

"That doesn't happen. It's part of our contract, the one we never violate, that employees can refuse to serve any table at our discretion. It's a promise that was made to me and that I make to every employee I supervise. It's one of the ways we help keep everyone safe and happy under very stressful circumstances," I said, knowing full well that Michael was not the one who made this decision. Still, I was unable to roll over, especially on something this important.

Michael sighed and leaned against the door jam. "I'm aware. Believe me, I cited the contract to both Anthony and the Council member who called on Margaux's behalf."

Oh shit, I thought. She had indeed called in a big favor. I took a deep breath. This wasn't Michael's fault. It was useless and unfair to take it out on him. I would have words with Anthony when he arrived. Anthony had his connections and was the only one I could appeal to at this point. I still had hours before I was expected to be on the floor. I would try to resolve this issue before then. If I couldn't ... I wasn't sure what I would do.

I made my way back to my office, greeting the kitchen staff as they arrived. I attempted to go through my afternoon as usual, but I couldn't concentrate. I had served Margaux many times before, and the last time had been one too many.

I always did my best to be professional, to please the client while also maintaining an appropriate distance. Margaux had different ideas. She wanted me. She knew that many people who worked at the bar longed for a different life. Any other staff member might have been more than happy to play along with her advances in hopes of moving up in the world—and many had—but not me. I loathed her. I couldn't stand her overly flirtatious nature, her entitled attitude, or her inability to keep her hands to herself. My skin crawled at the thought of having to serve her again and endure all that it entailed.

I shook my head, trying to clear my thoughts, and glanced at the clock. While I had been brooding, time had sped up. It was almost time to open. I slipped into a suit jacket I kept in the office and went to check on everyone.

The aroma of rare spices, rich sauces, and perfectly seared meats wafted from the kitchen and staff dining room. I noticed that most of the employees had already finished dinner and were in the lounge area at the back. Several long sofas, a big-screen TV, and overstuffed chairs created a comfortable place to wait until they were called. I stopped by to talk with a few of the newer hires to ensure they were ready for opening, and then went to find that evening's hostess.

Jessica was already on the main floor, talking to Michael. They both looked up, halting their conversation as I approached. "Everything okay out here?" I asked. I knew I sounded a bit hostile, but I couldn't help it. I was on edge, and they both knew why.

"Yup, everything's fine. We're ready to open. Is everyone in the back of the house ready?" Jessica asked.

"They are," I replied more softly, offering her a smile that I hoped would lessen the impact of my rudeness.

Jessica gave Michael a look that I couldn't interpret, then turned toward the door that opened to the passage from the bookshop above. She pressed a button on the wall to signal to the employee in the bookshop that we were open for business.

I turned toward Michael, feeling resentment at the look of pity I saw there. I composed my features and returned the stare. "Will Anthony be in soon?" I asked.

Michael nodded. "I expect him within the hour."

I nodded in return. There was nothing more to say. I left the floor and returned to the employee lounge. Leaning against the wall, I observed the staff. People sat alone or in small groups. Most chatted comfortably, but some of the newer employees tapped a leg or fiddled with something nervously. Even the newbies had worked at least a few shifts by this point, and I wasn't worried about them. They would do fine tonight, I thought.

Jessica hurried past the doorway, carrying the first stack of menus. They were printed daily and would be reprinted throughout the night to reflect the remaining availability after clients made their selections. I waited with the others for Jessica to return.

She was back moments later, and I met her at the doorway to take an order. After receiving it, I turned and spotted the person I was looking for. "Becca," I said, loud enough to get her attention. "You're up. Table three, and take Devon as backup."

The pair nodded and got to work. I maintained my post for the next thirty minutes. As the bar started to fill up, another hostess joined Jessica, and I was tapping more and more staff to work the floor. However, as I worked, I shifted closer and closer to the hall until I realized that instead of watching for orders to come in from the front of the house, I was staring at the employee entrance, waiting for Anthony instead.

When the next shift began arriving for dinner, I grew agitated. It was forty-five minutes after opening, and Anthony was still a no-show. My stomach twisted. Maybe he wouldn't show up in time. Perhaps he was avoiding me on purpose.

I glanced at my watch. Margaux was due in thirty

minutes. My palms began to sweat, and I wiped them on my trousers. It wasn't like me to get rattled, but there was something extraordinarily dangerous about that woman, and I wanted to keep as far away from her as I could. Serving her this evening would make that impossible, however. I rechecked my watch. I knew I had to prepare. Sighing, I turned and went to the dining room for my assigned meal.

I was certain the food was delicious. I had eaten this exact dish of spiced lamb tagine several times before and remembered enjoying it. I barely noticed the taste as I forked it into my mouth. It was an exercise in efficiency, rather than enjoyment, given my current state of mind. I was surprised that I could get it down at all, considering how tight my stomach felt, but this was part of the job, and skipping dinner was a bad idea, especially on a night like tonight.

I finished my meal and drank a glass of water just minutes before my booking. I returned my plate and hurried out into the hall, intending to go up to Anthony's office, but Michael stood at the bottom of the stairs talking to Tamara, the other shift supervisor. I raised my eyebrows in question, but Michael just shook his head.

I swore out loud this time and took a deep breath. I had no choice now. I turned my head and looked out over the main floor just in time to see Margaux enter the bar. She wore a tight, calf-length red dress that probably cost more than all the clothes I owned put together. A man and a woman accompanied her, both dressed just as expensively, but it was Margaux who drew everyone's attention. Not only her clothing but her very attitude demanded that every eye be on her. I instinctively took a step back, but not before Margaux's eyes flicked to mine. Her face transformed as she pinned me in place with her gaze. She smiled in a way that made the hair on my body stand on end, and then she turned and followed the hostess to her regular table.

2

BRUCE

I swallowed the lump in my throat. Glancing down at my hands, I noticed they were clenched into fists, and I shook them out. Looking back up, I saw Jessica coming toward me.

"You ready?" she asked, her voice holding a note of regret.

I nodded and began to head for the main floor, but Jessica stopped me with a hand on my shoulder. "You need to choose someone else to accompany you to serve the other two," she said, and now there was a clear apology in her tone. "Margaux has requested that you select someone your-self for her guests."

I thought this couldn't possibly get worse. I was wrong. Not only would I be humiliated this evening, but I also had to choose one of my employees to witness my humiliation up close.

I turned my back to the floor and stepped forward to survey the prospects. I skipped over the newbies; there was no need to subject them to a gross violation of protocol. I didn't want to scare them into running off, nor did I want to give them the wrong impression of this place. Finally, I spotted Chelsea sitting alone with a book. She was a good choice—professional and discreet.

"Chelsea," I said, and it came out as a bark. Her head whipped up, and she met my eyes and nodded. She dropped the book on the table and straightened her uniform as she approached.

I cleared my throat and made an effort to soften my tone. "I need you to come with me. We have a three-top," I said, lowering my voice even further. "Margaux and two guests. I'll serve Margaux, and you will serve the other two."

Her eyes widened slightly at the mention of Margaux. She knew who she was and that the woman had previously acted inappropriately toward me.

"You want me to take Margaux?" she asked, and I loved that she would offer. She was good people.

"I've been requested. But thank you."

"Ew. Can't the woman take a hint?"

"Apparently not. You ready, or do you need a minute?" I asked her.

"Let's get this over with, shall we?" she said.

I nodded and led the way out to the main floor. Chelsea was right; this was our job, and I needed to get it over with and put it behind me. How bad could it be? Margaux knew that I was not interested and that I wasn't looking for other employment opportunities. I had made that very clear the last time she was here.

Maybe it was time for me to stop serving customers and focus on my supervisory role. I liked the extra cash I made from serving, both from the bar and in tips, but it wasn't worth it if my wishes and boundaries were not respected. It was too bad that this would be the last table I served. I liked my job, both on and off the floor, and it was a crime that Margaux might be my last.

I didn't look up until we stood in front of the table. Margaux and the two others stopped their conversation as Jessica addressed the group. Jessica introduced Chelsea and me before turning to attend to other customers. She offered me a tight smile as she passed, and I had to keep myself from grimacing in return.

Chelsea held the couple's attention as I stepped close to Margaux.

"Bruce, it's so lovely to see you again," Margaux said. Her voice was pitched low in what I imagined was meant to be a seductive tone, but it made my skin crawl. She leaned back, stretching her arm out across the back of the booth, pulling the fabric tightly over her ample chest. I held her gaze. She smiled and patted the velvet fabric next to her. "Come. Sit. I won't say that I don't bite; we both know that would be a lie." She chuckled at her own joke.

I took a deep breath and then did as she asked, sitting beside her while leaving as large a gap between us as I could manage. As soon as I sat down, however, she scooted closer, let her arm drape across my shoulders, and began stroking my neck.

I made no effort to move away. I knew better. It was best to get on with it and leave as soon as possible. This was not how the job was meant to be. Even when clients were rude and ignored me, I could still feel good about what I did and where I worked. This crossed the line by a long shot.

"It was surprisingly hard to book you for tonight," she whispered in my ear, her fingers playing with the hair at the nape of my neck. "They told me you were busy for weeks. Good thing I knew who to call to free up your schedule."

The rage building in my chest was tempered a bit by the

knowledge that my employer had tried to shield me from this. It was a small comfort, but a comfort nonetheless. "I expected you might prefer someone else, given our last conversation," I said with as much politeness as I could manage.

"I still can't believe you would turn me down. I mean, isn't that why you work here?" she asked, waving her free hand to indicate the bar. "I thought you all wanted to be whisked away from here and onto bigger and better things."

"I like my job," I said flatly. "I would prefer to stay here. Thank you all the same."

"Hmm." She chewed on her lower lip and looked me over. "You're upset, aren't you?" She lowered her eyes in mock sorrow. "I don't like being told I can't have something I want." Now, her voice was hard, and the threat was implicit. "You think I took something that belonged to you, but if he had truly belonged to you, he wouldn't have come with me."

I flinched at the mention of what she had taken. She knew exactly what she was doing. Noticing my reaction, she smiled, and the display made my insides twist.

"Jake misses you, you know? You could join me, join us, and we could all be happy together."

I remained still, unwilling to give her the satisfaction. "I'm content where I am."

There was nothing she could do if I continued to refuse her. She had hoped that by seducing my boyfriend, I would be tempted, but there wasn't much more she could take away.

She dropped her smile then and reached for my arm with her free hand. My sleeve was already rolled to my elbow, exposing the one blank, untattooed patch where I allowed clients to feed. I gritted my teeth and waited. I was ready for her to make it painful. I was prepared for some sort of foul play. She still managed to shock me, however. She grabbed the back of my neck faster than I could blink and sank her long fangs into the artery in my throat.

I struggled against her strong grasp. I was trained better, but I couldn't help it. What she was doing was such a shock. Quickly, though, I managed to control my muscles and remain still as she pulled at my throat. I couldn't slow my rapid heartbeat or my fast breathing, and I could tell it excited her. She held me immobile with one hand on the back of my neck and the other clamped down on my thigh. Fighting would only cause more damage, and I might not survive if someone didn't get to me in time.

I stared straight ahead as she drank. I tried to distract myself by glancing around the bar. The other tables were mostly full. The staff I oversaw were feeding some customers directly from the wrist, while others delivered glasses full of ruby red blood. Several employees glanced in my direction and quickly looked away. Even though this was in no way my fault, I was embarrassed that they saw me in this position. It was not how things were done here. This was not the kind of place that allowed this type of feeding. It was too intimate and too dangerous. No sooner had the thought entered my mind than my vision began to go slightly blurry. I felt dizzy. She was taking too much. I looked around for my backup but remembered too late that in my haste to get this over with, I hadn't tapped anyone to watch the table.

I had a terrible thought then. What if she killed me? And what if Chelsea were similarly in danger? A danger I had put her in, with no one to help. The bar had bouncers; they were vampires who helped keep the rowdy customers in order, but none of them were in sight.

Panic rose in me, dumping adrenaline into my system,

which helped clear my mind, but I knew I was in trouble. It was then that I spotted Anthony making his way through the crowded room. His expression was calm, but he was moving quickly, and I had never been so glad to see him.

"Margaux," Anthony said. His tone was cordial, but his volume was louder than necessary to get her attention. That, in itself, was a measure of his alarm. "Your time with Bruce is up. If you'd like, I can bring someone else to the table."

She withdrew her fangs and leaned back. I attempted to raise my hand to apply pressure to the wound, but my arms were heavy, and my movements were uncoordinated. My hand slipped off the slick skin of my neck, where blood continued to pump. Before I could try again, Anthony was at my side, lifting me out of the booth. I felt Anthony's fingers pressed against my wound, and I breathed a sigh of relief. Anthony would have scored his skin to allow his blood to flow directly into the punctures, closing them with his vampire blood.

"No, thank you, Anthony. I ate before I came," Margaux purred. "I just missed Bruce."

I shuddered, and Anthony tightened his grip around my waist. "I'll just take him to the back then," Anthony said.

"Or you could leave him with me, and I could take care of him."

"No exsanguinations or transformations on the premises. You know the rules," Anthony said. "And so does your sire. He's been reminded. Recently."

I could hardly focus on the conversation. I might not have been bleeding anymore, but I still wasn't out of the woods. I closed my eyes and allowed Anthony to take more of my weight.

It was then that I must have passed out because the next

thing I knew, I was lying on a bed in the clinic just steps from my office.

I cracked my eyes open to the glare of the all-white room. A monitor beeped somewhere behind me and sounded surprisingly steady. I supposed that was a good sign. Lifting my head, I looked around. Troy, the nurse on staff, sat in the corner of the private room reading a magazine. I cleared my throat. "Is Chelsea okay?" I asked. I hadn't been able to assess what had occurred at the other end of the table after Anthony had stepped in. I needed to know that Margaux's guests hadn't punished her for my stubbornness.

"She's just fine," Troy said, setting his magazine aside and rising to check the monitors. "Her feeding was textbook, while yours ..." he trailed off.

"Who am I getting?" I asked, raising the arm with the IV that supplied the transfusion I was receiving.

Troy glanced up from the machine he was examining and raised an eyebrow. "Your own. We had several units left."

I nodded. We each donated for use at the bar, but sometimes, it came in handy for situations like the one I was in. Not that there were many situations like mine. But the blood was useful when a client took a bit too much. I let out a sigh and leaned back on the bed.

This would definitely be my last time on the floor. I still couldn't believe she had gone for my throat, let alone taken so much blood that it put me in danger. She was as spoiled and entitled as any other vampire, but she also hailed from one of the major Houses. Someone of her station was supposed to behave better. Her sire sat on the Council, for God's sake. It would look bad for one of his to flaunt the law so blatantly. I didn't doubt that she was capable of killing, but I never suspected she would try it in public or with so many witnesses. I shivered when I realized how close I'd come.

A soft knock sounded at the door, interrupting my thoughts. Troy answered it, revealing Anthony standing in the hall. His expression was softer than I had ever seen, and I wasn't sure if it was due to what had happened or what he was about to say. Either way, it made me uncomfortable to see him like that. Troy stepped out into the hall to give us some privacy, and Anthony shut the door behind him and moved closer to my side.

"That should never have happened, and I'm sorry," he began. "I spoke to Margaux, and she assured me that it won't happen again. I also wrote to her sire for good measure. It will probably piss her off, but I don't care at this point." He let out a breath and ran a hand through his usually perfect reddish hair. He was upset, and I was glad to see it, but Anthony was the only protection I had, and I didn't like the idea that he was overwhelmed or outmaneuvered in any way.

"I'm giving you the whole week off. Go home. Get some rest. But watch your back. I've rarely seen someone as obsessed with a human as Margaux seems to be with you." He took another breath and let it out, but before continuing, he dropped his gaze and looked down at the sheets instead of meeting my eyes. "Have you considered taking her up on her offer and joining her House? I mean, I know a lot of humans would literally kill for a chance at what she's offering you."

We had had a version of this conversation before, and my response had always been the same. I was content with my life as it was. I didn't want to become a vampire or join the staff of one of the Houses, beholden to the vampires residing there. Each human signed a contract that granted any House member the right to feed on them whenever and however they pleased. I didn't want that. I wanted to have the option to choose. I enjoyed being part of this secret world. I liked knowing what few humans knew, but I wanted my independence.

"I can't. It may not make sense, especially to a vampire, but I just can't. No offense."

"None taken," Anthony said, raising both hands to wave off the comment.

"I think it might be best if I stick to the back of the house from now on. If I'm off the menu, maybe Margaux will get bored and lose interest," I said with a sigh.

Anthony sucked air between his teeth. "About that. I was able to get assurances that Margaux would act appropriately from now on, but after I hung up with her sire, I received a call from Mr. Emmerson."

Oh shit, I thought. Margaux had her sire go directly to the owner of the Tap House, someone I had never met in all my time there. The vampire who held my contract. Was she trying to get me fired? I wasn't sure where this was leading, but I knew it was nowhere good.

"I don't know what strings were pulled," Anthony continued. "But he instructed me to place you on reserve for her indefinitely."

I stared at Anthony as the words sank in.

She had done it. She had finally achieved what she wanted.

I was hers, at least in part.

3

SARA

My mom fell asleep in the front passenger seat about fifteen minutes before we arrived back in our valley. I knew this because her head—with its neat black and grey bun—which had been nodding for several minutes, finally fell forward, her chin resting against her chest. She had been my rock throughout the day, throughout my life, if I was being honest, and I wasn't surprised she was worn out.

It wasn't my first funeral. My father died when I was young, and both my grandparents passed away in the last ten years. I thought I had experienced the full range of emotions one feels at these events, but I had no idea how difficult it would be to attend this particular funeral. The funeral of my best friend was something else entirely.

The sadness and loss were expected. I mourned alongside the others for all that was taken away and for all that could have been. I nodded and agreed that she was so young and that something like a hit-and-run shouldn't rob someone of the bright future they had barely begun to live. All of this was true.

But it was her mom and her little brother who broke my heart.

I watched the teary-eyed woman I had known since high school lay her daughter to rest, and it shattered me. I wanted to go to her. I wanted to offer words that could make it better. I wanted to ease her pain. But I couldn't. I was as helpless as she was to change what had happened, and paralyzed to do anything but stand and witness her anguish.

All during the ceremony and the interring of the cremains, she sat in her seat weeping quietly, only rising to speak about her daughter and all she had meant to the world. How she got through the speech, I will never know. She spoke beautifully about the short life she had brought into the world and witnessed grow into adulthood. She even managed a smile or two in recounting that life.

Sitting beside her was her younger son, Oliver. When I first met him, he was just a little kid. At this point, he had to be around seventeen or eighteen. He sat quietly next to his mother, offering silent support. His eyes were swollen, but he didn't cry—not until his mother began to speak. Then the tears rolled down his face, his expression remaining one of blank, shocked silence.

And I was there to witness it all.

I had my mother and aunt beside me, as well as Silas. Whether he was there as my friend or my boyfriend was hard to say, but he was there to support me. As if he knew that the most challenging part of the day would be standing there, watching it all unfold, and not saying a word, not telling the truth about what happened to my best friend.

Silas stayed until the end and walked me out to the car. He drove himself, however. My family liked him okay, but it wouldn't have been appropriate for him to ride with us. My aunt would have thrown a fit, and my mother would have backed her up. Neither of them was happy about the time we spent together or the obvious attraction between us. But given all that had happened, they kept their mouths shut. In the end, he squeezed my hand and told me he would stop by later. His voice was low enough that my family couldn't hear, and for that, I was grateful.

I glanced over at my aunt, who was driving the car. She sat ramrod straight, as always, staring straight ahead. While my mother was my rock, my Aunt Lucia was the stone on which the entire family rested.

She came today to offer her respects, but she also provided me with something else I needed. She didn't cry or show any emotion throughout the event. She nodded at me once or twice, approving of my silence and acknowledging my struggle. It was she who helped keep me in check. My mom was my source of comfort and solace, but my aunt was there to shore me up, prevent me from making mistakes, and strengthen my resolve.

And I played my part.

When I climbed into the back of my aunt's old Subaru, I practically collapsed. I was emotionally exhausted and wanted nothing more than to crawl into bed and sleep for a week. However, there was always more to do, and my aunt and mom had been leaving increasingly more of it for me. I wished they would return to work full-time at our family's shop, but so far, I had spent most days alone. I understood their reasons, but it still made me sad.

The sun was beginning to set as we pulled into the parking lot just outside the shop, rather than the house. That in itself was a statement from my aunt. They would not be coming into my home. As the car came to a stop, though, I couldn't help but ask, "Would you two like to come in? I could make some tea. You could say hi?"

My mother raised her head and looked at her sister, blinking away sleep.

My aunt sniffed. "Maybe another night," she said. "I'll be over tomorrow afternoon with the new batch of oils. I'll see you then."

My mom looked down but didn't add anything further.

"Okay," I said and climbed out of the car.

I may have shut the door a bit harder than necessary before turning toward the attached house. It was more of a lodge, really. I purchased it less than six months earlier and was in the process of renovating it to serve as both a home and a shop for our family business. Once, it had been a B&B for skiers, but it hadn't lasted long. The people who built it weren't locals, and the townspeople didn't take too kindly to outsiders in the valley. It was only a few years before the property sat empty and began to decline. But the abandoned hotel was perfect for our needs.

The house portion of the property was huge. It was constructed from massive timbers and featured a basic A-frame design for the central space. There were tall ceilings and beautiful glass windows that overlooked the surrounding forest and mountains. It had a large kitchen with an industrial stove and a massive fridge. There were four bedrooms on the upper floor, all with attached bathrooms, and Silas was remodeling the walk-out basement with even more rooms. The living room was spacious, featuring a stone fireplace and several smaller seating areas. It was really too much house, but it was warm and inviting and had quickly become home.

I paused on the front porch before going inside and glanced down at my attire. I was dressed all in black, which wasn't unusual, but I was also wearing a dress—something I typically wouldn't wear. I looked up through the trees at the dimming sky. I needed to change quickly.

I grabbed the front door handle and went inside. It was quiet. My roommates wouldn't be upstairs for at least another thirty minutes. I suspected Kate was already awake but still in her room. I didn't drop my purse; instead, I took it with me to my bedroom. I quickly stripped off the offending dress, hose, and shoes, tossing the whole mess into the back of my closet. I pulled on some old sweats and a T-shirt, along with fuzzy socks. Then, I rifled through my purse and pulled out anything related to the funeral. There was a folded paper program and some tissues I had used to wipe my eyes. I took them to my trash can but thought better of it and hid those, too, in a drawer.

As I worked to conceal the evidence of the event I'd attended, I realized it was probably a good thing that my mom and aunt hadn't taken me up on my offer for tea. There would have been no hiding where we had all just come from. It wasn't that Kate didn't know about the funeral —she did—but I wasn't sure she remembered what day it was scheduled for, and I didn't want to remind her. She had enough going on, enough to worry about.

I looked myself over in the mirror before heading downstairs. Kate would be up soon, and I wanted everything to seem normal. I would usually be making my dinner by now, and that is where Kate would expect to find me.

When I hit the bottom of the staircase, I glanced around the corner, down to where the stairs to the basement ended in a heavy wooden door. It was still shut tight. I had a few more minutes.

I kept myself busy preparing a simple meal for one. I found some leftovers in the fridge and heated them in a pot on the stove while I turned on the oven to warm some bread. As I waited for the food to heat, I reminded myself to calm my emotions. Kate might overlook some changes in my behavior, but she would know right away that I was trying to hide something if I didn't get my feelings under control. Nobody could read a person like Kate. It was her special gift, as my mother called it.

I heard the door creak open and shut downstairs and took a calming breath. I cleared my mind and thought of all the orders that needed to be filled in the shop next door and all the inventory I still had to log.

A moment later, a figure appeared in the doorway. I saw it was Marcus, and I let out a long breath.

"You're going to have to do better than that if you want to fool Kate," he said and flashed me a grin.

My shoulders slumped. "How did you know?" I asked.

"I have a better memory than she does, and I know what day it is," he said, heading over to the fridge and snagging something to eat. "When you didn't say anything last night, I figured you weren't going to tell her. But, you're a nervous wreck; she's going to know right away that something is up."

I shot him a dirty look. "I'm trying, okay. I just got home, and I'm still a bit flustered." I turned my attention back to my food and stirred the soup that was beginning to simmer.

"I'm just saying, if you don't want her to know what you were up to, you need to hide it better," he said and sat down at the kitchen table to break his fast. "I don't know why you would keep it from her in the first place. She's a big girl. I think she can handle it."

I scowled at him again. "You didn't say anything, did you?" I asked.

He shook his head and sipped at his meal.

"You don't get it," I said. "She would feel bad if she knew

the funeral was today, and it would only upset her that she'd forgotten. No. It's better if she doesn't remember."

"She's going to remember eventually, and when she does, isn't she going to be mad that you didn't bring it up?"

I bristled a bit at his question. He was right. She would be upset either way. "It doesn't matter," I said a little defensively. "I'll deal with it then. There was no need to tell her. It's not like she could have gone."

Just then, I heard the door downstairs open and close again. I shot Marcus a warning look and brought my finger to my lips. He shrugged and made a zipping motion over his mouth. Satisfied, I turned back to my soup.

I took one more steadying breath and relaxed my body just as Kate came into the kitchen.

"Good evening, everyone," she said cheerily.

I gave her a smile over my shoulder. "Morning," I said, and winced at the inadvertent reference.

Kate didn't seem to notice and went to the fridge to get her breakfast. Sleeping through the day meant that dinner was her first meal, but she always referred to it as breakfast, even though it took place well after most people had finished work for the day and settled in for their supper.

After shutting the fridge, Kate paused on her way to the table. I could feel her just behind me, and I stiffened without meaning to.

"Sara," Kate said, her voice gentle and soft. "Are you okay?"

I glanced at her over my shoulder again, not wanting to turn around. She stood watching me with her large brown eyes. Her long, dark hair was pulled into a ponytail, and she wore jeans and a cream-colored sweater. "I'm fine," I said, hoping she couldn't hear the lie in my voice. "It's just I've got a lot of work still to do, and I'm a bit stressed." That part wasn't a lie.

She narrowed her eyes but nodded. She walked past me to go to the table, but stopped and pivoted toward me. Faster than I could track, she moved. I felt the rush of air, and then she was there in front of me, only inches separating us. I breathed in and tried to step back, but she had me pinned between her and the stove. I wasn't afraid, only startled.

She lowered her head and shoulders until we were eye to eye, and she took a deep breath in. Then her face crumpled, and her eyes filled with blood-red tears. "Where have you been?" she asked in a small voice.

"I ... I ..." I stammered. I didn't know what to say. There was no hiding it, though.

"It was today? Wasn't it?" she asked, and her bottom lip began to tremble.

I heaved a sigh and felt my own eyes begin to fill. "Yeah, honey. It was," I said, reaching forward and pulling her into a hug. "I just got home," I said, and rubbed her back as she began to shake. "How did you know?" I asked softly.

She turned her face into my neck, where my hair rested on my shoulder. "You smell like my mom," she whispered.

She pulled back to look into my face. Sniffing, she wiped away her tears.

"So," she said with a forced smile. "How was my funeral?"

4

KATE

I looked at Sara through my haze of bloody tears. She was crying, too.

"Your funeral was very nice," she said, and swallowed some of the grief I felt rolling off of her.

"You saw my mom?" It wasn't really a question, but I wanted to hear about it.

She nodded. "Yeah. She's about how you would expect."

My eyes flooded once again, and I wiped at them with my hands, not wanting to get blood all over my sweater.

"And my brother?"

"He was holding up," she said, and placed her hand on my shoulder to offer comfort. Unfortunately, the only thing it did was amplify her emotions to the point where I couldn't shut them out. Her grief. Her pity. But also her love.

I took a shuddering breath. It made sense why she didn't tell me. I understood. I would have been a mess for days had I remembered the ceremony was today. "Thank you for going," I said, regaining some composure.

Sara scowled at me. "Of course. I couldn't *not* go. You're my best friend."

"Yeah, but it's a lot, and I'm not dead," I said.

"To your family, you are," Marcus said from behind me. "It's important for them to have this closure."

I knew he was trying to be comforting, but it made me angry.

"Why?" I asked, turning to him. "I don't understand why I can't just tell my mom what happened. I know it would be a shock, but she would get over it."

He sat up straighter then, and his handsome features took on the hard look he got when he wanted me to know he was serious. "No, Kate. It's not possible. No matter how much you miss her, it could be devastating if she were told."

I began to shake my head. "You don't—"

"No," he said more forcefully. "Think about it. If you told her, a human, you would be responsible for her. She would be monitored, and if she ever let it slip, you would be the one who would have to deal with it. I know you haven't considered this, but would you want to hold her accountable? Or stand by while an enforcer like me held her accountable?"

His words and the threat implied in them made me shudder. I knew he was a good man, and I understood he wasn't trying to hurt me, but I hated the restrictions on who I could talk to and who I couldn't. It wasn't fair. Yet, he was right; as long as the rules were in place, she would be in danger, and I couldn't live with putting her there.

Walking over to the table, I sat heavily in one of the rickety chairs. I knew I was pouting, but I didn't care. The night had gotten off on a bad foot, and there was no salvaging it at this point.

I sat in silence while Sara continued to prepare her meal, and Marcus finished the blood he was drinking. After a while, he set aside the bag and asked, "Hey, how did you sleep?" I knew he was fishing around for a neutral topic, and I appreciated the attempt.

I glanced up. He was dressed in his usual black tank top, paired with jeans for the evening. His dark hair was cropped close on the sides and longer on top, with a slight wave to it. He looked at me with kind, grey eyes, waiting for my response.

"Okay," I said with a sigh. "I woke up early," I admitted. I don't know why I told him now, with everything else still so raw. Maybe I was just too emotional to lie to him. At first, I hadn't wanted him to know that I was waking up early, something he had said only older vampires did. I was only weeks old, not centuries, after all.

Marcus tilted his head to the side as he regarded me with his shrewd gaze. "How early?" he asked as Sara joined us at the table. She cut a glance in my direction, and I just shrugged. She had known for a while and was aware that I had wanted to keep it quiet.

"I don't know," I said. "Over an hour ago, I guess."

"How long has this been happening?" he asked.

I shrugged. The truth was, I had been waking up earlier and earlier since my confrontation with my sire, Alexander. I suspected it had something to do with his attack and the surging of my abilities. I had been hesitant to lay it all out for Marcus. I never wanted to be a vampire in the first place, but now that I was, I didn't like the idea of being some sort of vampire anomaly. "A while," was all I said in the end.

Not only was I concerned about my early rising, but I was also feeling the stress of being the head of the House of Ward, my House. I hadn't intended to found a House, let alone lead it. My only intention had been to free myself from Alexander. Marcus had led me to believe that he would be in charge of the new House we were forming. It was a shock to discover that I was responsible not only for a hundred-year-old vampire but also for my best friend, Sara. Sara's membership was still a secret we kept from the Council, the governing body of vampires. I wasn't sure how they would react if they ever found out that a witch was a formal member of a vampire House. I hoped that the small size and insignificance of our House would prevent this from becoming an issue. Marcus worked for the Council as an enforcer, and if he wasn't going to inform them, no one was likely to.

I glanced at Marcus. He still studied me; his eyes narrowed as he considered. "Would you mind if I brought this up with Felix?" he asked. "He's older than me and might have some idea why this is happening. Or it could have to do with ..." he trailed off.

Ahh yes. The thing we didn't talk about. At least since the attack. The fact that something seemed to be wrong with me. Besides my ability to feel others' emotions—a trait no other vampires seemed to have, no other witches possessed, and that I had had long before I became a vampire—and apart from my waking early, there was some-thing wrong with my blood. Something about the smell of my blood made other vampires view me as prey. I had seen it with Alexander, and even Marcus had been affected at first.

I wondered if that was part of the reason James had been attracted to me. I sighed. James, the vampire who had hidden me from my sire after my change and attempted to control me, was gone. He was the reason I was a vampire. He didn't turn me—that was Alexander—but he had been the one behind the wheel of the car that plowed into me. Whether it was all part of some insane plan he had or some obsession with me, I would never know for sure.

I didn't like the idea of being different. I had been different my whole life. And I liked the idea of being hunted by other vampires even less. So, partly because of the mess with James and partly out of fear of being attacked again, I had stayed away from all other vampires besides Marcus and my lawyer, Felix.

"Sure. Why not?" I said. "Tell Felix, but tell him the info is confidential."

"Will do," Marcus said.

Felix would be a good choice, I thought. He was odd but discreet. Besides his aversion to eating bagged blood and his constant pressure to get me to "eat natural" with him, I liked the vampire. I was surprised to find out he was older than Marcus. If I had to guess, I would have bet that he was a nineties surfer kid before he was turned.

"Hey. You okay?" Sara asked, her dark curls bouncing into view as she leaned forward to get my attention. "You're not hungry?" She pointed to the untouched bag I had been staring at.

I marveled at how nonchalant Sara was about the bag of blood on her kitchen table. It was strange how normal it had all become.

"Oh. Yeah, I am, actually," I said, picking up the bag. "I can put this in a mug or something."

"Not on my account," Sara replied between spoonfuls of soup. "Then someone just has to wash a bloody mug."

"You sound British," I teased, but I appreciated the economy of it and the acceptance Sara exhibited. While I sucked my meal from a bag, I watched Sara enjoy her soup and sourdough bread, realizing how much I missed food. I missed the companionship of dining out and the ritual of sharing a meal. I no longer had a reason to use any dishes other than cups and glasses. The thought made me feel even sadder.

"Hey, I got that," Marcus said, reaching for my empty bag. I handed it over and thanked him. He smiled at me, and I tried to smile back. "You want more," he asked.

"No. I'm done for now," I said, regretting the sound of my voice.

"Okay," he said. "I have some work to do before I head out. Just let me know if you need anything." With that, he left the kitchen and disappeared back down to the basement, leaving me with Sara and feelings of guilt.

I had every reason to be upset that evening, but I hated being the one to bring everyone else down. I wasn't surprised that he would retreat to some other part of the house. None of this was Marcus's or Sara's fault. I hadn't asked for what had happened to me, but these two had gone out of their way to make my life easier and deserved better than a sulky roommate and House leader. House leader. It was almost laughable. I didn't lead anything. I was stalling out here, just like I had in my human life. I needed to figure out this new life quickly before I drove away the only two people I had left.

Just as I started to consider my options, I was interrupted by the sound of a car slowing and turning onto our drive.

"Is the shop still open?" I asked Sara.

"Nope. We closed down early due to ... you know," she said with a wince. "Why, do you hear someone?"

"Probably. Were your mom and aunt going to stop by?" I asked. The question was innocent enough, but I watched closely to see how Sara would respond. Since Sara's abduction by James before Christmas, and my failure to notify her family, I had been on their naughty list. When they saw me, they were polite, but there was a distance that hadn't existed before. I hoped it would lessen with time, allowing us to reclaim the closeness we once had. Separated from my own mother, I desperately missed my two witchy mother figures.

"No," Sara said and gave me a smile that didn't reach her soft brown eyes. "They had to get home."

I nodded. "Is Silas coming over?" I asked, wanting to move on from the topic of her family.

"Yeah, but I don't expect him for a while. He promised to come by and help with the inventory."

"It's probably a customer who doesn't know you're closed or someone who is lost," I said, shrugging. "Have you been busy in the shop?" I asked.

Sara tilted her head from side to side, making her curls dance around her face. "Not many people come to the store directly, but the online orders are going great. Better than great. I'm having a hard time keeping up, and the stress has led to me frying two computers since New Year's." She crooked half a smile and wiggled her fingers at me. Blue electricity sprang up, dancing from fingertip to fingertip and spreading down the back of her hand.

"Maybe I could help?" I offered. It would be great to contribute and not feel useless in my own home.

"Can you build me a new website?" Sara asked, pulling the energy back and dropping her hand.

"No. I can't," I said, watching Sara's magic wink out with my hope. "I just wish there was some way I could help around here."

"You have. The artwork you've provided has been a huge boost. I love the new packaging and signage. I've used a lot of your work on the existing website as well. Although it looks better, it still needs a major overhaul.

Sara got up and cleared her place, going over to the sink.

I followed behind and leaned against the counter, crossing my arms. "Well, let me know if you can think of any way for me to be useful, please," I said.

I was just about to ask what Sara had planned for the rest of the evening when I heard footsteps coming up the porch stairs. The shop was off to one side of the house and clearly marked. There would be no reason for a customer to come up the steps to the main house. Whoever had pulled in was there to see us, not the shop next door.

"We have company," I said, pushing off the counter to head for the front door.

"Can you tell who it is?" Sara asked, setting her dish in the sink and turning to follow me out.

I approached the front door and leaned toward the inset window. "No idea," I said, peering out the glass at the man coming up the steps. When I caught a glimpse of his face, I wasn't sure I was seeing correctly. My surprise turned to frustration and then anger as I yanked the door open.

"Did Felix send you?" I asked, my tone insistent. I tried to remind myself that whoever had sent him, it wasn't his fault. I took a deep breath, but then caught the familiar scent of his blood and stopped breathing altogether.

The man reached the top step and came to a stop. He was just under six feet tall with short-cropped black hair that was spiked up on top. Wearing jeans and a black wool coat to guard against the cold, I noticed his neck tattoos peeking out from the thick collar. His bright blue eyes were wide with surprise. "Felix?" he asked. "I don't know who that is. No. I came here on my own."

"To feed me?" I asked in confusion.

The man stiffened and lowered his brows. "No. I came here to ask for your help."

5

SILAS

Despite having had a long day, I was looking forward to helping Sara that evening. I knew that if I was tired, she must be exhausted. The funeral had been a trial, and I knew that witnessing Kate's family grieving had taken a toll on her. I was glad I could be there for her, even in some small way.

I turned up the drive to Sara's place. Nestled in a clearing among the pines, it was a beautiful spot, and I had to admit the house was lovely, too. It seemed to belong there. Sara asked me to help her with some basic repairs, and I was happy to assist. It was a pleasure to work on a building like this. In the end, she needed more than just repairs, and I was glad for the excuse to linger here, spending most of my free time making the place livable for Sara's new roommates.

Sara's housemates, however, made me uneasy. I knew Kate had been her best friend since high school, but she was a vampire, and I found it hard to trust vampires. It might not have been too bad if it had just been Kate moving in. But now there were two of them. Marcus moved in just after

Sara's abduction. And while he had played a key role in bringing Sara back, he was still a vampire.

Remembering the abduction made my skin prickle, and I felt my bones sliding, urging a change. I rolled my shoulders and pressed down on my wolf. He was even less happy than I was about everything that had happened. I knew Sara trusted her housemates, and my wolf and I trusted Sara, but old prejudices died hard.

The lights in the shop were out, and Lucia's car was gone, but a strange black sedan sat next to the house. I parked beside it and scanned the surroundings before getting out of the truck. My senses sharpened, and my wolf peeked out through my eyes, on alert. I knew there was most likely no danger and that the witches' wards were strong and effective, but I couldn't help it.

I took a deep breath of the air around the strange vehicle. The visitor was human; I was certain of it. My shoulders lowered, and I felt my muscles relax slightly. I wasn't sure who was there, but they were no threat to a witch and a house full of vampires.

As I crossed the ward and stepped inside, my skin broke out in goosebumps. The smell of the human was stronger here; they had invited them in. A human wouldn't get through the wards without assistance any more than a witch or vampire, so it was a good sign. I heard voices coming from the great room and went to see who the guest was.

I found all three roommates and a human man sitting around the fireplace. Despite the chill in the room, no one had lit a fire. I glanced at the group. Sara and Kate sat huddled together. Marcus had adapted a casual pose, but his muscles were taught, and much of his weight was resting on his feet. He was prepared, and it eased me a bit to see it. The human was leaning forward, and everything about him was tense. I suspected the chill I felt had more to do with the grim faces than the cold fireplace. Something serious was being discussed.

The man sat with his back to me as I approached. I cleared my throat to avoid startling him. He turned his head at the sound, and his eyes widened slightly. He quickly recovered, though, and nodded in acknowledgment before returning to the group.

Sara and Kate glanced up simultaneously. Sara smiled, and warmth spread through me to see it. Kate's expression remained unchanged, but she spoke up in greeting. "Silas, this is Bruce. Bruce, this is Silas. He's with Sara," she said. Her words and matter-of-fact tone caught me off guard. It was true that Sara was the reason I was there, but none of us had discussed the relationship—a relationship I was still uncertain about.

I crossed the room and pulled a chair up next to the sofa, where Sara and Kate sat side by side. The scent of Sara so near got my wolf's attention, and he breathed in deeply through my nose, savoring the electric smell of the sky after a storm and the sweet scent of orange blossoms that was Sara. He stretched inside me and relaxed into blissful contentedness. My wolf had no misgivings whatsoever about our relationship with Sara.

As I sat down, I met Marcus's eyes, and he gave me a brief smile before turning his attention back to the stranger in the room.

"Bruce was just telling us that he wishes to become a member of Kate's House," Marcus said, leaning back and crossing his legs. It was a compliment that the vampire took a more relaxed posture upon my entrance. It did not go unnoticed or unappreciated. It didn't escape me, however, that he had positioned himself so that he had a clear view of everyone in the room and all exits. Despite my misgivings about vampires in general, I had to admit that Marcus was a professional, and it was nice to have him watching over the house.

Bruce remained quiet, and Marcus looked toward Kate. She swallowed and worked her tongue around in her mouth before answering. It was then that I smelled her hunger. My wolf perked up a bit at this piece of information, not in alarm but more out of curiosity. I groaned inwardly; he might be interested in seeing Kate lose it and attack this human, but I was not going to let that happen if I could help it. My wolf snorted at the thought and went back to observing.

"I tried to explain that we aren't accepting applications at the moment," Kate said, scowling. "But he won't listen." Kate clamped her mouth into a tight, thin line and glared at Bruce. Bruce, on the other hand, looked calm but serious. I had to admire his self-control and poise in the presence of the vampires. I hadn't witnessed many vampire-human interactions, but I suspected most humans would tremble if a vampire looked at them the way Kate was looking at Bruce just then.

Bruce cleared his throat and turned his gaze to Marcus. "I have nowhere else to go," he said. His voice was as calm as his demeanor, but he sounded tired. "I was forced to leave my position at the Tap House and have been refused employment at all other licensed venues downtown."

Marcus raised an eyebrow. "Hmm. What did you do?" he asked, tilting his head.

Bruce shifted his weight where he sat, and his expression grew even more grim. "I refused the wrong vampire," he said.

Marcus pushed back in his chair even farther. "Must

have been someone pretty powerful to earn you a city-wide ban."

Bruce sighed heavily. "It was Margaux. I assume you've heard of her."

Marcus nodded and let out a small laugh. "Yeah, she's got quite a reputation." He narrowed his eyes at Bruce. "You wouldn't feed her?" he asked.

"I wouldn't join her House."

Marcus nodded. "And she wouldn't take no for an answer? She doesn't like to be denied what she wants. I can see the position that would put you in."

"I don't," Kate said. "Why can't you go get some other job? I'm sure she doesn't have that kind of influence in the human world."

Marcus shook his head and turned to Kate. "He can't. He's part of our world now," he said. The reminder that Sara was also part of the vampire world now, as a member of Kate's House, made me uncomfortable.

"He has to maintain a contract with a Council-approved business or House," Marcus went on.

"And if he doesn't?" Kate asked.

"There is no quitting or leaving for humans. You stick around under someone's authority, you get turned, or you die. Those are the only options," Marcus replied.

My wolf started to growl, and a low rumble filled my mind. I tried to soothe him, reassuring him that no matter what any vampire thought, we wouldn't let any harm come to Sara, no matter who she chose to live with.

At Marcus's statement, Bruce nodded, but Kate looked horrified. "You mean they would kill him if he doesn't show up to work?" she demanded.

"An enforcer would track him down and lay out his options," Marcus said.

"Wait. You've done this before? Hunted down humans and ..." Kate trailed off.

Marcus stared at Kate. "That's my job, Kate. It doesn't happen often, and I can usually talk them around, but yes, I have occasionally had to perform that function. Part of my job is to ensure that the human world doesn't discover us. And we can't have knowledgeable humans loose in the world."

Kate glanced at Bruce. "You knew all this when you went to work there?" she asked incredulously.

He nodded.

"You would rather die than join Margaux's House?" she asked.

Bruce considered. "I would do whatever I could to preserve my ability to choose for myself," he said.

Kate's face softened, and she smiled at Bruce. It wasn't one of her best, but it was genuine. "I understand about wanting to make your own choices. But why would you want to join our House? I understand that Margaux isn't a good choice, but what makes you think I would be any better?" Kate asked.

"I'm not sure," he admitted. "But, from our limited contact, you don't seem like the type I would have to run from. I've heard some of our clients talking about your new House. I knew it was small and that Marcus, who still works for the Council, was your only member. I guess I thought that this would be a safer environment." Bruce cleared his throat again and looked down, his cheeks flushing. "I'm not just asking for a place in your House but a place to stay as well. Maybe not for good, but for now," he said, glancing back up to meet Kate's eyes. "Margaux sent people to my apartment. I was able to get away from them, but I'm not sure it's safe for me to return to the city until I've worked things out. I had hoped you would be able to help. And that you would ..." He paused, pressing his lips together before continuing. "Think kindly of me," he finished.

I didn't know the history between the two of them, but Kate's posture loosened, and she took a deep breath at the mention of it. She huffed out a sigh, but her features held her answer. "Well. I'm not going to turn you away if you need help," she said. "But I'm not convinced I want another House member, either."

Kate turned her head to look at Sara. Sara glanced at Bruce and then back at Kate. "I'm okay if you are," Sara said. "It would be nice to have someone else around during the day, and we have more than enough room."

I bristled a bit at the mention of Bruce being around Sara during the day, but I knew that she could take care of herself.

Kate reached over and squeezed Sara's hand. She turned back to Bruce. "Sara is a member of this House, too," she said.

Bruce cocked an eyebrow. "She works here?"

"No. She owns this place. And she's a House member like Marcus is," Kate said.

"And she's human?" he asked.

Kate looked at Sara to answer.

"Nope," Sara said. "I'm a witch. I helped put up that ward you crossed over to get into the house. And we don't like being exposed any more than vampires do. If you get my meaning?"

Bruce smiled. "I understand perfectly, and I assure you I can be very discreet."

"Okay then. It's settled. You can stay here for now until you get things figured out. We have plenty of rooms, but none are fixed up just yet," Kate said.

Bruce raised a hand. "Not to worry. I'll take care of it."

Kate stood, and everyone else got to their feet as well. It was a subtle nod to the fact that she was in charge, whether she was aware of it or not.

By standing, the distance between Kate and Bruce closed to just a few feet. Kate's nostrils flared, and I knew she was smelling the human and the blood in his veins. My wolf twitched his ears, and I hushed him again.

There was a pause, and then Bruce spoke up. "Are you hungry?" he asked warily. "I would be willing to ..."

I hadn't been the only one to notice Kate's reaction.

Kate covered her mouth with her hand and shook her head. She stepped back and waited for a beat before answering. "No. I'm fine," she said with a fangy accent. "Marcus has us well stocked." She snapped her gaze to Marcus, and he nodded.

Having Bruce around could get complicated. I decided I would need to spend more time observing how they all got along before my wolf and I would feel comfortable with this new situation.

Sara wrinkled her nose and narrowed her eyes at Kate. "I'm glad we got that settled," Sara said. "Bruce, maybe you would like to wait in the foyer, and I'll show you the empty rooms. If you would give us a minute?"

"I think that would be a good idea," Bruce said and slowly walked toward the front of the house. He kept his gate steady with no sudden movements. At least the human had good instincts. And it took a lot of courage to turn his back on a hungry predator. *He might work out all right after all*, I thought.

Kate took several deep breaths and let her arms fall back to her sides.

"You okay?" Marcus asked, casually edging himself between Kate and the retreating human.

"Yeah. I'm fine. It's just I'm still a bit hungry and well ..."

"I get it. Don't let yourself go hungry. Like you said, there's a fully stocked fridge," Marcus said. "Unless you would prefer a hot meal. Bruce said he'd be willing."

Kate shot him a glare and stalked off toward the kitchen.

Marcus glanced at Sara and me and shrugged. "I had to ask," he said, his voice tinged with humor. "I'll keep an eye on her. I'm sure she would never forgive herself if she killed the poor guy." He turned and followed Kate into the kitchen.

Sara's body went rigid, and I placed a hand on her shoulder. "Don't worry. I'm sure it will be okay," I assured her, though I wasn't entirely convinced myself. Only time would tell.

Sara and I followed behind Marcus, putting more distance between us and the human waiting in the foyer.

"Besides fighting the urge to eat him, Bruce's presence could be a problem, you know?" Marcus was telling Kate as we entered.

"How so?" she asked, grabbing a bag from the fridge. She paused before shutting the door and grabbed another. I looked away from Kate and her meal. I understood biological imperative better than most, but I still didn't want to see Kate feed.

"Well," Marcus began, leaning back against the counter. "You are now responsible for Bruce—not just accountable for his actions, but also for keeping him safe. If that is your intention, and if Margaux or her people come after him— and they might—you will have to deal with it."

"Deal with it? But I'm just letting him stay here. I haven't said he can join the House," Kate said. I glanced at her, and her eyebrows were raised almost to her hairline. It was clear she hadn't considered this angle.

"It's up to you," Marcus said. "You could either claim him and rebuff her or hand him over." He shrugged. "Once a House officially claims him, she might lose interest, but you never know."

Kate's shoulders slumped. "I'm not going to turn him away. And I have no plans on giving him over to anyone he doesn't want to go with." She sipped from the bag she held, and I cringed, looking down at the old wooden floor.

"He helped me once," Kate said. "When I was trying to get away from James. It wasn't much, but he was kind to me."

"Why did you go to him? Did you know him?" Marcus asked.

"James took me to the Tap House the night you and I met," she said in a quiet voice.

Sara stepped closer to me and leaned back against my side. I moved my arm and draped it over her shoulder. I wondered if she had heard this story before or if we were both hearing this for the first time. Either way, I was glad for the warm weight of her pressed against me.

"I fed from Bruce," Kate said.

Sara flinched, and I pulled her closer.

"He's the only one I've ever fed from," Kate continued. "When I ran from James, I went in search of food, and Bruce pointed me in the right direction."

Kate's reaction to Bruce made more sense now. It wasn't just that he was a human. He smelled like food because she had tasted him before. I took a deep breath, inhaling Sara's sweet scent. It did much to steady my nerves.

"Don't worry," Marcus said. "We'll work this out. I need

to get to work. Are you going to be okay with Bruce in the house?"

Kate squared her shoulders and smiled. "Yeah. I'm fine. I wouldn't do anything to hurt him."

Marcus rubbed Kate's arm in reassurance and then turned toward Sara and me. "You guys good?" he asked.

Sara nodded, and Marcus locked eyes with me. I lifted my chin, and he smiled. "Good. I'll be back as soon as I can," he said. "And I think we need to get Kate's lawyer over here. However this ends, there's going to be paperwork."

6

BRUCE

Every hair on my body stood on end as I walked from the room to wait in the foyer. I wasn't exactly worried, but my adrenal system reminded me that there were beings behind me that ate humans. I was grateful for my extensive experience with vampires. I thought it would be helpful in this new living arrangement.

I spent several minutes admiring the gorgeous woodwork and the wrought iron chandelier before I heard footsteps, and the witch, Sara, and her companion, Silas, appeared. The two made for an interesting pair. She was short, just over five feet, with dark skin, black curly hair cut just above her shoulders, and lovely brown eyes framed by dark lashes. She gave off a friendly impression, but it didn't surprise me that she was the one who spoke up and took charge at the end of our little meeting.

Silas, on the other hand, stood well over six feet tall with chestnut brown hair, tan skin, and striking yellow eyes. He hadn't spoken a word since our introduction, but he observed everything and everyone with a keen eye. I wasn't sure what he was, but I would wager every penny in my bank account that he wasn't human. Not a vampire either, but definitely not human.

"Bruce, sorry to make you wait," Sara said, smiling as she approached, with Silas quietly in tow.

"It's not a problem," I assured her.

She turned to Silas. "Do you want to go on the tour with us, or would you like to wait for me in the shop?" she asked.

Silas looked at her then, and his features transformed from the blank mask he'd been wearing to a look of pure adoration. Even his eyes seemed to change from bright yellow to soft gold. "I'll be waiting in the shop," he said softly but in a deep rumbling voice.

Sara beamed back at him, and then the two parted.

I smiled to myself, enjoying the sweet moment.

Once Silas was out of sight, Sara glanced over and waved for me to follow her up the stairs to the second floor.

I was pleased with how things had gone so far. But I felt equal parts relief and apprehension. Kate was right; I didn't know if this would be a better situation than the one I was trying to escape. I had looked for other ways out of my predicament. I had gone to several different businesses, some blood shops, and even the tattoo parlor where I had first entered the employ of a vampire. All had turned me away.

The tattoo shop owner had been especially kind about the whole situation, but there was nothing he could do to help. Margaux had made it known around town that I was hers, and she was waging a pressure campaign to bring me in. No one I had spoken to had been willing to go up against her, not until I approached Kate.

I wasn't sure what I would have done if she had turned me away. I needed this to work in any way possible. I was betting on Kate and this House as a place where I could find safety.

We reached the landing, and Sara turned. "There are three large bedrooms up here, besides mine. They each have their own bathrooms, but things haven't been updated yet. And none of them have beds." She smiled again, but it looked more like a grimace.

"It's no problem, as long as you don't mind me having some things delivered," I said.

"Not at all. Anything you like," she said with enthusiasm. "I'm not much in the way of muscle around here, but I'm sure the others would help if you needed it."

I smiled to myself. "I'm sure it'll be fine. Thank you for agreeing to let me stay. It means a lot. Let me know if there is anything I can do to help out around here."

"Don't worry about it," she said and then cocked her head, studying me. "You don't know anything about computers, do you?"

"Umm. Not much, I'm afraid," I admitted. I used one at my previous workplace, but only to send emails and fill out time sheets.

"Too bad," she said with a shrug. "I'm looking for help in the shop."

"The one I saw next to the house?"

"Yeah, it's my family's business. We relocated here when I bought the property last year."

"Do your other family members live here as well?" I asked.

"No. It's just my mom and aunt, and they live in the valley farther up the highway. They come and help out at the store, but it's been mostly me since the relocation." She sighed.

"It sounds like a lot of work."

She shrugged. "It keeps me busy."

I had spent enough time among vampires to know of the existence of witches, but I had never met one before. Sara seemed nice, and I hoped her family would be the same. As far as I understood, vampires and witches usually kept apart from one another. This was an odd arrangement.

I glanced at Sara, who was waiting for me to pick a room.

"Um, I'm sure any of the rooms will be fine," I said.

She turned the handle of one of the large wooden doors that lined the hallway and held it open. "I'm at the end of the hall. I usually get up around eight, but I can be quiet if you're a late sleeper."

"Thanks. I usually get up around 3 or 4 p.m., but I don't know what my schedule will be while I'm here."

"You worked nights, I take it?" she said. "Kate mentioned she met you at a vampire bar." She fidgeted uncomfortably.

"Yep. I was both a supervisor and a blood source."

She nodded, her face turning red, but she didn't meet my gaze.

I suppressed a chuckle at her squeamishness. After all, she was a member of a vampire House. I thought she would be accustomed to the realities of their feeding habits.

"Do you have any staff working here?" I asked her.

She glanced at me, her brows creased. "Staff?"

"You know," I said. "Cleaning staff, food sources, a butler?" I hadn't seen anyone else around, but you never knew.

She waved a dismissive hand at me and grinned. "It's not like that," she said. "You'll see. We aren't that sort of House." She waved goodbye and left me to explore the room on my own. I was glad for the privacy.

Not that sort of House? I wasn't sure what Sara meant by

that. Things were obviously different here, though. Besides having no staff and witches around, it was the most relaxed vampire environment I had ever been in.

I surveyed the room. It featured a honey-colored wooden floor and off-white painted walls. Two large windows overlooked a side yard, and there was an attached bathroom that seemed to have remained unchanged since the late 1990s. The room contained no furniture except for a large wardrobe in one corner, but everything was clean and well-maintained. This space would do nicely with some furniture and personal items.

I took off my coat and hung it in the wardrobe. I felt better having most of my skin covered around Kate—not that a wool coat would have protected me from a hungry vampire. I rested my shoulder against the wardrobe and took out my phone. Within thirty minutes, I had ordered enough furniture to fill the room and several essential items, such as towels and bedding. I had all those things back at my apartment, but I wasn't planning to return there for some time.

Satisfied that I had done what I could upstairs, I decided to go back down and check in with Kate. I glanced at the wardrobe and considered putting the coat back on, but ultimately decided not to. Kate and I needed to get comfortable with each other, and I couldn't always wear a coat.

I was dressed in a black button-down shirt, jeans, and black dress shoes. I pulled my sleeves down over my tattooed arms, running my thumb along the bare patch on the underside of my left arm. It was the only spot on my arms or neck not covered in ink. It was where the clients I fed had bitten me. I remembered how Kate had struck my arm when she visited the Tap House. Then my thoughts drifted to Margaux, and I felt anger building in my chest.

The uninked rectangle was my way of asserting boundaries, boundaries that had been violated. I breathed out heavily. I was making the right choice. I was sure, but I still didn't know how this was going to turn out. I smoothed the fabric down and buttoned the cuff, and then the other—no need to tempt Kate more than necessary.

I made my way back downstairs and found Kate in the living room. She was sitting in a corner of the large room in a pink, overstuffed chair. Her legs were drawn up, and her arms were wrapped around her knees. The sleeves of her sweater covered her hands completely. I wasn't the only one using clothing as a defense.

"I don't mean to disturb you," I said. "I just wanted to know if there was anything I could do for you. Or get you?"

She blinked up at me from wherever her mind had been a second before. "Oh. Um, I don't think so. It's nice of you to ask," she said, hugging her legs tighter.

"Is Marcus—"

"No. He took off. He has to work most nights. He'll be back around three or four, though."

I glanced at my watch. It was only 8 p.m.

"I'm going to head back into the town I passed on my way here. I need to pick up a few things. If you're okay?"

"I'm fine. I don't have much to do most nights." She gave me a small smile that looked more sad than reassuring.

"Would you like to come along?" I offered. I wasn't sure if I should be shut in a car with her, the way she had vamped out earlier, but it felt rude not to ask.

She shook her head. "No, that's okay. I'm going to read or maybe do some more sketching," she said, pointing to a small table next to the chair that held a notebook, several pencils, and a beat-up eraser.

I stepped closer. "I can leave you my cell number, and you can text me if you think of anything?"

She nodded and shifted in her chair, unfolding her legs and reaching to pull a cell phone out of her back pocket. Unlocking it with her thumb, she held it out. I leaned forward and took the phone. It was only slightly warmer than the air in the room.

I entered my number and handed it back. "Anything at all. Just text. I'll be back soon."

"I am fine. I don't expect to be waited on, especially by a guest in my own home," she said, a sad smile still in place.

Her answer was not something I ever expected a vampire to say. I would try to change her mind about needing to be waited on and about my status as a guest. My survival depended on it. I needed to be able to make myself useful.

"Will I have trouble getting back into the house?" I asked, curious to know how the wards worked.

"No. You should be fine. I pulled you across the first time, and now you're all set. We don't lock the door. It seems redundant." She shrugged.

"Got it," I said.

Kate frowned as she looked down at her phone.

"I just wanted to say," I began, and Kate glanced back up. "Thank you again. For taking me in. For letting me stay here."

She smiled at me then, her face lighting up like it hadn't before. "Of course. I'm not making any promises yet, but you're welcome here, Bruce."

I smiled back before slipping out of the room and heading upstairs to grab my coat, then exiting through the front door. As I stepped onto the porch, I felt a slightly uncomfortable tingling on my skin. If I were going to stay there, I would have to get used to the feel of magic. However, compared to getting used to being bitten by vampires, it shouldn't be too difficult, I thought. What a strange life I had found myself leading.

Several miles back down the highway, I found an open camping goods store. They had exactly what I needed until my internet purchases arrived. In the same shopping plaza, there was a grocery store, and I figured I should stock up on food and toiletries as well. I hadn't had time to pack a bag when I left my apartment; I had been more concerned with evading Margaux's human goons than grabbing my toothbrush.

I packed the back of the car with groceries and got back on the highway. There were few cars on the road, and even fewer headed deeper into the mountains, as I was. I kept my eyes on a pair of headlights behind me. After all that had happened, I was alert to any possible threat. At one point, I was almost certain that I was being followed.

I slowed down and put my blinker on as if I were about to turn onto a small bridge crossing the river alongside the highway. The silver sedan swerved around me and continued on its way. I relaxed my arms and loosened my grip on the steering wheel. I was being seriously paranoid, I thought. But who could blame me?

I waited until the car disappeared from view, then got back on the road and headed toward the house—the House of Ward. I shook my head. I had never imagined myself joining a House. I briefly thought of my ex, Jake, who had accepted Margaux's offer. He was undoubtedly living in luxury on a vast estate with everything he could desire— except free will, how he would laugh to see me now.

Jake had worked for the Tap House precisely for the reason Margaux had mentioned. He wanted to be swept away to something bigger and better. But not me. And now here I was in the middle of nowhere, begging for admission to a House of three. It was a step down from where I had been just the day before, but I was determined to make the best of the situation.

I was determined to survive.

7

KATE

I moved my pencil over the contours of the design I was working on. It wasn't a drawing of anything particular, just a doodle that turned into an overall pattern of leaves and flowers with some small woodland creatures tucked in here and there. I darkened the spaces between the leaves and sharpened the detail around one particular rabbit I liked. Holding the notepad back to get a look at the design as a whole, I decided I was done.

Sara hadn't asked for more art for the shop, but I couldn't help myself. It felt so good to draw, to create. As I sketched, I focused on my mood. I hated the residual emotions that lingered after an upset. Given the circumstances, I don't think I could have reacted differently, but I desperately wanted to move past those emotions. I longed for some calm, some peace.

As I drew, I felt the tension drain away. I put all my swirling frustration, grief, and fear into the crawling vines, the twisting leaves, the blooming buds, and finally, the small birds, insects, and rabbits that hid among the foliage. I felt immense relief when I placed the notepad back on the small side table. The drawing was done, and I was done with all that had gone into it.

Feeling much lighter, I climbed out of the chair I had been sitting in for the past two hours and stretched. I looked at my watch; it was 2 a.m. Marcus wouldn't be home for another couple of hours. Sara had come back from the shop around eleven and gone to bed. Bruce had returned from his shopping trip and had gone upstairs, presumably for the remainder of the night.

And I was alone. Again.

What a strange situation the whole Bruce thing was. I still had a hard time understanding why someone would sign up to be part of this world when they knew there was no way out. But maybe that was the point. Just because I hadn't signed up for all this didn't mean others wouldn't want what I had. I suppose Bruce's goal could be to become a vampire eventually. The thought made me queasy. The idea that Bruce might not just be seeking sanctuary, but also looking for someone to turn him, was too much. I didn't think I could ever bring myself to do that to someone else. Ever.

I was about to go down to my room when I heard a car approaching. A few minutes later, Marcus came in through the front door with Felix in tow.

I walked around the corner to greet our guest, who was already standing in the house. Felix was just as I remembered: tall, rather lean, with long blond hair down to his shoulders, and dressed for a day at the beach in shorts, a t-shirt, and flip-flops this time, despite the thirty-degree weather. But then again, vampires didn't get cold, so we could rock whatever we felt like. It was hard to believe that he was older than Marcus. He dressed like my teenage brother and all his friends, I thought.

"I figured the house was the best place for your meeting, given the late hour," Marcus said. We typically met in the shop because it had a nice counter that we could all gather around, but the shop was closed, and we were all here.

I nodded. I was just about to tell them, however, that Bruce was asleep when I heard the door to his room open and close. A moment later, Bruce appeared at the top of the steps.

I glanced up and waved hello, noticing that Bruce stood still instead of coming down to join us. I looked over at Marcus and Felix. Marcus was as relaxed as ever, but Felix had his hazel eyes locked on Bruce with a look that could only be described as hungry.

Without thinking, I launched myself forward, stopping just before Felix, my socked toes hitting the front of the giant vampire's flip-flops. "Bruce is not for eating," I growled, craning upward, my lips pulled back from my teeth. I was surprised by my own vehemence. I didn't know if I was misstepping or not. Felix was much, much older than I. I could be getting into something I was unprepared for, but the impulse to place myself between Bruce and this vampire was overwhelming.

Instead of challenging me, Felix took a step back and lowered his head in a bow. I could sense his emotions shutting down, becoming smaller. All I felt from him was contrition and regret. I realized I'd let my walls slip during my outburst and quickly put them back in place.

"I apologize," he breathed from behind a curtain of blond hair. "I did not mean to offend."

I stepped back, too, shocked by my actions. *Had I really just done that?* It was possibly one of the most vampirish things I had ever done—besides drinking blood, I mean.

"It's okay," I said, regaining my composure. "I'm sorry. I just ..."

"No need to apologize," Felix said, lifting his head. "This is your House. I was in the wrong." He stood completely still, hands loose at his sides, eyes downcast, which just made me feel more guilty.

"How about we just start over," I suggested, stepping to the side and taking a deep breath. "Felix, this is Bruce. Bruce, Felix." I glanced up, and Bruce took the cue, walking down the steps to meet us.

I watched him as he descended. I wasn't sure how being stalked by a stranger or my outburst would affect him, but his gait was steady and his features calm. I reached out with my gift, but all I sensed was curiosity and a sense of relief. I was glad to be able to defend him, but I was also annoyed at the need to do so. Felix would have to watch his step if he visited regularly.

When Bruce reached the foyer, he extended a hand to Felix, a gesture that both surprised and impressed me. It reminded me that Bruce probably knew a lot more about vampires and vampire life than I did. I needed to remember that and see if he could help me navigate future interactions.

After the introductions, we adjourned to the kitchen table, the only one large enough to accommodate all four of us. We had done a lot to make the house livable, but we hadn't bothered with a large dining table, given that only one of the roommates actually dined. I was confident that we would eventually fill the house with everything it needed, but that would have to wait. Sara was our primary breadwinner, and although Marcus contributed to the house finances, I doubted his salary was substantial enough to furnish a place like this. And then there was me. I was supposed to be the leader of this House, and yet I made no money, had no job, and felt rather like an extra appendage.

When we were all seated, Felix spoke up. "Bruce, Marcus told me about your situation on our way here," he said. He turned to me. "He also explained that you don't feel ready to expand the House beyond the three founding members. Here's the impasse. Bruce needs protection and sanctuary; you need time to consider the arrangement. Do I have it correctly?" he asked.

Bruce and I both nodded.

"Good. Well, in that case, I have a proposal," he continued. "In some instances, individuals are brought into a House on a probationary basis. The idea is to see if they are a good fit for the House before permanent arrangements are made. These agreements are typically between sires and potential future vampires. Is that the situation we are dealing with here?"

"No," both Bruce and I said at the same time.

Surprised, I glanced at Bruce.

He met my gaze and shrugged. "It's not what I'm after," he said. "I want a job and a safe place to live. I'm not asking for anything more."

I nodded at him. "A safe place we can do. For now," I said.

Felix looked back and forth between Bruce and me. "Okay. I think that can still work. I don't see a problem with changing some of the wording in the existing documents to omit the parts about being changed at the end of the proba-tionary period."

While we waited, he fished around in his bag and pulled out a legal pad and a pen. "What do you think? At the end of a period of no more than thirty days, the applicant will either be released to pursue adoption into an alternate

House or ... what? Employed by? Join with? What would you prefer?" Felix asked me.

"Umm. I don't know; let's put 'be contracted to', will that work?" I asked.

Felix considered, tilting his head from side to side. "Yeah. I can work with that. Bruce?"

"Yes. That works for me," he said. "On the condition that I will be allowed to read over the contract before it's accepted."

I met his worried gaze. "Of course," I said. "How would it be fair to make you sign a contract before you'd even read it? I mean, I would think you would want to be involved in drafting the thing. It is *your* life we're talking about."

I looked around the table at three pairs of eyes staring back at me, blinking as if I were crazy.

"What?" I demanded. "Am I missing something?"

Was I missing something? I wondered. I figured I had just stepped into one of those situations where everyone knew more than I did about the job I was supposed to be doing.

Marcus finally spoke up. "No. It's fine. It's just that humans typically don't get a say in the agreements they're offered. It's unusual for the leader of a House, even a minor House—no offense."

"None taken," I assured him.

"—to give any say to a member of staff or, even a newly turned member of the House," Marcus continued. "The sire's will is law within their own House."

"Well, that must suck for everyone who isn't the sire," I said.

Felix barked out a laugh, startling the rest of the table. "Sorry. It's just this is the most fun I've had in a while," he said, grinning like a loon and making notes on his pad.

"You must not get out often," I grumbled. "Can we get

back to the document or whatever? I want this settled, at least for now, so that Bruce doesn't feel like he's blowing in the wind."

Again, blinking and blank stares.

"Ugh, Felix. You know what I want, yes?" I asked, growing thoroughly fed up with the process.

"Umm, yeah. I think I get the picture," he said.

"Great," I said, standing up from the table.

As I did, the other three quickly stood up, accompanied by the scraping of chairs and a flurry of movement. "Seriously?" I demanded. "I think I've had enough for one night. A person shouldn't have to deal with all this on the same night as their funeral," I said with more heat than I intended.

The faces of the others took on various expressions of regret and shock.

I waved a hand. I was done with the evening. "Felix, maybe you and Bruce can figure out the paperwork? You're my lawyer. I assume you will work in my best interests, and Bruce has the biggest stake here. I trust the two of you will come up with something I can live with. Okay?"

All heads around the table nodded in approval.

I let out a breath. "Good. Well, I'm going to my room and don't plan on coming back out until tomorrow night."

Felix cleared his throat in an obvious attempt to get my attention.

"Yes," I groaned.

"There is another matter I wanted to speak to you about," he said, giving me a knowing look. Unfortunately, I didn't know, so I just stared blankly, hoping he'd fill me in.

"Marcus mentioned you had some questions ..." he continued. I just shook my head. "About the typical sleeping habits of vampires."

Oh, right. Marcus was going to consult Felix about my little "waking up early" problem. I waved a hand again in his direction. "Sorry, yes. Can we talk about it later?" I asked.

Felix bowed his head. "Of course. Whenever you have time," he said. "Until then, Bruce and I will hammer out the details of the contract, and I'll leave a copy with Marcus for you to review and sign." He glanced at Bruce from the corner of his eye, and a slow smile spread across his face.

I was well aware that Felix only fed straight from the vein. But I thought I had made it clear that Bruce was off-limits. The man was in a desperate enough situation, and I didn't want him to feel he had no say. I would not tolerate him being used or pressured in that manner.

"Sure," I said. "As long as you remember what I said about Bruce. And the fact that he is not here to meet your nutritional needs."

Felix smiled, showing an enormous set of fangs. "Not to worry. I'm a professional. I promise I will keep my teeth to myself."

"Bruce, you good with all this?" I asked.

"Absolutely," he replied. His cheeks were bright red at that point, and I marveled that he hadn't run screaming from the room already.

"Awesome. You're a trooper, Bruce," I said, and then glanced at Marcus, who was smirking at me from beside Felix. "Marcus, do you need anything before I go?"

His smirk widened into a grin. "No, Sire. I'm good for now."

I narrowed my eyes. "Don't you start. I'm not in the mood," I growled. However, I did appreciate the obvious attempt at levity.

I trudged back down to my room. All the work I had done to improve my attitude was for nothing. I just had to accept the fact that it was just one of those days—or nights. But I also had to admit that I was glad that Bruce would be safe, or as safe as I could make him with documents and a roof over his head.

I supposed I had been able to do something good that night, something real that helped someone else. Did it complicate my life? —Yes. Did I regret helping? —No. It was the least I could do. And providing a kind man a place to shelter in a storm was more satisfying than any drawing or sketch I had produced.

I went to my bed feeling satisfied after all.

8

———

SARA

Pulling tape across the forty-third box, I set aside my tape gun and wiped the sweat from my brow. Silas and I worked until almost eleven the night before and barely made a dent in the number of orders I had due to ship out. But it wasn't the number of orders that was the problem. It was the organization of the information, or lack thereof, that kept me busy until late.

Every online order—and there were many—had to be manually entered into a separate system, cross-referenced with my inventory, and then re-entered to create a packing slip. Then, everything was selected, packaged, and sent out by mail. It was an archaic system. I knew there had to be a better way, but I didn't have the time or energy to sort it out.

To top it all off, my website was outdated, and I was constantly dealing with customer messages complaining about glitches, links that didn't link up, or the entire system crashing. I knew nothing about websites and didn't care to learn. It wasn't that I wasn't curious or capable, but with my particular "gift," getting frustrated was likely to lead to my frying out the computer before I had the chance to figure it out. Electronics and I were somewhat at odds, which was ironic.

Taking a break, I glanced around the quiet shop from behind the wooden counter. The new shop was beautiful. It had everything I loved about the old place: the mishmash of antique wooden kitchen tables and hutches that displayed our wares, yet it was roomier and more modern. The images Kate provided gave a stylish touch to all the packaging, making it feel more like an Instagram picture of a cool boutique rather than a run-down old store. It was unfortunate that hardly anyone got to see it.

It wasn't unusual to have no customers at this time of day—or really at any time of day—and I appreciated the stillness. I enjoyed being able to work uninterrupted for long stretches. But I felt lonely. I would have loved for Silas to be around during the day to lend a hand or sit and talk with me, but he had his own business to manage. His family business was construction. He, his father, and three brothers worked on projects throughout the mountain pass and beyond. They did a great deal of work in both the human world and the communities of Others.

I think what I truly missed was working alongside my aunt and mother. They had mainly been absent since the vampires arrived. While I understood their struggles, it made me sad and more than a little frustrated. They didn't blame Kate for what happened to me, or for the abduction itself, but it was difficult for them to be here in our new location, which also happened to be home to two vampires. Although they loved Kate, being close to the vampires was a struggle for them. They still didn't know the details of Kate founding her own House, and they had no idea that I was an official member of that House. It would take time for the relationships to heal, and I didn't think that piece of information would help expedite the process.

Maybe I should take Bruce up on his offer to help, I thought. It would be nice to have someone else around. I glanced at the clock; it was twelve-thirty. There had been only silence coming from his room when I tiptoed past at eight-thirty that morning on my way downstairs, and I hadn't seen him all morning. I sighed. It made sense for him to still be asleep, but it was a bit disappointing to have yet another night owl as a roommate. I had hoped, given that he was human, I might have some company during daylight hours.

I found myself staring at the far wall, lost in thought, and when the chime above the door sounded, I nearly jumped out of my skin. My aunt Lucia pushed into the shop backward, carrying a large box. I sprang up and came around the counter to help. She turned, and I relieved her of the box of oils.

"I was hoping you would have met me at the car," she said, a sour look on her face. "This stuff is heavy, and I'm old."

I snorted. No one would have considered my aunt old. She may have been in her mid-fifties, but she was as healthy as a horse and strong as an ox. She almost always wore loose, flowing linen clothing that concealed her toned, muscular frame, yet the way she carried herself suggested a woman decades younger. She moved with quickness and fluid grace. I suspected her gift of fire helped keep the spark alive within her and contributed to her truly awful moods.

"The day someone calls you old is the day I retire," I said. I walked the admittedly heavy box over to the counter and peered inside. "You guys have been busy," I said. And it was true. She and my mom had managed to produce nearly twice the usual amount of inventory.

"Well, we've had plenty of free time," she admitted, sniffing and glancing around. "The place looks nice." She crossed her arms and surveyed the nearest display of crystals, nodding. "Not bad."

I raised my eyebrows. That was high praise from my aunt. "Thank you," I said. "I forgot that you haven't seen it since I reorganized everything. Doesn't the new packaging look nice?" I pulled one of the new bottles of oil out of the box and held it facing her, as if she hadn't noticed while filling it.

She tilted her head. "Yes. It's an improvement," she admitted and looked away.

I nodded and smiled to myself. I knew I was pushing it, but I missed our banter.

"I should get back," she said, shifting her weight from one foot to the other. "We should have some tinctures ready by the end of the week."

"Already," I said, feeling disappointed. She'd only just gotten there, after all.

"Yes. Like I said, we've had the time."

"No. I meant, do you have to leave already?" I clarified. "You know, since you have all that extra time."

She shot me a glare, but then her face softened. "I'll be back soon," she said. She shook her head. She opened her mouth again to speak, but then hesitated. "How are you doing?" she finally asked.

I wouldn't beg for her to come back to work. I missed her and my mother, but they had to want to be here. I had to wait for them to want to be part of my life again. "I'm doing okay," I said. "I won't say that I don't need help. I do. I'm overwhelmed with the increase in orders lately, and I need to hire someone to overhaul the website." I set the bottle of oil aside and glanced up at her.

She was looking at me, but I could see the wheels turning in her mind as she tried to solve the problem. I was unsurprised a moment later when the glaze disappeared from over her eyes, and she said, "Give me an hour. I'll have someone here." With that, she turned on her heel and left the store.

I stared at her departure; that was just like my aunt. I had no doubt that whoever showed up in the next hour would be able to help. I realized I should have gone to her earlier. She might not have been willing to come in herself, but she was a great resource. Maybe she had been waiting for me, too.

I sighed and got busy unpacking the new product. There was quite a bit. If we had a better system, we could have sold a lot more than we did at the time. The idea made my stomach slightly queasy. I was already stretched so thin.

Sure enough, not forty-five minutes later, the bell over the door sounded again. Instead of my aunt, a young woman entered the store. She had long, dirty blonde hair and bright blue eyes. She wore a flannel shirt the same color as her eyes, a pair of jeans, and sturdy hiking boots. She also wore a huge smile, and I instantly knew I would like her. I hoped she was the help my aunt had sent and not a customer.

"Hello," I greeted her. "Welcome."

"Hi. I'm Beth," she said. "Your aunt sent me."

"Yes!" I said a bit too loudly. But honestly, I could have kissed her! "I can't say how happy I am to meet you." I held out my hand as she made her way over. "I'm Sara," I said, shaking her hand. Her energy was steady and calm and not witchy. I blinked for a moment. How was this going to work out, I briefly wondered.

She must have noticed the blank look on my face. "I'm not a witch," she said, grin still in place. "I just moved to town this winter when my mom married a witch. Louis Carter. You know him?"

Relief washed over me. Not a witch, but part of the community. This was going to make things a thousand percent easier. Doing business with a non-witch wasn't unheard of, but having a human in a witchy shop and dealing with our particular customers could be dicey.

I nodded. "Yes. Louis. Water Witch, I believe.

"Yes! That's the one," she exclaimed. "He and my mom met windsurfing in the Gorge in Oregon on the Columbia River last summer. They've been inseparable ever since. I just moved up here from Oregon myself, and I'm between jobs," she explained.

I just nodded enthusiastically. I didn't care what brought her here; it was such a relief to have another young person around, and some help in the shop would be a huge bonus. "What do you do?" I asked. I was sure that whatever it was, she could help with packaging, shipping, and organizing inventory if nothing else.

"I'm a web designer and social media consultant," she said.

No sooner had the words escaped her lips than I flung myself at her, grabbing her into a huge hug. "Oh, Gods, I'm so sorry," I said, pulling back and trying to compose myself. "But you're exactly what I need."

Beth stood there looking a bit stunned and shook her head. "No, no apologies. It's good to be needed," she said, still grinning.

"And I can pay you, of course," I stammered. "Whatever you charge, I'll pay. Business is great, but 'The Business' is a mess." I winced and hoped she wasn't signing on for more than she bargained for. It was 1990 back there, given that my mom and aunt set the whole system in place, and they knew even less about computers than I did.

"No worries," she said. "When do you want me to start?"

"Last month would have been great," I said. "But how about now?"

She straightened up. "Lead me to your office," she said, but before I could show her the way, the door to the house opened, and Bruce appeared in the doorway.

"I don't mean to interrupt," he said. "I just thought I'd check to see if I could help with anything." Instead of the dress shirt and shoes he had worn the night before, he was now in a black t-shirt with his jeans, and had switched to more practical black street shoes.

"I won't say no," I called to him. "Come meet Beth."

I introduced the two and asked Bruce to wait while I showed Beth to our office.

Bruce helped me unpack the oils my aunt had brought while Beth cracked her fingers and got to work on our computer in the back room. She had been surprised by the ceramic keyboard before I showed her my little parlor trick, and then she expressed more sympathy for my plight. Although I had to purchase new computers regularly, I hadn't updated our methods. The two qualities I looked for in a new computer were that it be used and cheap.

I truly hoped she would work out. I thought it would be great to have her company for as long as it took to finish the job. She even asked if she could bring her dog with her the next day, and I immediately agreed. Not only did I adore dogs, but having an animal's energy around would be delightful. They were so vibrant and resonated on a whole different frequency. I think it's because animals live in the moment and aren't wasting their energy on the past or the future.

"Are you averse to buying new equipment?" Beth called from the back room.

"Not all," I called back. "I'll buy whatever you need as long as I don't have to touch the thing."

Bruce cocked an eyebrow at me. "I'll just kill it," I explained in a normal tone. Lowering my voice even further, I said, "By the way, Beth is human, so ..."

Both his eyebrows rose at that little piece of information, and he nodded.

"Mom's married to a witch," I whispered.

Beth might know about witches since she was part of the community now, but she was still human, and vampires were a different story. Her new stepdad might have mentioned something, but for the most part, we didn't discuss the existence of other creatures with humans. Given how many legal documents Kate had received over the past few weeks, I didn't want to risk Bruce or me spilling the beans and causing Kate even more worry. Since the two vampires in the adjoining house slept all day, there was no reason to inform her.

Bruce mimicked, zipping his lips, and I nodded. I was glad he felt the same way.

"You know, if you're not comfortable with computers, I could lend a hand with some of the basic business tasks. I could help with online ordering for supplies, basic accounting, taxes, and that sort of stuff," he said.

I just stared back for a moment, not quite believing my luck. "Um, yeah, that would be awesome. The part of the job I love is the packaging, design elements, and the special personal touches. I would love to get help with those other tasks."

"No problem. Once Beth has an idea of what she needs, I can discuss the accounting side of things with you and place the orders with the correct vendors. It's not a bar, but I think I can figure it out all the same," he said.

"If Kate doesn't want you, can I adopt you?" I asked, but then instantly regretted my words.

Bruce's expression turned grim. "I'm afraid not," he said with a tight-lipped smile. "I go where the you-know-whats are."

I reached over to where he was placing another bottle of lavender oil on a shelf and squeezed his tattooed forearm. "Don't worry, Bruce," I assured him. "I've known Kate for years. She's a good person. She won't let anything bad happen to you. Not if she can help it."

He gave a dry chuckle. "Then let's hope that she can help it," he said and went back to stocking the shelf.

9

SILAS

My truck protested as it climbed to the top of the Pass. As I crossed over and made the descent toward home, the truck caught its breath, and the dense pines gave way to a rockier landscape. It was much drier on this side. We didn't get nearly the rainfall that they did in the west, but it was beautiful in its own way.

The road turned and twisted as I made my descent, and soon, the landscape transformed once more into clusters of forests scattered among rolling hills, flat valleys, and farmland. It was in those valleys that most of the shifters in the state resided and where I'd grown up.

The driving time between home and Sara's was just over one hour, and I had made the journey many times over the past month or so. My work often took me to the other side of the mountains, and I had never minded the drive. Since Sara asked me to help her with the new property, I had found every excuse I could to make the trip.

This particular day, however, I hadn't been able to stop by on my way back home, and the disappointment sat heavily in my chest. I had another appointment to get to that wouldn't wait. I'd put off dinner with my parents for over two weeks, and my mother was not happy. So, my disappointment would have to take a back seat to my mother's growing insistence that I make an appearance.

My wolf, on the other hand, didn't handle disappointment well. He'd been pacing and panting in the back of my mind all day since I realized I didn't have time to stop by and see Sara. I tried to reason with him, but he wasn't interested in listening; he wanted what he wanted, and what he wanted was to see Sara and make sure she was okay.

Before too long, I pulled up the drive toward my parents' house. As it came into view, I smiled at the familiar structure. It was nothing special, just a house. It had four bedrooms, a three-car garage, and a living room with a two-story ceiling. Pretty standard American home. What made it special was that I had helped my dad and brothers build the thing when I was sixteen years old.

At that time, my dad and my oldest brother, Lucas, were already working together in construction. My other older brother, Beau, was eighteen, and it had been on-the-job training for him and me. Beau and I made many mistakes while building that house, but we also learned how to fix them, and that was the whole point. When I graduated from high school, I went to work full-time with my dad and two brothers. Our younger brother, Elija, had only been eight when we built the house. He was a member of the business now, too, but he'd had a lot of catching up to do.

I parked next to Lucas's SUV. I was willing to bet that his wife, Lara, who was a nurse, was working the evening shift. Elija was the only one still living at home, but it wasn't a surprise to see Lucas there. He often stopped by to visit and bring his two kids to see Mom and Dad when Lara was away, especially around dinner time. Mom was a very enthusiastic grandmother, and if I thought the pressure campaign she waged to get me mated was bad, it was nothing compared to what happened if she didn't see her grandchildren regularly.

Sure enough, as soon as I stepped out of the truck, I spotted clothes strewn across the front walk. It wasn't long before I heard branches breaking, and two long-legged juvenile wolves shot out of the underbrush and came racing toward me. I stopped walking and extended my hand as they slowed, lowered their heads, and began whining and wagging at my feet. I bent down to scratch my niece's white-speckled wolf first, then my nephew's grey and black wolf. I felt the warmth coming from my own wolf at the greeting. He loved these two as if they were his pups. They both licked and jumped until I stood up straight and huffed at them that I'd had enough. Turning tail, they raced off back in the direction they'd come from, playfully snapping at one another as they went.

My nephew, Brooks, was fourteen and had been able to shift for two years now. Emma, his little sister, was twelve and had managed her first shift the previous fall. It filled me with joy to see them running around together, learning what it meant to be wolves. Until adolescence, our animals lie dormant inside us. We meet our animals for the first time when the shift comes upon us. Young shifters must spend a significant amount of time in animal form during this period. It solidifies our relationships with our animals and helps us build pack bonds with others our age.

Typically, youngsters spent every waking minute outside of school in animal form, tearing up the countryside with their peers, harassing the local wildlife, and testing their boundaries. It was a thrilling time for a young shifter, but also a source of worry for parents and grandparents alike.

Not all shifters survived the first few years after their initial change. My niece and nephew had both established quick and harmonious bonds with their wolves. It was a good sign, and I was confident they would come through their adolescence just fine.

I stepped over the clothes on my way to the front door, didn't bother knocking, and let myself in. They would all be aware of my presence; shifter hearing was quite sharp.

Once inside, the smell of my mother's cooking enveloped me and melted away any annoyance that lingered. Even my wolf stopped pacing and sniffed the rich aroma wafting from the kitchen. He could be stubborn when he set his mind on something, but the promise of food was sure to capture his attention.

Despite my grumbling stomach, I suspected that heading directly to the kitchen would be a mistake. So instead of turning right, I continued straight ahead to the living room, where I heard the TV. My dad and Lucas were both settled into leather recliners, watching a prerecorded college football playoff game. It looked like UW was leading in the third quarter. I had no idea how the game had turned out, so I didn't know what kind of mood those two would be in by the time dinner was served.

I waved hello as I sat on the loveseat. They both smiled and said hello.

"How's the bathroom remodel in Monroe coming along?" my dad asked, eyes still on the game.

"Good," I said, leaning back into the leather cushions. "Should be able to finish it up tomorrow."

My dad nodded, looking like an older version of me. He had thick, greying brown hair and yellow-gold eyes. My brother shared the same brown hair, height, and build as the rest of the men in our family, but he had our mother's clear blue eyes. I sat with them, watching for a few minutes before I heard my mom's voice coming from the kitchen.

"You aren't going to come say hello to your mother?" she called out over the din of the game.

I glanced at my dad, who just shrugged, and then at my brother, who smirked at me. *Great. Something was up.*

"Is Beau coming tonight?" I asked before standing up.

Lucas shook his head. "Nope. He's got a date," he said, his smirk turning into a knowing grin.

I exhaled and closed my eyes briefly. That was the last thing I needed. Beau was usually my backup, the one who took the brunt of my mother's prodding and poking about mating and starting a family. He was two years older than I and unmated at thirty. If he was dating, I was screwed. Pushing to my feet, I steeled myself before heading to the kitchen to see how bad it was going to be. I glanced back at my dad and brother; they were both happily mated and would be of no help whatsoever.

I edged into the kitchen. My mom had her back to me, chopping vegetables on a board placed in front of her on the counter. She wore jeans and a gray T-shirt. Her dark brown hair, threaded with silver strands at the temples, was braided down her back. Standing five feet eight inches tall, she was still a head shorter than her sons and husband. At fifty-six, she was still lean and strong.

"Don't just stand there," she said without turning around. "Come over and give me a hug."

My wolf lay down and made himself small in the back of my mind. He wasn't eager to tangle with her if she was in a mood. I was relieved to see her put the knife down before she turned to accept a hug and a quick kiss on the cheek.

"Hi, Mom," I said softly, hoping to keep things calm by the tone of my voice alone.

"Hmmm," was all she said in greeting. She looked me over from head to toe, her blue eyes narrowed, and her hands on her hips. Finally, she relaxed and glanced away. "So, how are you doing? I don't get to see much of you these days," she said, her tone softer.

"I'm okay," I said. "Busy, you know, with work. But okay."

She nodded. "My grandbabies are here. Did you see them outside?"

"I did," I said and smiled. "They greeted me when I arrived. Brooks's wolf is getting big."

"They both are," Mom said, returning my smile. "And I'm not surprised, given how much those two eat." She leaned over to check something in the oven. It smelled like a lasagna—one of my dad's favorites.

"Can I do anything to help?" I offered.

"Sure, you can chop those peppers to go in the salad," she replied and grabbed two loaves to begin preparing the garlic bread.

I did as she asked, happy to be of help. I enjoyed cooking almost as much as I enjoyed working with wood. I had spent countless hours in the kitchen preparing food for our family. Being back at the chopping board with my mother beside me was nice. It felt like old times when I still lived at home, and life was simpler.

"I'm glad you came," she said from where she spread butter over the sliced bread. "I was beginning to worry that you'd run off."

"Mom, I see Dad and the guys almost every day," I said. "I think they would tell you if I had disappeared."

"Hmm," she said again. "Well, I miss you. I wouldn't mind seeing you almost every day as well."

I didn't respond. I kept cutting the pepper I was working on into thin slices, noticing how transparent they were in the late afternoon sun's rays streaming through the kitchen window. The pepper, the cutting board, and even the reflections off the knife all glowed in warm, butter-yellow tones. It was quite lovely. I set the pepper aside and reached for a red one.

"I know you're busy," she said. "I just think it would be nice if you took more work on this side of the Pass. We would get to see you more often for meals around here. I like the help in the kitchen, you know?"

"I know," I sighed. I also knew that she was aware that the bulk of the work I had been doing on the other side of the Pass was for Sara, with Sara. And she disapproved. My mom's primary goal was to see her sons happily mated. Her opinion—and that of most, if not all, shifters—was that you didn't, under any circumstances, form a mating bond with a non-shifter. It was an unwritten rule.

Not that it was impossible or had never been done, but it was risky and didn't always work out for the shifter in the relationship. Shifters, particularly wolf shifters, mated for life. Once that bond was in place, there was no other person for us, period. Occasionally, if the bond was new and one of the partners died, the other bonded member could move on. But it was rare. Most often, the bonded partner remained alone for the rest of their days, always mourning their lost mate.

It was bad enough if both people in a relationship were shifters; the loss was devastating. But if a shifter bonded with a non-shifter—someone who didn't bond the way we did, someone who expected to date or even marry and walk away if it didn't work out—it was a tragedy. There was no divorce in the shifter world, no casual dating, and no one-night stands. Mated was mated. Sure, going out with someone a few times was possible until you both knew it wasn't a match, at which point the shifters would go their separate ways and try again with someone new, but it was always with the intention of finding your mate. Two shifters always bonded at the same time. If it was a match, it was a match—the end. It wasn't the same if you got too close to a non-shifter.

"I feel like maybe you've been avoiding me," she said. "Could it have anything to do with the phone number I asked your dad to pass along?"

I sighed, putting my work down and wiping my hands on a faded kitchen towel.

"What?" she exclaimed playfully. "I'm not asking you to get mated. I'm just asking you to go out for coffee or drinks with a few of my friends' daughters. It wouldn't kill you. In fact, you might enjoy it. And who knows ..." she trailed off as she looked over to the side, avoiding my gaze that was now fixed on her.

She sighed. Clasping her hands in front of her, she met my stare. "All I'm saying is that I don't think it's a good idea to be spending so much time with the witch. Nothing can come of it," she said. Her tone was low and even—the one she used when she was laying down the law. "She isn't one of us. She's an entirely different species. There is no future for the two of you. Please listen to reason." She waved her hand toward the living room, where the rumble of the game still sounded. "Look at your brother and how happy he is to be mated," she began when Lucas piped up from the other room.

"Leave me out of it," he called.

"He and Lara mated when they were babies," I said, trying to keep my frustration in check.

"They were the same age as your father and I were when we mated," she protested.

"It's not like that these days, Mom. Plenty of people wait until they're in their thirties before they get mated," I said.

"So, that's your plan? Just wait until you're in your thirties to start taking this seriously?" The playful tone was gone. She was growing irritated.

Before I could answer, the front door slammed open, and my niece and nephew came running into the kitchen, back on two legs and fully dressed. I was happy for the interruption. The conversation was going nowhere good, and I'd heard it all before.

"Uncle Silas. Uncle Silas," Emma called as she came barreling toward me. She flung her thin arms around my middle. "My wolf is getting so big," she squealed. "Wasn't she big?"

"Yes, I saw you, pup," I said, hugging her back. "She's so big. Almost as big as your brother's."

"Yeah, I know," she said happily. "Isn't my wolf pretty?"

"She sure is. The prettiest one I've ever seen," I assured her before she took off for the living room to see her dad and grandpa.

My nephew waited patiently until his little sister finished, sneaking in for a quick one-armed hug before following her out. Neither of them greeted their grandma. It wasn't that they didn't adore her—they did—but even young shifters could sense when an elder had their hackles up.

When I glanced back at my mom, she was pulling the lasagna out of the oven. The line of her shoulders and back remained tense. I didn't want to upset her. I wanted to be happily mated, too. I just needed to figure out what that meant for me and how to go about it. If Sara had only been born a shifter and not a witch, I thought, then I quickly corrected myself. It wasn't Sara's fault, and I wouldn't want her to be any different. But things would certainly be a lot easier.

Dinner was a peaceful affair. My little brother, Elija, ventured out of his room to join us. The Huskies won, so my dad and Lucas were in a good mood, and my mother preferred not to argue in front of the kids. The food was delicious as always, and by the time dessert arrived, I had nearly forgotten about the argument in the kitchen.

I was spooning up the last of my tiramisu when my mother spoke up.

"Silas, we're having a family dinner on Saturday. It would be nice if you would join us," she said pleasantly enough.

I set my spoon down. "Um, well. I'm not sure what I have going on. I'll have to check," I said. I glanced up to see her disappointed blue eyes locked onto mine. She didn't say anything, but it broke my heart just the same.

I had a decision to make, and I needed to make it soon.

10

KATE

When my alarm went off at 6 p.m., I figured it was safe to come out of hiding. That's what it felt like. It felt like I was hiding downstairs from the sun and from the fact that I should still be asleep. I was curious to see what Felix had to say about it.

I sensed Sara before I saw her. With the enhancement of my abilities, I began to learn to recognize the emotional landscapes of those around me. Sara was typically optimistic, bright, and happy. Today, her mood was dialed up to eleven. I hurried faster than usual up the steps, through the foyer, and into the living room, where I found her on her phone.

"I want to hear all about it!" I exclaimed as I raced to a stop in front of where she sat.

She shrieked, clutching her phone to her chest, and then swore loudly. "Gods damn it, Kate," she panted. "You scared the crap out of me." She pulled her phone away from her body and looked at the screen. She scowled deeply and turned it to face me, showing a blank screen with some yellow and brown discoloration around the edges.

I sucked in a breath and hunched my shoulders. This was why I needed to keep my guard up around my housemates. Not only was it unfair for me to know everything they were feeling, but it was getting me into trouble. "Sorry," I said, cringing. "I didn't mean to. I just couldn't wait to hear what happened today."

She set the phone down and sighed. "It's okay. I need to learn to control my gift better," she said, cocking half a smile at me.

I was relieved to see that she wouldn't hold it against me. I examined her mood, and she was still flying high.

"So," I prompted. "Was it Silas? Did the two of you finally make it official?"

Her face fell, and I knew I had said the wrong thing. Whatever this was, it had nothing to do with her stalled relationship.

"Shit, Sara. I'm sorry. I'm messing with your awesome mood," I said, settling into a chair across from her. I placed my hands in my lap and tried to wait patiently.

"Don't worry. I don't think anything could mess with the mood I'm in," she assured me. Then she went on to tell me about her awesome day, her new employee, Beth, and how Bruce had offered to help her with the business side of things.

"You trust him, right?" she asked. "It's not like I'm about to hand him all my banking info, but I don't know the guy."

I tilted my head and recalled what I sensed about the man. So far, he was what he appeared to be. He was straightforward, well-meaning, and honest. "I think he's alright," I said. "I'll make sure to keep an eye on him, but I don't get the sense that he would cheat you."

She nodded. "Yeah, he seems like a good guy. I get zero

creep vibes, and I think he wouldn't want to mess up a future here if he's looking for protection."

"Agreed."

"So, what are you going to do about him?" she asked.

It was a good question. I didn't want to be responsible for another person, especially a human, given how the vampire laws treated humans. I also couldn't turn him out. I knew how vicious vampires could be, and the thought of Bruce being taken or handed over to one of them made me shudder. I thought of Sara and the shape she'd been in when we got her back from James, and she had only been in his hands for a few hours.

Of course, I was a vampire now, too. I wasn't *that* kind of vampire, though. I tried to comfort myself with the thought, but then I remembered how I had acted less than twenty-four hours before. I had threatened Felix without a second thought. I got in his face and growled at him, flashing my fangs, ready for a fight. I might have different thoughts about right and wrong, but I could be dangerous. I needed to remember that, especially around those I cared for.

"I'm not sure," I finally said. "I'm glad I have some time to think about it. Whatever it is, we'll have a House vote before anything is decided for sure."

She nodded and curved her lips into a tight smile. She understood my hesitation better than anyone. I was so grateful we were in this together. I honestly don't know what I would have done if I didn't have her.

My thoughts were interrupted by the sounds of Marcus emerging from his sleep in search of food, which reminded me I was starving.

"You had dinner yet?" I asked, getting to my feet.

She shot me an odd look. "No," she said hesitantly. "Bruce is cooking tonight."

My eyebrows shot up. "He is?" I asked. It was then that I noticed the smell of cooking food wafting from the kitchen. "That's good, I guess. For your sake, I hope he's a good cook." I wasn't surprised he had jumped in to help around the house. I knew he wanted to make a good impression and demonstrate that our lives would be better with him around. I just hoped it didn't step on Sara's toes. She was my partner in all this, and her opinion mattered greatly.

We rounded the corner and greeted Marcus just as he reached the top of the steps.

"How is everyone doing?" he asked.

"Good," we replied in unison as we entered the kitchen.

I stopped and stared, shocked by the transformation since I had been there the night before. The kitchen had been fairly utilitarian. Sara was the only one in the house who actually consumed food until recently, so I never gave the kitchen much thought. She had filled it with some second-hand items she needed, but it resembled a roughly stocked rental more than a real kitchen, until now.

Not only were all surfaces clean to the point of shining, but new small appliances adorned the countertops, a new round wooden dining table replaced the wobbly old one, and bowls of fresh fruit and vegetables were artfully placed throughout the room. Bruce stood at the stove, wearing a grey and black striped apron over a black t-shirt and jeans, stirring a pot of what smelled like a rich curry.

He glanced over as we entered. "Hey," he said in a low but friendly tone. "Have a seat; everything's just about ready."

I looked at the new table. A full place setting occupied one spot: a white placemat, a plate, a bowl, silverware, a crisp white napkin, and a drinking glass. In front of two other chairs sat black placemats, wine glasses, and black embroidered napkins. I wandered over to one of the settings clearly intended for vampires and pulled out the unfamiliar gray upholstered chair. It looked quite comfortable.

The three of us took our seats, shooting surprised looks at one another. Bruce came over and set a salad plate in front of Sara, filling her glass with ice water before coming to the other side of the table and pouring warm blood into the two wine glasses.

When he finished pouring, he set the pitcher between Marcus and me. Before he could step back, I put my hand on his forearm. "Bruce," I said, glancing around the table. "There are only three place settings. I hope you plan to join us."

The others nodded enthusiastically.

"Oh, no. That's okay. I don't think that would be appropriate," he said. Wiping his hands on his apron, he looked flustered.

"I told you, Bruce," Sara said. "We aren't that kind of House. None of us expect to be waited on, and we wouldn't dream of eating a meal you prepared without you."

"Please," I said, patting an empty spot between Sara and me.

"Well, alright," he said. "Just give me a moment. And, please, go ahead and eat before the blood gets cold."

I hesitated, but really, blood is way better warm than cold, so I lifted my glass and sipped. It was delicious. O-negative, just the way I liked it.

He finished dishing up some fragrant white rice and curry into serving pieces, pulled fresh naan from the oven, and grabbed an extra set of dishes before bringing them over to the table.

Sara was forking up her salad, and Marcus and I were on

our second glasses by the time Bruce settled down and served.

"Bruce," I said, setting my glass down and leaning in. "The kitchen looks amazing. I can't believe you pulled this all off in one day."

"Thank you," he said with a gracious bow of his head. "I was happy to do it. I enjoy cooking, and this kitchen has real potential—no offense," he added, shooting a glance at Sara.

"Not offended," she said, raising her hands. "I've been meaning to do more with the house. I've just been so busy. And thank you again for your help in the shop today. I appreciate it." She flashed him a wide smile before reaching for the rice dish. "Oh, and for cooking," she said brightly. "I'm terrible at it. My mom or aunt usually did all the cooking before I moved in here. You would not want to eat my food." She cringed.

"She's being too hard on herself. I remember her food being quite good," I said. "But, Bruce, you have to let us pay for all this. I'm sure it wasn't cheap to outfit the entire kitchen."

He shook his head. "No. It was truly a pleasure. I made plenty of money at the Tap House, and I haven't had a chance to spend it in quite some time. This was fun. If I stay on," he continued, "maybe you'd allow me to take a crack at the rest of the house? Nothing too major, but I could update the decor and make everything a bit more functional."

"Oh, yes, please!" Sara exclaimed. "Silas has been great for our construction needs, but decorating hasn't been on the top of anyone's list."

"What do you think, Marcus?" I asked. I didn't want any of the House members left out of decisions regarding the home we all shared, and I wasn't sure I wanted to give my consent just yet. I like the idea of Bruce helping out while he was here, and, in truth, I did want him to stay, but I was scared of what that could mean.

Marcus's eyebrows shot up. "Umm, yeah. That sounds great. But if we're going to spend money fixing the place up, I want to contribute. I've got savings to burn as well."

Sara beamed, and I smiled back but kept quiet.

Everyone fell silent, concentrating on their meals. I looked around the table at my housemates—House Members. Then there was Bruce. I considered him; he was one of the first people I met when I was thrust into this world. He'd always shown me kindness and respect, and he chose me when he needed help. That showed a lot of trust. I sighed. This was going to be hard on everyone if it didn't work out, I thought.

When dinner/breakfast was over, Marcus insisted on helping with the dishes. Bruce gratefully accepted, and Sara and I went back to the living room to give them some space.

"The improvements in the kitchen make the rest of the house look pretty dumpy," Sara said, glancing around at the sparsely furnished room full of second-hand pieces and piles of our clutter.

"Well, we could tidy up the place a bit," I said, grabbing a stack of books next to the loveseat and carrying them over to our single bookcase. I was placing them onto a tilting shelf when I heard Sara exclaim from behind me. It wasn't her cry that startled me; rather, it was the surge of grief, fear, and anger coming from her that broke through my defenses and got my attention.

No sooner had I turned to find out what had happened than her emotions righted themselves and were replaced with curiosity and awe.

She stood beside the chair I usually sat in at night, and my sketchbook lay on the floor at her feet. She stared down at it, her lips forming an O, and her eyes open wide. She started to tilt to one side.

"Sara," I said, racing to her side and taking hold of one of her arms to steady her. "Are you okay? What happened?"

She shook her head and then looked up at me. "You made a Relic," she breathed.

"A what?" I asked. I had no idea what she was talking about, but she sounded like she was in shock. "Let's sit down. Okay?" I walked her backward until she was in front of the loveseat and then gently helped lower her to the worn cushions.

"Kate," she said, turning her head toward me again. "This is incredible—"

"Hey," Marcus interrupted, coming from the kitchen. He glanced at the two of us on the sofa and the look on Sara's face. "Everything alright out here?"

"I'm not sure," I said. "I was putting away some books when Sara yelped and ..." I shrugged.

"Kate made a Relic," Sara said, her voice now sounding excited. "I can't believe it, but that has to be what it is." Her eyes were fixed on my sketchbook, still lying on the floor, the pages crumpled painfully on one side.

I got up to retrieve it and save the sketches from permanent damage.

"Careful!" Sara cried.

I glanced back at her alarmed expression before reaching down to pick up the book. As my hand made contact with the creased page holding my latest sketch, all the emotions I'd struggled with the night before flooded back at once, and I gasped.

These were my emotions, and yet they weren't. I reacted instinctively, shoring up the wall of space inside my mind and pushing back against the onslaught. It was enough. I was able to shield myself from the intensity of it, leaving only an echoing impression radiating from the drawing of leaves, flowers, and tiny animals.

I turned and placed the book carefully on the coffee table in front of Sara, who backed subtly away from the thing. "Can you feel it now?" I asked.

She shook her head. "No. Only when I was touching it."

Marcus walked over and peered down at the book, open with the sketch facing up. "It's nice," he said, cocking an eyebrow. "May I?" he asked, indicating the book.

I nodded, and he stepped forward and placed his palm flat on the drawing.

I didn't need my gift to know that he was affected. His whole body jolted, and he staggered back, breaking the contact with the paper.

"I told you," Sara said. "Have you ever seen a Relic before?" she asked Marcus, her features alight with excitement.

He shook his head, a look of wonder on his face. "No, but I've heard of them," he said.

"Could someone please explain what a Relic is and why both of you are so shocked?" I asked, growing frustrated.

"It's a magically infused object. But not any magic," Sara went on. "I don't know why I didn't think of it before, but a Relic is a magical object that can affect someone's thoughts, feelings, or perceptions."

"Why is that a big deal?" I asked. "I'm sure witches make stuff like that all the time. You sell magically enhanced stuff in your shop."

Sara shook her head, sending her curls bouncing wildly. "No. Not like this. The witches I know of only channel natural magic," she explained. "You know, air, fire, water, earth, and electricity. No living witch can directly affect the mind, at least not that I know of. That's why, when we met and I realized what you could do, I was pretty sure you weren't a witch.

"But this, this is something that hasn't been seen in decades, centuries maybe," she continued. "That's why we call them Relics. These objects are old. Super old. And extremely valuable."

"And you think my drawing is like these Relics?" I asked, unconvinced.

"Not, like one. It is one, Kate. I'm sure of it," she said, pushing her stray curls back from her face. "What else could it be?"

"I don't know," I said, irritated. "I don't know what kind of magic this is. I'm not a witch."

"What are you?" a voice asked from my left.

We all glanced toward where Bruce stood in the kitchen doorway, the towel in his hands forgotten.

Shit. This was going to complicate things.

11

BRUCE

Marcus narrowed his eyes as he studied me. "How much of that did you hear?" He crossed his arms, waiting for a reply. Looking at him, it was no surprise that he worked in law enforcement—or the vampire equivalent.

I cleared my throat. Instinct told me the truth was the only correct response here. "Pretty much all of it," I admitted.

Kate tilted her head and exhaled loudly through her nose. I thought she was going to shoo me away, but instead, she gestured for me to come closer. "You might as well join us, Bruce. If I'm leaving bits of stray magic around the house, you should probably be aware."

I nodded and stepped closer. The object on the table appeared to be a normal sketch pad with a lovely botanical illustration on the top page. I glanced at Kate, who sat watching me.

"As for what I am, aside from being a vampire, I honestly have no clue. But apparently, I can make that," she said, pointing to the drawing.

Bending over the page, I cocked an eyebrow at Kate, who

nodded in response. "You can touch it if you want to. I don't think it's dangerous. It just makes you feel shitty."

I reached forward and touched a single finger to the page. The effect was immediate, and Kate was right; it was shitty. I took a shuddering breath as fear and sadness overwhelmed me. I quickly broke contact and stepped backward, distancing myself from the source. As soon as I did, the negative emotions faded away, as if they had never existed.

"That's ... How did you do that?" I asked.

"I'm not sure," Kate said, leaning back on the sofa and crossing her arms, mirroring Marcus's posture. "I drew that last night. I was feeling pretty bad after everything that happened yesterday, and I guess I must have somehow pushed those emotions onto the page. I did feel a hell of a lot better when I was done."

"That was what you were feeling last night?" I asked softly. I stared down at the page, recalling the flood of despair that had swept over me. "After I arrived, after you were forced to make a choice?"

"Oh, no," Kate said, sitting up straight, a pained look on her face. "Bruce, it wasn't you. I promise. It's just everything right now. The funeral, missing my family, the Council, and their stupid rules. It was just a lot."

"So you think you pushed the emotions onto the page, into the drawing itself?" Marcus asked. "Like how you pushed against me when you were bleeding on the way back from your fight with Alexander?"

He had lost me on that one. I had heard rumors about Kate having a fallout with Alexander, but I didn't realize there had been an actual fight. At the time, I wondered how a newly turned vampire could stand up against someone as old as Alexander. I supposed this was the answer.

Kate sighed again. "Not just then," she said, sounding sad. "I'm constantly pushing at both you and Felix."

Marcus started. "You are?" He readjusted his arms, clutching his chest tighter, along with the muscles in his jaw. "And, just what kind of emotion are you pushing at us?"

"Disinterest and calm mostly." She looked down at the floor, not meeting Marcus's eyes. "I just don't want it to be hard for you to be around me. And I don't want to get bitten either," she said, her mouth pulling into a small smile.

Marcus nodded, but his face was still a mask of worry.

"So you can affect people's emotions?" I asked. "And other vampires want to feed from you?" As strange as that all sounded, I could believe it after what I'd just experienced.

"Yeah. My blood is like vampire catnip for some reason." She shrugged. "As for the emotional stuff, even when I was human, I could tell what other people were feeling. It's just become more intense since I was turned," she said. I must have looked worried because she quickly added, "But don't worry. I try not to. I keep myself blocked from the people in the house—when I remember to. And now you know my secret," she finished.

Suddenly, all eyes were on me. I shifted my weight, trying to think of something to say that would reassure everyone in the room that I would not reveal what I had learned. It was hard to know what more I could do beyond signing the stack of non-disclosure agreements and the interim contract Felix had given me the night before. "Of course, I—"

"Don't sweat it, Bruce." Kate waved a hand at me. "I trust you. And, as you now know, I'm a pretty good judge of character." She smiled at me. "Plus, you're not going anywhere. Unless you want to, that wasn't a threat or anything," she stammered. "I mean that, unless there are objections from the others, you have a home here for as long as you want."

I glanced at Sara, sitting beside Kate. Her grin told me she was on board. Marcus was harder to read, but he nodded slowly. "No objections here," he said in a firm voice.

I couldn't quite believe it. This was unexpected in a world where decisions like this move at a snail's pace. I had been prepared to wait out the full month for her decision, if not longer. "I don't know what to say besides thank you. I'll work hard and make sure you don't regret your decision."

"Well, don't work too hard. I can't exactly afford to pay you," Kate said. "Besides, if you stay here, you're one of us. I won't have you being a servant in your own home."

Her words were like a foreign language coming from the mouth of a vampire. But then again, she wasn't your average vampire. Still, I was shocked. I looked over at Marcus to gauge his opinion on the matter, but he was staring at Kate with a look that could only be described as impressed. I know I certainly was.

"Okay," I began. "But I want to contribute and be an asset to the House. If it's not interfering with what you already have in place, I would very much like to be a sort of House manager. I can see several ways I could help out, both here and in the shop. If that's okay with you, Sara," I added.

"More than okay." Sara beamed at me.

"Well, I suppose we should get Felix back over here and make it official," Kate said.

"He'll be by later this evening," I blurted out. There were curious stares, but no one added anything. I could feel my face grow warm. "He told me last night that he'd be back by," I rushed to explain.

"That's good," Marcus said. "Kate, I think you and I need to talk with him." He'd relaxed his posture, but his voice still held a note of concern. I was looking forward to seeing the lawyer again, but decided I didn't want to be around for that conversation.

"Yeah, I suppose you're right," Kate agreed. "Speaking of Felix, though ... Bruce, are you okay with having him in the house? I'm sorry about last night. I hope he didn't make you uncomfortable. You say the word, and we'll meet with him somewhere else."

Once again, I found myself at the center of attention. "Um, no. He's fine. I mean, it's fine." Why was my face so hot? I hoped Kate was blocking my emotions at that moment. I didn't want her to know how the tall, blond vampire with the European accent made me feel. I wasn't entirely sure myself, and I didn't want Kate's perception of the situation to complicate matters.

"Good. I also wanted to apologize for how I acted last night," she said, shaking her head. "I can't imagine that seeing me snarling at Felix was a pleasant experience. I didn't intend to jump all over him. I'm just glad it didn't escalate. Hopefully, I'll get better at controlling my emotions with time." She looked at me with wide eyes. "You're probably wondering what you signed on for. A crazy House with a half-mad, strangely magical leader." She laughed dryly. "I have no idea what I'm doing."

"There's no need to apologize to me," I said. "You were defending me, after all. Most sires would have let an older vampire drain whomever they liked, member of their staff or not."

She gaped at me. "I would like to say I don't believe you, but after meeting my own maker, I get it. But please don't use the "S" word." She cringed. "It's old-fashioned and creepy. I'm no one's sire. Nor do I plan to be, by the way. In case you weren't serious about staying human."

"Actually, Kate, you won't be able to turn another vampire until sometime after your tenth year," Marcus said with a bit of hesitation. "I probably should have mentioned it before now."

"Oh, great," Kate snorted. "So, not only is this a messed-up House, but the leader can't even make more vampires?" she continued. "Sorry, Bruce. If you want to run for the door, now is the time. I won't stop you."

Marcus barked out a laugh. "Don't worry, Kate. Sire or not, you're doing just fine. Your little display of fangs last night proves that you have what it takes. You were willing to go up against a vampire much older than you to defend someone you thought of as yours. Bruce is right; not many would have done the same. If Bruce had wanted a traditional House, he would have had options. I think he came here for the very reason you're apologizing."

I nodded at Marcus. No, this was nothing like a traditional House, and that *is* why I'd come. At that moment, I felt happiness for the first time since arriving at the Tap House days earlier. I looked around the room at the other members of this "messed up" House with wonder. It could be that Margaux had done me a favor.

In all my years, both before entering the supernatural world and afterward, I had never met a group like this. These were good people trying their best to help those around them. It seemed like a low bar, but in my experience, it was something special, and I was glad to be a part of it.

Kate pressed her lips together and lowered her brow. I noticed her bottom lip begin to tremble, and I stepped forward, pulling a black handkerchief from my pocket. She smiled gratefully as she took it. "How do you always have one of these when I need one?" she asked, sniffing through her tears.

"Well, they come in handy when working among vampires," I said, returning her smile.

"Not working," she corrected. "Living. This is your home now, Bruce."

"Even so," I said. "I'll make sure to stay well stocked."

She choked out a half-sob, half-laugh at that. "Good idea."

"Now that we have Bruce all sorted and Kate's in tears, are we going to talk about that?" Sara said, pointing at the drawing still lying on the table, forgotten.

Kate stopped sniffing and glanced at the sketch. "You said they're valuable?"

"Yeah, like priceless," Sara replied.

"I'm not sure what someone would use it for," Kate said.

"It's not just about the usefulness. They're artifacts from the past. They contain magic that doesn't exist anymore," Sara explained.

"Well, it clearly still does," Kate argued. "Do you think you could sell it?"

Sara looked thoughtfully at the drawing. "I'm not sure. These things are handled at an entirely different level than my family's magical supply shop. We're talking Sotheby's level."

"Why don't you see what you can find out?" Marcus suggested. "Not just about selling a Relic but where they originally came from, and I'll make similar inquiries among the vampires."

Sara agreed, and the matter was settled for the time being. I was about to excuse myself when Kate and Marus both whipped their heads up in unison, glancing toward the front of the house.

"I'll get the door," I suggested.

"Do you want one of us to?" Kate asked, with a look of concern.

"No. I got it," I said, leaving the group to see who was arriving. I took off the apron I was wearing and tossed it on the kitchen table, along with a dishcloth I was apparently still clutching, and headed to the front door. My stomach tightened at the thought that it might be Felix already. He told me he lived nearby, but I was never sure what that meant to a vampire. Distance was relative when you could move faster than the human eye could track.

By the time I opened the door, an orange Jeep was pulling up in front of the house. And sure enough, out stepped the lean vampire, his hair tied back in a knot and a gleam in his hazel eyes. He climbed the steps to the porch and walked to where I stood, holding the door open. But instead of coming inside, he leaned into me. I swallowed hard but didn't move as he brought his mouth closer and closer to the side of my neck. My heart tripped as he brushed his lips against the shell of my ear.

"Hey, gorgeous," he whispered in his smooth, accented voice. "Waiting for me?"

12

KATE

"It must be Felix," I said, pausing to listen. No one was talking, but I distinctly heard a gasp, and then someone spoke. "You're needed in your professional capacity this evening, and I'm afraid that wouldn't be very professional," Bruce said. His voice sounded strained.

Oh, for crying out loud. "Felix!" I yelled. It was unnecessary to raise my voice, but I wanted to make sure I had his attention. "Leave the man alone and get in here."

I turned to Marcus. "Are you sure that vampire's okay? He doesn't seem to be taking the hint," I snarled.

"From whom?" he asked with a smile. "Don't worry. Felix is a good guy. Easily distracted, but a good guy. And you've warned him. He won't hurt Bruce, I promise."

"If you say so," I mumbled as Felix walked into the room, followed closely by Bruce. At least Bruce wasn't acting afraid. I would have to keep an eye on Felix, however. I might trust him as my lawyer and quite possibly with my secrets, but Bruce's safety was another matter, and I didn't want to take chances.

"Good evening," Felix said. "Bruce tells me my services are required."

I nodded. "Yup, it's time to make it official with Bruce," I announced.

Felix halted his progress and clapped a hand to his chest in mock surprise. "Already? It's only been one night."

"I know, but he grows on you quickly," I said.

"Indeed, he does," Felix smiled, and I answered him with a scowl. His expression cleared. "But in all seriousness, and as your lawyer, do you not want to take more time to consider? Not that I disapprove of your choice, but these things typically take a lot of time and deliberation."

"No." I sighed. "More time isn't going to change anything. I'm not letting Margaux get her hands on him."

"Very well. I don't have it all with me, but I'll ensure everything is drawn up properly and review it with you all later." He turned to Bruce. "Congratulations. I hope this means we'll be seeing more of each other."

Bruce nodded but looked away.

"Hey," Sara spoke up, breaking the tension. "Bruce, why don't you and I go over to the shop and discuss your thoughts on the business? We could give these three some time to talk."

"Yeah," Bruce said, brightening at the idea. "That would be great. I have several ideas I want to run past you."

"Great," Sara said, rising. "Good evening, all. You know where we'll be if you need us." She squeezed my arm as she passed. *Thank God for Sara.* Bruce followed her out, leaving Marcus and me alone with Felix.

Marcus cleared his throat. "Felix, come join us," he said. "There are other things we wanted to talk about besides the Bruce situation."

We settled into the mismatched furniture, and I thought

about how wonderful it would be if Bruce were serious about making over the house. I would love to see the potential this place had, I thought. It was good that the others in the House were willing to contribute. I hoped Sara would find a way to profit from my newfound talent. It would be nice to contribute my share, which sparked a thought.

"Felix," I blurted out. "Who pays you?" I felt foolish for never thinking to ask, although I admittedly had a lot on my mind since meeting him.

He chucked while lounging in my favorite oversized pink chair. The six-foot-six Scandinavian vampire made the thing look small. "Pro Bono, my friend." He flashed me his fangs. "Marcus told me about your problem with Alexander, and I jumped at the chance. You're unique, and I don't have many expenses these days." He shrugged. "Even if I needed the money, I would probably work for you for free."

"Speaking of unique." Marcus flicked his gaze to me and raised an eyebrow.

"Whatever." I shrugged. "It's not like we're getting anywhere on our own at the moment. And ... I probably do owe him an explanation."

Marcus's mouth hardened into a thin line, but he nodded.

"Well, now I'm intrigued," Felix said, leaning forward.

I took a deep breath, steeling myself, and proceeded to lay it out for him. I told him about the early rising, my ability to sense moods before my change, and other vampires' attraction to the scent of my blood. Finally, I admitted what I'd been doing the few times we'd met. The only thing I left out was my creation of the Relic that still lay on the table between us. I made a point of not looking at the thing.

"Fascinating," he breathed. "So you've been manipulating my emotions every time I've come here?"

"Not totally." I twisted my hands together. It sounded bad. It *was* bad. But it was also an attempt to keep myself safe, given my experience. "I've just been giving you a bit of a nudge to keep you feeling ... disinterested."

"I'm afraid you're not as talented as you think," he said and gave me a wink.

"Well, disinterested in biting me. I've been working to keep myself from seeming appealing," I clarified. "Although I don't know why I didn't consider shielding Bruce, too." I nodded to myself. That could be a solution to the problem of keeping Bruce safe around hungry vampires, at least when I was present.

Felix held up his hands. "Let's not get carried away. I'm interested to see what it would be like to be around you without your little nudges," he said.

"Agreed," Marcus said. He'd taken Sara's place beside me on the sofa. I glanced at his stern face and felt guilt wrap around my middle. I hadn't intended to hurt him, quite the opposite.

"Okay," I said, feeling uncertain. Pushing against them had become second nature. It felt uncomfortable to consider dropping that barrier. Even though Marcus had been around me without it before my attack, ever since he'd smelled my blood, I hadn't wanted to tempt him. And who knew how Felix would react? I'd already seen how the scent of human blood affected him. "If you're both sure?"

"You were able to defend yourself against Alexander when he meant you harm," Marcus said. "Neither of us wants to hurt you. But if things go wrong, feel free to do whatever you must."

I nodded again but pushed myself back, putting some

distance between Marcus and me before I let go. I took a deep breath and let the pressure I had on both men ease. As the outward force dropped, so did my barrier against their emotions. I didn't put that piece back in place. It was probably a good idea to keep an eye on what they were feeling.

No one spoke. I glanced between the two, but their expressions were blank. I listened with my other senses. Neither was feeling homicidal, which was a good thing. Curiosity, fascination, and warm affection were all I felt. That last one was coming from Marcus, and it made me wonder if he felt that way all the time or just when I had my guard down.

Marcus smiled. "Interesting," he said. "It's not that I couldn't smell your scent a moment ago, but I have to admit it is more alluring now."

Felix cocked his head and furrowed his brow. "Do you mind if I get a bit closer?" he asked. "I promise not to bite." He said the last bit with his familiar teasing, and it went a long way in convincing me he was under control.

Marcus got up, and Felix took his seat on the sofa. I didn't move. I thought it best to let him come to me. Felix leaned forward, closed his eyes, and breathed in deeply through his nose. I didn't watch his face. Instead, I studied his emotions. He was delighted, radiating joy and wonder, with no hint of longing or desire. I relaxed my shoulders and took a relieved breath.

Felix flicked his eyes open and grinned at me. "You smell wonderful. Simply wonderful. I can see now why James went mad for you and why Alexander was loath to give you up. You are special, aren't you?"

I was glad, of course, that no one was trying to kill me. But there was a bit of disappointment, too. Was this what I'd been so worried about for the past weeks? Had I been keeping myself sequestered from other vampires for nothing, not that I had met any other vampires I wanted to spend time with? But still.

I gazed at Felix, waiting to see what else he would say, but he just stared back at me with a blissful expression.

"So," I demanded. "What's wrong with me?"

"Who says there is anything wrong with you?" He raised a blond eyebrow and quirked a smile.

"I mean, why am I different?" I asked.

"Hmm. That's a bit harder," he said, his hazel eyes growing soft. "Why are any of us different from each other? Why was your friend born a witch and her boyfriend a shifter? Why does she carry magic that smells of a storm while other witches carry the smell of cool water or damp earth? Magic is strange and sometimes unpredictable. I suspect that one of your parents had a bit of lost magic, or what some call 'old magic'. Although most people believe that old magic is a myth."

I perked up at the mention of old magic. "I don't think it's my mother," I said. "She's normal, as far as I can tell. And I don't remember my father. He left before my brother was born."

"How old were you?" Felix asked.

I shrugged. "I don't know. I must have been about eight or nine."

"Surely you remember back to when you were eight or nine years old. Besides the fact that your childhood was just yesterday, I remember things from my third and fourth years."

I glanced at Marcus, who merely nodded in confirmation. I thought back to my childhood. I remembered my elementary school and the house we moved to when I was in third grade. I tried to think of anything before that time, but I was drawing a blank.

I shook my head. "My first memory was of going to see my new baby brother in the hospital after he was born. My grandparents—my mother's parents—took me, and I remember looking at him through the glass window with embedded wire mesh where they kept all the newborns. My grandma brought two stuffed bears, one for me and one for my brother. That's as far back as I can go."

"Well, I think we have our answer," Felix said, smiling.

"What?" I asked, not following his logic.

"You possess some sort of old magic that influences people's minds, yet you cannot recall one of your parents, who contributed half of your DNA. I think it's a safe assumption that you inherited this magic from him and that he's the reason you have no memories before he left the family."

I considered what he was saying. On some level, it made sense, but it left me with a hollow feeling. I'd never questioned not remembering things from when I was small. It never bothered me. But now it felt wrong. Had something been done to my memory like Felix suggested? Had I been robbed, not only of a parent but of my life before I was nine years old?

"Sara says I'm not a witch," I said, staring into his eyes. "What am I?"

Felix sighed. "I'm not sure. I wouldn't want to guess until we had more information," he said.

I narrowed my eyes and studied him. But there was no ill intent that I could feel. Concern, interest, and a certain protectiveness, but no malice. Fine. Answers would have to wait.

"I suggest you go speak with your mother. Assuming

your father didn't work over her memories, she might have the answers you seek," Felix said.

"No," both Marcus and I said at the same time. Marcus smiled and motioned for me to continue.

"My mom thinks I'm dead. I don't want to disrupt her life or put her in any danger by revealing our world to her." I shifted in my seat. "You know the rules better than I do, and while I don't agree with them, I don't want my mother subject to vampire law."

Felix nodded. "That's a tough one," he agreed. "Okay. Well, do you need me for anything else tonight? I have a few other appointments," he said.

"Oh, no. Thank you," I said, getting to my feet as Felix rose to tower over me. "But, I did want to apologize for messing with your emotions. I see now that it wasn't necessary. I'm sorry."

Felix shook his head. "Don't ever apologize for protecting yourself or those you care for," he said.

Marcus and I saw him to the door and said goodnight. I noticed him glance over at the shop before going down the steps, but moments later, I heard the roar of his Jeep's engine and knew he hadn't gotten sidetracked.

"I could use a snack," I said to Marcus. "You want anything from the kitchen?"

He shook his head but followed me to our newly decorated space. It felt so much better. It would be nice, I thought, to have Bruce as a housemate. I smiled as I poured myself a glass of O-negative and then joined Marcus, who had taken a seat at the table. I glanced at his face. "We still need to talk, don't we?" I asked.

"Yeah, we do," he said. He looked down at his hands clasped in front of him on the table and took a deep breath. "Kate, I know I said before I was going to need you to push back at me from time to time if things got rough. But when I said it, you were soaked through in your own blood from the attack. I didn't consider that you would dampen my emotions each time we were together. I can only imagine it's been exhausting for you to maintain that sort of vigilance, and that was not my intention. From now on, don't try to influence me emotionally without me first asking, okay?"

A lump had somehow found its way into my throat. Not only did I feel as if I had been caught doing something wrong, which I had, but I could sense how hurt Marcus was. This, in turn, reminded me that I wasn't shielding his emotions from myself as I knew I ought to, which made me feel even guiltier ...

I cleared my throat and put my wall back in place, but I didn't do anything that might push against Marcus. I stayed behind my shield to give him some privacy and allow myself time to process my own feelings. He was right; it was exhausting. I was wrung out.

"I'm sorry," I began, but stopped to clear my throat again. "I promise I won't act unless you need me to, ask me to," I amended.

He nodded, and some of the stress eased from his face. He reached over, placed his hand on mine, and gave it a gentle squeeze. With the contact, I couldn't help but feel what he was feeling, whether I wanted to or not.

It was the same warm affection I felt from him earlier, but tinged with wistful regret.

13

SARA

Glancing at my watch, I marveled at how quickly the day had sped by. It was nearly four in the afternoon, and Beth and I were still sorting through old computer files, deciding what should stay and what to put into the tiny trashcan of death. Bless her. She'd offered to help with some of the tasks I could probably do on my own, but had been putting off for a very, very long time now. With each folder we trashed, I felt lighter and more in control.

The bell over the front door rang, bringing us out of the digital world and back into the shop's office. Beth glanced at me, but I wasn't ready to stop just yet. I was almost done with the inventory backups from 1993 and wanted to see it through. "Would you mind seeing who that is? Tell them I'll be right there."

"Sure. No problem," she said, hopping up from her chair. As she did, her dog, Arrow, jumped to her feet to follow. "No. Sit," Beth commanded. She held out her hand, fingers splayed. "Wait." Arrow complied, a grin on her doggy face, her eyes tracking Beth's every movement.

I happily agreed to let Beth bring her dog to work, but I

admit I was a bit hesitant when the eighty-pound German Shepherd walked into the shop that morning. I hadn't spent much time around dogs, and to me, she initially seemed huge and intimidating, despite Beth assuring me she was *on the smaller side*. However, my opinion changed as the morning went on and I got to know Arrow. Not only was she one of the most beautiful dogs I'd ever seen, but she was also incredibly well-behaved and as friendly as they came. Beth said Arrow was a trained HRD dog—whatever that meant. Either way, I was impressed, and I did not doubt that Arrow would stay right where Beth had parked her for as long as it took for Beth to return.

As it turned out, that wasn't very long. She reappeared a moment later, eyes wide, and mouth hanging slightly open. "You okay?" I asked.

She nodded, pointing over her shoulder. "There's a ... a man out there asking for you. He's huge. I mean, huge," she said, sounding as rattled as she looked. "And his eyes. Oh my God, Sara. I've never ..." she trailed off.

I grinned, my cheeks instantly heating. "Thanks, that's probably my friend Silas," I said, shooting to my feet and brushing past Beth.

"Does he have any brothers?" she called after me.

It was Silas, and I was glad to see him. It had only been one day, but I'd gotten used to him being around. I felt the loss when he was gone. Silas waited on the other side of the counter, and I went around and gave him a hug. He put his arms around me and drew me close, holding me there longer than a casual friend would. He put his lips to the top of my head, and I felt his chest expand as he breathed in deeply. I squeezed him tight, but felt him stiffen and freeze.

"You got a dog?" he asked in his smooth, low voice.

"Umm, not exactly," I said just as Beth cleared her throat

from the doorway. "Oh, yeah." I pulled back out of his embrace and glanced over to see Beth staring at the two of us. "Silas, this is Beth. She's the one I texted you about, who just started working here."

"Hey, nice to meet you," Beth said with a small wave and a crooked smile. "You guys mind if I let Arrow come say 'Hi'? She's losing her mind back here."

I glanced up at Silas.

"I don't mind," he said. "I like dogs."

I bit my lip and nodded to Beth. A moment later, the German Shepherd came around the corner of the counter and immediately dropped low to the ground. She let out small, high-pitched whines and crawled across the floor on her belly toward Silas and me, tail wagging. It was the strangest dog greeting I'd ever witnessed.

Silas stepped forward and crouched down. Arrow tilted her head to look up at him and pressed herself closer to the ground as she drew near.

Beth followed behind Arrow, brows furrowed. "I swear, I've never seen her act this way," Beth said, shaking her head.

"Don't worry, dogs like me, too," Silas said softly as he extended a hand toward Arrow. She jumped to her feet at the invitation to lick Silas's face. He accepted a few kisses on the jaw before gently holding her back, and then he stood to get out of range of her tongue. He patted her a few times, and the whining died down. She sat wiggling and staring up at him.

"Seriously?" I asked. "You have that effect on dogs, too?" I chuckled.

Silas shot me an exasperated look but smiled and shrugged. "What can I say?" He turned, putting his side toward the dog, and she lay down, head between paws, still giving him the doggy equivalent of goo-goo eyes.

"It's nice to meet you, Beth," he said politely. "I just wanted to stop by to see how things were going," he continued.

I beamed up at him. The last twenty-four hours had been transformative. There was so much I wanted to tell him about the shop, Kate, the Relic, and Bruce becoming an official member of the House. I glanced at Beth. Now was not the time. "Things are great," I said. "How about you? How was dinner with the family last night?"

Before he could answer, Beth whistled, and Arrow's head whipped around. "Come on, girl, let's give these two a minute. They don't need a third wheel," she said and patted her leg. The dog rose, casting a sad dog eye at Silas before obeying and following Beth into the back room.

I snorted. "Dogs do like you."

He sighed and rolled his eyes. "It's not like that," he said in a soft tone, so as not to carry to the office. "She knows I'm a ... bigger dog," he cringed at the word dog. "And she's trying to ingratiate herself. That's all."

"Sure," I said sarcastically. "Makes perfect sense. Big Dog." I patted his muscled shoulder, which, admittedly, was at the same height as my head. There was no arguing his size.

He narrowed his eyes but smiled at me. "Dinner was good," he said. "It was nice to see my family. My niece and nephew were there." His face softened as he spoke of them. I had only ever met his father and brothers; they had all worked on our old shop or family home over the years. However, the rest of his family remained on the other side of the mountain range, along with most of the shifters in the state.

I nodded. "You missed them." It wasn't a question. "You've been spending so much time over here lately," I said. "I'm sure they miss you too."

The yellow of his eyes turned brassy, and the smile slipped. "Yeah. They do," he admitted.

I looked up into his handsome face. *Why did he have to be so beautiful?* I wanted to reach out and touch him, but I took a deep breath instead. "I would understand if you couldn't stop by as often, or spend so many evenings here." I bit my lip. I knew what it was like to be torn between two worlds. I hated that I was putting pressure on him to stay away from his family, those he loved and clearly missed. "I have Beth here to help during the day now, and Bruce was in here last night keeping me company and helping me with the financials." I paused. "The work on the house is nearly done. So ..."

He looked down and shifted his weight. "Um, yeah. I'm glad you have the help you need. It might be better if I spent a little more time at home." Even though he was agreeing with me, his words still stung. The last thing I wanted was to see Silas less often than I already did.

After the incident with James, I had hoped the distance between us would close completely. It seemed like it would for a while. And even though we were closer now, with lingering hugs, touching hands, and gazes that set my blood on fire, there had been little else. I was starting to doubt that he was seriously interested. It was true, I had little dating experience and zero experience dating shifters, but Silas and I were warm-blooded adults, and I wanted more.

I'd attempted to move things forward. Besides shamelessly inviting him to sleep with me after my abduction, which he had turned down gracefully, I'd tried kissing him on more than one occasion, only to be rebuffed with equal skill. I knew he was unmarried—unmated—but he was keeping me at arm's length for some reason, and it was becoming increasingly frustrating.

Why had I suggested he spend less time here? I should never have opened my mouth about it. I was about to say that exact thing when the door between the house and the shop opened, and Bruce walked in. I wasn't sure if I was grateful for his timing or not. I filed away everything I wanted to say for later, promising myself that Silas and I would work this out. I wasn't ready to give up. It was fine if things moved slowly. I reminded myself that everyone was entitled to their own pacing, but Gods, I wanted him. I wanted to be with him and know he wanted to be with me.

"Hey, Sara, Silas," Bruce said. His black hair was wet, like he'd come right from the shower, and his clothes were fresh. I was pretty sure he'd just gotten up. It wasn't surprising that he kept near-vampire hours. It also made me grateful that I had Beth here during the day to talk to.

Beth took that moment to stick her head out of the office and greet Bruce, which also turned into a meet and greet with Arrow. She was way more chill about her introduction to Bruce. Just as she had with me, she booped his hand and gave him a polite sniff and tail wag. Nothing like the way she'd fallen all over herself at Sila's feet. I suppressed a giggle just thinking about it.

"Bruce has joined us more permanently, by the way," I said to Silas. "He signed the ... lease last night."

Silas raised his eyebrows at the news, and his body stiffened. "Congratulations," he said, but his usually smooth tone was a bit strained. "I'm glad it worked out."

"Uh, thanks," Bruce replied, running his hand through his damp hair. "I am, too. It was nice of Kate, Sara, and Marcus to offer me a place."

"Are those your other roommates?" Beth asked from where she leaned against the counter.

"Yup," I replied. "They work nights, so you probably won't see them much."

"Oh, what do they do?" There was nothing but polite interest in her wide blue eyes.

I groaned inwardly. Now I had to make up jobs for my vampire housemates. Something that would sound plausible. I decided to stick as close to the truth as I could. "Well, Kate is an artist and keeps strange hours, and Marcus is in law enforcement."

At that news, Beth squealed with delight. "Oh, man, I would love to meet him. I worked closely with law enforcement in Oregon, with Search and Rescue. Arrow is an HRD dog, and I was both a volunteer and her handler. I've been meaning to make contact up here and get together with their local team."

"Oh, ugh ..." I fumbled with something to say that wouldn't sound rude.

"What exactly is an HRD dog?" Bruce asked, saving me from having to make up some other lie.

"Human Remains Detection," Beth answered brightly. "She is trained to help investigators with their searches of crime scenes."

"She finds bodies?" I asked.

"Well, she could," she explained. "Some dogs work in disaster areas, but others, like Arrow, are primarily used to find weapons or trace evidence. You know, sniffing out blood. She can even smell blood on clothing that has been through the wash several times."

I glanced at Bruce, who was wearing an expression of mild alarm, and my eyes snagged on the door to the house that he had left open behind him. "Um, where is Arrow?" I asked, trying to sound as normal as possible.

"Oh. She was here just a second ago," Beth said. She looked around the room, scowling, and then ducked into the office to check there.

Just then, we heard loud barking coming from the house.

14

SILAS

Before any of us had time to react, Beth dashed for the door of the house, disappearing inside after Arrow. The three of us exchanged glances before bolting after her. Discovering that Arrow was trained to sniff out blood evidence was alarming, considering the household included blood-drinking vampires. I had spent enough time in the house, with my shifter's sense of smell, to know that, no matter how fastidious the vampires were, there was always a lingering scent of blood from recent meals.

Bruce was the first to reach Beth. By the time Sara and I arrived, he was staring down at the empty blood bag Beth held in her hand, while they stood beside an open kitchen trash can that had at least half a dozen more bags on top. "It's not what you think," he was saying. However, I couldn't understand how he knew what she was thinking. Judging by the look on her face and her body language, I guessed she was struggling as badly as Bruce to come up with a plausible explanation.

Arrow, on the other hand, looked very pleased with

herself. She sat at Beth's feet, tail wagging proudly. She'd done her job well.

Bruce glanced at Sara and me, a pleading look in his eyes.

Sara huffed out a sigh. "Guys, she's pretty much a witch. I say we tell her," Sara said, crossing her arms. "I mean, she works in the same building. It was bound to come up."

It was none of my business what the members of the House decided to share with Beth, but I doubted the vampires would be too thrilled that the human had stumbled into their lives. The thought of "House members" made the hair on my wolf's neck rise again, and he let out a low snarl from the back of my mind.

"Someone should start telling me something. As far as I know, there aren't any sanctioned witch practices that call for the use of human blood, and I was told you ran a clean business," she said, tossing the bag back in the trash on top of the others. "I don't want anything to do with blood magic. And I think the others in the community would want to know if you were practicing something like that. Give me a good reason I shouldn't go to one of the Elders, or I'm out of here."

I thought her speech was particularly brave in a room with two large men and an actual witch. I was impressed.

I glanced at Bruce. He was slowly nodding, but the grave look he gave Beth told me he wasn't so sure this was a good idea. "Beth," he began. "I promise, nothing bad or illegal is going on here." He motioned toward the table. "If you would have a seat, I think we can explain."

Beth's glare flicked between Bruce and Sara and finally landed on me. I offered what I hoped was a reassuring smile. She glanced back at Sara. "Fine, I suppose I'm fairly new to all this. I'll listen, but I won't promise not to go to my stepfather if I don't like what I hear."

Sara waved her hand. "He already knows, I'm sure."

This bit of knowledge softened Beth somewhat, but her scowl remained as she sat down at the table. Arrow followed her over and lay at her feet, tucked underneath the table like she knew the drill. Sara and Bruce sat too, while I chose to stand behind Sara, resting my hands on the back of her chair.

It wasn't for me; it was for my wolf. He'd been snapping and snarling since Sara mentioned Bruce joining the House permanently. Before that, he'd been quiet and sulky as we discussed spending more time apart. The only way to get him to calm down enough so I could focus on what was being said was to stay as close to Sara as possible while still respecting her apparent desire for more distance. My chest tightened as I thought of what she'd said earlier about my work here being done.

Bruce and Sara gazed at one another expectantly. Bruce shook his head slightly, and Sara finally spoke up. "So, I'm sure when your mom got together with your stepdad, they probably sat you down and broke the news to you about witches. Am I right?" Sara said, steepling her hands in front of her on the table, tapping her fingertips together in a soft rhythm. I wondered if it was a way for her to dispel some energy or if she was trying to keep her gift from crackling to life from the stress.

"Yeah, something like that," Beth admitted. She sat all the way back in her chair, her arms protectively across her chest.

"Well, there are more than just witches in the world," Sara went on. I knew this admission made her uncomfortable. It was usually up to the individual to decide whether or not to reveal what they were and the abilities they possessed. It was frowned upon to out another creature, but this was a special circumstance.

Beth's eyebrows rose, but she didn't respond.

"Um, yeah. So, my other housemates are vampires." Sara clasped her nervous hands together and leaned back. I squeezed her shoulder, and she reached up, covered my hand with hers, and squeezed back.

Beth glanced at Bruce, who nodded. "It's true, and now that you know, you will be expected to keep that secret, just as you have about the witches," he said. His posture remained stiff, and his jaw was clenched tight. He'd spent a lot of time in the vampire world as a human and understood the risks to any human who violated their rules. "I hope, for your sake, that you're handled like a witch in this instance. Humans who enter this world are bound very tightly."

Beth flinched, and her brow dropped again. "What does that mean?" she asked.

"As a human who works and now lives among vampires, I'm bound by a strict contract that lasts for life. No one in my position would dare share what they know with other humans."

"But, isn't that what you're doing right now?" she asked. I had to admit, it was a good question.

"Technically," Bruce said slowly. "It was Sara who told you." He glanced at Sara, his lips pressed together in a tight line.

At this, my wolf lowered his head and bared his teeth. I felt my skin prickle as he pushed for a shift, but that was the last thing this situation needed. I pushed down on him and breathed slowly through my nose, trying to understand what this would mean for Sara. I knew little about how the vampire Council would handle a witch who revealed their secrets, or how her Elders would see the situation.

Sara shrugged. "It's fine. I'm going with the fact that you are part of our community. You're covered as far as I'm concerned. I wouldn't sweat it. Plus, you're not going to discuss this with anyone on the outside, right?"

Beth shook her head. "I wouldn't. I swear." She paused. "There are seriously vampires? They're real? I mean, I saw the blood bags, but ..."

"I know, it's a lot," Bruce said seriously. "It takes some getting used to, but yeah. They exist. But don't worr—"

"Can I meet them?" Beth interrupted. She'd uncrossed her arms and was leaning forward, her eyes bright and alert. "I mean, if it's okay. I would love to meet an actual vampire." Her voice was excited, with no hint of reservation or worry.

"Umm," Sara looked at her watch. "Yeah, it might be a good idea." She glanced at Bruce.

"I think you're right. I'll send a text to Felix too, just in case." He took out his phone and began typing.

"Sara," I said, getting her attention. "Is everything okay? There isn't going to be any trouble for you over this, is there?" I asked. If there was going to be trouble, I was sticking around, no matter how little work I had left to do on the property.

Sara turned in her seat. "No. Everything will be fine. Felix might insist that she sign an NDA, but there is nothing for me to worry about. The witches police their own, and I've not overstepped." She smiled warmly up at me and patted my hand in reassurance. I hoped she was right.

"Hey, you can go if you need to," Sara said, tilting her head. "You don't have to hang around for House business if you don't want to." She still smiled, but her soft brown eyes looked a bit sad.

My chest seized up again. Did she want me to go? She was right. This was House business. She and the vampires would have to take care of it, and Bruce now, too. My wolf growled again, and I reminded him that Bruce was a good man. My wolf didn't care. He didn't like any man getting too close to Sara. I ignored him.

I glanced at the human again. He was chatting softly with Beth, trying to temper her enthusiasm, but not making much progress. I instantly liked him when we met. He was straightforward and brave. And he'd been a great help to Sara, it seemed. It was good that she had someone around during the day to talk to—someone who lived here. Or so I told myself. Deep down, I wanted to be the one who was there for her. But how would that work?

I thought back to my conversation with my mother. She wanted me to date and find my mate so badly. And here was the woman I wanted, and she was a witch. How would it work between our two communities? What did we really know about each other's cultures? And, even if we could overcome all that, how would she feel about it when I bonded to her and couldn't leave, not without ripping myself apart? Where would it leave me if we started a romantic relationship and she changed her mind? I felt a wave of nausea just thinking about it.

Sara had turned back to the conversation with Beth. They were now trying to guess when the fabled vampires would make an appearance. I watched Sara's animated face as she chatted. Her deep brown eyes and full lips, her high, rounded cheekbones, and the curve of her delicate chin. She was so lovely. So very beautiful.

I cleared my throat. "Um, Sara," I said.

She glanced up, raising a perfectly sculpted black eyebrow. "Yes?"

"Yeah, I'm going to go," I said. My whole body felt strangely heavy.

"You okay?" she asked with concern.

"Yeah, I'm good," I replied, not feeling good at all.

"Okay, well, text me later. Would you?" she asked, worry lining her gorgeous face.

"Okay," I said. I waved a quick goodbye to the others before turning and leaving Sara behind, sitting at the table with the people in her life she needed most at the moment.

I went to my truck and sat for a long time. I stared at the house I had helped renovate, where Sara and I spent countless hours together over the past several months. It was a good home, a solid home, and not just the building. What Sara and Kate were building was something special, something that fit both of them perfectly. Something that provided them with the lives and choices they wanted. And that was important: choices.

If I stayed, if I kept coming around, if I risked a bond with Sara, one she had no say in, it could ruin everything. It could wreck everything she was working toward. She was a good person, and I believed she liked me—possibly loved me. But how would she feel if I bonded with her, and her feelings changed? Would she tell me? Knowing I would never fall out of love? Or would she sacrifice her own happiness to keep me whole? That I couldn't live with either. There was only one smart choice.

I turned the key in the ignition, backed my truck out, and drove away. When I reached the highway, I turned left toward the climb that would take me through the Pass to the side of the range that I called home, where a thriving community of shifters lived and worked. A place I knew I belonged.

My wolf remained silent while I sat and debated which

direction my life should take, but as I turned the truck and headed for home, he let out a mournful howl that echoed in my skull and shook my entire body.

He would get used to it. This was the best way. The only way.

I activated the hands-free calling and dialed my parents' house. I stared ahead at the breathtaking landscape. The mountains were snowcapped, but the roads were clear and the view was amazing. When the phone picked up, it was my mom who answered.

"Hey," I said, my voice sounding as if it were not my own, outside of my body somehow.

"Hey, Si," she said cheerfully. "What's up?"

I gripped the steering wheel more firmly and took a deep breath. "You know your friend you were talking about? The one with the daughter?" I said.

"Yes?" She dragged the word out, making it a question.

"Would you mind getting that number for me?" I said.

"Sure, no problem," she replied quickly. "Silas, where are you? You sound strange."

"I'm coming home, Mom."

15

KATE

Barking from upstairs jolted me awake. Blinking, I rolled over and plucked my phone from beside the bed. It was only four-thirty. There were still several hours before it would be safe for me to go check it out. Instead, I sent a text to Sara.

> Is that a dog I hear in the house?

There was no immediate reply, so I tossed my phone on the bed and headed for the shower. My bathroom was a standard affair: a sink, a tub and shower combo, and a toilet. I appreciated having my own bathroom for washing up, and was grateful I didn't have to brave leaving my room before sunset to bathe. I showered, brushed my teeth, especially the pointy ones, and towel-dried my hair.

I wore my usual jeans and oversized sweater, pulling on some fuzzy socks. This look was quickly becoming my uniform, I realized. But when you never left the house, there was no need to put together a real outfit.

Tugging the duvet up to the headboard and fluffing the pillows, I crawled into my made-up bed and grabbed a book from my nightstand. Ever since I moved in with Sara, my TBR pile had grown out of control. Sara loved romances; through her, I'd discovered quite a few subgenres I had no idea existed. I was familiar with the typical historical romance, modern small-town romance, and contemporary romance. But now, I also had a wide range of time-travel romance, rockstar romance, billionaire romance, and of course, paranormal romance to choose from. The girl loved her books, and I was perfectly happy to take any suggestion she offered. Plus, the books were the only romance in my life at that moment. Cracking open the latest fantasy romance I was working on, I settled back into the pillows with a contented sigh.

A knock at my bedroom door brought my head up just as the two main characters were about to try something on the back of a dragon that I was pretty sure was impossible—at least without a really good saddle. "What?" I called out, somewhat annoyed.

"Kate? You going up? It's dark out," Marcus said from the hall. The last part was unnecessary because if Marcus was awake, it was already dark outside.

"Sure thing. Just give me a minute," I called back. I set the book aside and patted the cover. Those two would have to hold on until I got back, I thought with a smile.

I opened my door, and Marcus was waiting for me, leaning against the wall and looking relaxed and handsome in his usual cargo pants and tank. He had his arms crossed, nicely showcasing the muscles of his biceps and chest. I shook my head to clear my thoughts. Too many dragon books, I chided myself, and attempted to pull my mind out of the gutter. Marcus was a friend, and even if we both had been interested in one another, I was not willing to let anything with fangs come remotely near my neck, which would make dating a vampire somewhat awkward.

"Hey," I said, glancing down, suddenly very interested in the hem of my sweater. "Thanks for waiting."

"No problem." He smiled at me and turned to lead the way upstairs. "It was on my way," he joked.

"By the way, did you hear a dog bark earlier?" I asked as we climbed the stairs to the main floor.

"Um, no," he said, but lifted his head and took a long breath through his nose as we hit the landing. "But one was definitely here, in case you were wondering if you were just hearing things."

"Thanks," I said wryly. "But I wasn't concerned."

Bruce waited for us in the kitchen. He sat at the table, sipping something warm and fragrant. *Turmeric tea?* The look on his face was serious to the point of being worrying.

"Bruce, is everything okay?" I asked. "Does this have anything to do with a dog?"

His eyebrows shot up. "Actually, yes. It does."

"Ooh. Did you or Sara get a dog?" I really hoped they got a dog. I would love to have a pet around the place, I thought.

"Um, no. We did not," he said, setting down his cup.

"Then whose dog did I hear barking earlier?" I asked as I snagged a bag of breakfast from the fridge.

"That was Beth's dog. She brought it with her to work today, and apparently, it has a special set of skills we didn't know about," Bruce began.

"Like Liam Neeson?" Marcus asked with a smirk.

"Yeah, pretty much exactly like that," Bruce huffed, and proceeded to tell us about what had happened in the kitchen less than two hours before.

"Where is Beth now?" Marcus asked, with more seriousness, once Bruce was finished with the story.

"She's in the shop with Sara. Beth asked if she could meet you both, and we thought it was at least a good idea for her to stick around until you were both up to get your take on things," Bruce said.

"I'm glad it was Sara who spilled the beans," Marcus said from under his dark, furrowed brows. "It'll make things easier."

"Is this about the stupid Council rules and prohibitions again?" I asked. "What's the big deal? Beth's mom is married to a witch. Doesn't that count for something?"

"*I* think it does," Marcus said, but his brows remained lowered. "We should probably call—"

"Already done," Bruce said. "He'll be here within the hour."

"Who? Felix? Do you think that's necessary?" I asked, growing more agitated. "I mean, poor Bruce. Haven't you had enough of that vampire harassing you? I like the guy. He's nice and super helpful, but I feel bad for any human he's around. Honestly."

Bruce swallowed hard and took another sip of his tea. Marcus just grinned at me, like I was being silly.

"Fine. I'm sure he'll be lots of help making Beth feel right at home here," I said sarcastically. "Shall we go meet her?"

Marcus and Bruce nodded, but a strange vibe lingered in the room. I could have dropped my defenses and sussed them both out, but I was trying hard to give my housemates the privacy they deserved. If one of them had a problem, they would have to come right out and tell me.

I hadn't even bothered to sit at the table to eat my meal, and I tossed my empty bag into the trash on my way out of the kitchen, both men following behind me. I reached the shop door and paused. I had gone through the passage to the shop dozens of times, but for some reason, I felt the urge to knock.

I realized I was nervous to meet Beth and Arrow. What if Beth or the dog didn't like me? What if Beth was scared? What if her fear triggered a response in me that I wasn't ready to handle? I thought back to the night of my transformation, after I'd finally drunk for the first time. I had been terrified to see Sara. I'd gone down to the lobby, and there was a receptionist at the desk. He'd smelled good, like food, but I'd focused on his emotions, and they had overridden my hunger and reminded me of his humanity. I wasn't hungry now, but I was prepared to drop the wall in my mind that blocked out others' emotions in case things got too uncomfortable.

"Umm, are we going in?" Marcus asked from behind me.

I glanced back at the two men who were waiting for me to open the door. "Yeah, of course," I said, refocusing on the task.

Cracking open the door, I braced myself and was greeted by a German Shepherd's nose, followed by the rest of the dog and a very waggy tail. She sniffed my hand and then turned and bolted away. I glanced back at Marcus and Bruce. "Maybe she doesn't like vampires?" I shrugged. But before I could enter the shop, she reappeared carrying what looked like one of Sara's shoes in her mouth. There was yelling from the office as Arrow dropped the shoe at my feet and stepped back, panting and wiggling.

A moment later, a woman with wide blue eyes and dark blonde hair stepped into view. "Oh, she likes you," the woman said, smiling. "Arrow only brings presents to people she likes."

"I just don't understand why the present had to be one of my shoes. I kicked them off under the desk, and she stole one before I could grab her," Sara grumbled from beside the woman. "Kate and Marcus, meet Beth. And I see Arrow has already introduced herself." Sara bent down to retrieve her shoe and gave the dog a scratch, nuzzling the top of its head. She might pretend to be mad, but she quite obviously liked the animal.

Beth stood quietly, staring at Marcus and me, wide-eyed. "It's nice to meet you," she said. "I'm a big fan. I mean … I've always liked vampires. Well, vampire books and movies." She blushed a bright red, but her smile stayed plastered in place. "This is just too cool. I thought that Sara was kidding me about the whole vampire thing at first. But there are real witches, so why not vampires? Right?"

"Right," I said, hoping that was the right answer. I had been prepared for her to be afraid and possibly run screaming, but what I had not prepared for was her going all fangirl. I glanced at Marcus, who had a tight but pleasant smile in place. Perhaps he had more experience with this than I did. "It's nice to meet you, too, Beth. I've heard how much help you've been to Sara over the past few days. I'm so glad she finally got someone in here who knows what they're doing when it comes to the technical side of things. We certainly were no help to her whatsoever. She's been bragging about you big time," I said and smiled back.

"Oh, no way!" Beth exclaimed, stepping closer. "Your teeth are so …"

"Oh, yeah," I said, hastily closing my mouth. "They are that."

"Okay," Sara said, laying a hand on Beth's arm. "Let's finish up in the back. We're almost done today, and I'm sure Felix will be here soon."

I mouthed a "*Thank you*" to Sara as she led Beth away. I

turned to the guys, my own eyes wide. "That was ... unexpected," I said quietly so that Beth wouldn't hear.

"It's not that unusual," Bruce said, and Marcus nodded. "Vampires are a part of pop culture. Every human who meets one has their own idea of what they're like. Some people, mostly younger people, think they're pretty cool."

I shivered thinking about some of the vampires I'd met, specifically Alexander. "If they only knew," I said.

"They find out," Bruce said, raising a hand to the side of his throat. He had told us that he refused to join Margaux's House, but he hadn't gone into detail about what had happened between the two of them. I wondered if there was more to that story.

A knock sounded on the shop door, and Marcus went to answer it. A moment later, the Viking vampire lawyer walked through the door.

"How are you already here?" I asked. "The sun set like fifteen minutes ago."

"Well, I am an early riser," he said, shrugging. "And I'm not that far away."

"It was Felix's place I was staying at when I was coming by to check on you each evening for the Council. He has a house about twenty minutes away."

"He must be a fast driver," I said.

Felix only grinned back at me, then turned his attention to Bruce. "Bruce, nice to see you as always," he said, giving him a small bow. "Thank you for texting."

Bruce cleared his throat. "Yeah, I thought the House could use your advice on how to handle *reading people in*, so to speak."

Felix nodded. "I can see, given your background, why you would be concerned for the House," he said. "But if Sara is willing to vouch for her, there is nothing that needs to be done."

"Why did you come then?" I asked. I realized the question came out a bit rude. "Sorry, it's just, if we don't need to do anything, and you already had the information about Sara, why drive all this way?"

Felix smiled. "I came to deliver your mail," he said, handing over a packet that looked suspiciously like the one our House charter had arrived in.

"What's this?" I asked, taking the very thick envelope and walking to the counter to open it up.

Felix, Bruce, and Marcus all followed me over as I tore the top open and started pulling out various documents.

"Think of it as your welcome packet," Felix said. "It has some basic guides for things like filing taxes, recruiting new members, and bringing business before the Council. It also contains your new IDs and documents permitting you to open accounts with vampire-owned businesses and banks."

As he explained, I pulled the forms, IDs, and several official-looking pamphlets from the pile and held them up to inspect them. "What about this one?" I asked, holding up a square envelope with a golden seal affixed to the back.

"Ah, yes," Felix said with a gleam in his hazel eyes. "That is your summons."

"My what?" I demanded. This was the first I'd heard about a summons.

"Now that you have established a House and you have been made official," Felix said, pointing to the pile of paperwork, and smiling like a loon. "You are required to go before the Council and thank them for the great honor of leading your own House."

"No. Fucking. Way."

16

KATE

Twenty minutes later, Felix and Marcus were no closer to convincing me to go before the Council to grovel and declare them High Lords of the Universe. I wasn't having it. Most of the issues I'd encountered since being turned stemmed from them or their arcane rules. Bruce's very life had hung in the balance only days before because of them. No. I had no intention of meeting with that group of entitled immortals.

"You have no choice but to respond to an official summons," Marcus said for the tenth time. "I'm not just saying this because it's my job. Believe me, things will go much more smoothly if you play along with their rituals."

Felix nodded. "Nothing is required of you, other than that you make an appearance."

I pushed the packet and all its contents farther across the counter away from me. I glanced at the pile. I had to admit that the IDs were cool. I got a little thrill seeing The House of Ward in bold letters across the top of each one. But still, I wasn't a fan of the Council or their rules, and when it came down to it, I didn't trust them. Which was a bit ironic, I thought, as I gazed at the two men standing alongside me. "You two work for the Council, can't you go instead?" I asked Felix.

"Madam," Felix said dramatically while clutching his chest. "I most certainly do not work for the Council. I am independent. And, currently, I work for you, among others."

"And how did you swing that?" I asked, more than a little annoyed. "I didn't know *independent* was an option. I would have gone for that over being the leader of a House any day. Especially if it meant I didn't have to appear before a bunch of old vampire bureaucrats," I huffed.

"It wasn't an option. For you," Felix said pleasantly. "It's an option for me because I'm very good at what I do and travel throughout the various territories practicing my craft." He smiled brightly, raising a blond eyebrow. "It also helps that I wrote many of those laws myself," he added. "Particularly the ones that pertain to solicitors and their status as independent entities. How would it be fair to represent individual vampires in disputes with local governments if I were beholden to those very governments?"

I snorted. "Very nice. For you."

"Getting back to you, Kate. You will have to respond and set a date to appear. It will be painless, I promise," Marcus said. There was more than a bit of empathy in his grey eyes as he reached for my hand. "And if you're worried about your safety, I'll be with you, if you want. I won't let anything happen. You'll be safe as long as you're with me."

His choice of words gave me pause. James had said something similar when introducing me to the vampire world for the first time. I knew Marcus meant well, but I didn't want anyone to have to protect me. I didn't want to be different. I didn't want to worry about how others would react to me. I didn't want to live in a society with laws that showed little regard for the lives of humans. I didn't want rules I never agreed to dictating who I could inform about my very existence. I glanced at Bruce. Of everyone present, he probably understood what I was feeling the most.

"What do you have to say about this, Bruce?" I asked, curious what his take on it would be.

"Me?" he asked, looking genuinely shocked that I would ask for his opinion.

"Yeah, I haven't had a chance to talk to Sara yet, as she's still working, but you're a full-fledged House member now," I said. "You get a vote."

"Umm, I'm not sure that's how this works," Bruce said, glancing between Marcus and Felix. "I'm pretty sure that you have to do what the Council says, for the good of the entire House. And everyone in it," Bruce finished quietly.

"He's right," Felix said. "You may not like the Council, but it's not just you, Kate. You're now responsible for three others. And like it or not, the Council holds all the cards here in their territory regarding vampires and their Houses. It would be good not to piss them off. I vote you go."

"You don't get a vote, Felix. No matter how much time you spend here," I said, raising one corner of my mouth in a half smile.

"Okay, then my professional advice is that you get yourself cleaned up, find something appropriate to wear, show up before the Council and give them that winning smile of yours," he said, giving me a mock smile and showing off his very long set of fangs.

"Thanks," I groaned. "I'll take that under advisement."

"Perfect," he said, like I'd happily agreed. "I'll request an audience for around two weeks from now." He paused and glanced at Bruce. "Can you get her looking ready by then?" he asked.

I glanced down at my uniform and then at the tattooed man in the black t-shirt and jeans with perfectly tousled black hair. I had to admit he had a lot more style than I did, but still.

"Yeah, no problem. I'll take care of it," Bruce said, like I was a home reno project.

"And, I think she needs a night or two out to get her feet under her before she goes," Marcus said. "She hasn't spent much time around vampires, besides those in this room. I think she could use some more exposure. It would also give her more confidence regarding her ... differences and how others perceive her."

"It's a good idea," Felix replied. "Bruce, you've spent a lot of time in downtown Seattle. I'm sure you have some recommendations. You and Marcus should discuss it and come up with a few suggestions—quieter places, but nowhere too upscale. Let's keep her off the radar for now, but not overwhelm her with too many vampires all at once."

The other two men nodded, and I stared at all three. "I'm right here," I snapped. "You're discussing my itinerary like I'm some dignitary you're trying to handle, instead of your housemate standing right in front of you."

"Kate, you're our s ..." Marcus began when I shot him a look. "Leader. The leader of our House. It's our job to do things for you. But I'm sorry. You're right. We should have included you in the conversation." He glanced at Felix.

"Yes, my apologies," Felix added. "But I think you should give going out a try before jumping into vampire society with both feet."

He was right. I'd been thinking just that night that I should get out more. Or at all, really. I'd spent so much time hiding myself, afraid of the unknown. If I had to answer this summons, I could see the wisdom in testing how others reacted to me and getting used to being in the company of other vampires.

"Fine," I conceded. "You're right. It sounds like a good idea. And, I would appreciate the help." I looked down at myself again. "With the clothes and stuff." I glanced at Bruce and gave him a smile. He nodded in his usual serious manner.

Felix turned to Bruce and began discussing the dress code for an official summons. I watched the tall blond lawyer and how he kept leaning closer into Bruce's space. I glanced at Marcus to see if he noticed what I did, but he wasn't paying any attention. Marcus was busy scooping all my new fancy paperwork into a pile and shoving it back into the envelope. Just then, Sara and Beth reappeared from the office, Arrow in tow.

"Hey, Felix," Sara said brightly.

"Good evening," he said, grinning. "And this must be Beth. Lovely to meet you." He extended a hand to the stunned woman.

She shook it, a bit breathless, then blurted, "I just can't get over this. This is the coolest thing that's happened to me. I swear. And I thought my mom marrying a witch was awesome, but that's nothing compared to this. Sorry, Sara." She glanced at Sara, who just shook her head.

"Not to worry. But you're going to give them a complex, and they're already hard enough to live with," she teased.

The click of nails on wood announced Arrow, who came around from behind the counter to greet Felix. The German Shepherd sniffed his hand, and he bent down to give her a scratch. "And this must be the doggy that caused all the fuss," he said in the friendly way people spoke to dogs or sometimes children. "What a clever girl you are. Very clever indeed." He glanced up at Beth. "I would love to hear more about her training and what exactly she's used for. I'm fascinated." He turned his attention back to Arrow and started working on her ears. She leaned into his touch, tilting her head so far that she collapsed to the floor with a satisfied sigh.

"I would love to," Beth exclaimed, launching into an explanation about Search and Rescue, HRD dogs, and Arrow in particular.

Bruce, Marcus, and I caught Sara up on the Council's summons and the plans to go out on the town to help me ease into vampire society.

"I wish I could go with you," Sara said regretfully. "I suppose these places don't see many witches, though."

Marcus winced. "I'm afraid not," he said. "I don't think there are any strict rules about it, but it would cause a stir and we're trying to avoid drawing too much attention."

"That's just stupid," I said. "It shouldn't matter—"

"No," Sara interrupted. "I get it. It's the same in my community. I'm sure more than a few eyebrows would be raised if I brought you to a gathering. I don't like it either, and maybe it won't always be that way, but I understand."

"Want me to take that?" Bruce asked Marcus, pointing to the envelope. "I can ensure it all gets filed away, and the tax information would be useful for later."

Marcus glanced at me, and I nodded. "Sure, if Bruce is willing, go for it."

The two of them left then to discuss the House's finances and Bruce's plans for the rest of the interior. I was happy to let them. The idea of finances still made me uncomfortable. I hoped Sara was right, that she could eventually sell some of the things I planned to make, but I was acutely aware that I hadn't been able to contribute anything to the running of the household. Marcus even bought the blood for the two of us.

After the two disappeared into the house, I reached out and squeezed Sara's hand. "I miss you," I said. "I know we live in the same house and see each other every night, but I feel like we hardly spend any time together."

She nodded. "Yeah, I'm pretty much done with my day by the time you're up. It feels like we're living parallel lives, not with each other," she admitted. "It's not quite what I envisioned when I thought of us living together."

I wasn't hurt by what she said. It was true. Our different schedules made it difficult for us to enjoy each other's company. And many of the things we used to like to do together, like hiking or dinner out, weren't an option any longer.

"What did you imagine?" I asked, curious.

She smiled and shrugged. "I guess I imagined it would be like a never-ending sleepover, like we used to have when we were girls. Is that silly?" she asked.

"Not silly at all," I said. "Maybe we could do a lot of those things we used to do: watch movies, stay up late, gossip. I'm afraid I'll have to skip the popcorn and soda, though."

"I'd love that," Sara said and tilted her head. "You know, now that Beth knows about you, and given that we only get a couple of actual customers in the store per week, I suppose we could change our hours a bit. There is really no reason to work 9-to-5. I could sleep until noon or later and spend more of my waking hours with you. Bruce is already on that schedule, and it seems to work well for him. I'm sure Beth can do whatever it is she does from home or later in the day."

The more she talked, the more excited I became. It

would be so nice to spend more time with Sara. I did miss her, and I was tired of spending so much time alone in the house with Marcus at work and Sara asleep upstairs. I did have Bruce now to keep me company, but it wasn't the same as having my best friend around. "Oh, Sara, it would be wonderful if it's not too much trouble. It would change my life, really." I smiled so wide my cheeks began to ache.

Sara returned my smile. "I'll check with Beth, but I'm sure it would be great."

"Check with Beth about what?" Beth said, glancing up from where she and Felix sat around Arrow, who looked like she was in doggy heaven with all the attention she was getting.

"I was thinking we could open the shop later," Sara said. "Around 3 or 4 p.m.? Most of the customers we get come in the afternoon anyway, and that would give me more overlap with Kate's schedule."

"Works for me," Beth said merrily. "Does that mean I'll be seeing more of the vampires, too?" she asked.

"Well, I do live here," I said, giving her a smile. "I'm sure I'll see you around."

"Wicked," she said. "I never would have believed. Witches and vampires." She shook her head and returned to talking to Felix, who was still wholly focused on Arrow.

I glanced at Sara. "*Does she know about Silas*?" I mouthed.

She shook her head. "*Nope*," she mouthed back and grinned.

"That will be fun," I whispered and grinned back. "Please make sure I'm there to see it."

Sara nodded and gave me a wink.

17

———

BRUCE

Marcus and I finished discussing my plans for the house and the budget for the upgrades. Silas had done a wonderful job with the necessary construction, but now it was time to dress it all up, and I was eager to start on more than just the kitchen. The house had a lot of potential, and I had a clear vision of how I wanted it to look.

Our tour of the house ended on the large front porch, just before Marcus left for work. He drove back and forth to Seattle most nights, which was over an hour away. I was surprised he was willing to commute such a distance, but what options did he have? He was a direct employee of the Council, and they were located in the city. I didn't suppose there was a lot for a vampire cop to do this far out.

I sat on the porch steps, enjoying the cold night air, and considered what Felix had suggested: taking Kate back to Seattle for an evening in the company of other vampires. I agreed that she needed the practice. She was so unlike any vampire I'd ever met. For one thing, she was nice. Not that vampires couldn't be nice—some of them were very nice— but Kate was just so normal, and vampires were never normal. I hoped getting to know others of her kind wouldn't change her too much. Extra abilities or no, she was special.

I hadn't brought a coat, and the cold was starting to get to me. I contemplated going back in when the door to the shop opened, and Beth and Arrow came out, followed by Felix. Felix walked them to the back of Beth's blue Subaru, where she tucked Arrow inside and then said goodnight. She waved to me from the car as she turned and drove off, and I waved back, but my attention remained on Felix.

The lean vampire stood in the gravel drive, long hair loose around his shoulders, his pale eyes fixed on me. He didn't move to come over. He just stood there, and I got the impression he wanted me to look at him; wanted me to see him standing there reflecting all that moonlight, like the unearthly creature he was. And he was breathtaking.

I let a slow smile cross my face, and his mouth turned up in response. He was some distance away, and I was sitting in the dark, but I knew he saw me in as much detail as I did him, and the thought made me self-conscious.

"Would you like to join me?" I said in a soft voice, pitched to carry to his sensitive ears. I placed a hand on the step beside me.

His smile grew wider as he crossed the distance between us and climbed the steps. When we were eye level, he paused and offered me a small bow, gazing up at me from beneath thick lashes. My breath caught at the intensity of that gaze. This vampire could very well be the death of me, I thought. He finished his climb and sat beside me, his thigh lightly brushing against my own as he settled himself.

"This time, I was waiting for you," I admitted.

He leaned back, resting his elbows against the porch behind us, and looked up at the night sky, offering me his profile. "I know," he said.

"Did you know I was out here?"

"I hoped," he said and smiled lazily, but didn't look over. "Are you going to go with us? When we go to Seattle with Kate?"

"Us?" I asked. "Are you planning on coming along?"

"That depends. Are you going?" he asked, glancing my way.

"I think I'd like that," I said.

"How did you and Kate meet, by the way?" Felix asked, tilting his head.

I chuckled and glanced down at the drive. "You know I worked at the Tap House?"

He nodded, and I could feel his gaze still on me.

"I was her meal," I said, smiling at the memory.

"You're kidding? Kate?" He shook his head. "I've teased her often enough about her awful eating habits. I had no idea she'd had a taste of something so much better." He drew out the last part of the sentence in a way that made it almost obscene. "No wonder she's territorial."

"No. It's not like that, I don't think," I said. "I offered myself to her when I first arrived here. Despite her obvious hunger, she turned me down." I thought back to that night and how I'd been willing to feed her if she'd asked. It wasn't that I wanted to, particularly, but I couldn't afford to be turned away. She'd surprised me.

"You mean to tell me that you don't serve any blood needs for the House?" Felix asked, sounding curious but not judgmental.

"Nope. I'm falling into the role of manager here. I was a supervisor at the Tap House, and it's not too different than what I did there. But no one bites me here," I joked.

"Yet," Felix smirked.

"You would risk the wrath of Kate?" I asked. "She looked

pretty serious the other night when she told you I was off limits."

"I'm confident I could defend myself against her," he said, rolling his eyes.

I reflected on what I knew of him from our brief time together. "But you wouldn't," I said. "If you were in the wrong, you would let her tear into you."

"Know me so well already? Hmm. You may be right. I wouldn't let her do any real damage, but I would take what punishment I deserved." He sat up and turned his body toward me, gazing at me in an open appraisal. "It would be worth it."

I swallowed hard and felt the tightness in my throat. "Are you sure you're not interested just because Kate told you to leave me alone? You wouldn't be the first vampire I've known who only wanted what they couldn't have," I said, hoping I was wrong. My feelings for Felix were confusing. I was attracted to him, but at the same time, it was tinged with more than a bit of danger. Not just because he was a vampire, although there was that, but because I didn't want to be used or manipulated. I was running away from one powerful being who tried to control me and use me for her own purposes, and I wasn't eager to run right into the arms of another.

His smile widened. "No. I wanted you from the moment I saw you at the top of the steps. For an empath, Kate got my feelings for you completely wrong." He reached forward and brushed his fingertips down the exposed muscles of my arm.

My whole body shivered at the feather-light touch. "You weren't craving me?" I asked, feeling desire welling up inside me despite not being sure this was a particularly good idea.

"I didn't say that," he said. "And Kate only said drinking was off limits ..."

"You're such a lawyer," I said with a smile. "And not my usual type, you know?"

"Blonds?"

"Vampires," I replied.

He drew back, as if shocked. "You've never been with one of us? In all your time in our world?"

"I didn't say never. I said usual." I was sure my cheeks were bright red at this point. "Relationships with vampires can be tricky," I offered.

"Hmm." He took my hand and turned my arm over, exposing the uninked patch on the underside—the spot where the clients at the bar used to feed. "You're not wrong," he murmured. Raising my arm, he placed his lips to my skin and tenderly kissed the spot, keeping his fangs tucked inside his mouth. "Being with me could be about so much more than servicing a vampire." He dragged his kiss up the inside of my arm, tracing the curve of muscle with his tongue. My blood heated, and the cold weather was forgotten.

"Does it bother you?" I asked, my voice coming out strangled as my need for him intensified. However, I figured we should address this if it were to go any further.

"Does what bother me?" he asked, raising his head from where he'd made his way up to my shoulder and was pushing aside the sleeve of my shirt.

"That I was used for blood. That countless vampires have fed from me over the years?"

"Does it bother you that I have fed from—and fucked—countless humans over the years?" he asked in reply.

"No," I said. And I wasn't bothered. I hadn't even considered the question. He was what he was, and it was to be expected. I just wasn't sure if he would feel the same.

Vampires typically had no problem with a double standard when it came to the purity of their human companions.

He shrugged, seeming unconcerned. "We are here, together now. Why let the experiences that have led us here keep us from enjoying what we can?" he said.

I pulled out of his grasp and twisted, bringing my hands up to cup his gorgeous face. I gently pulled him closer and kissed his soft, cool lips. He remained motionless, allowing me to press against him as hard as I wished and control the experience for myself. After a moment, his lips parted and his tongue darted out against the seam of my mouth, tasting, asking, and I gladly opened for him. Then we were crushed against each other, our mouths and bodies entwining, desperate hunger replacing simmering desire. My hands tangled in his blond hair as I gripped the back of his head, trying to get even closer, pull him even deeper as he stroked the inside of my mouth.

A moment later, Felix pulled back and gently pushed against my chest, leaving me panting and wanting. "Kate and Sara just exited the shop into the house and are about to walk past the front door," he said, his eyes glassy and breath coming fast. "I thought, if you wanted to continue this, we might go up to your room? I could easily meet you there."

I huffed out an amused breath. "I'm thirty-three years old, I don't have to sneak around like a teenager," I said.

"Well, I may look twenty, but I assure you I'm quite a bit older. I don't want to set off your fearless leader. She's under enough stress; there's no need to push her over the edge."

"She'll figure it out eventually," I said. "But I see your point. And yes, I do very much want to continue this upstairs. My room is—"

"I'll find it," he said, disappearing quicker than I could track.

I stared at the clearing momentarily, knowing I wouldn't spot him, and shook my head. *What was I getting myself into?* I wasn't sure, but I didn't want to stop either.

Standing, I took a moment to clear my head and adjust myself before heading inside.

Sara and Kate were in the living room when I passed by on my way upstairs. I paused to inform Sara that there were leftovers in the fridge and to let both of them know that I would be going to my room for a while. Thankfully, neither of them needed anything or indicated that they suspected what I was up to.

Despite Felix's reasoning about keeping things between us a secret, I still felt like we were two kids sneaking around. It was a bit thrilling, in a nostalgic way. When I pushed open the door to my room and found him already in my bed, I wasn't at all surprised. And the fact that he was already naked was more arousing than shocking.

I closed the door, clicked the lock, and shed my clothes as I went to join him.

18

KATE

Two nights later, I was in the back of Bruce's black BMW, headed down I-5 toward Seattle. Marcus sat beside me, while Felix sat up front with Bruce. I was more than a little nervous about returning to the city and to the district where I had my only night out with James. Not that I hadn't enjoyed myself—I had. I glanced at Bruce in the driver's seat and fought back the feelings of hunger and desire I'd experienced that night. Not a desire for Bruce himself, but for the blood that had run warm and full of life from his vein. A shiver ran down my spine. Sticking to something in a glass this evening might be a good idea, I thought.

I reminded myself that my main concern should be the other vampires I'd encounter, not what I'd be eating. The primary purpose of this exercise was to observe how others of our kind reacted to me and how I would respond to them. I needed to focus on that and stop my fantasies about what, or who, I might be able to sink my fangs into. The fangs in question had descended when we pulled away from the house and were still crowding my mouth in a way that made me hesitant to talk. Luckily, Felix did enough talking for the rest of us, and I was content to sit back and listen to him prattle on about everything and nothing throughout the trip down. At least he wasn't drooling over Bruce, and I hoped he'd find someone to chew on to keep his mind off my newest House member.

We left the car in a city parking garage and made our way to a tapas restaurant in the same general area I'd visited before. I agonized over what to wear that evening. Sara had been kind enough to lend me a green blouse with fine Swiss dot embroidery. It looked nice with my dark jeans, and Bruce assured me that the place we were going to was not as fancy as the Tap House had been. I was grateful. Fancy wasn't my scene, and I didn't have any clothes suitable for anything nicer than your average restaurant.

Bruce and Marcus wore variations of the same outfit: jeans and black tops. Bruce wore a crisp, ironed button-down, while Marcus opted for a fitted T-shirt. I was curious to see what Felix would turn up in. So far, I'd only seen him in cargo shorts and well-worn graphic Ts. Tonight, he was dressed in jeans and an earthy-toned flannel open over a white T-shirt. He even wore brown leather loafers instead of flip-flops. It was quite an improvement.

When we entered the tapas place, I was surprised to see that it was full of humans. I scanned the tables and couldn't identify anyone who gave off the vampire vibe. I was about to ask if we were in the right place when Bruce spoke to the hostess.

"We have a reservation for downstairs," he said.

"Under what name?" she asked politely.

"Fitzgerald, Bruce," he replied, and handed over his new ID card.

Seeing the small, white plastic card surprised me. I

knew establishments in the vampire world were careful not to admit those without the proper ID, but I hadn't stopped to think about bringing mine. A jolt of fear ran through me. What if I got in trouble for being out without it? Then I remembered who I was with. Marcus, a Council enforcer, stood right beside me.

"Yes, here it is," she said. "Can I see the others' IDs as well?"

"Of course," Bruce said and passed her three more cards. Two of them I recognized, and the third, which I assumed was Felix's, was green. I sighed. Naturally, Bruce would know what was required and have everything taken care of. *We really should be paying that man*, I thought for the hundredth time.

Everything must have been in order because she led us to a set of roped-off stairs. She unlatched one side of the rope, with a dangling private party sign attached, and ushered us down to the floor below.

When we reached the bottom, we stood in what looked like a café, except that instead of tables scattered throughout, there were low seating areas with couches and chairs. It looked a bit like a dozen living rooms arranged around a central bar space. It was decorated in a similar style to the one above, featuring reds and golds, with soft overhead lighting. This time, the clientele was more what I'd expected —mostly vampires with a few humans scattered throughout.

I kept my eyes on the strange vampires in the room as the hostess led us to our reserved seats. A few of them looked up as we passed, but no one seemed overly interested or bothered. I breathed a bit easier after passing the third group without incident.

I glanced back toward the hostess as she stopped beside

an arrangement of two sofas and a large chair, clustered around a low coffee table. A petite blonde vampire was seated on one of the sofas. As she stood to greet Marcus, I realized she had been waiting for us.

She was short, maybe five-two, with a pixie cut, a heart-shaped face, and soft green eyes. She wore a red, sleeveless top and black leather pants fitted like leggings. I had to admit, if you were introducing me to a new vampire, there was no better choice than this tiny creature. I wasn't sure she could be intimidating if she tried.

The new vampire embraced Marcus, and he bent down for her to kiss him on both cheeks. A part of me bristled at the gesture and how familiar the two of them seemed. Then she turned to me.

"Hi," she said brightly in a high, clear voice as she extended her hand.

"This is E," Marcus said, smiling at both of us.

"E?" I clarified. It wasn't the oddest name I'd heard, but I wanted to make sure I got it right.

She nodded and beamed back at me.

"Kate," I said, shaking her hand.

"Oh, I know. Marcus talks about you all the time," she replied.

Strange, I thought, *he hasn't mentioned you at all.* I just smiled in reply, but kept my thoughts to myself.

Introductions were made, and we all took our seats, making ourselves comfortable. E moved to the chair, leaving the two sofas for the four of us. Felix sat beside Bruce, leaving Marcus and me on the remaining sofa. Part of me was glad that E and Marcus didn't end up on one together.

"E is ... one of my colleagues," Marcus explained as we sat. "I asked her to come tonight so that you could meet some new people."

"That was very thoughtful," I said.

"I'm sure it gets lonely up there in the mountains," E said. Her tone suggested that "the mountains" were like a foreign planet. But, I had to admit, she was right. It did get lonely.

"Yeah, I don't see too many vampires up there, that's for sure."

"You guys should get a house down here in the city," she said. "It would be such fun, and I would love to see more of Marcus." She reached over and squeezed his knee. "I don't ever see you outside of work anymore," she pouted in her girlish voice.

I glanced at her hand on his leg, and my fangs tingled in response. It was just one squeeze, and she withdrew her hand, but I didn't like it. It wasn't that I was jealous; Marcus and I weren't together in any way, but there seemed to be a history there that I was unaware of, which made me uncomfortable. I felt like I was an outsider with someone who was a member of my own House, and I realized I knew very little about Marcus and his life in Seattle.

Just then, a waiter stopped by to take our drink order. Flustered, I reached for a menu off the table and scanned what was available. There was plenty to choose from. It wasn't as fussy as the only other menu I'd looked over. With a slight shock, I remembered that James had ordered Bruce for me off that other menu, and I flicked my gaze up at him. Bruce, noticing my movement—or thinking along the same lines—looked up from across the table and gave me an amused smile.

I tried to smile back, but the muscles of my face were frozen with embarrassment. I glanced back down at the menu just as the waiter came around to me, and hastily pointed to something off the house's selection of O-negative by the glass. The waiter nodded, scribbled on his notepad, and took my menu before I had a chance to change my mind. Looking around, I spotted a few vampires who had ordered the whole bottle, so to speak, and my mouth watered as I watched them nursing from the wrist or throat of a human sitting beside them.

I looked away, not wanting to be rude or crave what they were experiencing. I was perfectly happy to drink from a glass or a bag, like I did at home. I'd been nervous when Bruce first showed up that controlling myself around him would be a struggle. But, as I had the first night of my transition, when I encountered the receptionist at James's apartment building, I knew I could always lower my defenses a bit and let in the emotions of the human I was around to help stem any craving I was feeling. I couldn't hunger for someone if I understood how they felt, if I saw the complexity of their human emotions, and recognized myself in their turmoil. So far, I hadn't had to resort to that with Bruce, and I was proud of my self-restraint. Being out among other vampires who were feeding, however, felt like a real challenge, and I took a steadying breath and refocused on our little group.

Felix and E were discussing Felix's many travels abroad, while Marcus and Bruce were talking about the numerous deliveries Bruce had scheduled for the House over the coming week. They had both moved quickly to outfit our home with everything it needed, and the boxes were already starting to arrive. Each evening, when I awoke, it felt a bit like Christmas as I discovered the new changes that had occurred while I slept. Bruce had asked if I wanted my room done too, but I liked it the way it was. Sara had cobbled together all the furniture and decorations for my room, and I didn't want to change a thing.

Our drinks arrived, and the waiter set wine glasses full of delicious-smelling, red liquid in front of each vampire and a tonic with lime in front of Bruce. I glanced at Felix with a frown. "I thought you never consumed bagged?" I said.

"This, my dear, is not bagged; it's collected in back, fresh. It allows me to feed in the company of others, without a body draped across my lap. It's more polite in mixed company. Human and vampire, I mean," he said, picking up his glass and taking a healthy sip. "Lovely."

Bruce shifted in his seat next to Felix. "I hope you're not changing your behavior on my account," he said.

"Oh no. I find I am completely myself these days," Felix said, swirling his glass, like one might swirl a wine. "It's such a refreshing change."

He was odd, but I had to admit, I liked the vampire. And he was behaving better lately. I had to give him that.

I sipped at my glass and was surprised to find that the taste was remarkably better than what I'd been drinking at home. I'd forgotten how non-bagged blood tasted. Not only did it seem fresher, but it also had delicate flavors underneath the familiar iron taste. I hadn't read the menu thoroughly, and I wondered if the doners were specially fed before collection, like they were where Bruce had worked. Whatever the reason, the blood was far superior to my usual fare.

I tilted my glass farther and realized I'd finished the entire thing in just two swallows. Feeling self-conscious, I glanced around at the others. E was the only one watching me, and she smiled and gave me a wink.

"Kate, let's split something for dessert," she said.

"Oh, I'm not hungry," I replied. I didn't know what she

meant, but I had a feeling she wasn't talking about a brownie sundae.

"There's always room for dessert," she said. "You boys don't mind? Do you?"

"Please," Felix grinned. "I think it's a great idea."

Bruce just shook his head.

I glanced at Marcus beside me. He smiled fondly. "It's up to you," he said. "There's no pressure."

I looked around again at the other vampires in the restaurant, feeding and chatting, none of them paying any attention. I licked my lips, and my mouth started to water, my fangs pulsing in my gums. I nodded, and E clapped her hands with delight, waving over our waiter.

I didn't hear what she said to him; the blood was roaring in my ears, and my face felt a bit numb. I was momentarily startled when Marcus got up and switched places with E. She leaned into me, grasping my arm. "Don't take too much, okay?" she said. "It's easy to go too far when you're sharing."

I glanced up at Marcus, who was watching me closely. I knew there was no small amount of panic in my eyes. "Not to worry," he said calmly, his posture as relaxed as his tone. "We won't let you do anything you'd regret."

I nodded again. Words were too much. The problem was, I knew what to expect. I knew how much I would enjoy what was coming, and I was frightened of myself. Despite my self-assurance that I was in control due to my empathic abilities, I was still scared. I was glad I was surrounded by people who wouldn't let me go too far, but at the same time, it felt like a private act, and I was nervous to feed for real in front of them.

Before I could chicken out, a man appeared beside me. He looked to be in his twenties, with deeply tanned skin, a beautifully handsome face, thick dark lashes, and curly black hair that brushed against the open collar of his shirt. He shuffled between E and me, and we scooted apart to make room for him on the couch. E was tiny, but we were still squeezed together, hip to hip. With the contact, I couldn't shut out what the young man felt, and it wasn't anywhere close to fear. I would have been grateful, but his emotions spilled into me, and I found myself breathing more quickly, a warm pressure building low in my belly. All my misgivings fled. I wanted this man.

My friends were momentarily forgotten as I looked down at his wrist, which was covered by a long sleeve that was buttoned tightly. I frowned and glanced across at E, who was sitting up straight and tugging down the open collar of the man's shirt. She looked across at me and quirked a smile before putting her mouth to the side of his neck.

I gasped at the same time he did, and paused to watch as E's throat moved with her rhythmic swallowing. I reached for the other side of his collar and pulled it aside. There was no hesitation as I moved toward the warm pulse under his jaw. He smelled wonderful, like honey and chocolate, and I wondered briefly if he had recently consumed those things. I remembered what James had taught me about making the experience more comfortable for the human, that our saliva had a numbing effect. But, I was too overcome to be patient and struck before I meant to.

The man gasped again but brought an arm around my shoulder and pulled me closer. I sighed. He tasted like honey and chocolate, too. I took just a couple of mouthfuls, savoring the sweet potency of the man. I was conscious of the moment when E stopped drinking and pulled back. It occurred to me that I, too, should stop soon, so as not to hurt him. I withdrew my fangs and opened my eyes.

The punctures in his neck were leaking blood, and my

first thought was, *What a waste.* My second thought was to help the poor man, and I bit my forefinger and sealed the wound. At the last moment, I leaned in and licked the side of his throat clean, just to be polite.

I realized then that I was leaning so far into the guy that I was practically on his lap, with one hand against his chest and my leg thrown over his knee. I jumped back, breaking contact with him, and glanced up. He had a satisfied smile and a glassy, far-away look. I had counted on my ability to sense emotion to keep me from going overboard, but in this instance, it had backfired, sweeping me up along with the man's desire. Separated from his emotions, I returned to being flustered and slightly embarrassed, but I was glad he was enjoying his job. And he tasted wonderful.

Our waiter was there when I glanced up, and he helped the man to his feet. He wobbled slightly but waved a friendly goodnight before leaving our company. I wiped my mouth with the back of my hand, not knowing if I'd made a mess of myself, but it came away clean.

E scooted back closer and put an arm around me. It was unexpected, but also welcome. I felt awkward, and the contact and her satisfied emotions were helpful. "Yummy, wasn't he?" she asked. I nodded and smiled at her. "I'm glad you came out with us," she said, sounding tipsy. I analyzed how I felt and found that I also felt a slight buzz.

"Was that guy drunk?" I asked.

"Yup," she replied. "Enjoy it while it lasts. It'll only be for a few minutes." She giggled.

I glanced over at the others. Bruce was staring down at the table, a slight smile on his face, but the other two were grinning at me with open delight.

"Not too bad, right?" Felix said. "I told you from the vein is best."

"You never mentioned the alcohol, though," I said, already feeling my head beginning to clear. E was right, the effects didn't last long.

E sighed and leaned her head against my shoulder. Then, her arm around me tensed, and her emotions shifted. She turned her face toward my neck and sniffed. My eyes locked with Marcus's over the top of her blonde head. His expression was guarded, and he raised a hand, motioning for me to calm down and wait.

She breathed in deeply a second time. "You smell nice," she said in a sleepy voice. "Like rain and flowers. Mmm ..." She leaned into the crook of my neck, and I jolted, but then she sat up and shook her head. "Sorry, the booze gets to me," she said, and shot me an apologetic smile. She scooted farther away and rubbed her face as if trying to wake up.

I eased out a breath and relaxed muscles I hadn't realized I'd been tensing, but my stomach remained in knots. Marcus nodded at me. I glanced at the two other men who'd been watching it all play out. Both sat across from me with masks of perfect calm. But I could feel their anxiety radiating off them, even with my guard up.

Marcus switched places again with E, and we ordered another round of drinks before leaving. I was grateful for the chance to settle myself, and despite being full, I did enjoy the extra glass of fresh blood.

Bruce settled our bill, and I said goodnight to E. She embraced me and kissed my cheeks, along with everyone else, but gave no particular reaction to me other than polite kindness. We walked back to Bruce's car and piled in.

"Well, I don't think that could have gone better," Felix said.

"I agree. I think we can chalk this one up as a win." Marcus smiled at me and squeezed my arm.

I just sat there, not sure what to say.

Bruce looked at me in the rearview mirror. "Kate, you okay?"

Of all the people, he was the only one who noticed that something was off. I heaved out a breath.

"She bit me," I said.

19

SARA

I was gradually getting used to my new schedule. Waking up at two in the afternoon wasn't hard, but staying up past ten was more difficult than I had imagined it would be. I'd been keeping the same hours for years and wasn't great with change. On the third day of my new schedule, I decided it was time for Kate and me to reconnect, which I desperately needed. She'd gone out with the boys the night before, and I was dying to know how everything had gone. It was a good excuse to have the girls' night we'd planned, and I needed her advice.

After putting on clothes, I shuffled down the hall and noticed that Bruce's door was cracked open. He usually left it closed only if he was in his room. I wondered what time they'd gotten back that morning. I fell asleep around 1 a.m. and didn't wake up when they returned. I was also curious if Kate had picked up on Bruce and Felix and the nature of their relationship. They hadn't come out and said anything, but the attraction between those two was clear. It was ironic that it was obvious to everyone except the person who could sense others' emotions.

When I reached the staircase, I heard the sound of several people moving about and the whurr of a drill. My heart picked up, and my stomach fluttered. I bounded down the stairs and ran into Bruce, who was holding a clipboard.

"Oh, hey, Sara. Good afternoon," he said, smiling as he looked up. "Sorry if we woke you."

I peered around the foyer and glanced into the living room. Two people were installing bookshelves, and a third carried a large rug in from outside. My heart sank; they were all strangers. "No," I said, trying to keep the disappointment out of my voice. "I slept great. What's going on? Who are all these people?"

"I hired some extra help for today," he said, tucking his clipboard under one large tattooed arm. "I have a team working on the kitchen, and another in the great room. There's a lot of heavy lifting today and some installation, and I needed extra hands."

"I'm sure Silas could have helped. He and his brothers do stuff like this all the time."

"I checked with him first, but he said they were booked this week. The deliveries were piling up, and I didn't want to wait. I hope that's okay?"

I waved a hand. "Of course," I said. A feeling of dread crawled through me, however. Even if Silas and his brothers were booked up, there is no way he wouldn't have offered to come over in the evening to help. "But how did you get them all in here?" I pitched the question so that only he would hear.

"I shook everyone's hand at the door as they stepped inside. A few noticed the 'static electricity' as they did. But I think we're good."

I nodded. There was no need to re-ward the house against the workers he'd hired. They weren't the ones we were trying to keep out. "How was last night?" I asked, attempting to distract myself from thoughts of Silas.

Half of Bruce's mouth curled up in a crooked smile. "It was ... informative. I think Kate had a good time, but you'll have to ask her."

"Hmm, that sounds cryptic," I said, tilting my head. "Speaking of asking Kate, tonight is supposed to be our girls' night in. Will we be able to use the living room, or ...?"

"It shouldn't be a problem. I expect all of this to be done around 6 p.m." He glanced at his smart watch. "Maybe closer to seven."

I nodded. "Is it okay if I get something to eat from the kitchen?" I asked.

"Of course," he said. "There are sandwiches in the fridge, help yourself. Let me know if you need anything you can't find." With that, he patted my shoulder and strode off into the main living space, leaving me staring after him.

I turned toward the kitchen, pausing when I reached the doorway. Inside, two men were placing a new industrial sink into a freshly installed white granite countertop. The cupboards had also been redone; instead of aging wood, they now featured stainless steel in some areas and open shelving in others. I glanced at a still-wrapped kitchen island in the middle of the space, which appeared to be another stainless steel addition, the kind often found in restaurant kitchens. I realized that's what it reminded me of —a restaurant kitchen. There was a new stove with six burners, two ovens, and a large flat surface that I assumed was for cooking. Directly across from the culinary monstrosity sat a commercial fridge double the size of the previous one.

I turned around and leaned out of the kitchen. "Bruce," I

called in a voice loud enough to carry. "How many people do you expect us to feed?"

"You never know," came his reply.

I shook my head. Either he expected us to host some major parties in the future, or he had a bigger appetite than I thought.

There were neatly wrapped sandwiches stacked in the new fridge, along with an assortment of beverages. I snagged a sandwich and a can of ginger ale and took them to the shop. There were too many people in the house for me to think, let alone enjoy a meal, and I thought it best to stay out of Bruce's way until the upgrades were complete. Luckily, there was plenty to do in the shop.

Beth migrated our inventory to the new system, and things were well on their way to running more smoothly. However, I still had to affix barcodes to everything in the store. We'd print the packaging with the barcodes already in place in the future, but we weren't there yet. I figured we were now up to twentieth-century technology. At this rate, it would take decades to reach the twenty-first, but maybe with Beth's help, we'd get there faster.

I ate breakfast in front of the computer while searching for information on Relics and where to acquire them. It was slow going. You had to know the specific sites to visit and the key terms that would lead to what you were looking for. Unfortunately, I had found very little. The last known Relic to be auctioned was over fifteen years before. It was a gold ring with an inset ruby, estimated to be almost five hundred years old. It was reportedly capable of calming the wearer and was sold for over $1 million. I suspected the price had something to do with the large ruby.

That kind of money would be life-changing, especially for someone who planned to live a very long time. But Kate couldn't make rings, at least not that I knew of, and we were fresh out of rubies. Unfortunately, I hadn't seen anything about paintings or drawings. All the Relics I found mentioned were jewelry or decorative objects. I wasn't sure if we had to pass her stuff off as ancient, but people would start asking a lot of questions if newer items were put up for sale. That was assuming I could get one of her creations into the market.

Beth arrived around four, and we discussed an upcoming photoshoot she had scheduled for our new social media accounts. She convinced me that, although business was good, there was a broader market for people interested in essential oils, candles, and basic herbal remedies. Beth found a photographer in the community to handle the job, and the shoot was set for the following week.

The changes in the house, the search for answers about Relics, and the improvements to the business all kept me occupied and helped take my mind off Silas. I hadn't spoken to him since the incident with Beth and Arrow, and I regretted every day what I'd said to him and that I hadn't made my feelings clear. We'd texted a few times, but even through the texts, I could sense him pulling away and felt a new distance between us. We needed to talk to straighten things out. I couldn't do it over the phone, and especially not in a text thread. I needed to say it in person if I ever got the chance.

Right around the time I started to get hungry again, the door to the house opened, and Kate appeared. She wore a sheepish grin and carried a large tray.

"Good evening, all," she said, closing the door behind her so as not to let Arrow into the house. "So, I'm not allowed in the rest of the house yet. Bruce handed me this," she said, lifting the tray higher. "And told me he'd come get us when he was done."

Beth jumped up from behind the desk and entered the shop's main room. "Do you need any help?" she asked. "That looks heavy."

Kate chuckled and shook her head. "Nope. I got it," she said, holding it easily with one hand. Beth lit up every time one of the vampires was in the same space. She wasn't quite as effusive as she had been during her first encounter, but her enthusiasm remained. "If my nose is correct, Bruce also included dinner for you guys." She set the tray on the counter and gave a theatrical whiff, wafting air from the tray with one hand. "Pot pies and fresh rolls," she guessed.

The tray held two covered dishes, two bottles of sparkling water, and a solid black insulated coffee tumbler with a metal straw. I removed the cover from one of the meals, and sure enough, it was a chicken potpie and fresh rolls, complete with silverware and a real linen napkin.

"I think I'm in love with Bruce," I sighed, picking up my plate and grabbing one of the water bottles. Beth and I pulled up stools from behind the counter and tucked into our dinners while Kate leaned against the countertop with her tumbler full of blood.

"What about you, Kate?" Beth asked between bites. "It looks like Bruce is spoken for, but is there anyone you fancy?"

Kate froze mid-sip. "Uh, no. Not recently. I'm still just getting used to this new life. I haven't had time to *fancy* anyone." She smiled, and her descended fangs peeked out from under her upper lip.

"What about Marcus?" Beth asked. "Is he seeing anyone?"

"Not that I know of," Kate replied. Her body shifted at the question, and I smiled to myself. Kate wouldn't admit it, but I'd seen her staring at him before and knew she was interested.

"What I want to know is," Beth continued, turning toward me. "Does your boyfriend have any friends he could hook me up with?"

"What?" I asked. "My boyfriend? You mean Silas?"

She nodded and shot me a look like I was being obstinate on purpose.

"Um, he's not my boyfriend," I said. The feeling in my middle, I'd been avoiding for days, came back. It made me feel like I was eating gravel instead of a perfectly cooked, flaky pastry. "I'm not so sure we will see him around here much anymore."

"What?" Kate demanded. She set her cup aside and came to stand in front of me. She leaned forward, elbows on the counter. "What happened?"

I pushed my dish away. I wasn't hungry anymore. "I think I screwed up," I said, and then told the two women about what I'd said to Silas about not coming around as often. I explained how he'd been pulling away, hardly texting.

Kate squeezed my hand. "I'm sorry, love. I know how much you like him. But don't worry, I don't think it's over. There's probably stuff going on in his world, too. I've seen how he looks at you. He'll be back."

Before I had time to reply, the door to the house opened, and Bruce stuck his head in. He looked tired but excited at the same time. "Ladies, the Great Room is complete. Would you care to see it?"

There was a scramble of chairs, and I think Beth squealed as we rushed to follow Bruce into the house for our new living room tour. I was not prepared for what awaited us.

Walking into the foyer felt like entering someone else's home or a charming boutique hotel. A patterned circular rug was now neatly placed beneath the wrought iron chandelier. An unfamiliar table in the center held a large potted white orchid in full bloom. Bruce led us around the table, and we got our first view of the finished living room, or Great Room, as Bruce had called it. And it was truly great.

The space was now divided into three distinct areas. Directly across from the foyer was a sitting area that featured tall bookshelves, a loveseat, and two large over-stuffed chairs that reminded me of Kate's old pink chair. These, however, were a tasteful dusty pink instead of the alarming shade of the last one. A plush cream rug tied the space together, along with several coordinating throws.

The middle section was a living room centered around the large fireplace. It had a long, brown leather sofa facing the hearth, two mismatched armchairs on one side, and a loveseat on the other, creating a sort of box around the fireplace. A five-foot-long, three-foot-wide coffee table with a black metal base and a glass top sat in the middle.

The last section, farthest from the door and nearest the kitchen, was a dining room. The dining table was made of wood that matched the walls and had live edges in a burnished brown finish. The chairs were modern but looked comfortable. The entire place could be described as modern-rustic, with homey decorative touches throughout the large room. Several freshly potted plants, soft lighting, small sculptural objects, and candles warmed up the space in a way the fireplace never could.

It was beautiful.

I stood back, taking it all in. I could hardly believe that

this was my house, our house. I'd discussed some of the changes with Bruce beforehand, but I'd just turned him loose in the end. He clearly had an eye for this sort of thing, and I hadn't been wrong in trusting him.

"Oh, Bruce," Kate said as she gazed around the new space. "It's so wonderful. I don't know how to thank you."

"You don't have to thank me," he replied. "This is my job." He smiled at her warmly. He might not want the thanks, but he looked very pleased that we were so happy.

We all took turns telling him how much we loved it, and he showed us the kitchen, which we also fussed over. The house was truly starting to look like the large B&B it had been built as. It now had a living room that could accommodate a large party, a table that would easily seat ten, and a kitchen that could feed an army.

An hour later, Beth had gone home, Bruce had gone upstairs for a well-deserved rest, and Kate and I were cuddled up on the leather sofa, watching "Practical Magic" on a new pull-down screen and projection TV. The movie was one we'd watched as girls and still loved. The irony was not lost on me that we used to watch witch movies but never talked about magic. It was still a good movie.

"I needed this," Kate said, leaning her head against mine.

"Me too," I said, meaning it. It had been too long since it had been just the two of us, when we weren't worried about some looming crisis or pending action from the vampires. "I forgot to ask, how did last night go?" Kate stiffened beside me. "Sorry," I said. "You can pretend I didn't ask."

"No. It's okay. It went alright. I guess," she said, sounding uncertain.

"Well, no one ate you. So that's good, right?" I joked.

"Um, well ..." she replied, and then told me about

meeting E and how tiny and cute she was. And how she'd been put at ease by her size and bubbly attitude. And how E had bitten her.

"She just bit you?" I asked.

"Yeah, it was quick, and I'm not sure how much blood she tasted. As soon as I felt her fangs, I pushed back against her with my ability. She stopped right away, but yeah." She sat up and put a hand to her neck. "Marcus and Felix weren't worried. They said if she were going to react, we would have seen it. Plus, she was super drunk."

"Drunk?" I blurted. "I didn't know vampires could get drunk."

"Neither did I." She squirmed in her seat.

"Kate, are you blushing?" I asked.

"Vampires don't blush," she said, narrowing her eyes at me. But then she relaxed and told me about the man she and E had shared for dessert.

"Oh, Gods, Kate. I mean. I know you're a vampire, but I didn't think about you … you know."

"I know!" she said. "But I did."

I looked at her. Really looked at her. The way she sat, the look on her face, the tightness in her arms and hands. "You liked it. The way you liked feeding from Bruce that first time," I said. There was no judgment in my voice. It wasn't an accusation. I was stating the facts.

She nodded.

"I think you are going to have to come to terms with that," I said. Her head snapped up, and she stared back at me. "You are what you are now, Kate. You're a vampire. If … feeding is something you crave or want or need, then it's something you should consider. I'm not saying I'd be cool with a stable of blood donors out back, but it's something to think about."

She bit her lower lip but nodded again. "Thank you for understanding," she said.

"I'm your best friend," I replied, pushing myself off the sofa. "Now, I think it's time for Midnight Margaritas. And I'm dying to use the new blender in the kitchen. Can I get you anything?" I asked.

She let out a long sigh. "Yeah. I'll take an O-negative. You don't need to heat it," she called after me.

A few minutes later, after playing with the awesome new kitchen gadgets, I returned to the living room and set a tray down on the glass tabletop. I handed Kate her drink, which I'd put in a margarita glass, and took my frosty lime cocktail.

"Cheers," I said, holding up my glass. "To best friends."

"Best friends," Kate repeated and took a sip. "Sara?"

"Yes?"

"Is there tequila in my O-negative?" she asked.

"Why yes, yes there is," I replied.

She made a face but took another sip as I restarted the movie.

20

SILAS

A chill blast of wind whipped through the valley beside my house, parting the fur along my wolf's side, making me shiver. It felt fantastic. It had been far too long since we'd been out on four legs, ranging the hills around my small cabin. Work, family, and Sara had kept me busy over the past few months, leaving little time to stretch our legs and ground our paws into the rocky soil.

My wolf panted, his tongue loling out, while trotting along a familiar path, avoiding the worst of the mud in favor of the slushy snow piles and bare ground. It had warmed up over the last few days, making the trails a mess, but it was still January, and there would be months of snow left before real spring arrived. We had hardly seen real winter yet. My wolf didn't care. He loved the cold weather; cold mixed with sunshine was his favorite.

He had been sullen and withdrawn lately, so this long afternoon outside was just what he needed. I didn't mind the break either. When we shifted and he took control, I got to rest. I was still aware, and we could communicate as always, but he made the decisions about where we went and what we did.

In human form, he granted me many of his abilities. I possessed heightened senses of hearing, smell, and sight, especially night vision. I was stronger and faster, had improved balance, and could withstand colder temperatures than most humans. When in wolf form, I had little to offer him besides my mind. Over time, as a wolf matured alongside their human, they developed human-like intellect and reasoning. Our wolves didn't need us to think for them, as some assumed. They managed well enough on their own by the time we reached adulthood. A shifter's main advantage in the relationship was that they could force the change, while the animal could not. They tried occasionally, and when a shifter was young, sometimes they succeeded, but not often.

That day, with the crisp wind and the warm sun overhead, my wolf was in heaven, and I was happy to take a backseat while he sniffed and ran his way through the mountainside. I closed my eyes, limiting my awareness to what my wolf was feeling, hearing, and smelling. There was so much information on the plants, across the ground, and in the wind. Animals that passed by, things that were growing or decaying, temperature shifts, and far-off scents, both human and animal.

Even though I could access his senses, his mind had been quiet for some time. Although he understood English perfectly, he didn't communicate in words; however, he got his point across just fine. I could sense his emotions and understand his thoughts and intentions based on how he felt in my mind when he wanted me to.

After more than an hour of muffled connection, I

noticed that the sun was particularly warm on our head and shoulders. He had been moving west for some time under the early afternoon sun. I came alert and peered out of his eyes. We were well past the trails in our valley and were headed uphill. The landscape was dominated by snow and rock, with little else in sight. *Shit.*

"What are you doing?" I asked, already knowing the answer.

He just huffed and shook his head, keeping his thoughts locked down.

"You can't possibly think I would let you run all the way to Sara's."

Nothing this time, just quiet.

"Don't make me turn this thing around," I warned. I would hate to have to jog back home, naked, in the snow, but I would.

I pushed outward, letting him feel the pressure in his bones and muscles. It was a warning, and he knew it. I expected him to stop or at least slow down, but he ignored my threat and kept going. I pushed harder, causing him to stumble. He regained his footing and growled, shaking his head and sending his skin rippling as he tried to shrug off the discomfort caused by my actions. He was fighting the shift.

I'd had enough. *"You're being ridiculous,"* I told him. I shoved, and he stopped, his body shaking. He dropped onto his stomach and relented. A moment later, I lay gasping in the snow. No warm layer of insulated fur between my skin and the icy bite of the wind or the slush I found myself resting against. Pushing to my feet, I brushed off the snow and looked around. We were over five miles from the cabin.

"Seriously? You thought I wouldn't eventually notice? Or did

you think that if you could get us far enough, I'd miss my date and head to Sara's?"

He huffed and turned his back to me, shutting me out again. *Fine.* I started walking. It was slow going, and I had to pick my way along on bare feet through the rock-strewn landscape, trying not to slip and tumble off the side of the mountain. After thirty minutes, I stopped to get my bearings. We were still miles from the valley. *"Are you speaking to me yet?"* I asked. My feet were freezing, along with other parts of my anatomy, and while I wouldn't get frostbite as easily as a human, it was very uncomfortable to have so much skin exposed to the bitter cold.

My wolf sighed, but I felt him relent.

"Okay, but if you turn us around, you won't be back on four legs for a month. I swear it," I warned him before crouching down. I placed one hand on the icy ground and shifted.

He heeded my warning and didn't turn back. However, he didn't move quickly, and with every sluggish step, I was well aware of his dissent. I understood. I missed Sara too, but I knew I was doing the right thing. I was giving us both a chance for happiness. I was ensuring she wouldn't get stuck in a relationship she didn't want, or that I wasn't trapped living without my other half. If I bonded a shifter, life would be less complicated for both parties.

We made it back to my cabin with only an hour to spare. I rushed through a shower and a quick shave, then threw on the clothes I had laid out. I buttoned my shirt, tucked it into my nicest jeans, added a belt with a simple silver buckle, and slipped into a polished pair of brown leather dress boots. I checked my reflection in the full-length mirror outside the bathroom. Everything looked fine, but it felt wrong. I tugged at my collar, adjusted the belt, and tried to ignore the growing knot in my stomach. My wolf had lapsed back into silence. It was probably good that he was quiet; I had enough turmoil churning inside for both of us.

I drove into town in my freshly washed truck. I'd offered to pick my date up at her house, but she'd declined, preferring to meet me at the restaurant. Perhaps her family was a lot like mine, and she didn't want so many people to be involved in our first date. I could respect that. It would also allow us to size each other up without so many eyes on us.

The first time two adult single shifters met could be telling. Sometimes you knew right away that it was a match, sometimes you knew right away it wasn't. Most of the time, you couldn't tell if the bond would develop until you'd spent some time dating and getting to know one another. Whatever we gleaned from our first meeting, if anything, would be between the two of us, and that was just fine with me.

I sat in my truck in the parking lot. I still had ten minutes before we were supposed to meet, and I needed that time to clear my head. I don't know why I was so agitated. It was just a date. I'd called the number my mom had given me and talked to Lacy, her friend's daughter. She seemed very nice. Like me, she was in her twenties, grew up in the same general area, and was searching for her partner at the urging of her parents.

It was a pretty typical story for a shifter. We'd met before, but had both been young at the time with only vague memories of the event. We didn't talk long, but agreed to meet for dinner this evening to see how things went. I don't know if I was hoping we would make a connection, or hoping we wouldn't. Either way, I was willing to give it a shot. For Sara, I told myself.

I spotted a young woman standing outside the German

restaurant. She matched the description: short, dark hair; tan skin; average height. She glanced around as if waiting for someone. That was my cue.

I got out of the truck and checked my reflection in the window again. I still felt off. The ball of anxiety in my middle had grown and was now threatening to choke me. I took a deep breath, walked around the vehicle, and approached the woman.

She spotted me immediately, and her face lit up with a pleased smile. The closer I got, the more agitated I felt, but I maintained a pleasant expression as I drew nearer. I didn't want to scare the poor woman away before we even shook hands. I was only a few steps away when I felt my wolf sit up and take notice.

I stopped just in front of her. "Lacy?" I asked.

"Yes, Silas, it's nice to meet you." She nodded and reached out a hand.

As soon as our palms connected, my wolf lunged in my mind, snapping his teeth and letting out a viscous snarl. We both jumped apart. From the look of shock on her face, I guessed that her wolf had reacted as well. I suppose that told us all we needed to know. It was an instant 'no connection' from our wolves.

"You are Silas, right?" she asked. Her look of shock was replaced with confusion, her brows creased as she studied me.

"Yes," I said. "Sorry about that. I guess it wasn't meant to be." I hoped she wasn't upset. It wasn't like it was something either of us could control. And now that I knew we weren't a match, I felt relief.

"Um, I think there has been some mix-up," Lacy said.

"Mix-up?"

"Yeah." She pursed her lips, and her brows lowered. "I

don't know what you were hoping would happen here," she said, sounding not just upset but pissed off.

I held up my hands. "I think you got the wrong idea," I said, stepping back. "I was just hoping for a nice evening over dinner, to see if we connected. I swear." I wasn't sure what she was talking about or why the incompatibility would bother her so much. It was a fairly common occurrence for two shifters not to match.

"Why would a bonded shifter be out looking for 'compatibility'?" she said, hand on one hip.

I just stared at her. What was she talking about? I opened my mouth to deny it, to tell her that she was mistaken, that I wasn't bonded, but no words came out.

Instantly, her face softened, and she breathed in. "Oh, Gods. You didn't know?"

I shook my head, grateful she wasn't still pissed off at me but not fully processing the revelation. My wolf huffed, and I could feel the smug satisfaction coming from him as he settled himself in my mind. "No," I finally managed.

"Well, congratulations?" she said with a small smile. "Whoever they are, I'm sure they're great."

"Um, yeah. Thank you," I said, but I still couldn't focus. Bonded. I was already bonded ... to Sara. As soon as I thought the words, the world clicked into place. My mind cleared, and my nerves stilled. I took a long, deep breath and let it out. "I'm sorry about this," I said to Lacy. "I assure you, I didn't mean to deceive you."

"Yeah, I can tell. It's okay," she said. She patted my arm, and my wolf remained docile. He'd made his point.

"Would you mind if we skipped dinner?" I asked. I knew it might be rude, but I needed to think, and I was certain I wouldn't be good company.

She laughed. "No problem. I can tell you're still in shock. You okay to drive?" she asked.

"Um, yeah. I think I can manage," I took another step back. "And, I'm sorry, again. I ..."

She held up a hand. "Don't sweat it," she said. "We're good."

I waved, then turned and climbed back into my truck. Pulling onto the road, I gripped the steering wheel. Bonded. Bonded. A new feeling bloomed in my chest. Joy? Excitement? Fear? Sorrow?

I hit my turn signal and headed for my parents' house. Before I did anything, I needed to talk with someone who knew what it was like to be a bonded mate.

There were no other cars besides my parents' in the driveway. I let myself in through the front door and called out, "It's me."

My mother came out of the kitchen, drying her hands on a towel. "Silas. I'm about to put dinner on the table. Your dad's in the shower. Everything okay?" she said, tilting her head. "I thought you were going out tonight with Bethany's daughter. Back so soon?"

I nodded. "It didn't work out," I said, unsure how to begin the conversation.

She crossed her arms and looked me over. "You know my friend Karen has a son—"

"No, Mom," I interrupted. I didn't need her to fix me up with anyone else. I needed the courage to say what I came here to say. I gazed down at the tile floor of the entryway. "It's too late."

Her gasp brought my head up in time to see her shocked expression. She quickly schooled her features and offered me a smile. "Sara," she said.

I nodded again. "Yeah." I swallowed. "I didn't know," I said. "Not until tonight."

My mother sighed, her eyes full of emotion. "Come on," she said, motioning to the kitchen. "I'll make you some tea."

I followed her to the kitchen table and fell into one of the sturdy chairs, as she rifled through the cabinet, pulling out a canister of chamomile tea and a chipped porcelain pot. She filled the kettle and set it on the stove to boil, then returned to the table and sat across from me.

"I assume it was your date's wolf and its reaction that tipped you off?" My mother said.

I nodded, feeling foolish for not figuring it out beforehand and for embarrassing myself in front of a stranger. "I thought I was being careful. I thought if I didn't even kiss her, if ..."

"Bonding has nothing to do with physical intimacy. The bond doesn't fall into place the first time you kiss or make love," she said. "Not even when you mark each other as mates." She reached up, unconsciously touching the spot between her shoulder and neck where I knew she bore the scar of my father's teeth marks.

I glanced down at the table, my face flushing. The thought of marking Sara in that way was overwhelming, especially in front of my mother.

"How is your wolf taking this?" she asked, getting my attention.

I chuckled dryly. "He's feeling pretty smug. I see now that he's known for a while; I just haven't wanted to listen."

She snorted. "Yeah, they do tend to catch on first." She paused, and I wondered if she was thinking about the fact that I was bonded to a witch, one she'd warned me against spending too much time around for this exact reason. "You know what you have to do now, right?" she asked.

My gaze snapped back to her. "I ..." I wasn't sure what to say.

Her eyes were soft, and her mouth pulled into a sweet smile. She looked at me like she had when I was young, when I'd needed her comfort and strength. She reached across the table and gripped my hand. "You go to her. And you do everything you can to make it work."

21

KATE

You learn new things every day. Or every night, if you're a vampire. For instance, not only are adult fun times possible on the back of a dragon, but also mid-flight. Who knew? I finished the first book in the dragon romance series Sara gave me and hoped to go upstairs to find that she had the rest, or at least the next volume. I had to know if the MC's dragon recovered from the last battle—and the trauma of all those "night flights" the two main characters used to hide their romance.

Sighing, I set the book aside and got off the bed. I'd been awake for hours again. This was quickly becoming the most boring part of my day. I knew Sara and Bruce were awake and busy living their lives upstairs, and I was itching to go up and join them. I did have a sitting room down in the basement that I could have gone to, but it felt strange being out there in front of all that covered glass. I knew I was safe as long as the covers were down, but it still gave me a nervous feeling.

I heard Marcus's door open and close, followed by his footfalls in the hall, and I knew it was time to go up. Despite my excitement to get upstairs and join my friends, I felt a reluctance that evening. It was the night I was supposed to present myself before the Council in Seattle. We wouldn't leave for hours, but going upstairs meant that the count-down had officially begun, and I was not looking forward to whatever the meeting might bring. Marcus and Felix assured me that it was only a formality and that it would be painless, but I wasn't so sure. None of my interactions with vampires, except for those in this house, had ever been painless.

I reached the top of the stairs and took a moment to enjoy my new surroundings. Bruce had truly transformed this part of the house. My eye was drawn to one of the newly installed bookcases in the sitting area. Instead of going to the kitchen as usual, I snuck across the foyer to check the shelves for the book I wanted. At some point during the day, Sara must have moved her entire collection because now the white shelves were bursting with color and crammed full of books I'd never seen before. They were all neatly arranged, resembling a well-organized bookshop, and I had to think that Bruce had something to do with it, too.

"Looking for book two?" Sara called from behind me.

I turned to see her at the large dining table on the other side of the living room. I smiled guiltily. "Maybe," I replied.

"Irina and Larz on the back of a dragon, am I right?" she said.

"You're not wrong," I mumbled. "Do you have it?"

"Next bookcase over, bottom shelf on the right," she said.

I found it right where she said it would be and pulled it free. The cover featured a dragon and a very half-naked man on the front. I tucked it under my arm and went to join Sara.

The table was set for five, and at first, I assumed Beth would join us. Then I noticed that three of the settings were what I referred to as "vampire settings." Nothing but a black placemat, napkin, and wine glass. I frowned but then turned to see Bruce, Marcus, and Felix coming out of the kitchen with various dishes and a steaming pitcher that smelled like vampire breakfast. I wasn't shocked to see Felix. Today was a pretty big day, and I was glad to have him here early.

Bruce set his dishes on the table and motioned for me to take the seat at the head of the table. It felt awkward, but I accepted and sat, realizing only at the last minute that I still had the book under my arm. I grabbed it and, not wanting to put it on the table, I dropped it under my chair.

Felix sat next to Bruce, with Marcus and Sara on the opposite side. "What are you hiding under there?" Felix asked. "Some great work of fiction?" His hazel eyes twinkled, and I was sure he'd caught sight of the cover as I'd stashed it.

"Ha," Sara laughed. "It's smut." She gave me a wide grin and helped herself to a serving of potatoes from the center of the table.

"I think she's blushing," Felix said.

"Vampires don't blush," I snapped, but my tone was playful. I looked at Felix's place setting and noticed he didn't have a glass in front of him, just a placemat. Of course, he didn't eat the bagged stuff, so it was no real surprise.

"How did you get here so early?" I asked. It had only been minutes since Marcus had awakened. "I know you drive fast, but not that fast."

He tilted his head and nodded. "You're right. No. I stayed here overday," he said.

That got my attention. I hadn't realized he'd been here. And I hadn't heard him leaving Marcus's room, the only other fully secured room in the house.

"Oh, cool," I said and glanced at Bruce. He was sipping

from a tall beer glass, his cheeks pink. He didn't look like anyone had drained him, which was good, but I worried that we had a hungry vampire in the house. I looked back at Felix, who sat regarding me as if he were tracking my thoughts. "I do hope you ate before you came," I said.

He smiled widely. "As a matter of fact," he said in a voice too sultry for the dinner table. "I did."

At that moment, my attention was drawn sideways as Bruce spat the beer he was drinking all over the table and began to cough.

I bolted to my feet and reached for Bruce. "Are you okay?" I asked, ready to pat his back or administer the Heimlich or whatever he needed.

He rose from his seat, his hands up to ward off any help. "No. I'm fine," he wheezed between coughs. "I'll just go grab a rag," he said, wiping the beer off the front of his shirt with both hands.

He disappeared into the kitchen, and I grabbed my napkin. I went to Bruce's seat and began to blot up the droplets that covered most of the area around where he was sitting. "You know this is your fault," I said, glancing up at Felix, who remained in his chair. "You could at least offer some help."

The look on his face was amused and something else. I had my walls firmly in place. Not only was it a bad idea to use my abilities to spy on my friends, but I didn't want to know what he was feeling at that moment. He grabbed the napkin nearest him and offered it to me.

As he brought his hand nearer, I caught a scent. A scent that shouldn't have been coming from Felix. A smell I knew well.

Bruce's blood.

A growl tore from my throat, and without thinking, I

lunged at Felix. I shoved him with both hands, and we tumbled backward, knocking over his chair and landing on the floor. We slid away from the table, Felix's back against the carpet. I straddled him, placing my palms against his shoulders to pin him down, and brought my elongated fangs close to his face. "I warned you," I snarled. "Bruce is not food. This is his home, and I will not have you feeding from him."

Felix lay still beneath me. His muscles were relaxed. He didn't even breathe. His face had gone blank as he stared up at me and my teeth, only inches from his blinking eyes.

I stayed where I was, my eyes locked onto him, waiting for some response. But he remained still. I was breathing heavily and still angry, but his lack of movement calmed me somewhat. I wasn't sure I could attack someone who wasn't fighting back.

Just then, I felt a hand on my shoulder. I flinched as Bruce leaned down so that his face was even with my own. "Kate," he said in a low, steady tone. "It's not like that."

I flicked my gaze to Bruce. His blue eyes were wide and pleading. He was scared. His fear, more than his words, penetrated, and I sat up, removing my hands from Felix. But I did not get up.

"He shouldn't be using you like that," I told Bruce. My voice still shook from the force of my anger, but I was under control.

"He didn't," Bruce replied. "He wasn't feeding from me." Bruce swallowed but looked directly into my eyes. "He's my lover."

I glanced down at Felix, whose face remained completely blank, and then back to Bruce. Bruce nodded and gave me a tight smile.

I leaped off of Felix, feeling mortified. "Oh, God. I'm ..." I stared down at Felix, who pushed himself up on an elbow.

"Is it safe to get up?" he asked, quirking the corner of his mouth up.

I clapped my hands over my face. "I can't believe I did that," I breathed. I dropped my hands and watched as Bruce helped Felix to his feet. Backing away, I glanced at Marcus, who was standing not too far away, arms crossed over his chest. "You knew?" I asked.

He nodded, and I glanced at Sara, who hadn't even gotten up from the table. "You're empathic. You didn't feel what's been going on between the two of them?" she asked, shaking her head.

"Did everyone know?" I asked incredulously.

"Pretty much," Sara replied and took a sip of wine.

I turned back to Bruce and Felix. "I owe you an apology. I'm so sorry."

"I told you, this is your House. No need to apologize," Felix said, bowing his head as he righted his chair and sat back down. "And I did promise you I'd keep my fangs to myself, which I admit I have not. Although it was more of a love bite than a real feeding—"

I held up my hand. "No, I don't need to know," I said, shaking my head and resuming my seat. "Would someone please pass me the pitcher?" I asked. I needed to eat, it would make me less grumpy, and I didn't need to think about Felix biting Bruce while I did.

Bruce reached over and poured me a glass of steaming blood. "I hope I haven't overstepped," he said in a hushed voice. "By taking up a relationship with your lawyer."

"Oh, no, Bruce. If you're happy, I'm happy. I'm just embarrassed I overreacted," I said.

"I suppose it proves you've been doing a good job

keeping our emotions blocked out," Marcus said before reaching for the pitcher.

"I have. I thought it was best to give you all some privacy. However, I see that I may not be great at reading people without it."

Marcus nodded. "It's good that you found that out now. Going into tonight's meeting, I suggest you loosen your hold a bit and keep tabs on how the others in the room are feeling. It would be good to get a read on the Council members and how they are feeling about our House."

"Are you suggesting I spy on the Council?" I asked with mock alarm. "And this from an enforcer."

He smiled ruefully. "I admit, it's unusual. But you are unusual, and the members of the Council can be ... well, like you were with Felix just now. It would be good for you to get a heads up if any of them feel likely to overreact."

I shuddered, remembering how my sire, Alexander, had reacted to me, how he had tried to school me with violence. I nodded. "Will do," I replied. "When do we leave, by the way?"

Bruce cleared his throat. "I have a stylist coming over in about an hour. She's bringing several outfits for you to choose from. The makeup artist and hairstylist will arrive around 9 p.m. We should be ready to leave by midnight."

I realized my mouth was hanging open and shut it with a click. "Stylists, plural?"

"Yes, I have no experience with such things, and I thought you might like the help," he said. "They were all hired from Council-sanctioned businesses. The makeup artist is a vampire, I believe. If you aren't comfortable with them in the house, we could have them meet us in the shop, I suppose. But that would be up to Sara, and it would mean ..."

Sara shook her head. "Nope, sorry. It would be fine except Beth and I are meeting tonight to stage the place for tomorrow's photo shoot. But I don't care if you guys do what you need to here in the house."

"Marcus, objections?" I asked. I had no problem with it, but it was our home after all, not just mine or Sara's.

"Whatever you guys need. The meeting is scheduled for 2 a.m. Let's go ahead and leave at midnight, though. Better to be early than late for these things."

"Sounds good," Bruce replied. "We can set up in here after dinner."

I breathed out heavily. This was happening. I would meet the Council that night, in just a few hours.

I glanced back at Felix, who would be going with Marcus and me to the meeting. He was looking at Bruce with a sweet smile. *How had I missed that?* I thought. Although, in my defense, most of the vampires I'd met, myself included, weren't as calm and relaxed as Felix. I'd assumed his motives toward Bruce were about food and power. I'd never been so happy to be wrong. I prayed my misgivings about the meeting were wrong too. I needed Felix and Marcus to be right about putting me in a room full of strange vampires. I hoped this wouldn't be a huge mistake.

22

———

BRUCE

After dinner, Sara bid us good evening and went to meet Beth, while Marcus left to fill his car with gas. Felix helped me with the dishes, and Kate went to shower and get ready for the first stylist to arrive. I was glad that Felix and I would have a minute alone before the meeting preparations began, especially after what happened at dinner.

"I'm sorry I didn't tell Kate sooner about us," I said, handing Felix another plate to load into the dishwasher.

He shook his head, his unbound hair waving around his face. "Don't worry about it. I could have told her, too, but I wanted you to be ready. This is your House, and I didn't want to complicate things for you."

"For me? I'm not the one who ended up on his back with a fledgling vampire snapping her fangs in my face," I scoffed.

"She was pretty great, right?" he said and chuckled. "She's got an impressive amount of control for one so young."

I didn't think I could be so blasé if she had attacked me.

But he had a point. She was handling way more than most new vampires and doing a great job. It was frankly amazing that she wasn't a homicidal wreck, but I supposed it had something to do with her ability to sense others' emotions. For whatever reason, she was unique. "Despite her reaction, she is one of the calmer vampires I've met," I agreed. "But you, by far, are the calmest." I cast a glance in his direction, but, true to his nature, he showed no reaction other than a small smile.

It was considered rude to ask a vampire how old they were. Many boasted outright about the many years they had lived, but some, like Felix, were very private about it. Just because we were sleeping together didn't mean I was any more privy to that information than anyone else. Maybe someday he would give me a hint, but for now, all I knew was that he was older than Marcus, who had stated that he was over one hundred years old.

"So, about tonight," he began, changing the subject. "We should be done shortly after 3 a.m. I could have them drop me at home, but ..."

"You could stay over again tomorrow if you like," I said. "If you don't mind sleeping in a room with only blackout curtains for protection."

"It didn't bother me today. I think I'll be fine. Maybe don't throw the drapes open when you get up, though. I don't want a sunburn," he joked.

Just the thought of it made me shudder. He seemed comfortable, but I thought he was putting a lot of unearned trust in me. "I could see if Silas has time to fix up another room downstairs," I said. "You know, if you want to make a habit of staying over. There is plenty of space."

Felix considered. "Maybe. But I'm fine in your room for

now." He placed the last of the dishes in the washer and leaned in for a kiss.

His lips and tongue were cool and soft, and I wished we had nothing else to do that evening than stay upstairs in bed. But, at that moment, the doorbell rang and I pulled away. "Later?" I asked.

His hazel eyes had gone dark, and he bit his bottom lip, letting his long fangs show, and nodded. "I should go get ready too," he said, looking down at his casual clothes. "I left some lawyer clothes in the wardrobe in your room. I hope you don't mind."

"No, I don't mind." I turned for the door. "Let me know if you need any help," I said over my shoulder. I heard a soft growl from behind me as I left the kitchen and smiled.

The first stylist arrived promptly, carrying three large garment bags slung over her shoulder. I helped her carry a collapsible clothing rack, a full-length mirror, and a box of shoes from her car. She set everything up in the living room, and I went to fetch Kate, who was presumably hiding in her room.

I tapped softly on her door and waited. A moment later, she cracked it open and stuck her towel-wrapped head out. "Bruce," she said, looking around behind me. "Are they here?"

"The woman with the clothing just arrived. She's waiting upstairs."

She licked her lips. "Okay, but you'll be there too, right? I mean, I don't know much about clothes and typically I'd make Sara tell me what looks good, but she's busy and ..."

"I'll be there. But don't worry. We hired this person to tell you what looks good. It's her job." I smiled reassuringly.

"Okay, just give me a minute. I'll be right there," she said, disappearing back into her room.

In under ten minutes, Kate was upstairs, wearing jeans and a t-shirt, her hair mostly dry and loose down her back.

The stylist walked around Kate, studying her like a specimen under a microscope. She looked at her from all angles and then nodded, going to the clothing rack. Kate looked half terrified and half amused. I gave her a wink, and she smothered a laugh. The woman returned with an armload of expensive suiting and a strappy pair of high heels. "Here," she said, thrusting the clothes at Kate. "Try these on and we'll start from there."

Kate took the garments and glanced around. "Okay, um, I guess I'll be right back?"

"Kate, there's a bathroom off the hall, just outside the kitchen," I said. "You could change there."

"Right, got it," she said, nodding, and headed for one of the less-used rooms in the house.

The stylist turned to me. "She's a bit unusual, no?" she asked.

I bristled at the comment. I knew Kate was different, but that was what made her special, and I didn't appreciate the woman's tone. "She is exactly as she should be," I said flatly. "And she is the leader of this House," I reminded her.

The woman just sniffed and crossed her arms. We would not be calling on her again, I thought.

Then Kate walked back into the room wearing a gorgeous black suit jacket, a pair of slim black slacks that ended at the ankle bone, and barely-there heels held in place with a strap across the toe and around her ankle. The look was immaculate and had it all, except a shirt.

Kate had one hand gripping the front of the jacket closed over her bare chest, even though it was already buttoned in the middle. "Um, I think you forgot to give me a blouse," she said, sounding embarrassed.

"No, no," the stylist said, approaching Kate and batting her hand away. "You'll wrinkle the jacket." Kate blinked down at the woman as she tugged, plucked, and arranged the clothing to her liking. "It is perfect," she declared. "What do you think?" she said, turning to me.

"What's most important is what Kate thinks," I said.

Kate just stared at me wide-eyed, pleading for help without saying a word.

"But," I continued. "While I agree that it is perfection, I think if she's uncomfortable, it won't send the right message. We need something that will make her feel confident." I could tell by the way Kate was squirming that she felt anything but confident.

"Hmm, alright. Let's try another one," the woman said, returning to her rack.

"Thank you," Kate whispered to me when I stepped close.

"You do look stunning," I said, and I meant it. She looked like a runway model in the expensive clothes.

"People can't actually go around dressed like this," she said under her breath.

"You would be surprised," I said just as the woman returned with another outfit for Kate to try.

It took four more costume changes, a parade of overly large shoulder pads, and a pair of shorts before she found the right combination. I could tell by the way Kate walked back into the room after change number five that this was the one. She wore another black suit, featuring a wrap-around jacket with silk lapels that revealed a deep V in the front. It was tied at the hip with a silk sash and was paired with long, straight-legged trousers that fell almost to the floor, making her legs look a mile long, complemented by the same strappy heels. Under the jacket, a black silk blouse peeked out, following the V of the jacket and showing just the right amount of skin.

She stopped in front of the mirror and turned from side to side, a smile tugging at her lips.

"It looks fantastic," I said, catching her eye in the mirror.

Her smile widened as she turned back to face us. The stylist tilted her head and pursed her lips before walking over to make a few minor adjustments, then declared that it would do. She showed Kate an assortment of jewelry, and Kate chose a long gold pendant that hung between her breasts, drawing the eye down nicely.

The stylist packed her things while Kate went to change into a robe for the next set of helpers who were due to arrive soon. I thanked the woman and helped her load her things back into her car. Before she drove off, I handed her my card and told her to send the bill. I'd looked at the price of the jacket and was grateful that the House accounts were all set up and still relatively full of cash, even after all the spending I'd been doing. I wondered what Kate would think if she knew the cost of the jacket alone was over $5,000. I grinned to myself. Some things were better left unsaid.

I shut the front door and turned just in time to see Felix appear at the head of the stairs. Now it was my turn to be at a loss for words. I stood there gaping as he stared down at me with hooded eyes. He had transformed. Gone were the jeans and ragged T-shirt, replaced by a dark blue suit that fit his long, lean body like a glove. He wore a light-blue shirt and a darker tie, and his long hair was gathered back into a neat knot. I swallowed hard as he slowly walked down the steps to join me, his polished dress shoes catching the light from the chandelier overhead.

I cleared my throat. "You clean up rather nicely," I said, my eyes traveling over him from head to toe.

"I do, don't I," he said with humor in his voice. "It's not my preferred attire, but there's an occasion for everything." He adjusted his cuffs, and I spotted a large silver Audemars Piguet watch that, despite its woven band, I was pretty sure cost more than all of Kate's new things combined.

I looked him over again. Not only was he gorgeous, but he looked like a serious professional. I knew he was a lawyer, but I'd never looked at him that way. "I'm glad you're going with her tonight," I said. "Not that she needs protection. I'm sure that Marcus won't let anything happen to her. It's just ... I worry about how they'll treat her. You should have seen how the stylist acted, and she's human."

His smile fell. "I heard her from upstairs. She sounded like a vile woman, but her attitude isn't unique. Typically, a vampire would be a seasoned member of the community before being granted a House charter. And they would possess the attitude that came along with that experience." He sighed. "Kate's not what people will expect, and she will have to get used to the judgment and ridicule."

I considered his words. It seemed so unfair that the Council members would judge Kate for not being like them. She'd had no choice in entering their world, and I liked that she was holding on to her humanity with both hands.

"You care for her, don't you?" Felix asked with curiosity, not jealousy written across his face.

I nodded. "I do, and for all the reasons that others'll judge her. No offence," I said quickly. "I don't mean to be critical of vampires in general, I've chosen to spend my life among them. I'm sleeping with one. It's only ..."

"No. I understand," he said with a sad smile. "I'm not sure I like what we've become as a whole. I thought by now we would have evolved differently, better. We could have learned more than just how to protect ourselves in this modern era. We could have overcome some of our bigger faults." He shook his head and smiled again. "Maybe with more time. But for now, you need to get the door, and I need to retrieve the book from under Kate's chair, where she left it. How am I going to truly tease her about her choice in literature if I can't quote the best parts during my taunting?"

I chuckled at him. "You just want to read the dirty parts for yourself," I teased. "Let me know if you get any great inspiration."

He winked at me and turned for the dining room just as the doorbell rang.

23

SARA

It was well past 10 p.m. when Beth and I finished. The photo shoot was scheduled for the next afternoon, but Beth had training with Arrow that day and wouldn't be available until just before. I suppose I could have set up the shop myself, but I was happy to have the help and company. Additionally, we had been opening each day around 5 p.m. and working most evenings until about 9 or 10 p.m. anyway, so it wasn't much different than our new normal. Our in-person clients didn't seem to mind the later hours. We were open when everyone got off work and accepted appointments for those who needed to stop by earlier. The new schedule was growing on me. I enjoyed sleeping in late, but I did miss the daylight sometimes. *It will be better in the summer*, I reminded myself.

I said goodbye to Beth and glanced at my phone to recheck the time. Kate was due to leave for Seattle at midnight, and I didn't want to miss her departure. She was busy being pampered in the main house, and as much as I would have loved to be there for her, the various stylists and one vampire hairdresser didn't need to know that Kate had a witch for a roommate. The vampire would probably pick up my scent in the house, but there was little we could do about that. The Council knew Kate was friends with witches and that she lived near our community, but they still didn't know that she'd adopted me as a member of her House. That was still a secret, as far as I knew.

Instead of sneaking into my own house, I went to the shop office to continue my research on Relics. The best idea I had come up with so far was to purchase something old, like a piece of jewelry, and have Kate add something to the object, hopefully imbuing it with whatever emotion she chose, perhaps not the doom and gloom she had put into the sketch, but something more uplifting. I wondered how she would feel about engraving or enameling. However, my lack of knowledge of art and jewelry production limited my ideas. Ultimately, I purchased an engraving kit and placed a bid on an antique locket on eBay. The price was reasonable, and it would give her something to work with while I looked for a place to sell whatever she created. We would use it as a test piece.

Picking up my phone once more, I shot Kate a text. I didn't want to miss the results of the makeover, and I wanted to wish her luck before she left. She responded immediately that the coast was clear, and I shut down the computer, about to head into the house, when my phone lit up again. It was a text from Silas.

My heart stuttered as I reached for the phone and thumbed it open. I had been hoping to hear from him. Our communication had dwindled to a text every couple of days. Part of me was happy he had texted, and part of me was heartbroken that he was no longer stopping by. I kicked myself again for opening my big mouth and trying to encourage him to spend more time on his side of the Pass.

I read the text and had to stop and read it again to make sure I'd gotten it right.

> Sara, would it be okay if I stopped by later?
> If it's too late, it's no problem.
>
> I need to talk to you.

He wanted to come by. He wanted to see me. I fumbled with a reply.

> Yes. Please do come over.
>
> It's not too late.
>
> I'll be up until around 3 a.m.

I debated adding a cute emoji or maybe an "I miss you," but I didn't know where we stood, and I didn't want to put any undue pressure on him or look like a fool if he was coming over to end it officially—not that it ever really started.

My stomach filled with butterflies. I needed to talk to Kate.

I went back into the house, and everything was quiet. Stepping into the foyer, I heard Kate call from the sitting area.

"Over here," she said. "I'm supposed to sit still and not wrinkle or smudge myself."

I followed the sound of her voice to one of the new reading chairs but had to stop halfway and stare at my best friend. She sat in one of the overstuffed chairs, her back and shoulders rigid, keeping her gorgeous jacket smooth and unwrinkled. Her silken hair was styled in soft waves and left loose down her back, and her makeup was Hollywood perfect: smoky eyes, pink cheeks, red lips, and long, thick lashes.

"You look amazing," I said. Taking in her House-leader look, I was reminded that tonight was a big deal for her and the other members of the House. She was going before the Council to present herself and represent the rest of us—even if the Council didn't know about all of us. She would be in a room full of vampires who were bound to have an opinion, not only about her as a leader but also about how she gained the House, the fact that she rose against her sire, and pressured a decision from them. I didn't envy her position, and it made my worries seem small in comparison.

"Thanks," she said, gifting me a red-lipped smile. "I've been plucked, primed, and painted. I hope it was worth it."

"I should think so," I replied.

"Too bad all those eyebrow hairs will be back tomorrow. Any change I make is just temporary, I'm afraid."

I waved a hand at her. "Well, at least you can experiment with confidence," I said, walking over and taking the seat beside her. "Are you nervous?"

She breathed deeply and placed her manicured hands neatly on her thighs. I wondered if the paint was still wet. "I am and I'm not," she said. "Marcus and Felix assure me that this is just a formality, and I try to remind myself that I shouldn't care what these people think of me. But it's hard. I want to get through it with little fuss. I don't want to give them any reason to single us out or look too deeply at what we've got going on here. I'd avoid the whole thing altogether except that it would put Marcus in a bad spot, and it could endanger Bruce if we're not seen as a strong, legitimate House." She sighed. "Truthfully, I have no idea what I'm walking into," she admitted.

I reached over and squeezed her arm, being careful not to muss her new clothes. "I think you're going to do great. And once it's done, you can come back home and relax."

She nodded. "Thanks," she said. "What about you? Are you ready for tomorrow?"

It took me a moment to remember what she was talking about—the photoshoot. "Oh yeah," I replied. "Beth and I have it all taken care of. Or at least Beth does. The shop looks great; the rest is up to her." I smiled at Kate, trying not to let the worry over my meeting with Silas show through.

Kate narrowed her eyes, and I knew I hadn't pulled it off. "Then what's bothering you?" she asked. "If you're worried about me, don't—"

"No," I interrupted. I didn't want her to think I was having doubts about her or how things would go with the Council. She needed confidence, not worry. "I'm sure everything will be fine. It's ..." I hesitated. I didn't know what it was. "Silas texted," I finally said. "He wants to come over and have a talk. Tonight."

Kate's darkened lashes rose as her eyes widened. "Oh. Is that good or bad?" she asked.

"The truth is, I don't know." I stared down at my hands. "Either way, I'll get a chance to tell him I'm sorry for pushing him away."

I felt Kate's hand on my shoulder and looked up. "You didn't push him away," she said, her voice soft. "You told him he had space if he needed it. Don't worry. It'll be okay. Will you stay up until I get home?" she asked.

I nodded. "Of course, I want to hear all about the

meeting and the infamous Council, and I'll let you know how things go with Silas."

She leaned back against the cushions like she would break if she moved too quickly.

I snorted a laugh. "You look like you have no joints. You're going to have to loosen up before your meeting."

She rolled her eyes. "I'm trying to keep everything looking nice. Bruce would be so disappointed if I messed it all up before I even left the house. Speaking of Bruce ..." She got up from her chair and smoothed the fabric of the swoon-worthy wrap-around jacket. "I think it's time to go," she said.

"You are keeping the clothes, right?" I asked, following her out to the foyer.

"Of course," she said over her shoulder. "And, yes. My closet is your closet."

I grinned in response.

As we reached the foyer, Bruce and Felix were coming down the stairs. Bruce's face was flushed, and Felix was straightening his tie.

Kate glanced at me. "Seriously, how did I miss that?" she whispered.

I put my hand over my mouth to smother a laugh.

"I heard that," Felix said, hitting the bottom of the stairs. "And, honestly, I have no idea."

"You look nice, Felix," I said, seeing him out of his surfer-wear for the first time.

"Thank you," he replied, bowing his head. "I'll just go get Marcus, shall I?" With that, he turned and descended the stairs to the lower level.

"Bruce, we all ready?" Kate asked, taking another deep breath and straightening her shoulders.

"I think so. You need anything before you take off? Another drink perhaps?"

She shook her head. "No. I feel fine and don't want to smear the makeup."

"Why don't I get a cooler fixed up for the ride home?"

"That would be great," she said and then took on the faraway look she got when she was listening to something the rest of us couldn't hear. "There's a car coming up the drive." She glanced at me, eyebrow raised. "I bet it's Silas."

I shrugged. "He just texted."

Bruce shot me a look, and I shook my head. "I'll get it, you go bag the blood." He smirked and disappeared down the hall to the kitchen.

Kate turned and took my hand. "It will be okay, I promise. And tell him not to text and drive. Okay?"

I smiled. "Will do." I gave her a squeeze and went to get the door.

I stepped out onto the porch, shutting the front door behind me. I hadn't thought to grab a coat, and it was freezing outside. I wrapped both arms around my body, trying to keep warm as a familiar white truck pulled up beside the house. A moment later, Silas stepped out, and then all I could think about was him.

He was dressed nicely, not that I didn't like the work clothes he usually wore, but the dress shirt pulled tight across his shoulders and nice dark jeans looked great. I felt severely underdressed in my old black slacks and simple t-shirt compared to everyone else.

He waved when he saw me, a tentative smile appearing on his face as he approached. He climbed the steps to the porch and paused at the top. "Hi," he said. "How have you been?"

From the moment he stepped out of the truck, I had

been trying to gauge how he felt. I had never wished for Kate's ability until that instant; it could have made this so much easier. "I'm good," I said, trying to sound cheerful. "Would you like to come in? I have to warn you, however, everyone is wound tight at the moment. Kate is heading off to present herself before the Council tonight, officially."

"Is this a bad time?" he asked, sounding concerned. "I could come back."

"No," I said a little too loudly. "They're just about to leave, and then we'll have the house to ourselves. Well, besides Bruce, of course."

His face went blank, but he nodded. "Okay. If you're sure," he said, heaving a sigh. "It's time we talked."

24

SILAS

Standing on the porch only feet from Sara, my senses heightened, and all my instincts roared. Even my wolf paced like a caged animal losing its mind, which was ridiculous. Nothing had changed since the last time I'd seen her, except that I now knew she was my mate. I was bonded—had probably been bonded for months—to this woman standing before me. And Gods, she was beautiful: her smooth skin, the tilt of her head, the look in her bright eyes. It was as if I were seeing her for the first time, smelling her intoxicating scent for the first time. But I knew she hadn't changed at all. She was as she had ever been. It was just that I now recognized her for what she was—home.

She was my home.

She turned from me and opened the door, walking inside and holding it for me to follow, and follow I did.

Once inside, I paused and blinked at the unfamiliar surroundings. In just a matter of days, the place had undergone a transformation.

Sara noticed my shock. "It was all Bruce," she said. "He's

been very busy since you were last here." I nodded, but the hair on my wolf rose, and he resumed pacing.

"Silas?" Kate said from behind a large blooming orchid. I peered around and saw her standing by the stairs, on the other side of the entryway. The house wasn't the only thing that had changed since I had last been there.

"Kate?" I asked hesitantly.

"Hey, Silas," she said, striding closer. "I know, I know. I look different." She grinned at me, and it was a relief to see she was the same Kate, just dolled up. "I feel ridiculous, but I've been told I look 'Fearce.'"

"No," Sara said from beside me. "You are fierce. And don't forget it."

Kate nodded. "Yes. Yes, I am." She straightened and squared her shoulders as movement from the staircase caught my attention.

Marcus and Felix joined us. Both were dressed in what I assumed was their professional attire: a black tactical jacket, pants, and boots for Marcus and a finely cut suit for Felix. I nodded to them both, and they looked at Kate.

"Ready to go, Sire," Marcus said with a smirk.

Kate's brows dipped, and her eyes darkened. "I warned you about that," she hissed, but the corner of her mouth quirked, and her body stayed relaxed.

My wolf, who was always ready to watch a good fight, stopped pacing and just sniffed as if bored. Even he knew the vampire was teasing.

"Just one minute," Bruce called from the other room as he came around the corner, carrying a picnic cooler on a strap. He handed the bag to Marcus. "For later," he said. Marcus took the bag, and the vampire trio moved toward the door.

Sara followed them onto the porch and gave Kate one

last hug. "Remember, you're a vampire badass. Don't let them give you shit," she said to her best friend before they left.

I waited inside utill Sara returned, shutting the door behind her. "You're worried for her," I said.

Sara smiled but nodded. "I know she'll do great, but I don't trust the other vampires. The ones that don't live or hang out here."

"Felix and Marcus won't let anything happen to her," Bruce said. Until he spoke, I'd forgotten that he was still there, and chided myself for being so unaware of my surroundings. It wasn't like me, but I couldn't focus on anything else with Sara in the room.

At the sound of Bruce's voice, however, my wolf sat up and narrowed his eyes. I felt a low growl in the back of my mind and had to place my hand on my chest to ensure it wasn't coming from my throat. My gaze flicked to Bruce, who stood on the other side of the room.

He caught my eye and smiled. "Silas, it's good to see you again," the large man said as he stepped closer. I watched his approach while my wolf pressed harder in my mind, sizing the male up. He was a few years older than me, muscular, with broad shoulders and a thick neck. He wore jeans and a tight black T-shirt that showcased his physique and numerous tattoos. And he was human—human, and living here with Sara.

I forced myself to smile back and shook his hand when he held it out. As I did, I caught a scent the man carried with him and stopped, not letting go of his hand. I leaned forward, tugging him closer, and took a deep breath. When I realized what I was doing, I immediately dropped his hand and took a step back.

I looked into his wide eyes. "I'm sorry. I didn't mean to be rude. It's just … you smell like the lawyer," I said, feeling a flush creep up my chest and into my face. It was embarrassing to get caught scenting a non-shifter, but my wolf felt so territorial that I couldn't help myself.

Bruce took a step back, too, and crossed his arms, looking from Sara to me. "Yes," he said. "Felix and I have become quite close lately."

Sara put her hand up to her mouth and coughed while muttering, "Very close."

Bruce shot her a look and then rolled his eyes. "I'm not apologizing, but I am curious," he said, turning me. "I showered, so you must have a very good nose, and I don't see any fangs." He tilted his head, waiting.

I glanced at Sara. "You didn't tell him?"

She shook her head. "Nope. I figured you'd drop that shoe when you were ready."

I turned my gaze back to Bruce. I had to admit, now that I knew he was not interested in Sara, I liked him a lot better. He seemed like a good man from everything I'd seen. And the House trusted him. "I'm a shifter," I said finally.

His eyebrows rose, and he nodded slowly. "Let me guess, if it's not rude, bear?" he asked, looking me up and down.

I chuckled. "No. But thank you. I'm a wolf shifter."

"Forgive my ignorance. I've never met a shifter, that I'm aware. Are you a skinwalker or …?" Bruce asked.

"No. It's more of a double or duel nature. My wolf lives inside of me until I shift, and then we trade places. If you meet him, it's not me, but I'm in there somewhere. The way he's here with me now," I said.

Bruce looked thoughtful but didn't respond. I glanced over at Sara, who watched me with wide eyes. "You *are* feeling talkative tonight," she said, and I realized it was more than I'd shared with her before. It was more than I'd share with anyone before.

I ducked my head and felt my face heat again. How could I have held so much of myself back from this woman? "I'm sorry, Sara," I said.

Bruce cleared his throat, getting our attention. "Hey, if you guys need anything, let me know; otherwise, I'm going to get a few hours of sleep. I imagine there will be a debriefing when they get back," he said.

Sara choked on a laugh, and Bruce gave her another eye roll. "You're killing me. I'm trying to be a professional here," he breathed before waving goodnight and heading for the stairs to his room.

"It's good for him," Sara said, staring after Bruce with a grin on her face. I loved her smile. She turned to me then. "Do you want to see the new living room? We could sit in front of the fire."

I swallowed, nodding, and then followed her into the familiar, yet entirely unfamiliar room. "You guys turning this place back into a hotel?" I asked.

Sara snorted. "It looks like it, but no. Bruce is just way good at this stuff, and Marcus gave him a bunch of money, so ..." She shrugged.

"Well, it looks great," I said as we both sat on the leather sofa, facing the fire, but angled toward one another.

We sat in silence for a while. I didn't know where to begin or how much to tell her. Instinct told me to lay everything out for her and let her decide what to do, but I also felt I couldn't do that to her, for all the reasons I'd decided it wasn't fair to bond with her.

Now that I was bonded, I didn't want to admit it. I didn't want her to be with me out of pity or because she knew I didn't have a choice. I wanted her to want to be with me, to want to commit to me on her timeline, without the pressure of the bond. Plus, she was the one who had initially pulled back. I wasn't sure she even wanted to explore a relationship anymore.

I'd made her wait for so long.

Finally, I glanced at Sara, and she looked up into my eyes. "Sara, I came here tonight to ... to tell you something," I said. I took a deep breath. "I like you—a lot. I want us to be together, but—"

"Yes," she blurted out, interrupting me. I blinked at her. She was smiling, and her brown eyes danced with the reflection of the fire. To my shock, my wolf, who had been trying to tell me for weeks to return to this woman, remained respectfully silent during this pivotal moment.

"Yes?" I asked. "You want us to be together, too?" I had to ensure I understood her correctly.

She nodded, and I watched her lips as she said, "Yes, Silas. I want to be with you. I have for a long time now. And I'm so sorry if what I said before pushed you away. That was not my intention. I—"

"No," I said. "It's okay. It was good for me to go home and spend some time figuring things out. It gave me a lot of clarity." My throat felt tight all of a sudden, and I swallowed. "Sara, would you like to go out with me sometime?" I asked, studying her face as she watched me.

Her smile widened, and the muscles in her jaw flexed like she was holding back a laugh. "Are you asking me out on a date?" she asked.

"Um, yeah. I guess I am," I said.

"I would love to go out with you, but isn't the purpose of dating to see if you want to be with someone? And didn't we clear that up?" she asked.

"Not that I've gone on many dates, but they're also

supposed to be about getting to know one another. And I realized tonight that I haven't shared much about myself with you. I've been holding back," I admitted. I glanced down and reached for Sara's hand. Before I left—before I tried to leave—, what connection we did have had been mostly based on proximity and simple touch. I craved that touch, and holding her hand in mine grounded me in a way that words never would.

"Silas," Sara said. I realized I was still looking down at our clasped hands, and I flicked my gaze back up into her warm eyes. "I do want to date you," she said softly. "I want to get to know you, everything about you—and your wolf." She smiled.

Looking at her, I wanted to lay myself bare. I wanted to pour everything I had, everything I was, out for this woman. And I realized, too, that I was afraid. I was afraid she wouldn't like what she saw, and I would be left adrift, homeless, without her. My body shuddered. My chest felt tight, and my eyes pricked with tears at the thought that I would ever be separated from her, but holding myself back from her wasn't the answer either. Balance and time. This would require both if I expected us to build something that would last.

"Are you okay?" she asked. She reached up to touch my face, and I realized she was brushing away a tear.

"Ah, yeah," I said, clearing my throat. "I'm good—more than good."

She brought her hand back and traced the tips of her fingers down the side of my face and over the stubble of my jaw. My skin was alive with her touch, lighting a fire in the wake of her fingers. I turned my face toward her outstretched hand, brushing my lips over her skin, and breathing in deeply. The warm scent of her flooded my senses and ignited my blood. My body shook now with want, not fear. She pressed her palm ever so gently against my cheek, bringing my head back around, and tilted her face up toward mine.

I met her eyes again and found them more than warm; they were heated with a look I didn't need to have seen before to recognize. I reached forward, sliding my hands up the sides of her neck and into her hair, burying my fingers in her silky curls and pulling her to me. The moment our mouths met, I stopped thinking.

Kissing Sara was the most natural thing in the world. It was almost like the exhilaration of running with my wolf through the forest, but I felt everything in sharp detail. I was experiencing the moment for myself, not observing. As I licked into her parted lips and felt her tongue slide against mine, my wolf finally sat up and made himself known. I had the sudden, overwhelming urge to push her backward, cover her with my body, and bite her hard between her shoulder and neck, marking her for all to see.

Marking her as mine, forever.

I gasped and pulled back, staring down at her gorgeous lips, trying to catch my breath. "That was ... that was perfect," I said. "But I think I'm going to need to stop here for tonight."

She shook her head but smiled, her eyes still blazing as she stared up at me from under her thick, dark lashes. "We can go as slow as you need, as long as we can do that again soon," she said.

"Promise," I said, and leaned in for another kiss. This one was softer, but no less passionate than the last. "I should go," I said. "I have work tomorrow. But I should be done around three. Can I stop back by? We could settle on the arrangements for our first date."

"Sounds great," she said. "I look forward to it." She sighed and got to her feet, pulling me up off the sofa with her. Her eyes flicked down and then back up to my face, and she smiled. I knew she could tell how much I wanted her, what kissing her and being so close to her did to my body, and I didn't care. I wanted her to see.

She grabbed my hand and led me to the door. Before I stepped over the threshold, back out into the cold, I pulled her against me and kissed her one last time, leaving us both breathless, then I turned and went to my truck.

As I drove home, I felt elated and bereft. Leaving my mate was more difficult than I thought it would be after touching her, holding her, tasting her.

I held on tight to the steering wheel and focused on what was important. I needed to learn more control around Sara if we were going to be physical with one another. If I thought telling her about the mating bond would scare her off, I shuddered to think how she would react if I marked her like my wolf wanted me to—like I wanted to. No, I needed to get a handle on those instincts. I wasn't bonded to a shifter. I was bonded to a witch, and I needed to remember that.

I thought back to that first kiss and how amazing it was, how wonderful it felt, and how glad I was that it was with Sara. I smiled to myself and wondered what she would think if she knew that was my first kiss ever.

25

KATE

We walked out to Marcus's car. I was relieved he was driving. I didn't own a car, and Felix drove an older Jeep that looked cool, but I wasn't sure if it would be particularly comfortable for the three of us.

"Hey, Marucus, you mind if I ride in back with Kate?" Felix asked when we reached the silver Honda.

"Not at all. I'm happy to play chauffeur." He winked at me before getting in behind the wheel.

I felt the butterflies in my stomach start to churn again, wondering what Felix wanted to talk to me about. There was plenty for him to choose from, given my outburst at dinner.

Once we were all buckled in, we resembled a well-dressed couple being driven by their bodyguard. I seriously hoped that would not be the case and that Marcus would not have to act in his official capacity that evening. I didn't truly have the confidence I'd shown Sara. I wanted to skip the whole thing and ignore the vampire Council in Seattle. But Marcus assured me that it would make my life more complicated and could endanger Bruce and eventually Sara if I did. It was in all our best interests to get the meeting over with as quietly as possible.

My goal for the evening was to keep aware of how everyone in the room was feeling, to act humble and thankful, and try not to let any of the vampires close enough to bite me—no big deal. After I'd accidentally let E sink her fangs in me, I'd been terrified that she would react somehow and out me as different, to the vampires she worked with. Marcus hadn't heard any rumblings along that front, however, and E hadn't mentioned anything unusual. He told me not to worry, but it was hard not to after my experiences with James and Alexander. I knew my blood had a certain appeal to other vampires, and I didn't want to end up defending myself against them, or causing Marcus to have to step in to defend me, and I knew he would.

"Hey," Felix said. "Just breathe. It's going to be okay." He smiled at me and patted my hand.

His kindness made guilt twist in my gut. "I'm sorr—"

He shook his head. "No, remember, no apologizing. You're the leader of a House. You were protecting your interests. You have nothing to apologize for."

"I don't know how you can say that," I breathed.

"Kate, I want you to listen to me. You are doing extraordinarily well, all things considered. You need to believe in yourself the way the rest of us do."

"But you saw me in the dining room. I was out of control. I could have hurt you, and I made a fool of myself for not asking questions instead of flying off the handle. How were you so calm? I was sitting on your chest for crying out loud."

His mouth quirked up on one side as he thought for a moment before he answered. "I'm a lot older than you. I've had years and years of practice." He shook his head. "You should have seen me in my first few years. I was terrible. If

I'd been upset about something, I'd have ripped out throats and asked questions afterward. No, you're doing beautifully. It's your temperament that made Marcus take a chance on you, hitch his fate to yours."

I glanced at Marcus. He was watching the road and seemed not to be paying attention, but I knew he could hear everything we said over the noise of the traffic. "What do you mean?"

"He vouched for you with the Council regarding the formation of your House. I, too, pulled my strings, but in the end, he put his neck out and wagered his future, his life, so that you would be granted the charter."

My eyes flicked back to the mirror, and I caught Marcus watching me. "What is he talking about?"

Marcus shrugged and turned his gaze back to the road ahead. "I didn't want to be the one to lead the House. It was important that it was yours, that you were the one in charge of your own life, after everything that happened. You were forced to become one of us, and I wanted you to have some control over your life. The Council agreed as long as I was willing to stand for you."

"In what way?" I asked. I didn't like where this was going.

"I promised that I would help you adapt to our society. And I accepted that if you got into any trouble, your fate would be mine as well."

"You mean, if I fuck up, you have to suffer the consequences alongside me, no matter what they are?" I frowned. "That doesn't seem fair."

"I trust you, Kate. I'm not worried." He glanced back into the mirror and smiled at me.

The butterflies in my stomach turned into bats, and I hunched in on myself, trying to relieve the feeling, then I remembered my new jacket and sat upright again.

"I'm sorry. I was trying to make you feel better, not worse," Felix said.

"It's not your fault. I should have known. I should have asked more questions from the very beginning." I blew out a breath. I was grateful for Marcus's help and Felix's, but it also added more pressure. I didn't like being responsible for the fate of others. "Formality. This is just a formality," I whispered to myself.

Felix patted my hand again. "That's the spirit. This will all be over before you know it."

When we reached the city, I expected we would go straight through to the neighborhoods with large houses or venture farther out to where the estates were hidden among the dense trees and shores of the sound. Instead, we drove right into the heart of the city's business district.

"Where are we going?" I asked as I peered out the window at the buildings that grew taller and taller the farther we drove.

"To the Council headquarters," Marcus replied. "Where I work." He flipped on his signal and pulled into a parking garage under one of the massive office buildings.

"You work here? I always thought the Council would be based out of an old Gothic mansion or something."

Marcus chuckled. "No. It's a governmental organization, not a secret society. Well, it is a secret, I guess, to humans, but you know what I mean."

"No. I don't," I mumbled as he parked and we all got out.

We rode an elevator to the lobby of what turned out to be a very fancy office building. Everything was made of white marble and glass, with oversized potted plants scattered throughout the space. From there, we took yet another elevator to a floor near the top of the building.

"What?" I asked. "They couldn't spring for the top floor?"

Marcus cleared his throat. "Um, no. The Council owns the whole building. My office is just below where we'll be meeting, but we have a few minutes, and I thought maybe you wouldn't want to show up too early."

The whole damn building? "Thanks," I said, feeling again out of my depth. "Yeah, it would be nice to see where you work."

Marcus nodded but didn't reply as the elevator came to a stop and the doors slid open. He held the doors for Felix and me as we stepped off into a bustling office. There was a normal-looking reception area, backed by a wall adorned with silver metallic letters that read "Enforcement." I noticed a glass-enclosed conference area with a meeting in progress, and several open doors that led to occupied offices. At first, I was surprised to see so many people—or, rather, vampires—but given the time, it was probably the middle of their workday.

A few people glanced our way, but most carried on with whatever it was they were doing. I was about to ask Marcus exactly what that was when a familiar face caught my attention. E had spotted us and was headed our way. I glanced at Marcus, trying to gauge what I should do, but he kept his eyes on E, a warm smile on his face.

"Kate," E said, a little too loudly. "It's so good to see you again." I thought she might stop to greet us, but no, she kept right on coming until her arms were around me in a tight hug, her face pressed into my neck. I stiffened out of reflex and fear of what she might do. Once bitten and all that ... But the embrace didn't go any further, and she pulled away with a dreamy sort of look on her face. "I have missed you," she said. "You're special, you know." She grinned at me, and I stood there at a loss for words.

"She is, isn't she?" Felix said, stepping forward and offering his hand to E.

She shook it politely and greeted Marcus before turning back to me. "This must be your first time here. Would you like a tour?" she asked.

"I'm afraid we don't have time for the full tour," Marcus said. "She has to be upstairs in a few minutes. I was going to take her to my office to wait."

E nodded. "Of course. Maybe another time. Council members have been arriving all evening. I think you are going to have a packed house," she said. "And, we should go out again sometime soon."

"Sure. I would love to," I assured her, before she strode off with a wave. I whipped around to Marcus. "A packed house?" I hissed low enough that maybe not everyone would hear me. "What does that mean?"

"It means many of the members, although not required to attend, have chosen to show up tonight." He lightly gripped my elbow and started to steer me down one of the side corridors when there was a commotion from the right. All three of us stepped back as two large men dressed like Marcus came marching toward us, holding a third between them. The man in the middle looked a little worse for wear. His head hung down, his clothing was disheveled, and his hands were behind his back. They were all vampires.

As they passed us, I noticed the man's hands were bound in an unusual pair of oversized handcuffs. "What's on his wrists?" I asked.

"Those are UV cuffs," Marcus said. "Most vampires could eventually break out of a pair of metal cuffs, but under any real amount of pressure, those emit UV light. It keeps detained vampires somewhat docile."

I shivered at the thought of what kind of burns those would produce as Marcus led the way down the corridor toward his office. He opened the door for us, and we stepped inside.

The office was a good size, but mostly empty. There was a desk with a computer, a phone, and little else. I noticed a black-and-white photo of a woman beside the computer, which was the only personal touch in the room. In front of the desk were two side chairs, and a sofa was positioned against one wall.

Above the sofa hung a large map of Seattle that immediately drew my attention. I noticed several of the buildings were highlighted in either blue or yellow. Stepping closer, I recognized the cluster of blue in the district where Bruce had worked.

"It's a basic map of the vampire business and the House address in the city," Marcus confirmed. "It's good to know where everyone is if we get called out to handle a dispute."

"Is that what you do?" I asked. "Arrest unruly vampires?"

He nodded. "Sometimes. Other times, we are called in to pick someone up who has a dispute with another House if the matter can't be resolved between the Houses themselves. The Council acts as a court in those cases."

"And you have a jail here?"

"We have several holding cells for vampires, yes."

"What about for humans?" I asked.

"Vampire law is for vampires only," Felix said from behind me.

I turned to face him, not sure I'd heard him correctly. "But what about all the rules humans are bound by in the vampire world?"

"Those are imposed by the businesses and Houses with which the humans are affiliated, not the Council," he said. "They are so strict because vampire law would hold the vampires involved in a security breach responsible. It is their way of protecting themselves against the Council and the law."

I shook my head, not understanding. "Why wouldn't the Council just vote on laws that would place the blame and responsibility on the humans? Why would they leave themselves so exposed in the first place?"

Felix smiled at me and nodded. "Because they, too, answer to a higher power. The same vampires that empower me to argue the law across territories. The reason I belong to no one territory or House."

"Like an international court? Or Council?" I asked.

"Yes, precisely," Felix replied. "They have the final say, and they have declared that no Council can pass any laws having to do with humans and can only intervene between a contracted human and the contract holder if there is a dispute. They are only then empowered to uphold the contract as they interpret it."

I sniffed. "Hmm, that's good, I guess. I still don't particularly like that they are okay with humans being killed as punishment for breach of contract, but it's good to know they are more concerned with the vampires themselves." I took a deep breath. The thought of what they were concerned with reminded me of why I was there. I was their concern, and I was expected to appear before them soon.

Both Marcus and Felix had coached me on what to do. Basically, I just needed to stand there to accept my House seal—whatever that was—and thank them profusely for the honor. *Ugh.*

I was about to have a seat on the sofa when there was a

gentle knock on the door, and a blonde vampire stuck her head in. "The Council is ready for you guys," she said, a tight smile on her face.

Felix glanced at his watch. "They're early," he said. "I suppose they know we're already here."

"Well, let's not keep them waiting," Marcus said, looking at me.

I sighed. "Let's get this over with."

Felix smiled broadly and offered me his elbow as we made our way back through the corridor to the elevator. My chest felt tight, and my throat was too narrow as we rode the short distance to the next floor. Not only was I not looking forward to this, but apparently, there was going to be a larger audience than I'd thought.

Marcus estimated that at least two of the Major House leaders would be in attendance, and maybe five or more of the Lesser House leaders. I was told that there were fifteen members in total: five from the Major and ten from the Lesser, but that few attended regularly and even fewer showed up to voluntary events like this one. He said no more than eight of the members would show.

He was wrong.

When the elevator door opened, it was clear that we were in a vastly different part of the world than we had been just one floor below. No expense had been spared on this part of the building. It had giant marble columns, reminiscent of an ancient temple. Marble panels on the walls, sported gold fixtures, and colorful inlaid stone on the floor created a beautiful circular mosaic that depicted a mountain surrounded by a forest and a blue coastline. On the other side of the chamber, across the mosaic, there were two massive wooden doors with intricate carvings featuring scrollwork and climbing leaves.

It was gorgeous.

"You can look later," Marcus whispered in my ear, urging me onward. He walked ahead, leading us across the floor, and pulled one of the ornate doors open, holding it for me to enter.

I looked up at Felix, who nodded. "We'll be right behind you." I let go of his arm and stepped inside.

The room was packed with vampires. Every seat around the long conference table was filled, and people stood against the wall as well. The room itself was as impressive as the outer chamber had been. But none of it registered. Instead, my eyes were drawn to one vampire in particular. He sat at the far end of the table, lounging as if he had not a care in the world, but his grey eyes bore into me with an intensity that made me shudder.

My sire was there.

26

KATE

My new strappy heels were glued to the floor. I blinked, hoping I was imagining things, or that the vampire staring me down would somehow transform into someone else, but no such luck. The corner of his mouth twitched as he observed my reaction, and that's what urged me to move. I would not let that man have the satisfaction. Not for a second would I show him the fear I knew he so clearly wanted from me. Would I be afraid?—Hell yes. Would I do what needed to be done regardless?—Absolutely.

I took a steadying breath, tugged my jacket into place, and stepped forward to the end of the table with all the confidence I didn't feel.

Without glancing back, I felt Marcus and Felix step up behind me. It was a relief to have them at my back—a solid wall of support. I didn't think that Alexander would try anything, and I was ready for him, but it was nice to know I wasn't alone.

I didn't recognize anyone else in the room, but I focused on the vampire sitting at the head of the table. Like every vampire I'd seen so far, he looked young, maybe in his late twenties, and had light skin and thick, wavy dark hair, like a young Elvis. Everyone was staring at me, yet he had the most expectation on his face, as if he was waiting for me to address him specifically.

The vampires at the edges of the room shuffled in anticipation. I swept a glance over the assembled crowd. There were over twenty vampires present, more than those officially on the Council. There was a variety of skin tones, heights, and hair colors, but they all appeared young, all beautiful, and all had expressions of curiosity. Bruce mentioned that word of our unusual House had gotten around, and it seemed he was right. I suspected they were there to take my measure and to see if sparks would fly between Alexander and me.

It was then that I remembered I was supposed to be using my other senses to gauge the atmosphere and everyone's intentions. However, something urged me to proceed carefully. I wasn't expecting two dozen vampires crowded into one room, and I knew that too many individuals could overwhelm me if I dropped my defenses. Instead, I established a connection between the head vampire and myself, then carefully softened my internal barrier until a gentle hum of emotion filled the room, leaving this one vampire's emotions standing out distinctly.

And despite the smile on his face, he was pissed.

But before I could open my mouth, he spoke. "You've kept us waiting, Ms. Ward." The smile looked plastered on, and the contempt in his tone did little to sell it.

"It's my understanding that we are early," I said. As soon as the words left my mouth, I wished I could call them back.

There was a collective gasp from the vampires around the perimeter of the room.

Elvis inhaled, his nostrils flaring. "You are here at our leisure, not the other way around," he said, biting off the last word and leaning forward as his displeasure increased.

I gritted my teeth but remembered my purpose. "My apologies," I said with a slight incline of my head.

He heaved out a sigh. "I am Étienne, leader of the House of Brogan, and current elected leader of the Council of the North Western Americas."

I wasn't sure what to say, so I bowed again.

It must have been the correct response because he continued. "To my right are Oswald, House of Callahan, and Louella, House of Rothbauer." He indicated the two vampires nearest him, Oswald, a sandy-haired man with a pinched face, and Louella, a beautiful woman with dark hair piled high on her head and shocking red lipstick. Both nodded in return. "And on my left, Ren, House of Hirata, and of course, your sire, Alexander, House of Ferenc."

As Étienne spoke, I glanced at Ren, a striking man of Japanese descent, but refused to look at Alexander as he was introduced. I knew what the vampire looked like. I'd seen his face as he'd come toward me weeks ago, mouth open to drain my blood. I wouldn't forget his dove grey eyes, his shoulder-length dark hair, or his trimmed beard. I straightened again and pushed my shoulders back. I stared at Étienne, making sure my face was a mask of indifference and calm.

I noticed the introductions stopped at five, presumably the five major Houses. There were still a good number of vampires in the room whom the leader hadn't acknowledged. I studied their emotions, but no one seemed particularly bothered or surprised by the snub.

"You have been invited here to accept your seal," Étienne

continued. "And to affix that seal to the official charter for your House."

At the end of the table, closest to me, there was a large document—the Declaration of Independence large—lying on the surface next to a small collection of objects. There was a shallow metal bowl filled with liquid, resting on top of a lit candle. Lying beside it was what could only be my seal —a round metal disk with a wooden handle attached. Felix had instructed me on how the ceremony was conducted. I was to step forward, lift the metal bowl, and then pour the wax onto the document before resting my stamp in the cooling puddle. While it cooled, I was expected to give a little speech about how honored I was to be allowed to have my own House.

Here goes nothing, I thought as I grasped the bowl between my fingers. And, damn, it was hot, but I didn't rush or let my discomfort show. I carefully poured the simmering red wax onto the space provided at the bottom of the paper, forming a perfect circular blob, and then replaced the bowl over the flame. Next, I placed my new seal directly in the center of the cooling pool.

I took a step back from the table and glanced up at Étienne. His smile was once again expectant, and he gave off a smug, self-righteous air. "Now is the time for you to say something if you wish," he said, gesturing toward me.

I knew I was supposed to be on my best behavior, but his bad attitude was rubbing off on me. I had spent so long shielding my emotions lately that I'd forgotten what it was like to be bombarded with the oily feelings of someone like him. I shot a glance at Alexander, who was sporting a smirk but waiting like all the rest for me to humble myself before those gathered, to prove that I was one of them and would behave as expected, to fall in line.

But, as my mother always said, "*If you can't say anything nice ...*"

"No," I said flatly and crossed my arms over my chest. "I've got nothing to say."

This time, the coordinated intake of breath wasn't limited to a scattering of individuals. There were murmurs and exclamations throughout the room. I felt the emotions shift from expectancy to outright shock and anger.

I'd had enough. I shoved my walls back in place and stared straight ahead.

"Ungrateful," Étienne said, pinning me with his hard glare.

"Ungrateful?" I exclaimed. "Damn right I'm ungrateful. A member of his House murdered me," I said, pointing a finger at Alexander, and then *he* turned me into a vampire, against my will. And you expect me to be grateful that I'm *allowed* to live under my own roof?"

Oh shit. I was supposed to be on my best behavior. What had I done? I glanced around the room at the shocked expressions. The anger radiating off of Étienne was palpable. I needed to get out of there before I did more damage.

Without waiting for a reply, I turned and headed for the massive double doors. I shoved them apart with such force that they sprang wide, one panel knocking into the wall as I stepped out into the front room and made a beeline for the elevator. I glanced back and saw Marcus coming after me, followed by Felix, who had thought to grab the seal on his way out.

"I'm sorry," I said between tight jaws. My anger was all my own, but it was enough to rattle me. I knew I'd messed up. I was madder at myself than at the vampires in the room behind me.

Marcus blew out a breath. His face was set with concern,

his brows drawn together. "That wasn't the plan, Kate. What happened?"

"I know. I know. I couldn't help it," I said, putting my hands up. "They were all so … self-congratulatory and superior. They were all waiting for me to grovel and prostrate myself before them. I couldn't do it."

He was about to say something else when the doors opened again, and Alexander appeared. He let the doors close behind him and then walked, at a measured pace, across the mosaic emblem to where we stood. His grey gaze was cool, and his face revealed no hint of any emotion. Marcus and Felix had both taken up places behind me as soon as they spotted him, so Alexander and I stood face to face, separated by only a few feet. I considered lowering my defenses to read him, but I was so wound up that I feared I would do something rash if I sensed his superior attitude at that moment.

"Kate," he said, tilting his head as he looked at me. "That was … unexpected." He smiled, showing his fangs. "I'm supposed to be out here talking sense into you and forcing you back inside to play your part as directed."

I tensed, ready to act if necessary. There was no way I was going back in there, especially with him.

He waved a hand dismissively. "Oh, don't worry. I don't care what they expect of me either. I just wanted an opportunity to ask you a question." He raised a brow, and when I didn't respond, he continued. "After our last encounter," he said in his smooth voice. "The strangest thing happened. I suddenly developed the ability to feel the feelings of those around me. It went on for days. It was both disturbing and curious. You wouldn't know anything about that, would you?"

"I have no idea what you're talking about," I lied. "And even if I did, I wouldn't tell you."

He nodded. "I thought so." He took a step closer and leaned in. I tried to back up, but the two men behind me prevented me from escaping. He inhaled, and I saw his teeth lengthen as the two vampires at my back started to move.

But I got there first.

I dropped my mental shields and shoved at him with a wave of revulsion. It was easy to summon the feeling. Alexander's eyes widened in shock as he took a step back, followed by another, placing his hand on his chest. Marcus and Felix stood beside me, ready to act, but I raised a hand.

Alexander's mouth curled into a slow smile. "Absolutely fascinating," he said, lowering his hand and composing himself. "You are, by far, the most interesting of my children."

"I'm not your child," I hissed.

He tilted his head from side to side as if it were up for debate. "Oh, I almost forgot," he said, reaching into the breast pocket of the grey suit he wore. He held out a cream envelope, but I didn't move to take it. He sighed as Felix stepped forward and accepted it.

"What is this?" Felix asked, holding it between two fingers.

"It's an invitation to a reception in your honor," he said to me. "To be held tomorrow night at the Council House."

"I'm not going," I replied, happy to let my anger seep through into my voice.

"Oh, I think you will," Alexander said. "Especially given your performance a few minutes ago. You need to repair some damage, and going to the party and making nice with the Council will help do that. For all your sakes," he added, glancing at Marcus.

I sighed and crossed my arms. I hated him, but he had a point.

rrow's fur felt warm and soft beneath my touch as I stroked her and watched the photographers work. It was incredible to see them together. They were a married couple from the area, both witches familiar with our shop and family. The person behind the camera, Gina, a woman in her late forties with medium-brown hair gathered in a messy bun, was an Air Witch, while her partner, Dale, a middle-aged man with a salt-and-pepper beard and gentle creases around his brown eyes, specialized in light. Together, they seemed to move and think as one.

"Okay, now ... Yeah, that's perfect," Gina said, as Dale channeled a bit of light by moving his hands like a sculptor in front of the display of bottles, creating reflections and shadows like a painter might. She snapped a dozen shots with her digital camera and shifted her position to take a few more.

I'd been watching them steadily for over two hours, absolutely captivated.

Gina took several more shots and then waved one hand

around herself, creating a circular motion in the air that fluttered the dried leaves and made the tablecloths sway.

"Does the moving air help with the shot?" Beth asked from the other side of Arrow. For the first hour, Beth had been giving the pair some direction, but found it was better to sit back and watch them cook. She, too, seemed captivated by the way they worked together.

Gina glanced back and chuckled. "Sometimes. When we're outdoors and working with a lot of fabric or doing portraiture and want flowing hair, for instance. Then my ability is awesome for getting the right effect." She paused for another shot before looking back over her shoulder again at us. "But my gift is also great for a witch going through menopause." She winked and waved her hand again, creating a cooling breeze. "I don't know how you other witches, or non-witches, can stand it," she muttered, bringing the camera up for another picture.

I grinned and glanced at Beth, who was nodding. "I wish I had magic," she said wistfully.

"It's not always that great," I said. "The only thing I've ever really done with my gift is fry electronics and zap a vampire."

At that, Gina and Dale stopped what they were doing and glanced my way, twin looks of surprise on their faces. I shrugged. "It sounds cooler than it was."

"One of your roommates?" Dale asked. I wasn't surprised that the witches knew Kate and Marcus lived in the house. I'd heard some rumblings and whispers from time to time about the vampires who'd moved into the valley.

"No. They're good people. It was a different guy, who most definitely was not a good person," I said.

Both witches nodded but gave each other a look that

said they doubted that any vampire could be considered a "good person."

Beth, who adored my roommates and Felix, patted my arm over the dog's back. I glanced at her and gave her a tight smile. It would take some time before the witch community as a whole accepted the vampires, if they ever did. At least no one had been outright hostile. We had lost a few customers, but nothing that hurt our bottom line, and so what if it did. I wasn't about to kick out my friends to make some small-minded witches comfortable.

I had to admit, there were some legitimate reasons to be wary of vampires, but no individual should be judged on the actions of the whole. Kate and Marcus should be given the benefit of the doubt, but old prejudices die hard. And our community was very isolated and traditional.

The thought made my stomach flutter and my mind go to Silas. There was less animosity toward shifters in our community, but they were still outsiders to most witches. Silas. I hadn't been able to stop thinking of him every minute since he'd stepped off my porch the night before. All my worries dissolved the moment he began to speak. He cared for me, and I was free to express my feelings. I'd been walking on a cloud all day, just waiting for this afternoon when I'd see him again.

Kate returned from the meeting around three in the morning, and it took a tremendous amount of self-control not to grab her and demand her undivided attention. I was dying to tell her what happened with Silas, and I eventually did, but she needed to vent about the meeting, and I let her. It was better to get the frustration out before I shared my good news. And she was carrying a lot of frustration.

She was mad at herself, as usual. She'd intended to make a good impression but had apparently blown it. It was made worse by the fact that she'd come face to face with her maker, Alexander—whom I remembered all too well—and was now expected to attend a fancy reception.

Felix and Marcus had very different views of how the meeting had gone. Felix positively beamed as he recounted how Kate managed the room full of older vampires. Marcus, on the other hand, appeared concerned for Kate. He stayed quiet while Kate and Felix shared their perspectives, his brows furrowed. I was particularly curious about what he thought of the entire affair, considering he worked for the Council and possessed unique insight into their thoughts and operations. I didn't want Kate to be in trouble, and I was more than a little worried that any attention drawn to our little House would shine a spotlight on the fact that we were more unique than the Council would likely appreciate.

Just another group of Others determined to keep the species separate. Vampires with vampires, witches with witches, and shifters with shifters. Each in our own lane. I sighed and glanced back at the photography team. They were "good people" too, but emblematic of the problem.

"Okay, I think we're about done here," Gina said with a smile. I glanced at my watch; it was nearly three in the afternoon.

Beth and I got to our feet, and Arrow jumped up too, excited by the sudden movement. "No. Arrow, stay," Beth commanded, holding out a hand. The German Shepherd yawned, letting out a doggy whine, and lay back down. *Man, she is a good dog,* I thought for the hundredth time.

We chatted with Gina and Dale as they packed their things away, but I couldn't help sneaking a peek at my watch every few minutes. They promised to send us the proofs in a few days, and we would follow up then. Beth walked the pair to the door and shut it behind them, jingling the bells overhead.

Beth turned back toward me and paused, hands on her hips. "What time is he supposed to be here?" she asked, lifting a corner of her mouth.

"Who?" I replied, trying to play it cool.

"Don't give me that. You know who." She walked back to Arrow and gave her the release command. The dog jumped back to her feet, tail wagging, and began to sniff the floor nearby, happy to be free.

I glanced up from the dog. Beth was watching me. "You've been happy all afternoon, and now you're checking the time every five seconds. That can only mean Silas finally stopped ignoring you and is on his way. Unless you've started dating someone else," she said.

I shook my head. "No, and he wasn't ignoring me. He was taking some time. And yes, he should be over soon. He came over last night and we talked." I took a deep breath.

"Is that what people are calling it now?" She grinned at me, enjoying her own joke.

"We just talked," I protested. "And, maybe kissed," I mumbled.

Beth nodded knowingly. "About time. But, seriously, does he have any brothers? He's dead gorgeous and as big as a house ..." Her face took on a wistful expression.

"Several," I said, and she brightened. I shook my head and gave my watch one more look. It was just after three. "I'm going to wait outside," I said, going to the office to grab my coat. I needed some air and didn't really want an audience when I saw Silas again. Plus, Beth was likely to corner him about his brothers, and I didn't want to have to stand in line with Arrow to get a kiss from my boyfriend. Boyfriend. The word felt both odd and thrilling. He was now officially my boyfriend, I supposed, but the word felt too soft, too weak for what I felt we had.

The front porch felt like a better place to wait than the front steps of the shop. I settled myself into a new rocking chair I hadn't seen before, but appreciated, especially since it had a cushion and a throw blanket draped over the back. *Thank you, Bruce.*

I didn't have to wait long. When Silas stepped out of his truck, he was wearing his work clothes, and I knew he'd come right from a job. I was delighted by the thought that he hadn't wanted to wait to go home and change. And Beth was right; he was dead gorgeous. Looking at him, he was a study in contrasts with his soft, dark curls, the hard bronze angles of his body, and the intense look in his honey-colored eyes. I got up from the chair, tossing the blanket onto the seat, and met him at the top step.

He stopped several steps down, bringing us eye to eye, a slow smile spreading across his face. "Hello, beautiful," he said and leaned in for a kiss. I wrapped my arms around his neck and pulled him close. The thrill of touching him, really touching him the way I wanted to, sent joy bubbling up through my middle. He was here, in my arms. He was mine. And when our mouths met, it was electric, sending a shock of awareness over my skin and heating me to the core.

He pulled back, the smile still on his face but now tinged with something more—something private, just for me. It reminded me that it wasn't just his looks that created a beautiful contrast. He was a blend of hard and soft, strong yet vulnerable. This man I'd known for years as a quiet, steady presence was opening up to me in a way that humbled me deeply. I thought of the gentle tear that had fallen onto the hard planes of his face when he'd looked at me the night before. Despite knowing him for years and wanting him for almost as long, he was wholly unexpected, a gift.

I kissed him again quickly and dropped my arms, reaching to pull him up the stairs onto the porch with me. "Would you mind sitting out here?" I asked, indicating the pair of rockers arranged precisely with a small table in between. "It's a bit cold out, but I'm enjoying being out in the daytime."

"The cold doesn't bother me," he replied, seating himself beside me. I gathered the blanket and wrapped back up, burying my hands in the warm folds. "How did last night go for Kate? And how was your day?" he asked.

I filled him in on the meeting, everything that accompanied it, and the photoshoot. I didn't mention that the witches had brought up my roommates or the look the pair exchanged. He understood, just as I did, the prejudice in the various communities towards outsiders. It reminded me that we would be scrutinized too. Our relationship was going to be the talk of not only my community but also his. I could deal with the pressure, but I had no idea what it would mean for him on his side of the Pass.

"So, about our date," he said, changing the subject. "I'd like to take you out tomorrow night if you're free."

"I am. I have to help Kate get ready for the reception tonight, but tomorrow I'm all yours."

"Great. Unless you have something specific in mind, I thought we'd go to dinner and then maybe a bookstore?"

"A bookstore?" I asked. "I thought you were going to say something like a movie or dancing."

"We could, if you'd rather. But, I must warn you, I'm not a great dancer. I noticed your new bookshelves and your impressive collection last night. I figured there was some room for a few more."

I smiled. I didn't realize he'd paid so much attention. "I would love any excuse to go to a bookstore, but is that where you want to go?"

He leaned closer, resting his elbow on the arm of the rocker as he looked at me. "I want to go where you're happiest. I want to see you smile and have a great time. That's where I want to be."

I flushed under his gaze. "Then it doesn't matter where we go," I replied. "As long as we're together."

28

KATE

By the time I came upstairs for the evening, two dozen dresses were waiting for me on a clothing rack in the middle of the living room, courtesy of Bruce. We had both agreed not to call the stylist back; she wasn't a particularly good fit, but she had sent over some delicious choices for the evening reception, and they all fit perfectly.

It was also nice to have Sara with me. Unlike the night before, she didn't have to hide in her own house, and I needed her opinion and support. We all agreed on a simple floor-length silk gown in the color of fresh blood. It felt appropriate for the occasion and was one of the least fussy options. Despite the underpinnings Sara insisted I wear, it still felt comfortable and allowed me to move easily.

She was styling my hair and telling me about her upcoming date with Silas—for the third time—when Marcus walked into the bathroom where I was being pampered for the second night in a row. Instead of his usual paramilitary gear, he wore a black tuxedo with a bow tie and cummerbund. He looked like a million bucks.

"Sorry to interrupt," he said, ducking his head slightly and looking uncertain.

"No, please come in. You look amazing, by the way." I waved at him in the mirror, beckoning him in.

He stood behind me, glanced down, and addressed my reflection. "Um, thanks. At least it's black." He tugged at the jacket and cleared his throat. "I wanted to go over the details for this evening, and we don't have much time before we have to leave."

"Sounds good. What am I up against tonight?"

"It shouldn't be too bad. It will be more casual than last night."

I raised a penciled eyebrow. "The ball gown and tuxedo would beg to differ."

"True, the attire is more formal, but you won't be expected to do anything tonight besides mingle and enjoy yourself."

"And how many people, or vampires, will I be mingling with?"

He winced. "I don't know. Every House leader is invited, and all are welcome to bring as many as three House members and attendants, of course."

"Of course," I replied. "What's an attendant?"

"Like a butler. They will all be human."

"Why, and why human?"

"Well, they will act as an assistant, see to our coats, bring us drinks, let us know who's approaching to be introduced, and serve as a hot meal if we should want one." He said the last bit quickly as if I wouldn't notice.

I just stared at his reflection for a moment before answering. "And who exactly are we supposed to take with us as our snack?"

He cleared his throat. "Bruce will come with us and serve as our attendant."

"We don't need one," I snapped. "There is no need to subject Bruce to the Council and their bullshit."

"It will be noted if we don't bring anyone." He looked down, breaking eye contact.

"There, I'm done," Sara said, interrupting our conversation at just the right time and patting the back of my hair that she'd artfully twisted into a lovely updo for the evening.

I stood and grabbed my matching clutch, which I'd stuffed full of items to touch up my face and resecure my hair if necessary. Marcus stood behind me, and I met his gaze again as I turned. I had my internal barriers in place and couldn't read how he was feeling, but the look in his eyes told me he was worried for me, or maybe worried I'd screw this evening up as badly as I did the last. I sighed and relented. "Okay, Bruce comes with us, but not for food. And, Felix sticks close to his side and keeps anyone else from bothering him."

Marcus nodded. "That was Felix's plan. I'm not sure you could have talked him into anything else. He was as unconvinced as you when Bruce agreed to come along."

I cocked my head and considered his response. "It's Margaux. She'll be there, won't she?"

"Yeah, I'd be willing to bet on it."

"How would she even know about tonight? I didn't see her at the meeting. She's not on the Council or a leader of any House. Right?"

Marcus let out a long breath. "No. But Étienne is her sire," he said.

The news shouldn't have come as a shock, given the number of surprises I'd faced over the past months, but it did. "Why did no one tell me?" I demanded. "It would have been good information to have going into last night's meeting."

I figured you had enough to worry about, and I knew she wouldn't be at the meeting. I didn't learn about the reception until Alexander handed you the invitation. Since joining the House, I've been excluded from decisions regarding you and the House. It makes sense, but doesn't give us any heads up." He paused. "I'm sorry. I should have told you."

"Yes, you should have. I know I'm new at this, and I know I'm a lot younger than you and Felix. Hell, even Bruce is older than me, but I deserve to know when something affects me or this House. It doesn't do us any good if I walk into these things unprepared or unaware of the information everyone else has. Don't leave me in the dark, and don't try to protect me from the very things I need to be aware of."

He looked down and then met my stare. "You're right. From now on, no more ... omissions."

I nodded and then walked past him without another word. I was pissed and tired of being handled.

Marcus and Sara followed me upstairs, where Bruce and Felix were already waiting. Both men were decked out in black tuxedos that were clearly tailored to fit them perfectly. Felix's tuxedo was the classic black and white, while Bruce opted for a black shirt underneath his black tuxedo. The first thought that crossed my mind was that it was so the blood wouldn't show. A shiver crept up my spine.

"I'll be joining you this evening," Bruce said from Felix's side.

"Marcus and I already discussed it," I said, crossing my arms. I turned to Felix. "And, no. I will not be sipping from your boyfriend between toasts."

Felix narrowed his eyes. "I don't think I would let you," he said, his tone far from his usual playfulness.

"Good," I replied in the same tone and walked out the open front door, only to stop on the porch when I saw what was parked in the driveway. "Seriously? Is this really necessary?" I called back over my shoulder.

Felix was the first to leave the house, patting my shoulder as he descended the steps to the waiting stretch limo. A chauffeur, dressed head to toe in black, including a cap, opened the side door for Felix to get in. Bruce followed, offering me an apologetic smile as Marcus and Sara stepped up beside me.

Sara squeezed my arm, getting my attention. "Try to have a good time," she said. "It's not every day you look this awesome." She nudged me in the side, and I relaxed a bit and smiled back at her. She was the only member of the House not going along. Part of me felt guilty that she wasn't invited, while another part was grateful that she would be safely at home. And she was right. I needed to loosen up and remember that the other members of the House were only trying to help me through this challenging situation. It wasn't their fault, and it wasn't as if any of us had a choice but to go and try to repair my already horrid reputation.

"It's no art show," I said, trying to lighten the mood.

"Nope, but this time the party is for you. Try to remember that." She leaned in for a quick side hug and then stepped back.

For me. The idea was daunting, but it also came with an advantage. I was the guest of honor; surely the other guests would cut me some slack, or at least not try to murder me at my own party—I hoped. After our interaction the previous evening, I wasn't as concerned about Alexander, but I didn't know the other vampires who would be there. I'd never met

Margaux. I had no idea how one acted at an event like this, whether human or vampire. Panic started to rise in my chest. I didn't want to do this. I didn't want to put myself out there again.

At that moment, Marcus reached down and took my hand. His emotions flooded into me with the contact. He was calm, confident, and he cared about me. I glanced at our clasped palms as he lifted my hand and tucked it into his arm. He met my surprised gaze, and I remembered that I wasn't alone. I had help; I had people who cared about me and wanted to see this work out.

"Are you ready?" he asked.

I took a deep breath of the icy air and nodded. "Yeah, let's do this."

The limo swayed gently as it slowly crept back down the gravel driveway and then turned onto the paved road leading out of the valley. After several long, silent moments, I shifted in my seat. "Okay, I was wrong," I said. "The limo is cool."

Marcus chuckled, and Bruce bit his lip to suppress a smile, while Felix's face broke into a wide grin. "You should get used to the finer things in life, you're a House leader after all," Felix said.

"Says the guy who drives a beat-up old Jeep the color of a traffic cone," I scoffed.

"Hey, I like my Jeep. And I'm not a House leader," he said, seemingly offended, and leaned back in his seat, putting an arm around Bruce. I glanced at the two of them together.

"You will watch out for him tonight?" I asked. But it wasn't a question; it was more like I needed confirmation.

Bruce bristled slightly, likely at the thought of needing to be watched over, but Felix's gaze sharpened in a way that made me hold my breath as he glared back at me. "I will not leave his side," he growled low in his throat, annunciating each word carefully. Every hair on my body stood on end, yet I managed a nod and felt a sense of relief inside. *One less thing to worry about*, I thought.

I glanced at Marcus, who sat beside me; he was also watching Felix with a blank expression. Then he turned to me and smiled tightly. I reached for his hand again. I needed the reassurance of his touch as much as I needed the influx of his soothing emotions. Thankfully, he didn't object, and we rode the rest of the way in silence.

The Council House was just that—a house. If by 'house' you meant a Victorian mansion with as many rooms as a typical high school. Light poured from every window, but it couldn't dispel the dark feeling of the place. It was where the Council wanted to sequester me months earlier, when my fate had yet to be decided, before I had been granted my own House. I was a bit breathless when I got my first glimpse of it from the limo window. Surely, a place like that would have swallowed me whole.

"You actually lived here?" I asked Marcus.

He squeezed my hand. "It's not as bad as it looks," he said. "E *still* lives here as an employee of the Council without a House."

I tried not to react to that. I wasn't so sure I liked thinking about the two of them living in the same house for all those years.

Our limo pulled up to the front of the massive structure, and the men got out ahead of me. Marcus waited and helped me out of the vehicle, just as you see movie stars being assisted onto a red carpet. And what do you know, there was an actual red carpet leading up the front steps and into the gaping front doors.

We arrived at the same time as several others, and no one in particular seemed to notice us as we stepped into the foyer. It felt like entering an old woman's jewelry box. The walls were covered in dark blue silk wallpaper adorned with crystal sconces; the woodwork was painted gold, and a kiddie-pool-sized crystal chandelier hung overhead, making me want to duck to avoid being skewered by the sharp, icy points.

We followed the crowd into the ballroom. Marcus walked beside me, close enough that a single swing of my hips would have brought us into contact. Felix and Bruce were directly behind us, and I could practically feel Bruce's shoes brushing against the hem of my gown. I was grateful. I had my game face on. No one looking my way would have known that I was quaking inside. But having my house-mates all around me gave me the strength I didn't feel.

As we joined the main assembly in the ballroom, I paused and scanned the faces for anyone familiar. I wasn't looking for anyone in particular, but I was curious about who was present and where they were lurking. It didn't surprise me that Alexander was the first person I recognized.

He stood by the far wall, bloody wine glass in hand, with a lazy expression on his handsome face. His eyes were fixed on me, and I got the distinct sense that he'd been waiting for me. The small nod he gave in my direction felt like more than just an acknowledgment; it was a private greeting. And although I still loathed him, I nodded back, unwilling to snub the one vampire who seemed to be making an effort.

The next familiar face I spotted was Étienne. He was engaged in an animated discussion with several others, and I couldn't help but wonder who they were performing for. I decided there was no reason to hide. Everyone would soon know we were here, and frankly, I wanted to get this over with. I strode toward the knot of men and practically elbowed my way to the head of the Council. The entire group fell silent as we entered the circle.

"Étienne, thank you so much for hosting this event. I appreciate the gesture and the hospitality," I said, choosing my better behavior for a change.

"Ah, Kate, the vampire of the hour. So glad you could join us," he drawled, extending his hand. I reached out to shake it, but he grasped my fingers, twisted my hand, and brought it to his lips. A jolt of alarm shot through me, and I found myself back in James's apartment, my hand caught in his grip as he bit into the back of my fingers, sucking my blood from the punctures. Before I could pull away, Étienne placed a chaste kiss on my knuckles and released me.

I nearly stumbled but recovered as Marcus and Felix greeted Étienne. As Étienne introduced his companions, I nodded politely and shook a few hands, failing to hear what anyone said or to remember names as they were given. I murmured something polite, and then we stepped back, allowing the group to close again, shutting us out once more.

"Are you okay?" Marcus asked softly under the rumble of the crowd.

I nodded. "Yup. Doing great," I replied.

"I thought we were going to be more honest with one another."

I twisted my fingers around my clutch. He had a point. "I was just reminded of James," I admitted.

Marcus nodded and extended his elbow, which I gratefully accepted. I wasn't sure if he realized the effect touching him had on me, but it was a relief nonetheless. I took a few deep breaths to steady myself and continued scanning the room.

I didn't see her at first, but I felt the impact on Marcus when he recognized her. His muscles didn't tense, nor did his step falter, but through the grip on his arm, I felt him bracing for conflict. I glanced in the direction he was looking and saw a stunning brunette in a silver gown, her lips painted bright red. She was on the arm of a young man who looked somewhat familiar, but I couldn't place him. We stopped moving and let the couple approach. I heard Bruce's sharp intake of breath behind me, confirming it.

This could only be Margaux.

29

BRUCE

As Margaux navigated through the crowd, I couldn't help but gasp. It wasn't that I hadn't been prepared to see her—I had. It was seeing my ex on her arm that caught me off guard. It was my fault. I should have expected it. I'd known her for years and was aware that she'd do whatever she could to achieve maximum impact.

I was surprised, however, that Jake had gone along with it. He was free to make his own choices, and I didn't hold it against him for accepting Margaux's offer to join her House, but I hadn't known that she'd turned him. It was a hell of a way to find out—seeing your ex-boyfriend walk over with that supernatural glow they all had, his eyes sharper than before, and his lips ever so slightly fuller as they concealed his new set of teeth. Then again, he probably had no idea that I was going to be there. I'm sure he wasn't privy to Margaux's games. Plus, Jake had never been cruel.

The moment Jake saw me, I felt a wave of relief as the shock registered on his features. I shouldn't have cared, but I did. I wasn't interested in him, not anymore, but I hated to think he was out to hurt me. No, I think the thing I feared the most was that she'd changed him so completely from the man I'd known. I was happy she hadn't twisted him as badly as she had herself. At least not yet.

I glanced at Margaux hanging off Jake's arm. She was watching me, and a small smile played on her lips as she stroked Jake's shoulder with her free hand. Chills rushed down my spine, not from her possessiveness over Jake, but because the sight of her fangs poking out from under her top lip made the skin of my throat prickle with the memory of her tearing into me the last time we'd met. Her heated gaze held mine for a split second before she snapped her attention to Kate, who stood just in front of me. "You must be the new House leader everyone is talking about. Kate, right? It's a rather pedestrian moniker. I would have gone with Kathrine or Katrina or something," she said by way of greeting.

Kate, to her credit, said nothing.

After a long, awkward moment, Margaux huffed out a breath and knit her brows together. She hated being ignored and despised being snubbed. She turned to Marcus. "Marcus, would you please have the courtesy to introduce us?"

Marcus took a half step forward and turned toward Kate. "Kate, may I introduce Margaux, of House Brogan?"

Kate gave a slight nod, and I didn't miss the glare Margaux shot Marcus for asking Kate's permission. My gaze flicked to Felix beside me, who had a grin on his face; he hadn't missed it either.

"Margaux, this is Kate, leader of the House of Ward," Marcus continued, gesturing toward Kate.

Margaux heaved a sigh and nodded. "Nice to meet you," she clipped out.

"I wish I could say the same," Kate said, her tone level

and bored. She might claim she had no idea what she was doing, but she was playing Margaux beautifully. That is, if she was looking for a fight.

The scoff and eye roll from Margaux were no surprise. But when she looked over Kate's shoulder to address me, I was caught off guard. "Bruce, so nice to see you again. I'd heard you went to work for some low-level House out in the middle of nowhere. I'm surprised to see you here tonight."

"I don't know why you would be," I replied. "If you knew our House was so small, then you would have guessed that few humans are working there. And this party is in our sire's honor, so naturally, most of us would be in attendance." I glanced around the room at all the attendants in full-black circulating through the crowd, and the two who were following Margaux and Jake. There was no way she wouldn't have guessed that I would have been brought along.

"Sire, that's funny," Margaux shot back. "Not only are you still human, but your 'sire' is a fledgling who couldn't turn you if she wanted to. You'll be forty before she can manage it." She laughed dryly. "You should have come with me." She stroked Jake's arm again and leaned her body toward him as she spoke. "You're missing out." At least Jake had the decency to look uncomfortable with her performance.

Kate shifted in front of me, blocking my view and capturing Margaux's attention. "I think we're done here. I've heard enough. You will kindly leave my House members alone." Her tone didn't shift, but there was something in her voice that reminded me of the way she'd flung herself at Felix when she'd thought I was being mistreated. It made warmth creep into my chest, and the nervousness I'd felt at seeing Margaux dissipated somewhat.

"Or what?" was Margaux's answer. The words came out

fangy and slurred, and I shifted to my right so that I could see her again. Her top lip was peeled back, and her canines extended for all to see. It was a direct challenge, and I feared what Kate might do.

"Or I will make you," Kate stated calmly. Her voice might have been steady, but she was clutching Marcus's arm as if she were holding on for dear life.

Margaux let out a growl, catching the attention of a few people nearby. Marcus subtly shifted his weight forward, while Felix moved beside me until our shoulders brushed. It was a reminder that he was there and wouldn't let her get to me. But as I stared at Margaux, a look of confusion crossed her face, and she took a step back, closing her mouth. "Come on, Jake, this is a waste of our time," she said, sounding somewhat dazed. Jake looked almost as confused as Margaux, but nodded and allowed himself to be tugged along as Margaux turned and disappeared back into the crowd of onlookers. As soon as she was gone, everyone lost interest, and the din of conversation started back up around us.

Marcus turned to Kate. "That was you?"

Kate nodded. "I know it was a risk, but I figured it was better than wrestling with her here in the middle of the ball-room. She looked like she could probably mop the floor with me," Kate murmured so that only we could hear.

Kate turned to Felix and me. "Well, she was delightful. I can see why you might not want to sign up for that. And I assume that was your ex you told us about."

"Yeah, that was him." I glanced at Felix. He seemed unbothered by Margaux, Kate's use of her abilities, and the sudden appearance of my ex—all points in his favor. "Whatever you did, is it permanent?" I asked. It would be great not to have to worry about the vampire anymore, especially if I was going to attend any more of these get-togethers.

Kate shook her head. "Afraid not. She went away feeling a calm, loss of interest, but I don't know how long it will last. I've never tested it out," she admitted.

We circled the room, thankfully avoiding another encounter with Margaux. Kate greeted several more House leaders and chatted politely, never needing to resort to violence or reach for her abilities. Marcus spotted E, and we had a brief, friendly reunion with Kate's drinking buddy before making our way back toward the exit.

We'd been there for over forty-five minutes when Kate asked, "How much longer do we have to stay here?"

She directed the question at Marcus, who shrugged. "It's your party. We had to make an appearance, but we can leave any time you want to."

"Let's get out of here before anything else goes sideways."

Marcus held out his hand, and Kate took it. I turned to follow, but was stopped by Felix, who held out his hand for me. I was surprised. Not that he wanted to hold my hand, but that as a vampire, here among other vampires, he would want to be seen holding the hand of a human. After a brief hesitation, I gratefully took his cool hand in my own, and we followed behind Kate and Marcus.

We had to wait for the limo to pull around, and while we did, Marcus and Felix kept their eyes on the other partygoers. I hadn't seen Margaux or Jake since Kate had affected them with whatever magic she possessed. It was impressive what she could do. I'd never seen Margaux turn away so easily from something she wanted, be it a man or a fight. I just hoped it would last long enough for us to get away.

The limo arrived, and we all piled back inside. Kate looked steadier than I had expected, and she was stunning in her red gown, her hair styled beautifully. I glanced over at Felix; he looked incredible, too. If I thought his suit was a nice upgrade, it paled in comparison to Felix in a tux. He noticed my gaze and flashed me a wide smile, crossing his legs as he rested a hand on my thigh.

Most of the time, what you saw was what you got with Felix. He was as calm and composed behind closed doors as he was with everyone else. But there had been moments, like when Kate wanted assurance that he would protect me if necessary, when the ruthless vampire peeked out from behind that smile I liked so much. The way he growled in response, the tone in his voice when he told Kate he wouldn't let her feed from me, was as unsettling as it was thrilling. *And what did that say about me?*

My reaction to him shouldn't have come as a shock. For all my complaints about vampires in general, and Margaux in particular, I had chosen to live my life among them. I covered Felix's hand with mine and laced our fingers together. I couldn't claim him as my own. I had no illusions that what we had would last forever; how could it? But I was glad he was in my corner, that was for sure.

Felix leaned toward me. "I'm going to be spending more time at your house if that's okay. I would feel better if I were there during nighttime hours. Not that Kate hasn't proven that she can handle things, but I would rest easier. Until we find out how Margaux will react to this evening and how Kate handled her," he said.

"Did I screw up again?" Kate asked with a crooked smile. I didn't think she had any regrets about being rude to Margaux. Neither did I.

"Not at all," Felix said. "I thought you were brilliant, but

I worry about that female. She's clearly spoiling for a fight." He smirked. "And I would dearly like to give her one."

"Better you than me," Kate replied. "I might have a few tricks up my sleeve, but she was right. I'm young and she's probably magnitudes stronger than I am."

"It's true, but I've seen how you react when you think someone you care about is in danger." Felix winked at her, and had she been human, she would have blushed.

We all lapsed into silence after that, and the trip passed quickly. As we were turning up the drive to the house, I leaned close to Felix. "You know, if you're going to be here each evening, you could stay overday too."

The pressure of his hand on my thigh increased. "I'll think about it," he said coolly.

We exited the limo and were all walking toward the door when the driver spoke from behind us. "Excuse me, Sir?"

All four of us turned around, but the chauffeur's gaze was locked on me. "Yes?" I asked, turning back, thinking I must have forgotten some aspect of the evening's contract with his company.

He stepped forward and held out a small white envelope. "A lady asked me to give this to you after I dropped you all off. She said it was a surprise." He shrugged like he wasn't sure whether he was doing the right thing or not.

I reached out and accepted the envelope, despite having no doubt who the "*she*" was. "Thank you," I said, and joined the others. We watched the limo drive off before any of us spoke a word.

"Do you want me to open it?" Kate offered.

"No. I got it." I tore the flap open and pulled out a folded piece of paper. It looked as though it had been roughly torn from a notepad. I unfolded it and read the inscription. I clenched my jaw so tightly it began to throb. Felix held out his hand, and I passed the note over.

"*I know where you sleep. Love, M,*" he read aloud. There was a big red lipstick kiss just below the M. Felix glanced over at me, and the look in his eyes held the promise of violence. "I think I'll be taking you up on your offer to stay over," he said.

30

SILAS

Dinner was better than I could have hoped for. We ate at a fairly nice chain restaurant that offered a wide range of options and a pleasant atmosphere. It was just nice enough to say "date" without the pressure of being fancy. It had a gas fireplace, low lighting, and soft music that was quiet enough for Sara and me to talk without shouting at one another.

It was wonderful to talk to her—really talk, without the need to strategize about an upcoming vampire meeting or an impending crisis. I learned more about her family and how she and Kate had known each other since Sara attended high school in a larger town outside the valley. We discussed my niece and nephew and how they were both adjusting to their wolf forms, as well as what it meant to be a shifter. I also shared details about my parents and brothers, as well as how I got started in construction with my dad.

And the whole time we sat there, I couldn't take my eyes off her. The way she tilted her head when she considered what to say, how she raised her eyebrows just slightly when she took a bite to eat, and the warmth in her eyes as she gazed at me from across the table. I was lost to her, and I enjoyed every moment.

If I thought watching her over dinner was captivating, it paled in comparison to watching her browse the local bookstore we went to afterward. I loved the simmering heat in her gaze when she looked at me, but there was something about the pure joy reflected in the way her eyes danced over the colorful spines of the books as she chose which realm to delve into, which love story to get lost in next. I stood back and took in her delight as she considered what to bring home with her.

She asked for a bag to hold her treasures, but on the way back, she promptly dumped the stack of books onto her lap so she could pet the covers. "Thank you, Silas," she said, grinning from the seat beside me. "I didn't intend for you to buy these for me, though. I would have paid for them myself." She traced her finger over the raised lettering on the front of a blue jewel-toned book.

"I know, but I wanted to. I want to spend every day making you happy."

"Every day?" she whispered, almost too softly for me to hear.

However, my hearing is better than that of any human or witch. *Damn, why did I say that?* I thought. My goal was to take things slowly and let her eventually choose forever without all the pressure of the bond. But the truth had slipped out. I hoped I hadn't just screwed things up on our very first date.

I decided to ignore my comment and change the subject. "You said you had to help Kate get ready for a reception last night. How did that go?" I asked, tossing out the distraction.

She winced. "Okay, I guess. She didn't piss everyone off

like last time," Sara said. She shifted in her seat and rearranged her books in her lap.

"But?" I asked, knowing there was more to the story, and whatever it was, she didn't think I was going to like it.

"But, when they got home, Bruce got a note from the crazy vampire chick that's been after him." She paused, staring down at her hands.

"What did it say?" I prompted when she didn't elaborate.

She let out a sigh. "'I know where you sleep.'"

I stopped breathing, and my wolf, who had been lounging peacefully in the back of my mind all evening, sat up straight. I knew where Bruce slept, too, three doors down from Sara.

"As you can imagine, it freaked everyone out a bit. Kate is ready to rip the vampire's head off, Felix is now basically living at the house, and Marcus promised to mention it to the Council, but the head of the Council is Margaux's sire, so ..."

I nodded and swallowed down the lump forming in my throat. "So they won't do anything," I finished for her.

"Yup, that's about the size of it," she said, looking out the window at the trees whizzing by.

"How strong are your wards?"

"Strong enough to keep a vampire out, but they don't protect against all types of mayhem. It depends on what she intends to do. They wouldn't stop her from setting fire to the place, for instance." Sara shrugged. "But Kate said the vampire was obsessed with Bruce; I doubt she wants him dead."

I wasn't as optimistic as Sara, and neither was my wolf, who was now pacing back and forth, trying to peer out of my eyes as if he might spot the danger ahead. I hadn't meant to spoil our evening with vampire talk, but I wasn't sorry I'd asked. Anything that put my mate in danger was information I needed to know.

At that moment, Sara reached over and put her hand on my arm. The feel of her fingers against my tight muscles grounded me. I let go of the steering wheel with that hand and reached for hers. She laced her fingers through mine, and I drove the rest of the way one-handed, grateful for her touch and the reminder that she was safe beside me.

When we got back to her house, I carefully scanned the surrounding woods as I stepped out and helped her with her stack of books. The sun had set hours earlier, and the darkness felt especially ominous as we walked up the steps to the relative safety of the wards. I rested my fingertips on her lower back as she climbed, not wanting to lose the physical connection. And not for the first time, I thought about how much living with vampires had complicated things for Sara and how much danger had been added to her life. It wasn't where I would have preferred her to live, yet it wasn't my choice to make, and I knew that Kate and the others had become family to her.

Sara opened the door, turned to me with a smile, and took the stack of books from me. "Do you want to come in?" she asked, and the smile on her lips grew into something else, something quieter but also deeper and more intimate.

"Yes. Yes, I do." There was no other answer. I wasn't sure I could have left even if I wanted to. Not only did I need the reassurance of her touch, but with the threat to the House, there was no way I could go far. Had she not invited me in, I knew I'd end up circling the house all night on four paws to ensure no one got close enough to test the wards. No, there was no going home for me that evening.

I followed her inside and closed the door tightly behind me. Sara made a beeline for her new bookshelves, and I watched with amusement as she found perfect homes for each of her new acquisitions. If there was a shelving system, it was well beyond my understanding, but Sara knew exactly where each book belonged and, in a matter of minutes, had them all tucked away. I noticed happily that there was still enough room for several more bookstore dates.

When she was done, she came to stand beside me to admire her work. "You're not going to keep one out to read right away?" I asked.

She tilted her head up toward me, and the private smile returned. "No. I thought maybe I could find something better to do than read this evening."

The tone of her words was enough to drive a heat and need through me that had me reaching for her before I realized what I was doing. Part of my mind wondered if this was too forward, if I was being too aggressive, but I didn't stop myself, and she came willingly into my arms. I bent down to capture her mouth in a kiss as I pulled her closer, wanting to feel all of her against me.

She wrapped her arms tightly around my body, gripping onto the muscles of my back, pulling herself even closer, and I groaned into her open mouth. "Sara," I said hoarsely, pulling back slightly. "Could we go somewhere more private? If you're comfortable with that. It's just that Bruce is in the kitchen, and I can hear Felix on his way down the stairs. Or we could tap the brakes. I could leave if you want." I was breathing hard and not sure I could make myself walk out the door, but I would give it a shot if she wanted me to.

"I don't want you to go," she said, just as breathless. "You could stay over, you know." She smiled again, but there was nothing coy or hesitant about it; it was pure suggestion, an invitation. And Gods, yes, I wanted to stay. My mate was inviting me into her bed, and there was no way I was going to pass up the chance. I hesitated, though —would I be able to be so close to her and not sink my teeth into her shoulder? Could I lie with her without marking her as mine? As she watched me, her smile slipped a bit and became softer. "Only if you want to," she said, an apology in her tone. "And you wouldn't even have to sleep on the couch this time. Bruce fixed up a guest room just down the hall from mine."

"I don't want to sleep in the guestroom, Sara," I growled out. "I want to be with you, in your bed." My body practically trembled just thinking about it.

"Oh, good," she said in a small voice. "That's what I want too."

She pulled away then and took me by the hand. She tugged softly, leading me toward the foyer. Felix was clearing the last of the steps as we arrived and opened his mouth, presumably to greet the two of us. Without meaning to, I flashed him a look and felt my wolf press hard through my eyes, my lip curling, and a low growl rumbling through my chest as the vampire regarded us.

Felix dropped his gaze to the floor and raised both hands in a clear gesture that he was not challenging me in any way. *What the fuck am I doing?* I thought. I knew Felix had no intention of getting between me and my mate, but instinct had taken over, and nothing besides her was going to stop me from taking her to bed.

Sara noticed Felix's odd behavior and glanced back at me. If I could have, I would have felt embarrassed by the display of wolfish dominance she must have seen on my face. But she just chuckled in amusement and tugged harder. "Come on, Silas," she said as she walked by Felix. "Sorry, Felix. Don't mind us."

I passed Felix and dipped my head in acknowledgment.

It was the most I could manage at the moment. And then I followed Sara upstairs.

Once we hit the landing, my body relaxed, and possessiveness was replaced with an overwhelming need to get my mate behind closed doors. I made myself walk slowly, calmly behind her down the hall. She opened her door, and the feeling of desire wasn't helped by the gorgeous scent of her that lingered in her room. It was the sky after a storm, and the sweet smell of orange blossoms. I breathed in deeply and felt drunk on the scent as she pulled me toward the bed, still clutching my hand.

And I wanted to go. With everything that I was, I wanted to go with her, but there were things to say first. Things she should know, I thought. I pulled back, not letting go. "Sara, wait," I breathed.

She paused, eyes round with worry. "Is something wrong? If it's too soon. I get it," she said in a rush. "I know it's technically our first date, but I've wanted you for years. But if—"

"No. Sara, it's not that. I want this as much, if not more than you do. I promise," I said, trying to calm my wolf, who was shoving at me to get on with it. He didn't understand my need for verbal communication when our mate was offering herself to us. "But I think we should talk first."

"Oh, yeah. I suppose we should," she said, wrinkling her brow. She didn't let go of my hand, though, which I appreciated. "I don't have a condom, but I've been tested, and I assure you I'm not carrying anything. And I've been drinking a contraceptive tea every morning since, well, since you started working on the house, actually," she said, looking down, a blush creeping up her cheeks.

I tugged on her hand to get her attention. "It's not that," I said. "I just ... I thought you should know, I've never done this before." I wasn't sure how much she knew about shifters. She'd spent time around my father and brothers, but I was certain none of them would have delved into the mating habits of wolf shifters with her. From the look on her face, she hadn't talked to anyone else about it either.

"Oh," she said. Her lovely black brows were now raised in surprise. "That's ... not a problem." I was sure that for a witch, twenty-eight was a bit old to be a virgin still, but she didn't look disappointed; that was a good sign.

"It's different with shifters, especially wolf shifters," I admitted. "We don't do casual sex. It's complicated. And in no way a moral judgment," I assured her. "It's more cultur-al." I wasn't sure how much I could get into without discussing bonding.

"Is this okay? With us, I mean? You don't have to ..." She shifted and bit down on her bottom lip, clearly conflicted.

"It's very okay, and I don't consider this at all casual," I said, my voice dropping lower, as I pulled on our clasped hands until she was standing against me.

She let out a soft sigh and stood on her toes to kiss me, pressing her body against mine in a way that reminded us both why we were there. I had no doubt she could feel through the layers of our clothing how much I desired her, how ready I was for her. As her tongue darted into my mouth, I prayed to the gods that I could get through this without scaring or scarring her.

Wrapping my arms around her, I lifted her off the ground and walked the few feet to the bed, laying her gently on the mattress, her legs straddling me, her hands reaching to push my shirt up, urging me to take it off.

Bare-chested, I lay beside her then and took my time undressing her. I was glad for the slowness of it. I needed the moments it took to unbutton her blouse and slide the thin straps of her bra down her arms to pace myself, to enjoy this first time with my mate. I wanted her more than anything, but I also wanted to remember this. I didn't want to rush, not this time.

With every item of clothing I removed, more and more of her beautiful skin was revealed to me, and I bent to kiss and touch every inch of her. I marveled at the softness of her, the gorgeous curves and lines. When she was completely naked, I traced my fingers down her stomach and across the inside of her thigh and deeper. She arched up into my hand and let out a soft moan that I captured with my mouth. She was so perfect.

"Now you," she said. "I want to see you too." She reached for the buttons of my jeans, and I complied. I stood up from the bed and let the last of my clothes fall to the floor.

"Oh," she breathed, staring down at me.

"This still okay?" I asked, crawling back onto the mattress to lie beside her.

"Um, yeah. It's good," she said, and then reached forward and grasped me in her palm.

Now it was my turn to arch my back and let out a soft hiss as she stroked me. "Did I mention this was my first time, Sara?" I panted and placed my hand over hers. "It's not going to take much more than that."

She smiled at me from under hooded lids but stilled her hand. "Come here," she said, rolling from her side onto her back and opening her thighs for me.

My breath stilled, and I held her gaze as I moved until I was lying over her. My weight braced on my arms, our faces inches apart, her sweet breath flowing into my lungs with each inhale. She tilted her pelvis, and my cock pressed up against her entrance. My arms tensed, and the muscles of my abdomen shook. "Sara, I love you," I said, unable to hold the words back. I needed her to know. I needed her to understand. I searched her face, looking into her deep brown eyes.

"I love you, too, Silas," she said and gave me a sweet smile and a small nod.

And I thrust inside of her.

She let out a gasp, and I tried to pull back, but she held onto my shoulders, holding me close. "No, I'm good," she breathed. "Move, Silas. I need you to move."

And I did. And oh Gods, she felt good.

I fisted the sheets in my hands, squeezing tightly, trying to even out my breathing and take it slow. But Sara moved underneath me, matching my rhythm and pushing herself against me in a way that urged me on, and I lost myself in the feel of her.

After some time, she wrapped her hands around the muscles of my upper arms, her nails digging in, and her face took on a pained expression. "Sara?" I said, worried I was hurting her.

"Don't. Stop," she ground out just before I felt a surge of electricity shoot into my arms from her palms, as the muscles of her body gripped onto my cock, squeezing me tightly.

I cried out as my own orgasm overtook me, the waves of pleasure rolling over me as I collapsed on top of her, my teeth clenched together, my body shaking.

"Oh, Gods, Silas," Sara nearly wailed. "Are you okay? I'm so sorry. I didn't mean to."

Her hands were in my hair, her muscles tense. I lifted my head from where it rested beside hers and pushed my weight off of her so she wouldn't suffocate. I wasn't ready to leave her body, though. "I'm alright," I assured her.

Then she burst into tears.

"I thought I killed you," she sniffed, her body shaking beneath mine.

I chuckled. "I would have died happy," I said. "But no, you did not kill me."

She laughed too at that point, sending strange vibrations through me where we were still connected. At least I didn't bite her, I thought with amusement. My wolf huffed in the back of my mind, like it was only a matter of time. It was the first I'd heard from him since I'd put the brakes on for Sara and my chat before, and I was happy with his silence. The only one I wanted to be thinking about at that moment was Sara.

I looked down at her and brought up a hand to wipe away a tear. "Are you okay?" I asked. "Was that okay?"

She nodded. "It was more than okay," she said. "But we're not done yet." She smiled and pulled me down for another kiss.

31

KATE

After two nights in a row dealing with the Council, I was looking forward to a night at home. I was even more excited to hear all about Sara's date when she got back. I didn't have to wait long; the distinctive rumble of Silas's truck echoed from the driveway well before ten o'clock. When I didn't hear it start up again, I figured Silas must have stopped by, so I went upstairs to say hello.

When I reached the first floor, I followed the low murmur of voices to the kitchen. Bruce was at the stove, and Felix was sitting at the small kitchen table, one leg crossed over the other, with a strange smile on his face.

"Hey," I said. "Where's Sara and Silas?"

Bruce raised the spoon he was using to stir in greeting, but didn't reply. I turned to Felix, whose smile had now morphed into a proper smirk. "I do believe the shifter is finally claiming his mate," he said. "I made the mistake of getting between them and the bedroom and nearly got my head bitten off." His words were a shock, but his tone was one of amusement.

I skipped the claiming part of his statement and focused on the threat of violence. "Are you okay?" I asked. "Did Silas hurt you?" I couldn't believe Silas would do something like that, but I didn't know shifters very well, and, well, I'd attacked Felix myself, so ...

"Oh no. Nothing like that. He was very polite for a shifter on his way to mark his mate. I was just in the wrong place at the wrong time."

"What is all this talk of mates and marking?" I asked. I knew that Sara and Silas liked each other, probably loved each other, but they were on their first date, for crying out loud.

Felix shrugged. "It was pretty obvious where they were headed, and when a shifter bonds, it's for life. It's my understanding that the first time a bonded pair ... mates, they mark each other."

"Mark each other?"

He snapped his jaws in demonstration. "Biting Kate. They bite each other in a place that shows other shifters that they're taken."

I shook my head. "Sara's not a shifter, and I can't imagine that Silas would ..." But then I paused. I didn't know what he would do. It turns out that pausing was a mistake. In the silence, my vampire ears picked up sounds from above that left no doubt about what my best friend was up to. I slapped my hands over my ears.

Felix chuckled. "You can't be that squeamish. If so, I'm sure you've heard plenty in this house that's made you blush," he said, shooting a look at Bruce. Bruce didn't even flinch; he just kept stirring the food on the stove.

"I try not to," I objected.

"Just tune them out," Felix said, grinning.

I let out a sigh. "I'm going back to my room," I said. Walking to the fridge, I took out several bags of blood and grabbed a travel mug from the cupboard beside Bruce.

"Kate," Bruce said. "I've got some work to do on the patio outside your room tomorrow. I'll try not to disturb your rest, however."

"Is this part of your super-secret project you won't let me see?"

"The very one," he replied. "It should be done in a few days."

"Good, I'm dying to find out what it is," I said. "In the meantime, if you need me, I'll be in my room with earbuds in, reading my book."

Felix's blond brows shot up. "Oooh, have you gotten to the part where they're trapped in the cave and their dragons can't get to them and the only way they can keep warm is to—"

"Hey, no spoilers," I said, shooting him a glare. "And I can't believe you've read that series."

"What can I say? I'm a man of diverse tastes," he replied.

At that moment, there was a deep masculine cry from upstairs, and Felix's gaze drifted back to Bruce, taking on a heated glow.

"Okay, I'm outta here," I said. "You all have a good evening." I turned and hurried out of the kitchen before either of them had time to reply. With my meal tucked safely under my arm, I shut myself in my bedroom and reached for my earbuds. I had never been so grateful for the noise-canceling feature. It wasn't that they were making that much noise; I would've bet that Bruce couldn't hear anything. However, as a vampire, I was not so fortunate.

After the shock wore off, I had to admit I was happy for

Sara and Silas. I liked them together, and I was glad they were finally taking their relationship to the next level. I didn't know what to make of Felix's comments about mating for life. I knew Sara was crazy about Silas, but she'd never mentioned marriage. I was pretty sure that if things had progressed that far, she would have said something. And I was convinced that while they were probably having a great time, one night didn't equal a lifelong commitment. At least it had never been that way for Sara. She'd dated a handful of guys since high school, one of them seriously, but even that relationship hadn't reached the marriage stage despite them being together for over a year. No, I was sure Felix was mistaken.

I put thoughts of shifters and mating out of my mind and settled in with my favorite dragon series. My book kept me occupied for the next two hours. I hadn't yet reached the cave scene, but now that I knew it was coming, I was looking forward to seeing how Irina and Larz got out of the cave ... eventually.

I pulled my earbuds out to blessed silence and decided it was safe to go upstairs. I wanted to give engraving a try, and my room felt too small for the project. I'd been excited when Sara had shown me what she'd bought for me to work on. It was a beautiful, metal locket with plenty of surface area for a design. She'd also bought a modern engraving pen with a very precise diamond tip. I'd tried it out on a few pieces of scrap metal first. It didn't take me much time to get used to it. It wasn't that much different from using a pen after all.

I retrieved the engraver from my dresser, where it had been charging, along with the locket that lay beside it. I had already drawn out the design I wanted: a simple repeat of flowers and leaves. I planned to trace the design with the engraver until the lines were deep enough, all the while trying to imbue it with some emotion. Sara and I agreed it should be something positive. The sketch I unintentionally created was full of fear and sadness, and I didn't want to put *that* out into the world. The question was, what did I want to put into this one?

Gathering my supplies, I went past the curtain of plastic that hid Bruce's secret project and upstairs to the dining table. The firm surface would be perfect to rest the locket against as I worked. Of course, I placed a cutting mat down first; I didn't want to screw up the new table.

Once everything was in order, I sat down and reflected on my feelings. I didn't feel sad or fearful. I felt content, but I wasn't sure that was enough of an emotion to put into the locket. Would anyone even notice? I considered what I wanted to feel. Focusing on the joy and love I wanted to create, I thought of my friends—those who were here in this house, who had devoted so much time and effort to make this place a home, to support me and our new House. I owed them so much.

Focusing on those feelings, I lifted the pen and began to trace the tiny leaves and delicate flowers. My vampiric muscle control was amazing, and I felt very happy with how the piece was turning out; I put all that into the locket as well. At least I hope I did. I'd never intentionally created a Relic before; I just hoped I was doing it right.

When the front side was complete, I flipped the thing over and started on the back. I was finishing up when I heard the telltale noises from above. Sara and Silas were awake again. Good thing the next day was a Sunday, I thought, those two were going to need to sleep in.

I looked at the locket and sighed. My thoughts went to Marcus of all people, and how it had felt to hold his hand, to have his emotions soothe and calm me when I was nervous.

As another moan sounded from above, I dropped the engraving pen and decided to call it a night. I looked at my phone. It was past three in the morning. Too early to sleep, but not too early to hide in my room until dawn.

By the time I'd put everything away, had a long shower, and changed into a t-shirt and sweats, it was only a few hours until sunrise. I tucked myself back into bed and read until my eyes grew heavy. I did make it to the cave scene, and it was a good one. I would have to mention it to Felix tomorrow night, I thought as sleep drew me down and I let the book fall closed beside me on the pillow.

A deep groan woke me from sleep sometime later. *Seriously?* I thought. I reached for my earbuds, but then the noise came again, and I froze. Something wasn't right. I sat up in bed and listened, really listened. There was grunting and the sounds of heavy impact, followed by a cry that was unmistakably pain, not pleasure, and the noises were coming from just outside my shuttered window.

Before I thought about what I was doing, I jumped from the bed and sprinted down the hall barefoot, tearing the plastic and curtains aside to reveal the sitting area in mid-transformation. My momentum carried me forward into the room before I could stop myself. I came to a stop in the center of the space, facing the wide, open sliding glass doors that allowed the morning light to pour through, bathing both the room and me in golden light.

I slammed my eyes shut and threw my arm over my head, crouching on the floor—as if that would help protect me from the burning sun's rays. I was about to throw my weight back toward my room and safety when I realized I wasn't in pain.

I wasn't burning.

It was then that the sounds that had awoken me registered again, louder and closer.

Without a moment's hesitation, I rushed out the door and into the bright morning light, where a horrifying scene confronted me. Two men circled Bruce, each wielding large hunting knives, their backs turned to me. Bruce was bleeding from a cut on his head, and blood dripped down one arm, which he held immobile against his body. He had a knife in his other hand, facing his attackers head-on with a look of grim determination. It was then that I noticed a body on the patio behind Bruce, lying still.

At the same moment, both men charged at Bruce, and I threw myself at the nearest attacker. Grabbing his head from behind with both hands, I screamed and twisted it to the side. There was a loud cracking sound, and I suddenly found myself supporting the man's full weight as it hung from his broken neck. I dropped him and turned.

A flash of movement by the house caught my attention. I thought it might be another attacker and was surprised to see Felix drop from a second-floor window wearing nothing but a pair of cargo shorts and a full beard. *Since when did Felix have a beard?* I wondered briefly. He landed on bent knees and sprinted past me toward where Bruce was still grappling with the remaining man.

I spun around to help when a scream tore loose from the knot of bodies. Felix ripped the attacker in two, dropping each half to the side. But it wasn't the cry of the attacker I'd heard; it was Felix's.

I crept closer as Felix dropped to his knees in front of Bruce, who now lay on the cold ground. It wasn't until I stepped up beside him that I realized what caused him to scream.

As quickly as Felix had moved, as fast as he'd reacted, he hadn't gotten there in time. I looked down at Bruce, the man I had promised to protect, the man who had helped me when I needed it most, and saw the handle of a hunting knife sticking out of the middle of his bloody chest.

32

KATE

"Bruce!" I rushed the remaining distance and dropped to the ground beside Felix, who was staring open-mouthed at the knife protruding from Bruce's sternum. "What do we do?" I asked, my voice tight. "How do we fix this? Should I call 911?" I didn't have time to marvel that both Felix and I were out in the open on this clear blue winter's day. The only thing that mattered was saving Bruce.

I glanced at his face. His eyes blinked, and his lips moved like he was trying to speak, but no sound came out.

"Felix!" I screamed, trying to get his attention.

He turned his head and caught my gaze; then his attention snapped back to Bruce, and he began to act. "Yes, I think there's a way," he said. His usually smooth voice was rough with emotion. "If he can just stay alive until it has a chance to work." He reached for the handle of the knife, and I grabbed his hand.

"No. Aren't you supposed to leave it in until help arrives?"

"Kate, we *are* the help. Look how much blood he's lost.

There isn't much time. And my blood can do a better job than any surgeon with a needle and thread."

At the mention of blood, I glanced down and saw it everywhere. It soaked through Bruce's shirt and open winter coat, pooling beneath him and coating his hair and hands. The smell was mouthwatering. I swallowed my craving and refocused on what Felix was doing.

"On second thought, I want you to get ready to pull the knife. As soon as you do, I'm going to use my blood to try to repair the damage. We have to move fast, got it?"

I nodded and numbly wrapped my fingers around the hilt as Felix bit into his wrist. I could feel the knife pulsing and wondered if it was touching Bruce's heart or lodged inside. The thought made me shiver, and I stole another glance at Bruce's face. He was no longer blinking, and his eyes seemed fixed on the clear sky above. It was then that the pulsing under my fingers ceased.

"Now, Kate. We're losing him," Felix cried as I yanked the knife free. He already had his slashed wrist positioned over the gaping hole in Bruce's chest, letting his blood drip into the open wound. Felix had to hold the skin of his wrist apart to keep it from closing and to allow the blood to flow freely.

I couldn't tell if it was working. There was so much blood. Everything was such a mess. But as I watched, I saw the blood well up in the wound and run over, and soon there was no wound at all, just smooth flesh where the knife had been. I listened, but there was still no heartbeat, no steady pulsing, and Bruce's eyes remained staring off into nothing.

Felix jumped forward and began performing chest compressions, trying to jumpstart Bruce's repaired heart. I scooted back to give him more space and watched, waiting for Bruce to take a gasping breath and sit up to tell us he was okay. But he didn't, and Felix kept pumping away at his chest.

"Oh, God. I've broken his ribs," Felix said, anguish lacing his words, but he didn't stop. He pressed on, trying desperately to save his lover.

It wasn't working. He was dead. How could Bruce be dead? *This isn't right*, I thought. *We can't lose him.* This wasn't how it was supposed to go. He was one of the kindest, most generous people I'd ever met. He was brave, strong, and capable in ways I only dreamed of being. He had quickly become the beating heart of our House, of our home. He couldn't be gone.

It was then I heard a noise and looked toward the patio door in time to see an enormous wolf rush out of the house. He came toward us, glanced at Bruce's body, and gave a soft whine before rushing off into the forest. Behind him, Sara hurried to where we crouched. She was dressed in nothing but PJs, a robe, and slippers against the cold. "Oh, Gods, Kate. Felix," she cried. Then she saw Bruce and shook her head. "No, no. What happened?" She grabbed my shoulder as Felix continued trying to get Bruce back.

"His heart isn't beating," I said. My voice sounded far away, like someone else was talking.

"Felix!" Sara shouted. "Get out of the way." She stepped around me and shoved at the vampire.

Felix's head whipped around, his lips raised and his fangs fully extended. I stiffened, ready to intervene, but it wasn't necessary. As soon as Felix registered who was pushing at him and the look on her face, he bowed his head and scooted away, sinking back to sit on the ground near

Bruce's head. He stroked Bruce's forehead as Sara pushed Bruce's shirt up, exposing his chest, and bent over him.

"Don't touch him," she warned. She brought her hands to Bruce's bloody chest, one hovering over his heart and the other under his arm. The expression on her face was one of intense concentration as she summoned her gift. Blue light built in her palms and flowed over her fingers, then she slammed her hands down onto Bruce's chest, releasing the energy into his body.

She pulled her hands away and glanced at Felix. "Anything? Can you hear his heart?"

Felix shook his head, his face stained with bloody tears, running from his eyes and gathering in his beard. "No. Nothing. Try again. Please, Sara," he breathed.

"Of course," she said, repositioning her hands. She brought her gift to bear and slapped her palms down again. This time, Bruce jolted with the impact.

We were all silent, waiting. And then I heard it. I steady thump, thump, thump coming from Bruce. I let out a breath, and Felix collapsed down, folding himself around Bruce's shoulders and head, whispering into his hair. Bruce took a shuddering breath, and we all sighed with relief.

Sara sat back as Silas trotted out of the woods. He stopped to sniff at one of the dead attackers before beginning to shake. Moments later, the wolf was replaced by a crouching Silas who stood up, his legs still wobbling slightly. Sara rose to her feet and went to him, wrapping her arms around his waist. He rubbed her back in slow circles, meeting my gaze over the top of her curly head. I nodded in response. "There's no one else out there," he said, glancing from me to where Felix still cradled a prone Bruce. "I circled the property and found their car parked up the road a ways. They came through the trees on foot."

I nodded again and squeezed my eyes shut against the light reflected off the pavement of the patio. They were starting to sting. "Felix, can we move him inside?" I asked. "The light is starting to get to me."

Sara turned around in Silas's arms. "How are either of you out here at all?" she asked.

I shook my head. "I have no idea. Besides my eyes, I feel okay." I glanced at Felix and noticed for the first time that his exposed skin appeared to move slightly. There was a mottling of brown and red that shifted and flowed back to his pale cream almost too fast to see.

Felix looked up. "Yeah, he should be okay. He's still injured. He was stabbed in the shoulder, and I know I broke several of his ribs, but I think he'll live."

Bruce groaned, drawing our attention. His eyelids fluttered, and he blinked, focusing his bright blue gaze on Felix. "Hey," he croaked out.

"Hey, yourself," Felix whispered back. "You gave us a scare, you know?"

"Sorry to worry you."

"I know you're still hurting," Felix said. "Would you do something for me? Would you let me give you some more of my blood?"

"More?" Bruce asked, his blood-smeared forehead wrinkling.

"I don't know if you recall, but you had a knife sticking out of your chest a moment ago. I used my blood to repair the wound. Now, I'm asking you to drink a little for me. To help with the internal injuries. Not enough to turn you, just a sip."

Bruce inhaled and winced, hissing through his teeth. "Maybe just a sip," he replied.

Felix nodded. "Thank you." He bit his wrist again, reopening the wound, and placed it to Bruce's lips.

Bruce's stare locked on Felix as he drew from his wrist. One quick pull, and Felix withdrew his arm. Bruce shivered all over and closed his eyes, but his breathing was easier and his muscles relaxed.

Felix lifted him into his arms, and we all went back into the house through the open glass doors. We didn't stop in the sitting room, though. Felix carried Bruce up both flights of stairs to their bedroom, with all of us following behind. I walked through the sunlight streaming in from the windows in awe. I extended my hand and gazed at my skin under the light, the actual sunlight, for the first time in months. *How was this possible?*

Felix lay Bruce on the bed in the darkness of their room, settling him gently before turning to us. Silas had disappeared, hopefully to find some clothes, but Sara and I waited patiently. "Is he going to be okay?" Sara asked.

"I think so," Felix said. "There might be some temporary changes because of my blood, but he'll be alright. He needs rest, and I need to feed." He stared at me, a strange expression on his face. "You are a surprise, Kate," he said. "I didn't expect to find you outside, although I'm grateful you were there."

"I didn't get there in time, though."

"Neither did I," Felix replied. "But if you hadn't screamed while attacking the human, I might not have woken."

I shuddered at the memory of killing the man. I'd never done anything remotely like that in my life. The most disturbing part of it was that I felt no guilt about it. None whatsoever.

Silas reappeared over Sara's shoulder, fully dressed.

"How is it that you two weren't burned up in the sunlight?" he asked. "Did I miss that part?"

"No, you didn't," Felix replied. "I don't know how Kate survived, but I was burned. I just heal faster than I burn these days." He shrugged, and I looked at his skin. It was back to being a pale cream, no indication of the strange mottling I'd seen outside. He was paler than I'd ever seen him, actually.

"Because you're old?" I blurted out.

Felix rolled his eyes. "Yes, Kate. I'm old. What's your excuse?"

I shrugged. "No idea."

He nodded. "I'm going to make it a priority to get to the bottom of that," he said. "As soon as I've made sure we don't get any more uninvited visitors, and after I've had something to eat."

"All we've got is bagged," I reminded him.

He winced. "Is Beth here—"

"No," I snapped. "It's Sunday, and that is not in her job description."

"I don't require much," he said with a sigh. "Fine, I'll have whatever swill you keep in the fridge."

"You don't have to. You could always go into the city and find a willing meal," I reminded him.

He shook his head. "I'm afraid being in the sun takes a lot out of me, and that's when I'm not bleeding into someone I love."

I looked at him more closely then. Not only was he paler than usual, but he was also leaning heavily on the dresser beside him.

"I'm on it," Silas said, leaving the doorway and disappearing again.

I inched closer to Sara, who stood in her robe, arms

crossed, as she regarded Felix. "Are you going to be okay?" she asked.

"Yes. I'm fine. And thank you, Sara. We would have lost him without you. How did you know how to do that?"

Sara took a breath, uncrossed her arms, and looked down at her hands. "I don't know. It's the first positive thing I've done with my gift." She shook her head, and a smile tugged at the corners of her mouth. "You know, I always wished I had a different gift? I thought it would be cool to wield fire like my aunt or control water or air, but I'm so grateful for what I have today, and what it allowed me to do." She hugged herself again.

Felix nodded. "I'm grateful, too." He glanced at the bed and Bruce, who was asleep, resting comfortably. Felix tilted his head as he looked at him and smiled sweetly.

"We should leave you both to rest," I said as Silas entered the room and handed Felix a steaming mug. Felix took it, thanking Silas. "You know where there's more if you need it," I reminded him.

"I can bring you more if you want," Silas offered. "Just call out. I'm not going anywhere today."

Felix bowed his head. "Thank you, Silas. I'll rest and we'll talk about this attack when the sun goes down. I'm sure Marcus will want to know the details, and we need to get to the bottom of who those men were and who sent them, although I have a pretty good guess."

"I do too," I said. Now that Bruce was going to recover, I felt rage building at the thought that someone had attacked him, wanted him dead. It had to be Margaux, and I would make her pay. I shook off the thought and followed Sara and Silas as they left the bedroom, closing the door behind me.

Standing in the hall, with winter sunlight coming in through the window, felt surreal. I walked to the glass pane, halfway down the hall, and looked out. It overlooked the backyard and patio. I could see the bodies—and parts of bodies—of the three men. "I suppose we should do something about that," I said aloud.

"I suppose we should," Sara answered, and I started. I'd honestly forgotten that Sara and Silas were still in the hall behind me. I'd been so lost in thought about sunlight, about the attack, and Bruce.

I glanced back at the pair. "I don't think we should call the police," I admitted. It felt wrong, but also an acceptable way to handle things. How would we explain the deaths and the manner of the deaths?

Silas took a step forward. "I can take care of it," he said in his soothing, low tone. "You've been through a lot."

"Thanks, Silas. I appreciate it." I looked out the window again. "Sorry it got so messy," I said.

"You should see my wolf take down a rabbit. He's usually a pretty neat hunter, but something about rabbits ..." he trailed off, shaking his head.

I didn't want to think about that, or what lay in the yard out back. I glanced at Sara and then down at the sunlight on my bare arms. "So I guess we have some new developments to catch each other up on," I said, smiling at her.

"Um, I'm going to go find a shovel," Silas said, excusing himself.

Sara cocked her head at me. "How is this possible?"

"How is any of it possible? How do I sense what people are thinking? How does vampire blood heal people? How does Silas turn into a very large wolf? Why can you summon electricity?"

"True enough," she conceded. "Does the light make you feel tired? Drained, like Felix?"

"No. It stings my eyes, but oddly, it makes me feel more awake. Energized even."

"Well, in that case, let's let Bruce and Felix sleep and go downstairs to talk," she said. "I do have a lot to tell you." She grinned and turned toward the stairs.

33

SARA

Seeing my best friend step into our living room in the bright daylight for the first time was a magical moment. And being magical myself, that was high praise. I'd always lamented that she never saw the space, and our incredible view, in all its glory.

"Wow," Kate said, standing in the middle of the room, facing the triangular windows. The golden hue of the wooden beams overhead glowed in the light.

"It's pretty great. Right?" I replied.

"It is."

I watched her and realized not only did the warm wood of our home glow in the sunlight, but Kate did too. And not in like, "She's so happy, she's glowing," type of glow. Her skin had a luminescent quality to it. It was unlike anything I'd ever seen.

"Kate," I said, getting her attention. "How do you feel? You okay?"

"Yeah, like I said upstairs, I feel wonderful." She sighed and continued to gaze at the snowcapped mountains and the blue sky. Then she shook her head and joined me in the library area of the great room. She curled up in the chair in the corner, which had quickly become her spot. I took the one beside it, wrapping my robe around myself, trying to shake off the chill from being outside, even while wielding my gift. We had both stopped by the kitchen to wash up as best we could with warm water, but I was still freezing; whether from the winter air or shock, I didn't know.

"This is so unreal," she said, sounding a bit dazed. And I could understand why. Not only was the attack a great shock, but here she was in the middle of the day, bathed in sunlight. She sighed again and then seemed to come back to herself. Her face split into a grin as she focused on me. "So, you know about all my recent revelations," she said. "But the fact that Silas slept over means I have yet to hear all of yours."

I smiled and looked down. It didn't seem right to kiss and tell, but she was my best friend and a vampire; it's not like she didn't know what we'd been up to. I gave her the broad strokes. Yes, we'd slept together. Yes, it was amazing. No, we hadn't planned it. Yes, I hoped it wouldn't be a one-time thing.

"I came upstairs last night to see how your date went," Kate said, still grinning from ear to ear. "Felix mentioned that Silas was upstairs bonding you or somesuch."

"Bonding me? What are you talking about?"

Kate's smile slipped, and her brow dipped a fraction. "I don't know. It's just something Felix said. He said that shifters bond for life, and the first time a bonded pair has sex, they bite and mark each other." She looked at me with a cocked head. "Did he bite you? Did you bite him? I know it's personal, but a vampire wants to know."

"No," I replied. "I have no idea what you're talking about. There was no biting."

She shrugged. "Felix was probably misinformed. Or maybe it takes a while to bond or whatever."

"Yeah, maybe," I said, but I couldn't help wondering about shifter bonding and why it hadn't happened for us. I knew I wasn't a shifter, but given how intense things had gotten between Silas and me ... Maybe I was feeling a bit disappointed that he hadn't bonded with me, marked me. But that was silly. We had only just established our relationship.

Then I thought about what he'd said regarding shifters and casual sex. We had slept together. He'd said he loved me. He was willing to go that far. Perhaps he hadn't been able to bond with me because I was human. *Is he feeling regret?* I wondered. Was he sorry we'd slept together when he realized there would be no bond? Would he have a chance at a real bond if he found a shifter he was compatible with?

My thoughts were interrupted by Kate. "Sara?" Kate said for probably the third time.

"Yeah, sorry," I replied.

"Seriously, don't listen to a thing I said. I'm sure I misunderstood." She cocked her head a me again. "I'm so happy for you."

I couldn't keep the smile off my face. Regardless of whether we eventually bonded, I was deliriously happy. "Thanks. I've never felt this way, Kate." I took a deep breath. "I think I really, truly love him. I think I have for a while."

"I know," Kate said softly as she reached over to squeeze my hand. She beamed at me for a moment and then, in a playful tone, said, "But, if he's going to be staying over regularly, we've got to get you some soundproof walls. Or maybe me ... No. It should be your room. I want to be able to use the rest of the house without hearing you two."

I put my face in my hands. "Ugh, you're kidding?" I lifted my head and glanced at my best friend. The look on her face said she was absolutely not kidding. "Gross. I am so sorry. I thought we were being fairly quiet. Kate—"

She held up her hand. "Don't apologize. You were being quiet. It's not your fault." She tapped the side of her head. "Vampire ears, remember?"

I groaned again.

"Yeah, I could use less of that," Kate said with a smirk.

I shook my head. "Sorry."

I cast around for something else to say. I needed a change of subject before I died of embarrassment, and there was something I wanted to know. "Um, Kate?"

"Yeah?"

I got quiet. Maybe this wasn't the time, and I knew that the rest of the House would want to hear the details for themselves, but I needed to talk to my best friend. "Will you tell me what happened before I got outside?"

It was her turn to get quiet. She sat up straight and looked down at her hands in her lap. It wasn't until then that I noticed that there was blood on the knees of her sweats. Then she told me what she'd seen. And what she'd done.

I considered what I'd heard. "How do you feel? You killed a man."

"I know," she said with a remarkably steady voice. "That's just the thing. I feel regret, but only because I didn't get out there sooner." She took a deep breath. "I feel regret that I didn't get to kill the other two," she admitted.

It wasn't a complete shock. Was it something that my best friend of a year ago would have said?—No. But I still wasn't surprised. I glanced her way. She was watching me.

Waiting for my reaction, and I suspected that meant more to her than what she'd actually done.

"Kate, you're a vampire," I said. "You have a vampire's instincts and reactions now. You can't hold yourself to the same standard you did as a human ... or whatever you were."

"But how could I feel happy that three people are dead?" she pleaded.

"Because they deserved what they got," Silas said from the foyer as he came toward us. "You were defending your people and your territory." He stopped in the wide doorway and leaned against the jam. "You were raised like a human. Had you been raised a shifter, you wouldn't have thought twice about it."

"That's just it," Kate protested. "I didn't think twice about it. I just acted. You saw what I did out there."

He nodded. "You acted to save Bruce's life. Are you bothered by what Felix did?"

"No, but he's a ..." she paused.

"Vampire," Silas finished. "And so are you, mostly," he finished.

Kate didn't answer; she just gazed back at Silas as he regarded her. "Actually, I think it was your girlfriend who saved Bruce's life," Kate said, a small smile playing on her lips.

Silas ducked his head, and when he looked back up, his yellow gaze was on me. His smile was equally subtle but filled with something else entirely, warming my whole body through. "Yeah, she's amazing," he said in a husky tone.

"Agreed," Kate said, pulling me out of the moment. "I'm going to go wash up and go back to bed. I might be able to be up during the day, but I'm running on very little sleep at the moment."

I got up as she did, and Silas and I wished her a pleasant rest.

Then we were alone.

"Hey," I said, placing a hand on his chest as I looked up into his eyes once more. I'd touched him so many times in the last twelve hours, but I was still thrilled by the feel of him, by the hard muscle under my fingers. And he was mine. At least, I hoped so. My mind flicked back to my conversation with Kate about bonding, and suddenly, I wasn't as sure.

"What's the matter?" Silas asked, and I realized my gaze had drifted down to my hand, and I was frowning.

"Nothing," I assured him, smiling again. "Everything is great—more than great. Granted, shocking someone's heart and burying bodies isn't how I thought we would spend the day, but I'm happy."

"Good," he said, encircling me with his arms and pulling me close. "I'm not done outside, but I wanted to come in and check on you before I go."

"Go?" I asked, confused.

"Not far. I found a shovel and wheelbarrow and thought it would be better to dig the hole deeper into the forest, rather than right next to the house. It might take me a little while, though."

"Ah, yeah. That's probably a good idea, and I'm fine. I'm going to go shower, and I probably need to burn this robe," I said, thinking of the bloodstained cuffs.

He squeezed me tight and then let go. I stepped back. "I'm sorry you got caught up in this, Silas. I'm sorry you have to deal with this stuff."

He shook his head. "No. Don't be. I'm glad I was here to help."

"I'm glad too," I said. "Come find me when you're done? We could talk or ..."

His gaze heated, and he nodded. "I'll find you."

I gave a small wave and turned to head back upstairs. I could sense him watching me as I climbed, until I vanished down the hall and out of view.

Back in my room, I faced the tangled sheets and blankets from our long night together. I liked the mess. I liked remembering the things we'd done to make the mess. There was an ache between my thighs that served as an equally potent reminder. He was incredibly sweet, yet there was something wonderfully untamed about him at the same time. I couldn't get enough. I sincerely hoped what we had could last. I didn't like the thought that this was temporary. I didn't want it to ever end.

I sighed and stripped out of my clothes, tossing them into the far corner of my room, and went to the shower. I couldn't get Kate's explanation of shifter bonding out of my head, and I realized that I wanted that. I wanted him to want me like that, to mark me, to bite me. I wanted to know that he wanted this to last as well. I soaped up and let the warm water soak into my skin. But what if he couldn't? What if he never would? What if he belonged with someone else?

I shook my head. What was I doing? I had only been with him one night. How could I have become so attached after only one night?

Because I loved him.

I loved him with all that I was. And if this wasn't forever, it was only going to get worse with time. If we weren't trying for forever, I was in way over my head. We were going to have to talk, and soon.

34

BRUCE

I woke up with a gasp, clutching my chest. My hand met with smooth bare skin. There was no pain, and I realized I was lying in my bed. My memories of the attack were hazy, but I recalled Felix mentioning that I had a knife sticking out of my chest. He'd healed me; that was the only explanation.

I breathed in and out, taking stock. My body felt fine, good even. I remembered being stabbed in the shoulder, my arm going limp at my side. I moved the arm in question, and it felt as good as new. I didn't know how long I'd slept, but I was completely refreshed.

Sitting up, I reached for my phone. It was 8 p.m. I turned on the bedside lamp. It was time to get up; the whole House would be awake. Then the thought hit me. Felix and Kate had been outside during the attack or shortly after it. No, I couldn't be remembering that correctly. Maybe they'd brought me inside? I wasn't sure; my mind was still muddled.

I looked down at myself again. Not only were my chest and shoulder completely healed, but I was also clean. Felix not only repaired my body but also washed me and tucked me into bed. There were definite benefits to having a boyfriend with inhuman strength.

Pushing the covers back, I swung my legs over the side of the bed as the door opened. I wasn't surprised to see Felix in the doorway. "How are you feeling?" he asked, walking into the room and turning on the lamp by the dresser. I knew he didn't need the light and was doing it for my benefit.

"I'm good. Better than good," I said, stretching my arms over my head. Nothing felt stiff, nothing ached, which was new. Now, in my thirties, and after years of regular exercise, weightlifting, and sports, I was usually a stiff mess when I woke up.

I glanced over at Felix. "I see you shaved again," I said. "You know, I kinda like the beard."

He waved a hand. "It has its uses, but lately I prefer a cleanly shaven face." He studied me. "Are you sure you're feeling well?"

"Yes, I feel years younger, in fact," I said. Felix had his bottom lip between his teeth, holding back a smile as he looked down at the floor. "Does the way I feel have anything to do with the blood you gave me?" I asked.

"Most likely," he admitted.

"Should I be worried?"

"No. I know your opposition to turning. The amount of blood I gave you, and how I gave it to you, shouldn't change you."

"Shouldn't?"

"I doubt it."

"You doubt it? But you don't actually know?" I pressed.

He met my gaze, and his hazel eyes were troubled. "I've never turned anyone. But as far as I know, it would take more blood, by mouth, to accomplish the task. Don't worry.

There is very little risk you will be stuck with me for an eternity." His tone had gone from his usual jovial tone to something bordering on hurt.

"That's not what I meant," I said. "You know that's not why I object. It has nothing to do with you or our relationship."

"Oh, I'm well aware," he said, sounding wounded.

"Felix," I demanded. "Where is this coming from? We've had this conversation before, and my desire to remain human never bothered you."

He let his arms hang loosely at his sides and gazed up at the ceiling. "I'd never had to watch you die before." He glanced back at me, and there was a red sheen in his eyes.

I stood up and went to him, both to prove that I was fine and to comfort him. He let me hold him, wrapping his arms around me as I did. "I didn't mean to scare you," I said. "If it makes you feel better, I didn't like dying any more than you probably liked watching it."

He stiffened. "I didn't just watch you die. I couldn't prevent it. I tried everything I knew, but it wasn't enough. If Sara hadn't shown up and shocked your heart back into rhythm, you would be dead," he said with a shudder.

"It seems like a lot happened that I'm unaware of. I would like to hear the whole story. Especially the part about how you were out in the middle of the day trying to save my life." I pulled back to see his face.

There were tear stains on his cheeks, but also a crooked smile on his lips. "Everyone else is downstairs waiting for you to wake up. Why don't you get dressed and come down so we can all share what we know? I wasn't the only vampire tromping through the backyard in full daylight, you know?"

"Kate?"

Felix nodded.

"I thought I dreamed that part," I said.

"No. There is something very special about your House leader, and I'm determined to get to the bottom of it. But first things first. There have been some developments regarding Margaux, and I want to tell the entire House about them," he said. "Now, I'll go wash my face, and you get dressed. They're waiting." I wasn't sure I liked the sound of that, but I did want to know what had happened.

Less than ten minutes later, Felix and I walked into the living room where everyone was sitting around on the couches, waiting. Sara and Silas were curled up on one of the loveseats, while Kate and Marcus were on the large leather sofa. Marcus's face was a stony mask of worry, while Kate looked completely at ease. As soon as she saw me, she dashed over and nearly lifted me off the ground with the force of her hug.

"Bruce," she breathed. "I'm so glad you're okay." I squeaked a bit, unable to get a deep enough breath to reply, and she dropped my weight back on my feet. "Oh, sorry. Did I hurt you?" She looked so worried; it made me adore her even more. She was quite a vampire.

"No. I'm fine. I just needed some rest. How are you doing?" I asked, looking her over. She appeared no worse for her exposure to the sun. "I heard you were outside, in the day."

She pursed her lips but nodded. "Yeah, it was a surprise to me too," she sighed. "Not that I'm complaining. It was great to be in the sunshine. It's just confusing, is all."

"We're going to figure it out," Felix said from beside me. "Don't worry. There must be someone who has seen or heard of this before. Frankly, I'm shocked that I've never encountered a vampire like yourself before now. There is a place I'd like to explore. It would mean a quick trip over to Europe—no more than a week. But I may know where to search for answers. There have to be more creatures like you. You didn't come from nowhere." He glanced at me and then at the rest of the House, waiting patiently. "But in the meantime, everyone is waiting to hear what happened from you directly, and I have some news I thought I would share with the group," he said. "Shall we?"

As I walked deeper into the room, I caught Sara's gaze. "Thank you," I said, placing my hand on my heart and giving her a slight bow. She beamed a smile at me in return, and Silas squeezed her closer, placing a kiss on the top of her head. "Thank you" was hardly an adequate way to express how grateful I was to Sara for being there when she was and jumpstarting my heart, but it would have to do for now.

Kate reclaimed her seat, and I took one of the chairs beside the sofa, as Felix stood in front of the riverstone fireplace where no one would have to crane to see him. "First, Bruce, would you like to tell us what happened. Before we got there, I mean."

"It happened pretty fast," I said. "I was outside on the patio, taking some measurements for my project, when three men showed up. They were smart and stealthy. I didn't hear them, and by the time I noticed they were there, one of them was already between me and the open door. I fought with one. He managed to get me in the shoulder, but I was able to wrestle the knife from him and stab him in the neck." I shrugged. "The rest you saw. It was probably only a minute or two before you and Kate showed up."

Felix nodded, and then he and Kate took turns telling the story from their points of view. It was pretty much what I'd figured out on my own. Hearing the story from them didn't so much shock me as it did wear me out. This had all gone too far.

When Kate was done sharing her part, Felix picked up with his news. "After this afternoon's little incident, I made a call to Étienne," Felix said. "I informed him of what happened and took it upon myself to lay an accusation against Margaux. I accused her of sending her human employees to trespass on your House's property and attempt to kill one of your employees."

"House members," Kate corrected.

"House members. Yes, well, of course, he denied she had anything to do with it. He insisted that he had no idea who the men were or what brought them here. I was able, thanks to Silas, to produce their House IDs and tell him their names. After that, the conversation ended quickly." Felix clasped his hands in front of himself and continued. "He phoned back an hour later to say that Margaux is holding us accountable for the loss of her employees and wants to bring suit against the House of Ward for compensation."

Kate snorted. "They expect us to pay them for stopping a murder? That's ridiculous."

"Agreed," Felix said. "And I don't think she will be successful. However, it will require you, Kate, to make another appearance before the Council."

"Fine. I look forward to giving them a piece of my mind … again," she said, crossing her arms.

"I also reminded Étienne of his responsibility to keep the peace and uphold the law, not only as a House leader, but as the head of the Council. He assured me he didn't know of Margaux's plans and he would watch her more carefully in the future."

"I don't think that will be enough to hold her back indefinitely," Marcus said. It was the first time he'd spoken up since Felix started talking. I had to wonder what he felt about all this. Being in the employ of the Council, and as an enforcer no less.

"I also agree with you," Felix said. "And, I'm not willing to leave it to Étienne to ensure Bruce's safety."

"I think we would all agree with you on that," Kate said.

"I think I could get some people here in the next week or so to ward off more of the property," Sara said. "It's not perfect, but it would help."

"Thanks, Sara," Kate replied. "Until then, Bruce, I think you should stay in the house, behind the existing wards."

I considered her request. I agreed that it was a good decision, although I hated the idea of being on lockdown. I didn't want the Houses going to war over me, though. I also didn't want Felix to put himself at risk for my sake. It wasn't his responsibility to keep me safe. "For now," I replied finally. "But there is going to have to be some long-term solution. I can't hide in the house forever."

"You won't have to," Kate said. "I understand what it's like being on house arrest. We need some assurance that Margaux will leave Bruce and the rest of us alone. Like her death, for instance."

"I think I can do that," Felix said. "Through legal channels. It is my job, too, to uphold the law and try to find a better, more civil way for vampires to exist."

"Says the vampire who tore a man in half earlier today," Kate shot back.

I flinched at the revelation. In Felix's recounting, he stated that he eliminated the attacker. I had no idea it had been so violent.

Felix's protests interrupted my thoughts. "I was well within my rights to defend this property and its inhabitants against a threat while I was a guest. You have to remember we are talking vampire laws, not human ones, Kate."

She huffed out a breath but didn't reply.

"Is there a death penalty for vampires?" Sara asked.

"Of course there is," Marcus said. "But not for killing humans."

His words sent a thrill of dread through me. I had come to this House for protection, to escape Margaux and her harassment. But perhaps there wasn't a place where a human could hide from a vampire bent on destruction. I glanced at Felix, standing by the fire, his shoulder-length blond hair glowing from behind. I thought of him rushing into the sun to save me, risking himself and losing his carefully honed control to protect me. He could walk in the sun, though it took effort. I had never heard of a vampire that old; he had to be at least six or seven hundred years old. And he had put himself at risk for me. It was flattering, sure, but it wasn't right.

"You said Kate has to appear before the Council. When?" I asked.

"Not for ten days," Felix replied.

"I think we can expect that Étienne will be more mindful of Margaux, at least until then. And if I stay within the wards, I would be reasonably safe, especially now that we know Kate is okay with daylight. She would have no trouble if Margaux were to send more humans. And, I think I can assume that Silas will be sticking close by as well?" I asked, glancing in his direction.

"Absolutely. I will be staying here for the time being—if that's okay with you all. I plan to patrol regularly at night and during the day. My wolf insists."

I nodded. "I think that's more than enough protection," I said.

Felix cocked his head at me. "What are you saying?"

"I think you should go on that trip you mentioned. To get more information for Kate. Now might be the perfect time, before the repercussions hit. Before Kate has to visit the Council, and before Étienne loses interest in keeping an eye on Margaux."

"I think that should wait," Felix said, his brow dipping as he studied me. I was glad he wasn't the one who could read emotion, or he would know I was terrified for both of us. "There will be plenty of time for research when this is all over."

"We don't know when that will be," I protested. "And the more this House knows about Kate, what she is, and what she's capable of, the better off we will be as a whole. The better she will be able to defend herself and the rest of us. She didn't know until just hours ago that she could walk in the sun. What else doesn't she know about herself?"

"He has a point," Marcus said. "And, I've taken off the next couple of weeks to be around. I'll keep watch at night, and I have access to weapons and restraints that civilians don't. I know I could fend off Margaux if she were to show up."

I glanced at Kate. She was the one I needed to convince. If she shot down the idea, there was no way Felix would agree, and I needed him to leave town at least for a little while. She bit her lip. "I think Bruce is right. It would be good to know more about what I am. It could help us, and I won't let anything happen to Bruce. I promise."

Felix's jaw muscles flexed. He struggled to balance his need to protect me with his need for information. He glanced at Kate, then scanned the others in the room. Among them were three fierce protectors and one very capable witch, whom I credited with saving my life. I couldn't imagine a safer environment.

Felix nodded. "Okay, I'll leave tomorrow night. But I'm stopping by Étienne's to remind him of his responsibilities on the way. And to get something better to eat." He made a face that broke the tension in the room. "I don't know how you stand it, Kate, really."

It was settled. He would go to Europe, and I would ensure that these people were protected.

One way or another.

35

SILAS

Sara's curls brushed against my face as she turned her head to hear what Kate and Marcus were saying. The House meeting had been going on for some time, and while I was sure the details were important, all I could focus on was Sara sitting in the crook of my arm.

My fears about the vampires and the danger their world posed to the House had come true. The House had been attacked, and Bruce was nearly killed. My mate had been drenched in blood up to her elbows, and I'd spent two hours burying body parts in the forest. Yet, I'd never been happier in my life.

After I'd finished in the woods, cleaned the tools, and rinsed off with icy water in the yard, I went to find Sara. She was asleep, freshly showered and tucked into a newly made bed. I crept to the bathroom and took some time washing and scrubbing myself thoroughly. I didn't want any trace of the mess from the yard to linger on my skin or hair. I would not taint the place she slept with the horrors of the day.

Sleeping next to Sara was nearly as good as the sex. Being warm beside her and feeling her body against mine brought me as close to peace as I could imagine, and I slept there until she stirred, waking us both. We'd made love again ... and again, unable to be so close without reaching for each other. I'd heard talk of how the newly bonded were. I never expected to find that with Sara, but I had. I worried that it was just me, and I was careful to make sure that when I drew her to me, she wanted me just as much. So far, we'd both been unable to get our fill of each other.

As we sat there on the loveseat, with the voices of the others filling the room around us, she reached her hand toward mine and threaded our fingers together. I glanced down as she tilted her head up to meet my gaze. "You tired?" I asked.

She shook her head. "No. You?"

"No."

"Hey," Marcus said, getting our attention. "Before the two of you go to bed, let's talk about schedules over the next few days. It would be ideal to have someone on watch at all times. It's better to be over-cautious than caught off guard again."

I nodded. "Sure. I called my brother and cleared my work schedule. I told him I would be needed around here for the next week or so. My wolf can run a pretty solid perimeter. He can easily pick up both human and vampire scents."

"Good," Marcus replied. "I'll go over some of my UV equipment with you, if you like. I have a pair of restraints and a baton that might come in handy if you take a vampire on in human form."

"Honestly, if a strange vampire rolls up on the house, I'll be in wolf form. I'm faster and stronger on four legs."

"Understood. Sara?" Marcus asked. "Any interest in a UV baton?"

She held up her hand and let a considerable amount of electricity jump to life in her palm. "It's not sunlight, but it will knock a vampire on his ass."

My wolf growled at the thought of Sara having to use her magic against a vampire. Not that he was at all upset by the idea of one of them getting hurt, but he didn't want her to get that close to danger of any kind.

"Noted," Marcus replied with a smile. "I'll remember that. And I assume it works against non-vampires as well?"

"I expect it would be even more effective, although I haven't done it on purpose to a non-vampire before," she said, and I could hear a strained note in her voice. I dipped my head and buried my smile in her hair as I thought of the many jolts of electricity I'd received in the course of our lovemaking. She was getting better at controlling it, but honestly, I didn't mind so much.

Marcus turned his attention back to Kate, and I was about to suggest we find something to eat, when Bruce walked over. "Silas, if you're going to be around for the next few days, I could use your advice on my current project."

"Sure, I'd love to help if I could. I like the improvements you've made so far. The house looks great," I said and meant it. The upgrades he'd done were just what the place needed.

"Thanks," he said. "I've got no experience, however, with things like moving walls or upgrading existing doors. I have most of the materials on hand, but I could use an expert."

I glanced down at Sara, and she smiled encouragingly.

"Consider it done. I want to be able to contribute while I'm here, and I'm a halfway decent cook if you ever need a hand in the kitchen."

Bruce pressed his lips together, looking like he was holding back a smile. "That would be great. It's usually just me in the kitchen," he said, holding up a hand to stop Sara mid-protest. "Because I enjoy it. And if I'm cooking for myself, I might as well make a bit extra for Sara. But with more mouths to feed, it would be nice to have company. I'm also going to need someone willing to do the shopping until this all gets sorted out."

"You got it. Before I left home, I used to help cook for a large family of wolf shifters. My challenge will be scaling down, so we don't end up with enough food for an army. I was going to suggest that Sara and I find something to eat now. Are you hungry?" Bruce agreed that he could eat and offered to show me the new layout of the kitchen, so we left the vampires to their machinations and went in search of food.

The new kitchen was a significant improvement, and I thought about how much my mom would have loved to have something like this when she was feeding three growing male shifters. She would have envied the size of the fridge alone.

We prepared a simple meal of sandwiches with freshly sliced roast beef and all the fixings, along with a side salad for each of us. Working side by side with Bruce, I wondered if he noticed how quickly he was moving for a human. It wasn't a complete shock to me; the scent of vampire coming off him was strong, even for him. Once our plates were ready, he excused himself, saying that he would take his in his room, leaving Sara and me to eat alone at the small kitchen table.

The food was good, and the company was better. It felt right sitting there enjoying the simple act of sharing a meal. Several times, however, Sara glanced up at me as if she wanted to say something, but then went back to picking at her salad or finishing her sandwich. I didn't want to pry or rush her. If she wanted to tell me something, she would.

Finally, she set down her fork and spoke up. "Silas, I need to go see my family."

It wasn't what I was expecting, and it took me a minute to understand what she was asking. "And you don't want me to come along?"

She winced. "I really should go alone to talk to them."

I nodded in understanding, but my wolf stood up and shook his coat in my mind. He lowered his head, panting slightly. He was uncomfortable with her leaving the wards for any reason while we still didn't have a handle on the danger. "Are you going tonight?" I asked.

"No. I thought I'd see them tomorrow in the late morning, before the shop opens. It's been a while since I saw the two of them, and a lot has happened recently. They should know about the attack. I screwed up last time by not telling them about the meeting with James, and I regret it."

"Would you mind if I rode along, not all the way to the house, but close enough that my wolf can have a good run around nearby? He and I both want to check out your family's property line if it's okay, just to be sure."

"I think that would be great. I would appreciate knowing that they weren't also being targeted."

It was a relief. I couldn't say that I wouldn't have gone anyway. Once my wolf got an idea in his head, it could be very unpleasant to ignore him. I was feeling a bit overprotective myself. And, while I understood it, I was nervous that she needed to speak to her mom and aunt alone. Neither of them had been particularly welcoming toward me ever since my interest in Sara had become apparent. I couldn't blame them. If the witch community was anything like the shifters, you didn't date outside of your lane. I finally got up the courage to ask her what I really wanted to know. "Are you going to tell them about us?"

She looked thoughtful. "I honestly don't know," she admitted. "I will eventually, but I don't know if I can drop all the news on them at once." She chewed on her lower lip for a moment before adding, "Especially since it's all very new and we don't know where it will eventually lead." She swallowed and gazed down at the table in front of her.

I didn't know how to respond. I couldn't breathe. The logical part of my brain knew she wasn't saying she didn't want to be with me. She wasn't breaking up with me or telling me she planned to leave. But my heart still cried out that she considered a future where she wouldn't want to be with me anymore. I remained quiet. Blurting out that she was my mate and that I would never want anyone else was what instinct told me to do, but I had to remember that she wasn't a shifter. The only thing a declaration like that would do was scare her off.

"So," she continued. "I'll call my mom and make sure they're going to be around, and we can plan to leave sometime after breakfast."

I nodded mutely.

"Silas, are you okay?"

I glanced up into her soft brown eyes, so full of concern. I gave her a smile. "Yeah, I'm great," I said, trying to sound as normal as possible. Balance and time, I reminded myself. I couldn't rush her. I knew she cared about me. She'd told me she loved me.

But the darker, less optimistic part of me wondered for how long?

36

KATE

The meeting concluded, and all the happy couples were tucked away for the evening. Marcus and I were the only two left in the living room. I appreciated that he stayed home from work. It was nice to have the company and his was especially calming.

I was still rattled by the attack, although not for the reasons I expected. I wanted to head out into the night, hunt Margaux down, and take my vengeance. The rational part of my mind knew this was a terrible idea, and the only defense I had against her was my ability to push her emotionally, which probably wouldn't save me in hand-to-hand combat. But the vampire side of me craved revenge for what she'd done. Considering Felix's initial reaction, I was surprised he had chosen the diplomatic or legal approach. I had hoped he'd be carrying a pitchfork right alongside me. But since I was in the minority, I kept my mouth shut.

I stared at the flickering flames in the stone fireplace. Instead of comforting, they reminded me of destruction. I was feeling anxious, itchy, like I needed to move, to run, to fight.

"Hey," Marcus said, drawing my attention away from the fire. "You doing okay?"

I shook my head. "It's just not right. She should pay for what she's done. She shouldn't be able to hide behind laws that don't protect humans as anything other than property."

Marcus breathed in deeply before answering. "Vampires have been mostly concerned with protecting themselves from humans, not protecting humans from ourselves. The laws do say that there should be no intentional deaths of humans except in self-defense or defense of one's property, but they're not perfect. And she didn't try to kill him herself; she sent humans to do it for her. Technically, our laws don't apply to humans. Had they succeeded and gotten away, it would have been a matter for the human police to follow up, if it could be kept separate from the vampires involved, of course."

"And what great crimes have humans been perpetrating against vampires?" I asked, my tone coming out a bit more sarcastic than I'd intended.

Marcus bristled. "Fortunately, not many recently, but that is because we work hard to keep the human population in general ignorant of our existence. Most of my work involves violations of laws protecting our anonymity and disputes between vampires." He sounded defensive, and I felt a pang of guilt.

"I'm sorry. I know it's not your fault. You don't make the rules. I'm just pissed off at the whole situation."

Marcus nodded. "It's going to be a while before this is resolved. I'm sorry, but that's how these things work."

"And what is Bruce supposed to do in the meantime?"

I glanced at Marcus in time to see him wince. "He needs to do what you suggested and stay put. It's the only way we can keep him safe until you and Felix get this sorted with the Council."

"You work for them. Do you think there can be a solution where Bruce is safe from her?"

"Honestly?" he asked, raising his eyebrows. I knew it was probably rhetorical, but I nodded. "I've seen these things play out before. Usually, the more volatile of the vampires in a dispute will do something to cross the line, something rash, and the other meets them with equal violence until one of them is dead. Enforcers like me try to keep that from happening, but we aren't always successful."

"The more volatile," I mumbled.

"You're the younger vampire, but you're also a House leader. You have to do whatever you can not to lose your head and go after her. You must remain calm. Follow Felix's advice and handle this through legal channels. I know it doesn't seem fair, but if Margaux doesn't abide by the rules, let her be the one who oversteps or acts out and gets punished or killed in the process."

"As long as she keeps her hands off my people," I seethed.

"Your people," he said with a smile. "You sound like a real House leader."

"I am a real House leader, if that's what it's going to take to keep everyone safe."

"Good. But in the meantime, is there some way to keep calm? Maybe some art therapy," he suggested, which gave me an idea.

"I think I might have just the thing," I said, brightening. "Wait here, I want to show you something."

It only took a minute to grab the cloth-wrapped bundle from my dresser and return to the living room, where Marcus waited. I could have tested it out in my room, but I was nervous that it hadn't worked and wanted to share the discovery, whatever it was. Once I was back in my seat next to Marcus, I carefully unwrapped the locket and gazed down at its engraved surface. "I made this last night, but with everything going on, I hadn't thought about it until now."

"It's beautiful. Does it work?"

I shrugged. "I have no idea. I put into it what I was feeling at the time, so it was hard to check, and I haven't touched it since. Wanna be my guinea pig?"

"Is this one going to suck like the drawing?"

"I sincerely hope not," I said.

Marcus reached out and gently plucked the locket from the fabric. He paused, his eyes taking a faraway look. Finally, he smiled. "Yeah, it works," he breathed out. "It's incredible, Kate." He glanced at me, his steel-grey eyes softening, his posture relaxing. "This is how you felt last night?" he asked.

I swallowed and nodded. "Yes, I was thinking about all of you. The people who live under this roof, and those we love. I...feel so grateful for all of you, for the support and kindness." I glanced down, unable to hold his gaze. I was glad the thing worked, but I suddenly felt exposed. It was one thing to share my gratitude and love for my new family; it was another for them to feel exactly what I felt for them.

I jerked in surprise as Marcus took my hand in his. Through the connection, I felt the love and contentment from the night before, but I also felt the longing. I was about to pull away when he turned my hand over and dropped the locket into my palm. "You should hold onto that for a while," he said. "It's just what you need to calm your nerves and to remember what you've got to lose if you let yourself get out of control."

Had I not been incapable, I know I would have blushed

at his words. I felt chastened. He was right. I needed to keep my mind clear, and he was correct about the locket as well. The moment it touched my skin, a familiar warmth spread through my body, smothering my anger and frustration. I turned it over, considering, and then undid the clasp, hanging it around my neck. It felt heavy against my chest, a weighty reminder.

I placed my hand over it, holding it tighter against my skin, and glanced up at Marcus. "I'm sorry for how I acted in front of the Council. I'm sorry you ended up with a hotheaded leader who breaks necks and longs for violence. I didn't think that's who I'd be. And, frankly, it scares me."

He gazed at me intently and placed his hand on my knee. I noticed that my feelings didn't change at all with the added contact. "I know Felix said it before, but he's right. You're doing a brilliant job, and no one blames you for defending Bruce," he said, tilting his head. "Sure, you could have been a bit smoother in front of the other House leaders, but you were amazing with Margaux at the reception. No one expects this much control out of you. It's probably the very reason that Margaux dares to challenge you in the first place. She thinks you'll screw up. Don't prove her right. Keep Bruce safe and let her be the one to overstep. You've got this. And you've got all of us backing you."

My vision went pink, and tears spilled down my cheeks.

"Oh, hey," Marcus said, reaching up with the dark fabric of his sleeve to wipe them away. "I thought that thing was supposed to make you feel good."

I sniffed. "It does. I'm not sad. I'm just so thankful for what I have. Despite everything I've lost over the past months, I've gained a lot too." I let out a small laugh that sounded a lot like a hiccup. "And now I can go back out in the sun. I haven't had time to process all that just yet."

Marcus leaned back, smiling. "I'm jealous. I haven't seen the sun in over eighty years. I mean, I've seen pictures and movies, of course, but not real sunshine."

"How long do you think it will be before you can stand it again? Like Felix."

"I don't know," he said, pursing his lips while he thought it over. "Maybe another several hundred years before I can stay awake long enough or wake early enough for it to be an issue. And then maybe a few hundred more before I can spend any more than a few seconds outside. I don't know any vampire, besides Felix, who can be out for more than a minute." He paused, then asked, "How long would you say that Felix was outside with you and Bruce?"

I considered. It was hard to remember how much time passed while we were trying to save Bruce. It had all happened so quickly, and yet it felt like it had gone on for hours. "Probably ten minutes or less," I said.

Marcus raised his eyebrows but didn't respond.

"Don't you know how old he is?" I asked. Marcus had told me that they'd been friends for over fifty years; surely something like that would have come up in all that time, but vampires were strange when it came to age, I was learning.

"No. I have no idea. Old. Much older than me. That's all I know." He shook his head. "But you don't have to wait that long," he said, changing the subject. "Will you go out tomorrow, you think?"

"Yeah, I think I will," I said brightly. I don't know if it was the locket or the thought of going back out into the daylight, but I was giddy just thinking about it. "I wonder if I would tan."

"I seriously doubt it," Marcus said. "You're body still seems to heal like a vampire's, and Felix didn't. His body healed itself of the skin damage. Tan included."

"Too bad. I look pretty good with a tan," I said. "Plus, it would help me blend in with the humans."

Marcus stiffened and sat up straighter. "You aren't planning on going out among people, though, are you?"

"I don't know. I might, now that it's an option."

"I know we keep saying this, but you don't want other vampires to find out you're different, Kate. It could be very dangerous for you."

"How would other vampires know? They'll all be asleep."

He sighed. "Just be careful, please."

"I will be," I assured him. "And it's not like I'm planning a shopping trip to Seattle or anything. I just thought it might be nice to do something normal, like go to the grocery store, or the post office."

"The grocery store?" He asked. "You plan on eating human food again, too?"

I wrinkled my nose at the thought of what had happened last time I'd tried to eat food. It had been before my complete transition, but it had been a disaster. "Ugh, I don't know if I'm ready for that, but it would be good to be back out in the real world."

"The real world," he repeated softly. "Kate, that world isn't any more real than ours. It's the human world, and I'm not sure what you are now, but I know you're not human."

My fingers still clutched the locket to my chest, and I pressed harder. The love and gratitude had faded. I knew I wasn't human. I knew there was no going back, and I had come to terms with that. But somewhere in the back of my mind, I'd always thought there might be some way to be a part of the human world again. Being able to go out in the day was like a confirmation of that idea. A promise that I could regain some of what I'd lost. His words turned my stomach and filled me with a loss I had only felt the edges of until then.

I thought of my mom and my brother, and all the other people I was avoiding so that I didn't put them in danger. He was right. I couldn't get that back, not with the world the way it was.

I didn't feel that I fit into vampire society, and I wasn't a witch or a shifter. If I wasn't welcome back into the human world, I wasn't sure where that left me. Was I destined to be stateless? At home, only here with my House? I didn't want to be trapped, but I also saw the truth in Marcus's words.

I reached up and unclasped the locket and let it fall into my waiting hand.

"Why did you take that off?" Marcus asked.

"I think I broke it," I said, holding it out and dropping it into his palm.

His body jerked. He reached over and placed the locket on the coffee table, then looked up at me with haunted eyes. "I'm sorry," he said.

"Don't be," I said. "It's not your fault. I'll make another one. Or try to fix that one when I'm feeling up to it."

He nodded. "Go out tomorrow. You never know. Order a coffee. Get an ice cream. You're unique. Maybe you do still belong out there."

I tried to offer him a smile. "Maybe," I said, but inside I felt bereft. There had to be a place for those of us who didn't fit. Things had to change.

37

SARA

S ilas and I spent another long night in bed with very little sleep. As a result, we didn't wake up from our last nap until around ten in the morning. I didn't mind. My days still started late and ended late, and I felt no guilt about sleeping in. However, it did leave us rushing around to get showered, dressed, and fed before leaving the house around eleven. I wanted to have plenty of time to talk to my mom and aunt and still be back at the shop by one to meet Beth.

My Toyota Corolla knew the way back to my family home like it had never left. Silas and I spoke very little as I drove. My anxiety was steadily building with each passing minute. I stopped just short of the ten-minute drive, in a spot off the road, sheltered by trees.

The door squeaked loudly in protest as Silas got out. "Do you mind taking my clothes back to your place?" he asked. "I'm going to let my wolf run after we do a security loop of your family's place. I'll meet you back at your house after."

I nodded and swallowed hard as he began to strip off his shirt. I'd just seen him completely naked not an hour before, but I couldn't tear my eyes away as he revealed more and more skin. He was about to tug down his jeans when he caught me watching him and paused. "You have to stop looking at me like that or you're not going to make it to your mom's house," he said.

His tone was playful, but his voice was pitched so low it made my blood warm and my fingers itch to touch the chiseled muscles of his bare stomach. I shook my head. "Nope, I'm here for the show," I said. "I know you shifters don't have an issue with nudity. Why are you suddenly so shy?"

"Not shy," he growled. "Interested." He finished undressing, and he was indeed interested.

I glanced at my watch to see if there was enough time to delay for a bit of fun, but there wasn't. "Later, I promise," I said and gave him a wink as he folded his clothes and tucked them into the back seat so they would be less obvious if someone happened to glance in. Then his massive body began to shake as he crouched, placing one hand on the ground. I couldn't pinpoint the moment when the change occurred. But it was all at once, and there stood, on all fours, Silas's oversized wolf.

He was beautiful. My feelings shifted instantly from heated wanting to awe. I'd seen the wolf before, of course, but never in a setting with just the two of us. He had always been on a mission, running off or toward me, never simply standing still. I opened my door and climbed out, determined to get closer.

He didn't move as I circled the car until we stood no more than a few feet apart. He was colored like a classic wolf, with shades that ranged from white to gray to black, and was tinged with russet brown on his nose, ears, and chest. Absolutely breathtaking.

I extended my hand like one would to a strange dog, and

he huffed, closing the distance between us, butting my arm with his enormous head. I brought up both hands and sank my fingers into the thick fur around his neck. He was unbelievably soft. Leaning down, I rubbed the side of his head with my own; it felt like the right thing to do. He pressed back against me gently. "Be careful and stay out of sight," I whispered.

He huffed again, sounding much like a scoff. I released him and ran my hand over his face and ear before he turned and dashed into the woods. I knew it wasn't truly Silas. I understood that the wolf was a distinct being, yet they were intertwined, and I felt that connection when the wolf gazed at me with his bright yellow eyes. I sensed that he approved of me and wanted me around, and a tension I hadn't realized I was holding onto fell away as I watched him disappear into the forest.

After brushing off as many wolf hairs as I could, I got back behind the wheel of my car, driving the final half mile to the house. I pulled into my family's driveway moments later. I cut the engine and stared up at the beautiful mix of Craftsman and Victorian architecture, which my grandparents had built when my mom and aunt were just little girls. I had lived there for eight years, since the end of high school, when my mother and I moved in to help with the business. A lot had changed since then. We'd relocated the business, I was the only one still working there full-time, and I no longer lived under this roof.

I glanced toward the underbrush as I walked up the steps to the front door, searching for a flash of yellow eyes among the evergreens, but of course, saw nothing. I don't know why I chose the front door. I had almost never entered this way during the entire time I lived here, but going around to the kitchen felt wrong somehow. I didn't live here anymore; I was visiting as a guest. The thought saddened me, yet filled me with a sense of pride. I suppose that was what growing up felt like.

My feet were strangely heavy as I climbed the familiar porch steps. I considered knocking on the door, but that felt too formal, so I reached for the knob and twisted it. The wards remembered me, but there was a bit of extra bite across my skin as I stepped into the house, as if the wards knew I had changed, that I wasn't quite the woman who had walked out the door weeks ago. And they were right. I wondered how much I could change before they refused to admit me altogether, and I would have to ask to be pulled across like some stranger. I shook off the thought.

"Hello," I called out, shedding my coat and hanging it on the tree in the hallway. I heard my mother's answering call from the living room and went to join her. She stood as I walked in and wrapped me in a hug. My mother, Sybil Heartwood, was just as she always was. Wearing a tan linen dress and her green apron tied snugly around her middle, she was warm and soft, and smelled of plants, earth, bergamot, and oranges. She pulled back to look at me, and I took in the grey-threaded bun on the top of her head and her deep brown eyes. "Hi, Mom."

"Hello, my darling," she cooed. "It's so good to see you."

"You act as if it's been months, not a week, since I last saw you," I chuckled. "The new sage is a big hit, by the way. Very fragrant and holds together well."

She nodded. "Of course, I told you it would be." She smiled, and the creases around her kind eyes made me long for simpler days, free from attacks, crises, and worries about the future. But then, had such a time ever truly existed? I had to think back quite a way to remember a time without any concerns, perhaps when I was a child.

"Where's Aunt Lucia?" I asked.

"Oh, she's cooling down a batch of her latest with a wort chiller in the kitchen. She probably has her earbuds in." My mother leaned in conspiratorially. "She says she's listening to travel books, but I think they're romances." She covered her mouth and gave a small laugh.

"Well, she's in good company," I said, giving her a wink.

The two of us went to the kitchen to find Aunt Lucia standing by the sink, water running through the chiller, and paying no attention whatsoever. She was staring off into space, eyes narrowed as she listened to whatever was playing through her earbuds.

"Hey," I said, grasping her elbow to get her attention.

She let out a shriek and clutched her hand to her chest, her round eyes meeting mine. I couldn't keep the smile off my face as she removed her earbuds and dropped them into a pocket, quickly composing herself.

"That good, huh?" I asked.

"Yes. It's a very nice piece on the islands in the Mediterranean," she said with a sniff. She turned off the tap, quieting the splash of the overflowing water. "I'm done here for now. Shall we sit? Your mother said you wanted to talk."

Right to the point, that was my aunt, and one of the reasons I loved her. "Yup, that sounds great," I said, swallowing down the lump in my throat. I pulled out a chair and noticed, with a feeling of warmth, that we instinctively took our usual seats. The same places we'd each sat while sharing countless meals around this table. It was reassuring to see that some things hadn't changed, and it relaxed me a bit.

"I wanted to update you on some things that have been going on at the house," I said. House with a lower case H, in this case, since neither woman knew about Kate's House as of yet. "There was an attack," I said.

"Vampires?" my aunt asked, her tone implying that the question was rhetorical.

"Is everyone okay?" my mother asked at the same time.

"Yes, everyone is okay, and no, it was humans," I said, and then grudgingly added, "Sent by vampires."

My aunt nodded smugly.

I ignored her. "Our new housemate, Bruce, whom you've met at the shop, has been targeted," I explained.

"Housemate?" my mother asked, and I realized I'd never told them about his moving in. "Is he a particular friend of Kate's? Or yours?" she asked with a raised eyebrow.

"No, he has another particular friend," I said. "But there is a vampire who wishes him harm. It's a long story, but she's a real piece of work and not easily dissuaded. So, we are all on alert for now, and I wanted to let you both know. It would be good to keep an eye out. Note anything unusual and let us know."

"What about these humans? Do you think they'll return?" my aunt asked.

"No. They were ... dealt with," I admitted.

"Oh, Sara," my mother said. "What happened?"

I sketched the picture for them, avoiding any unnecessary details. I mentioned that Kate had acquired a new skill and was immune to the sun's rays. I also shared how I had shocked Bruce's heart back to rhythm with my gift. I left out the part about Felix and skipped over Silas's involvement.

My mother beamed at me while my aunt gave me a small smile. They were proud, and I felt pretty proud of myself. It wasn't every day we got to use our gifts to save a life directly, and it felt good.

"I didn't know you knew how to do that," my mother said.

"I didn't," I replied. "It was a gamble, but there was nothing else to be done. I couldn't let him die."

My aunt nodded. "And the bodies of the would-be murderers?" Lucia asked, ever the practical one.

"Gone and buried."

"Good," she said. "And what is to be done about the vampire who started this whole thing?"

"That's more complicated, but Kate is seeking a legal solution. For now, Bruce is staying behind the wards, and I wanted to see if I could enlist you both to find me another Air Witch to help extend them farther around the property."

"Of course," my aunt said dismissively. "They'll be there tomorrow at the latest." Once again, she was stepping into her role as head of our family, the one who got things done when we needed them. Our matriarch.

"And," I hedged. "After all this is over, it would be great to see more of you two around the shop. I know it's a change, but I miss you both."

My aunt sighed, but my mother looked thoughtful. I wasn't surprised when she was the one who answered. I was surprised, however, at what she said.

"I know we've been hands-off lately, absent," she said. "But we felt it was important to let you lead now, take charge of the business. And you have; you've made it your own." She leaned forward, placing her arms on the table. "It took the ... incident," she said, carefully avoiding the word abduction. "And you moving out, for us to see how much we were holding you back. You deserve your own life. We haven't meant to leave you lonely or shorthanded."

"I thought this was about the vampires, and about my not telling you before I went after Kate and James," I said.

My aunt shook her head. "We aren't keeping away because we're scared of vampires," she scoffed. "Or because of some grudge. We're not that petty. We were trying to do you a favor." She leaned back and crossed her arms.

"Does Kate think we're staying away because of her?" my mother asked. There was a look of real worry on her face.

"Well, kinda," I admitted.

"That's just terrible," she said. "I can't believe either of you would think that."

I sighed. "We didn't know what else to think because you never talked to us about it. It's been a recurring theme with the two of you. My whole life, you've held things back. About the vampires, about what you're thinking, about shifters," I added.

At the mention of shifters, Lucia lifted her head sharply. "Is Silas still coming around your place?" she asked. Her tone was level, but the question was pointed.

"The repairs to the house are mostly finished. He's not been around as much over the past couple of weeks," I said, feeling like a total hypocrite. I had just accused them of not being forthcoming, and here I was leaving out a significant detail. I needed more information, however, and if this was a way to get it, I was going to play my cards close to my vest. "What did you have against him anyway? Were you worried that a shifter wouldn't be an appropriate choice for me?"

"It was never really about that," my mother said, sounding tired. "It was about the bonding."

At the mention of bonding, my ears perked up. This was something they'd never mentioned before, the very thing Kate was trying to explain.

"I don't know what you mean," I said, trying to draw her out without sounding too eager.

"We were worried that if Silas spent too much time

around you, he'd bond. In the way shifters do," my aunt explained, as if I should know all about it. "And if you, like many young women, changed your mind, he would be left without his mate. Forever."

"It wasn't that we didn't want him for *you*," my mother said, her brown eyes full of compassion. "We never wanted that for *him*."

38

BRUCE

Felix was asleep in what I had come to think of as our bed. Like all vampires, except perhaps Kate, he looked dead when he slept. He didn't breathe or move. His body was as cold as the air around him. But even in his false death, he was beautiful.

I gazed down at his relaxed face, his beard almost fully grown out, as it did each night, his blond hair splayed across the pillow. Beautiful and older than he seemed. It made more sense now why he wasn't bothered by sleeping in a room without shutters, with only blackout curtains between him and the daylight. I had never expected to meet, let alone sleep with, a vampire old enough to walk in the sun. I shook my head as I closed the bedroom door behind me and slipped downstairs.

Felix was scheduled to leave in the evening, and until then, I needed to act as if everything were normal. I knew he would disagree with my plan to keep everyone safe, which is why I hadn't mentioned it to him. Once he was on a plane over the Arctic, there would be nothing he could do about it. I believed that Kate, Marcus, Sara, and Silas would fight to defend me if Margaux or any of her henchmen showed up, but I didn't want them to have to. While Felix seemed to believe that Étienne would keep Margaux in check, I knew her. I understood what she was capable of and what lengths she would go to if she didn't get her way. I didn't want anyone to get hurt because of her or because of me.

I glanced at my watch. It was nearly one in the afternoon. With Felix and Marcus asleep, Kate was "on duty" for the day until Silas and Sara returned from their errand. Marcus had ensured that everyone was on the schedule and that all slots were filled to keep me safe. I found Kate in the living room, curled up in one of the reading chairs.

"Hey, how's the book?" I asked as I entered the room, trying to keep my pace slow and steady.

"Oh, hi," she said, smiling up from the pages of what appeared to be yet another fantasy romance, judging by the cover.

"Dragons still?"

"Yup. I figure if I get far enough ahead in the series, then Felix won't be able to spoil it for me. Sara said he hasn't read past this one," she said, holding up the thick tome.

I smiled back. I didn't have the heart to tell her that Felix had snatched all the volumes off the shelf two days ago and read them while Kate was in her room and Sara was busy with Silas. It had only taken him a couple of hours to get through all four of the remaining books.

"Well, don't let me bother you," I said and turned for the kitchen.

"Bruce," Kate called after me. "You aren't bothering me. Did you want something?" She pushed herself forward to disentangle from the nest she'd made, but I waved her back down.

"No, no. I just stopped in to say 'Hi'. I'm going to grab

some food, and when Silas gets back, I'll be downstairs working."

She gave a small wave goodbye, and I hurried to the kitchen, hoping she wouldn't follow me. It wasn't that I didn't appreciate her company; I just wanted her and the others to get comfortable with me being out of sight. Everywhere I had gone since waking the night before, I'd felt eyes on me. It was understandable, but I didn't want anyone trailing me today. I hadn't lied; I did plan to work on the special project for most of the day. I aimed to complete the bulk of it and walk Silas through the rest of my plans. I wouldn't tell him that I might not be around to finish with him, but I wanted to see it through as much as possible.

Another sandwich sounded good, so I made it to go, wrapping it in wax paper and grabbing a bottle of water from the fridge. I headed to the shop first to log in and check on the financials I had been working on. There had been a significant increase in traffic on Sara's site since the new advertising launched. I wanted to be there when Beth arrived to ensure everything was running smoothly.

The shop was empty, so I made myself at home in the office to have lunch and catch up on work. I finished my sandwich about the time I heard a car door shut outside. Opening the shop door, I was greeted by Arrow. She whined and wagged her tail in greeting.

I spotted Beth over the top of the Subaru as she closed the hatch, but before she could come back around the car, Arrow's head whipped toward the forest. She let out a low growl and darted into the treeline at full speed. I was so shocked that I didn't have time to think about what might have startled her.

A flash of movement caught my attention just as Beth began to yell for Arrow. Kate had heard the commotion and stood on the front porch. Although she wore her usual jeans and baggy knit sweater, she looked ferocious. Her face was set in a snarl, and her eyes narrowed on the forest where Arrow had disappeared. Her long, dark hair, lifted by the wind, blew out behind her as she crouched, ready to run or fight. Her skin absolutely glowed in the overcast daylight.

Beth was halfway across the clearing when Kate spotted her. "Stop!" Kate yelled and launched herself off the porch vampire-fast to come to stand between Beth and the forest.

Beth's face was a mask of confusion and fear. "Kate? What the hell?" Beth glanced back at me, needing confirmation that she wasn't seeing things. By this time, I stood only a few feet away. If whatever was coming out of the woods was meant for me, I wouldn't let Kate and Beth face it alone. I nodded to Beth, and we all turned to see a large form move from the shadows of the trees and into full view.

Immediately, Kate and I relaxed, although Beth squeaked in alarm. Silas—because it had to be Silas—stood on the edge of the forest in wolf form with Arrow happily running circles around him, trying to lick at his muzzle with each pass.

"Arrow!" Beth screamed. "Come! Oh, my God. What do we do?" Beth grabbed onto Kate's shoulders, digging in her fingertips with panic.

Kate reached up and patted one of her hands. "It's okay," she said and then called out to the wolf. "I'm going to tell Sara you were kissing another girl," she said. The wolf snorted and lifted his head out of Arrow's reach for the dozenth time.

Beth looked at me, eyes wide. "It's Slias," I told her. "He's a shifter." I shrugged. I'd never seen his wolf before, and I couldn't blame Beth for freaking out. He was huge, not just huge, he was enormous. Next to him, her full-grown German Shepherd looked like a scrawny adolescent.

"I'll assume you're back and on patrol," Kate said. "I'm going to go get some sleep." The wolf huffed in what could be interpreted as an affirmative.

Kate turned and grinned at Beth. "Pretty cool, huh?"

Beth just nodded, eyes still wide and mouth hanging slightly open.

"Well, you guys have a good day," Kate continued. "Bruce, say goodbye to Felix for me, and please get back into the main house and behind the wards."

I winced. I hadn't considered when I'd gone to the shop that it was unwarded. But of course it was. It would be challenging to run a business if no one could step inside. I nodded. "Will do."

Kate patted Beth's shoulder before going back inside. Silas trotted past us, allowing a still-shocked Beth to grab hold of Arrow's collar. Then he locked eyes with me for a beat and took off again for the trees.

"Sara should be back any minute, but why don't you and Arrow follow me back to the main house, and I'll fill you in on what's been going on?" I suggested.

"I think you'd better," Beth said a little shakily.

And I did. I told her everything except for Felix's involvement in my resurrection. Kate had already outed herself as a day-walker, and Silas had shown up in fur, so those felt like safe topics. However, it wasn't my place to reveal that Felix was old enough to move about during the day. I hoped we hadn't made enough noise to wake him from his sleep.

Beth took it all in stride. I told her about the deaths of the humans who'd come after me. I warned her that there might be some spots on the back patio and in the woods that would be of particular interest to Arrow, and she might want to keep her on a leash while outside. I expected her to have a moral objection to the deaths, but she set her jaw and nodded.

By the time I was done, Sara had returned, and Beth followed her back to the shop, bombarding her with questions about Silas and shifters. I smiled as I watched them go. It would be a miracle if Sara could steer the conversation back to business anytime soon.

I finally got down to the main task of the day: my special project. All the furniture and decorations were already on site, but I made some significant changes after discovering that Kate could tolerate daylight. I rushed-ordered a solid wood door blank, which would be arriving any moment. There was plenty of framing material, drywall, tape, mud, primer, and paint left over from earlier projects for the wall I wanted to install. I also decided to keep the original glass patio doors and had a landscape crew coming over at two to finish the outside. There was a lot to accomplish.

Silas returned from his run around the property—in human form and fully dressed—at the same time as the landscapers, and I walked everyone through my plans for the back of the house. It was the first time I'd been out on the patio since the attack, and I was glad to have Silas by my side and a task to focus on. There would probably never be a day when I could step out that door and not think about what had happened. But the space I was creating wasn't for me. It was for Kate, and I wanted it to be just right, so I set aside my discomfort and concentrated on what needed to be done.

By the time the sun set, I was covered in sweat and sawdust, and feeling much steadier about my project as well as my final tasks for the evening. I left Silas bent over the router, finishing the work on the door, and headed upstairs to clean up.

When I returned to my room, Felix was awake and packing. I hadn't realized how many articles of clothing he'd stashed away in my wardrobe over the past few weeks, but it was enough to fill a vintage leather carry-on bag.

"When do you expect to return?" I asked as I stripped out of my filthy clothing and headed to the shower.

Felix watched me with hooded eyes but continued filling his bag. "Probably four or five days," he replied. "I don't want to leave you too long."

"Don't worry about me. I'm perfectly safe here. Just do what you need to and come home," I said as the water began to warm up. I stepped into the glass enclosure and was about to pull it shut behind me when Felix's hand caught the edge of the glass. I quirked a smile at him. In the time it took me to step into the shower, he had shed all his clothing to follow me inside.

"Home?" he growled. His tone was low but not upset.

I let the water run through my hair, ignoring the naked, wet vampire, with his hands on my chest. "Um hmm," I said. "If you want. I like having you here. Just because I don't want to be a vampire doesn't mean I don't want to be with you." I reached for the shampoo, but he caught my wrist, stopping me.

"You want me to stay here? After we've sorted things with Margaux?" He took a half-step closer, leaning his face down to mine.

"Yes," I said, leaning in and nipping at his lower lip. "But please let's not bring her in here with us?"

He growled again, wrapping his free arm around me and pulling me against him. We didn't leave the shower, much less the bedroom, until it was time for him to head to the airport.

"May I take your car? I could always call for a ride, but this way's easier." Felix said as we descended the staircase to the main floor. I'd noticed he hadn't brought his Jeep and had anticipated his request. I saw it for what it was: a test to see if I'd stay put while he was gone. I pulled the keys from my pocket, already detached from the others on my keychain.

I dropped them into his palm. "Of course. I figured you would, since I won't be using it until you get back," I said pleasantly. He nodded and pocketed the keys, but gave me a searching look.

I didn't walk him to the porch; I just said goodbye from the foyer. He gave me a tight hug, a lingering kiss, and then he was gone. I hoped it wouldn't be the last time I saw him. I was counting on his skill as a lawyer, along with his affection for me, to help me when the time came. However, I was gambling on too many variables to be certain it would all work out as planned.

I asked Felix which airline he was flying. It would be nice to know when he'd be airborne and out of communication. He explained with a chagrined smile that he had connections and was taking a private plane to avoid any complications or a daylight layover. But he told me what time he should arrive in Oslo and assured me he'd text. I figured I had two hours before his flight took off. He was cutting it close, but I guess that was another perk of flying on a private jet.

Two hours felt like an eternity while waiting to act. I decided to tidy up the house and ensure everything was running smoothly. There was very little for me to do, and I ended up back in my room, contemplating whether I should pack my own bag. Ultimately, I decided that sneaking out of the house with a packed suitcase would be too difficult, and it wasn't worth the effort.

As I crept back down the stairs, the two-hour window was closing, and I took stock of where everyone was. Silas was still down working on the project, Kate was asleep in her room, and Sara had taken the late dinner I'd made out to the shop for her and Beth. The only person I hadn't accounted for was Marcus, who was sitting in the living room watching television, with a clear view of the foyer if he bothered to look. This was going to be more difficult than I expected.

Entering the living room, I did my best to act normal. I greeted Marcus and let him know that I was turning in early, as I was still tired from the day before and the healing that had taken place. He wished me a good night, and I trudged back upstairs, feigning exhaustion.

In reality, I felt wonderful. I'd worked my body hard all day, and despite that, and the exercise in the shower, I was full of energy. I'd felt this way ever since waking with traces of Felix's blood in my system. Felix assured me the effects would fade and I would be back to my usual achy self soon, but for the moment, it was an added tool in my toolbox.

I got to my room and went to the window. I cracked it open and could hear the router going below. That was good. It was just enough noise to mask what I intended to do. I glanced down to the patio two stories below and then pulled back and shut the window tight, drawing the curtains as I usually did before sleep. Then I slipped out of my room and into the guest room across the hall.

Going to this room's window, I unlatched it and pushed

it up as far as it would go. Peering down over the sill, I was glad to see that the landscapers hadn't left any equipment directly below and that, as expected, the drop was half what it was on the other side of the house since I was no longer over the walk-out part of the basement. Taking a deep breath and praying that I wasn't overestimating the new limits of my body, I swung my legs over and, before I could consider what I was doing, I pushed off and dropped to the ground below.

The landing was surprisingly easy. My knees ached a bit when I hit the ground, but I was unharmed. I'd probably pay for it later, but I didn't have time to stop and regret my decision. I pulled out my cell phone and tapped on the ride-share app. The car was nearly at the pickup point. I skirted the light from the house, sticking to the darkness of the trees, and moving much faster than I should have been able to.

I made it to the car just in time and thanked the driver for agreeing to meet on the abandoned sideroad in the middle of nowhere. It wasn't until we were on the highway heading for Seattle that I breathed easier. I wasn't sure if it would work, but at least I knew that at that point, there was no one to stop me.

The drive took over an hour. My racing heart calmed considerably throughout the drive, but as I left the car and approached the front doors of my destination, my stomach flipped. Getting inside was no problem. I explained who I was there to see, showed my ID, and was allowed upstairs with very little discussion.

As I stepped forward toward the familiar female vampire, my anxiety spiked. There was no going back.

"Hello, Bruce," she said, giving me a fangy smile. "It's so good to see you again."

I swallowed hard. "You as well," I forced myself to say.

She quirked an eyebrow at me. "But I'm a little confused as to why you're here?" she said.

I looked at E and sighed. "I would like to be taken into protective custody."

39

KATE

Noise from the foyer told me Sara was on her way downstairs. My vampire ears had no trouble picking out her lighter steps from those of my other housemates. I'd taken over from Marcus just before sunrise. It was now almost noon, and I was getting desperate for company.

"Hey, Kate," Sara greeted me, coming over to where I was working on the third novel in the dragon series.

"What, no Silas?" I set my book aside.

"No. I went up to bed around two, but he was still downstairs at work. I have no idea what time he came to bed. I thought it best to let him sleep. Unless you need to rest?" she said. "He would prefer someone with better ears than mine to be on duty at all times."

"Nah, I'm good." I climbed out of my chair. "Can I join you for breakfast or lunch? I wanted to talk to you about the locket."

She eagerly accepted, and I filled her in on my creation of the locket and subsequent re-forming of it. "So, I'm not sure I need to do the actual art, or if I just need to hold onto something. It will take some experimentation, I think."

Sara nodded and poured herself a cup of coffee from the fancy coffee maker. I leaned in and took a whiff of the fragrant steam coming from her mug.

Sara looked up at me with a bland expression. "Does it smell okay?"

I sighed. "Yeah, it smells fine, just not appetizing."

"Did you expect it to?"

"I'd hoped that because I'm different from normal vampires in other ways, maybe I could still eat food. I really miss coffee," I admitted. "Or at least, my memory of coffee."

"Want a sip? Just to be sure?" She held the mug out, her eyebrows raised.

I reached for the coffee and noticed how the piping-hot ceramic mug felt extremely uncomfortable. I was still getting used to the way my body felt—but didn't react to—temperature shifts. There was pain, but it was tolerable.

I brought the rim to my lips and stifled a grimace as I took a small sip of the dark liquid. It didn't smell remotely good to me. And, unfortunately, it tasted even worse. I shoved the mug back into Sara's hands and turned and spat the coffee into the sink. I ran the water and tried to rinse out my mouth, but the whole inside felt coated with the stuff.

"That bad, huh?" I turned to see Sara leaning against the counter, sipping from the mug. "It's too bad, Bruce orders really good coffee."

I groaned and went to the fridge. There was only one thing that would get the taste out of my mouth. I popped the bag in the microwave for a few seconds to take the chill off and then poured it into a mug of my own. "I guess I'm stuck with this," I said, raising my mug in Sara's direction.

"Ugh, sorry," she replied.

"Don't be. It tastes great to me. You can keep your bean water." I smirked at her.

"Will do." She took another sip of coffee. "So what happened to the locket? Is it ruined, do you think?"

I pulled at the neck of my sweater so she could see the locket dangling from the chain around my neck. "No, it's fine. I re-worked it as close as I could to the original emotion. I've found it helpful for me to wear it. It's been keeping my spirits up."

"It's a good idea," Sara said. "Like setting an emotional intention for yourself. Nice."

"It was Marcus's idea," I reached up and unclasped the locket, and held it out for Sara. As soon as I touched only the chain, the warm glow of love and happiness I'd felt all morning dimmed a bit.

Sara took the locket in her palm and stared down at it for a few moments. "I hate to tell you this, Kate, but I don't think it's working."

"No, it works just fine. I suspect that the tone of the locket just matches what you're already feeling too closely."

"What am I supposed to be feeling?"

I smiled broadly at her. "Love, happiness."

Her answering smile was warm and bright. "Yeah, I think you're right," she said and handed the locket back. "But how am I going to sell it if you're wearing the thing? I don't want to take it away from you if it's helping." She tilted her head. "Feel like making another?"

"Yeah, I could do that."

"Great, I've had my eye on a pocket watch with plenty of room for embellishments. I could probably have it here in a couple of days."

I nodded. "Sounds great," I said. I pulled out my phone and checked the time. "Do you know what time Bruce went to bed last night? I wanted to see how his project was coming along and how he was feeling."

Sara shook her head. "No. He was in bed when I went up. I chatted with Marcus. He said Bruce was feeling tired and went to bed early."

It was just past noon, but that was still a lot of sleep if he'd gone to bed long before Sara. I hoped he was okay. He'd been through a lot. *Maybe I should check on him?* I thought.

I'd learned over the past few months to dampen my senses to give my housemates privacy and keep myself sane. It had not been easy lately, with so many people in the house and their various … activities. But I'd improved significantly at it.

I knew I should allow Bruce his privacy. Still, I felt responsible and knew that if anything happened to him, not only would I never forgive myself, but Felix would probably kill me, so I concentrated on seeing if I could hear his heart in its normal steady rhythm. A slow rhythm would mean he was still asleep; a faster one, and he was awake. Too fast, and he might be sick or injured.

I strained and heard the slow, steady thump of two hearts. One was Sara, standing before me, and the other, a fainter one, was coming from upstairs. "Sara, you saw Silas upstairs, right?"

"Yeah, he was in bed beside me when I got up. Why?"

"Because there is only one beating heart upstairs," I said, hating the fear I heard in my voice.

Before Sara could respond, I rushed out of the kitchen, up the stairs, and threw open the door to Bruce's room. The bed was made, the lights were off, and Bruce was not inside. I checked the bathroom just to be sure and dashed into the hall, nearly colliding with Sara, who was panting to catch her breath at the top of the stairs.

I felt a cold tendril of air brush over my foot, and my

gaze snapped to the guestroom door across the hall. I shoved it open so hard it bounced off the inside wall with a loud bang as I sped into the room. The window stood open, the curtains flapping in the breeze. A loud noise behind me brought me around to find Silas in the doorway, bare-chested, and clutching Sara's sheet around his waist. "What's going on?" he demanded. His face was stony, no hint of sleep, and his chest was heaving from the adrenaline I could smell coursing through his system.

"Bruce is missing," I said. "I only smelled him and Felix in his room, and there is no other scent in here besides his."

Silas nodded. "I'll check outside, you two stay here." With that, he disappeared downstairs and out the front door, leaving the sheet behind and a stunned Sara staring after him.

"You didn't smell anyone else, though. That's got to be good, right? I mean, no one took him. Maybe he just needed to get out and didn't want us to worry," Sara said.

"So he jumped out a window?" I shook my head. "We have to find him. Even if he did leave on his own, he was trying to hide it from us, which means he intended to do something we wouldn't like. Something dangerous."

Sara and I went downstairs to wait for Silas. She told me that she'd seen Felix drive off in Bruce's car around 8 p.m. the night before when she'd come from the shop to get dinner. Bruce had been there at the time and given her a tray to take back to Beth. That was the last she'd seen him.

Silas returned a few minutes later to report exactly what I'd suspected: Bruce had left on his own sometime during the night. Silas then left Sara and me to get dressed before we discussed what to do next.

I tried calling Bruce's cell phone, but it went straight to voicemail. Next, I tried Felix's phone, but it wasn't ringing at all, just dumping me into his inbox. I knew he had to have landed by now. He was probably just somewhere without a signal.

"Do you think Margaux has him?" Sara asked.

"I'm not sure. I don't think he'd go to her, knowing that she just tried to kill him. Maybe he's hiding somewhere? But why wouldn't he tell us?"

"Because he didn't want us to follow," she said.

I glanced at Sara, whose face reflected the panic I felt. "I'm going to go wake up Marcus," I said. "Maybe he'll know what to do."

"You could try," Sara said. "But even if you could, what would he be able to do? He'd be stuck in his room, and all his contacts are asleep. I think we're going to have to wait until nightfall. After that, Marcus can call into work and see if anything's been reported. Surely they would know if there'd been an incident involving the Council leader."

"How can I sit around here and wait? I could go to Seattle. I don't know where Margaux's House is, but I know where the Council House is and the offices."

"And out yourself as a vampire that can be out in the day? And if he's in trouble, or being held by Margaux, what do you intend to do?"

I shook my head. "I don't know. But sitting here is unbearable."

Silas returned just then and went to stand by Sara, placing a hand on her shoulder.

"I'm going to call my mom and aunt," Sara said quietly, covering Silas's hand with her own. "Our Elders have some Council contacts, maybe they can help. Why don't you start calling anyone else who might have seen Bruce? The place he used to work? The tattoo shop he sent you to? Those places might have some staff members who could have seen him. Then, if that doesn't pan out, start calling hospitals."

Hospitals. I thought of the last time I'd been in a hospital. I'd woken up in the morgue. A chill worked its way down my spine, but I refused to think that Bruce could be dead. Sara was right, we needed to get more information and do what we could from here.

So I started making calls. I looked up all the numbers I could find. The Tap Room was unlisted, but I found the number for the bookstore above it. Unfortunately, they hadn't seen Bruce since he'd quit. The same went for the tattoo place he used to work. I was halfway through my list of hospitals when the doorbell rang.

I looked up from where I'd been working to see Silas make eye contact with Sara. "Do you want me to leave?" he asked. "I could slip out the back."

"No. Don't be silly. I want you here," Sara said and stood to go get the door.

A moment later, Sara returned, her mother and Lucia following behind her.

I'd never been so glad to see those two women. They were the closest thing I had to family, besides my mother and brother, who were now no longer part of my life. I felt tears prick my eyes as I locked gazes with Sybil. After a beat, she opened her arms, and I rushed to her, letting her wrap me in a mother's hug. "Sara told me you're not angry with me, but I wanted to tell you again how sorry I am for everything," I choked out.

"Shush now," she said and rubbed my back. "Everything's going to be alright." I let her hold me until I feared I was dripping bloody tears onto her shoulder. I pulled back and wiped at my face. "It's a treat to see you out in the daytime," Sybil said, smiling at me. "Sara told us, but it's still a shock."

I nodded. "Yeah, there have been some developments," I said.

"I should say so," Lucia replied from behind her sister.

I glanced her way to find her staring past me. I turned, but I was fairly certain of what I would see. Sara stood facing us, her expression one of challenge as she stared at her aunt. Silas stood behind her, both hands on her shoulders in what was a very possessive gesture.

"Any developments between Silas and me are our own and no one else's business," Sara said in a tone brokering no argument.

To their credit, both older women nodded and didn't say a word on the subject. Finally, Sybil spoke up. "We have news," she said. "About your friend Bruce."

My stomach dropped, and I felt my knees begin to shake. Sybil grabbed my elbow. "Have you eaten, dear? Maybe we should go sit down?"

I nodded numbly, and the five of us went to the living room and arranged ourselves on the new furniture. Sybil was solely focused on Sara and me, but Lucia's eyes grew wide as she took in the new decor. "Developments indeed," she muttered under her breath.

By the time we were all seated, I was nearly out of my mind with anticipation. I grabbed Sybil's hand and squeezed as gently as I could. "Please, tell us what you've heard."

"Well, one of our Elders was able to talk to someone over at the Council building, who transferred her to Enforcement. Unfortunately, there was hardly anyone there, because all the regular vampires are asleep—"

"Yes," I interrupted. "But she was able to get some information?" I prodded.

"Oh yes. She finally spoke to a human who works there during the day, and he confirmed that they have Bruce."

"What do you mean, they have Bruce?" Sara asked.

"He's being held there. He turned himself in sometime last night, asking for protection."

"And so they're keeping him there? He's there now?" I asked.

"Yes, as far as I understand. The man on the phone said he's being looked after personally by one of the Council leader's own House members. A Marjorie, or Margaret. Yes, I think it was Margaret."

"Margaux?" I asked in alarm.

"Yes, that was it. He's being looked after by Margaux."

40

SILAS

At the mention of Margaux, Sara gasped and pressed against my shoulder. I wrapped an arm around her, stealing a glance at her aunt, who was watching us both, less interested in the conversation than in the two of us across from her. I gave Lucia a quick nod, and to my surprise, she nodded back.

Kate jumped to her feet, wringing her hands. "We have to get over there. We have to do something. She's going to kill him," she said. "He could be dead already."

From the look on Sybil's face, she'd caught on to the issue at hand. Her soft eyes grew shrewd, and her body tensed as she considered Kate's words.

"Those bloodsucking bastards," Lucia cursed.

Sybil grabbed Kate's sleeve as she paced in front of the coffee table. "Sara mentioned a lawyer. Have you been in contact?"

Kate shook her head. "No. I've been trying to call, but it goes straight to voicemail."

"You think he would help if he could?" Lucia asked.

"Absolutely," Kate said. "I think he'd do just about anything for Bruce."

I pictured Felix bent over Bruce's prone form, trying desperately to restart the man's heart. I'd seen him through my wolf's eyes, his bare skin rippling as it burned and re-healed under the midday sun. Yes, I think Kate was right. Felix would do all he could if he managed to get there in time.

Sara nodded beside me. "I checked the Norway cell-coverage maps. There are very few places that are out of range, mostly the mountains. If he's up there, we have to hope he has a way of calling out and checking in soon. He's been gone for less than a day, but when he can't get in touch with Bruce, he'll reach out."

"Okay, but until then, we can't just sit here. Anything could be happening to Bruce right now."

"No," I said, drawing all eyes my way. "Think about it. It's daytime. And with very few exceptions, all vampires sleep during the day. If Margaux is with him, she's passed out right now. For now, he's probably safe."

"If he's still alive," Kate mumbled.

I nodded. There was no reason to pretend he might not be dead. We'd seen what Margaux was capable of from a distance. I shuddered to think what she would be like close up.

"When I talked to our Elder, he seemed to believe that Bruce was not only alive but doing okay. The Council is aware that you're interested in his welfare and that you've a legal representative. I don't think they'll kill him," Sybil said.

"I think we should wait until Marcus wakes and then go to the Council offices," I said, earning a smile from Sybil and a look of disbelief from Kate.

"He's right," Lucia put in. "We'll all go. Show them that

it's not just Kate and her lawyer who are interested in what happens to the human."

Kate looked around the room. "You would all go to try to help Bruce?" she asked.

"Yeah, we would," Sara said. "He's part of this House, part of our family." Her comment drew a sharp glance from both Lucia and Sybil. Sara sighed. "Kate's been granted her own House," she said, emphasizing the H in house. "That's how she's able to live here and not in some stuffy mansion with a bunch of old vampires hanging around."

Sybil nodded. "I see. An interesting detail to leave out. We just assumed a permanent guardianship had been given to Marcus, as long as they stayed together."

"Nope," Sara took a deep breath, her body growing tense against mine. "Kate is the leader of our House—Marcus, Bruce, and mine."

"You've joined a vampire House?" Lucia said slowly, as if she wanted to ensure she was getting it right.

"No," Kate piped up. "She's joined my House, a House of friends, a House of people who care about and support each other."

Lucia sniffed and didn't reply, but Sybil nodded. "I can see that," she said. "And yes, we will all go with you, Kate, and get your House member back. But we need to wait for Marcus. Not only is he a vampire, with more knowledge of the situation than we have, but he also works for the Council. Are you sure he's going to be inclined to side with the House in this matter, though?"

"Yes," Kate said without hesitation. "He's not like some of the other vampires I've met. He's fair and honest. I trust him."

Sybil nodded. "Then we wait."

Waiting around when you knew someone you cared

about was in danger was difficult. All of us wanted to know what was happening at the Council building, and none of us lacked imagination. Around 3 p.m., Kate's cell phone rang. It was Felix.

He was just as upset as we all expected when Kate informed him of what had happened. He was still far from Oslo and a flight back to Seattle, but he promised to get there as soon as possible. He was also determined to reach out to Étienne and try to sort things out along the way. When Kate got off the phone with him, she looked shaken but hopeful.

Around that time, I offered to prepare something to eat for the four non-vampires. Sara followed me to the kitchen as I began to assemble a spread of cold chicken, sliced vegetables, cheese, and a loaf of crusty bread that looked fairly fresh.

Sara was helping me with the vegetables when Lucia entered the kitchen. She peered around, clearly impressed with the new setup. "Did you do all this?" she asked, glancing at me.

"I wish I could take credit, but this was all Bruce. He's something of a House manager and decorator, I guess."

She nodded and crossed her arms. "How far has this gone?" She pointed back and forth between Sara and me.

Sara stopped slicing carrots and pointed her knife at her aunt, clearly preparing to confront her over the question. I raised my hand. Her aunt had a valid point; we were asking them to help us and to trust us, yet we weren't being completely honest with them. Or with each other, I thought. "Sara," I said, meeting the stern gaze that was meant for Lucia. "Is it okay if I answer this honestly?"

Sara snapped her mouth shut, and her eyes widened slightly, but she nodded.

I had seen how brave Sara was in front of her mother and aunt, admitting that she belonged to Kate's House and not asking me to leave, despite knowing they might disapprove of my presence. I decided that I could be brave too. I could trust Sara and her family.

"As far as it goes," I admitted.

Lucia tilted her head and scanned Sara critically. "I don't see any marks."

Sara started at the comment and snapped her gaze to me. Perhaps she thought my answer was about sex. I turned my attention to my mate. "Sara," I paused. It was harder to admit than I'd expected. I truly didn't know how she would react. "I'm bonded to you. I have been for a while, but I know you're not a shifter. There is no expectation that ..." I trailed off. I couldn't get the rest out. I couldn't even say the words, letting her know that she didn't have to stay with me, that she was free to walk away at any time she wished. It was true, but my heart seized up, and I couldn't push the words past my lips. I just stared at her open-mouthed, unable to go on.

"You see how dangerous this situation is for him?" Lucia prompted. "This is what we warned you about."

Sara whipped her head toward her aunt. "No, it isn't," she said harshly. Then she turned back to me, and not only did her tone change, but her whole being softened. "You don't have to be afraid," she said. "I love you. I want to be with you for as long as possible. I'm honored to be your mate."

The relief washed over me so strongly that I thought my legs would give out. I gripped the edge of the kitchen island and dropped my head as tears filled my eyes. Then, Sara's arms were around me, and I realized we were alone in the kitchen, just the two of us.

I held her, breathing in her soft scent and finding comfort in the feel of her body. "Thank you," I breathed. "Thank you for loving me back."

She jerked away from me to look up at my face. "You never have to thank me," she said, her own eyes filled with tears. "I feel like the luckiest woman alive just to be here with you, let alone be loved by someone like you."

I pulled her to me again. My wolf felt very satisfied and very smug at the moment, yet he was also pushing me toward her, urging me closer to our mate to make it more official. I realized she could undoubtedly sense my feelings with her body pressed so close. I also recognized that this was not the right time.

I cleared my throat and gently pulled away from her. "We should probably let the others know that the food is ready," I said.

She nodded and wiped her face, then placed a hand on my chest and gazed up at me with understanding. "Later, when this is through, I want you to tell me more about this marking thing that shifters do," she said.

My hands rose to her shoulders involuntarily, and I nearly pushed her to the floor to show her right then and there what it was all about, but I stopped myself. Instead, I squeezed her shoulders and took another step back, my breath coming fast. I was anything but composed. "Yes," I managed hoarsely. "Why don't you go tell them about the food. I need a minute."

She smiled and patted me on the arm on her way out.

By the time the three women came in to fill their plates, I was back in control, but still felt like my chest might explode with happiness. I knew I had a goofy smile on my face and couldn't take my eyes off Sara, but I didn't care.

Sara loved me. She wanted to be with me. She was proud to be my mate.

Sara's mother, Sybil, was the last to get food. The others carried their plates to the dining room, leaving the two of us in the kitchen. I gazed through the doorway to the dining room after Sara, watching as she took a seat at the far end of the table.

"We've always liked you, I hope you know that," Sybil said, getting my attention. She stood across from me on the other side of the island, watching me with a tilted head and an unreadable expression.

"I ..." I didn't know what to say. "I would never force her ... to stay, I mean. I need you to know that." I looked down, unable to meet her eyes. "I would rather spend the rest of my life alone than make her unhappy," I breathed.

Her warm hand covered mine where it rested on the top of the island. I glanced up. Her eyes were kind and understanding. "I know, Silas. You're a good man. I'm happy she has you. And I know she loves you very much."

I breathed easier and nodded at Sara's mother.

"Now," she said, letting go of my hand and straightening up. "We just have to survive a den of bloodthirsty vampires, so you and Sara can have your happily ever after." With that, she picked up her plate and walked out, leaving me alone and wondering just what we were getting ourselves into.

41

BRUCE

I had miscalculated.

I'd come to the Council thinking it was the best place for me to wait out the hearing and keep my House safe. I hoped at least one of those things would still be true. I wondered how long it would take for them to realize I'd left and figure out where I'd gone. Despite how this was turning out, I hoped it would be a while. I would accept the consequences for my actions, for my mistake, but I didn't want Kate or Marcus to do anything rash.

My leg ached, and I thought about moving it. It was the least of my worries at that moment, but the ache was growing increasingly uncomfortable, and I longed to shift out from under the weight pressing down on it to get some relief. But was it worth it? And even if I decided it was, could I trust my judgment anymore?

The only experience I had with the Council up until then was through the contracts I signed with my former employers, Marcus, whom I respected, and Felix. Felix, who acted as a go-between in his role as a lawyer, had led me to believe in the power of vampire law. He'd dedicated his time as an immortal to help uphold that law, and I assumed that the Council would have the same aims. From my limited experiences, I'd formed a picture of the organization as a steadfast entity that took pride in its unquestionable laws and formality. I should have known better.

If I moved only slightly, maybe it would go unnoticed ... I thought. The ache in my thigh was turning into a throb that matched the dozens of healing punctures across my body. I stared at the ceiling of the cell where I lay. There was a wire mesh covering the top that no human could break through, not that it had been designed for a human. Above that mesh, and tied to sensors that would trigger them if the mesh was breached, were large UV lights that would flood the small space in the event of an attempted escape. It was the same for the walls, the door, and even the flooring. The whole place would light up if a vampire tried to break out from any direction. But it wasn't easy. I'd tried and failed to trigger those lights dozens of times since arriving. Not that I could even attempt it now, bound and trapped as I was.

I hoped by turning myself over to E, someone I'd met briefly and who Marcus considered a friend, that I was placing myself in the hands of the enforcers, who would, presumably, enforce the Council's many laws. In that, I was also mistaken.

It wasn't E's fault. She'd done her very best to do what I asked. She was on her way to providing me with the physical protection I sought when Étienne was notified of my request. Then E was gone. In her place was a male vampire who not only didn't know me but also had little regard for humans and ultimately didn't care what happened to me. It was made clear that I was no longer there for my protection; I was being detained. He had no qualms about allowing the very vampire I sought protection from full access to my cell.

She'd waltzed in with a note for the enforcer and a smile for me, her red-painted lips pulled into a gruesome curve that showed off her already elongated fangs. I knew I was in trouble long before then, but I hadn't truly been afraid until that moment.

I had no idea what time it was now. After years of working around vampires, I knew they were the hardest to wake in the middle of the day. When I'd calculated that it was sometime around noon, I'd tried to move out from under my burden, hoping to have enough time to work on my restraints and make another attempt to trigger the lights overhead. Margaux's eyes had popped open, just inches from my own. Her pupils dilated as she focused on me, and then she clicked her tongue. "Be patient, love. Let me have my rest, and we'll pick up where we left off," she'd said before dropping her head back to my chest and closing her eyes. I hadn't moved since. I needed the rest, too.

It had been hours since then, and my body was now screaming out to move, to shift her hip off my thigh, to bring some relief to my bound hands trapped between her body and mine. I'd finally had enough, I couldn't lie still any longer. Holding my breath, I rolled my left leg inward and pushed up. Her hip skidded down the inside of my thigh, her weight redistributing uncomfortably onto my bound wrists, pressing them into my stomach, but my leg was free. I bit my lip to keep from crying out as the blood flowed back into my thigh and calf, pins and needles stabbing into every nerve as they rewoke. At least Margaux lay still, unbothered by my change in position.

Air rushed back into my lungs as I sighed in relief, bringing with it the noxious smell of her expensive perfume. Then, I felt her nails dig into my sides where her hands rested. *Shit.*

"Ummm, Bruce," she purred as she stretched against me. "Did you sleep well?"

I clenched my jaw so tightly my teeth ground together audibly.

"Oh, don't be like that," she said, pushing herself up and off my body to kneel beside me on the hard platform. New aches and pains began to make themselves known with the removal of her weight. I gazed up at her, and the smug look on her face. She wore a loose red skirt and a sheer lace bra in matching red. Glancing down at my naked body, I felt neither shame nor embarrassment.

She'd stripped me soon after locking herself in. Luckily, she wasn't after sex. She knew I didn't desire her that way, and I had no idea what she desired, besides control. She wanted to get to as much of my skin as she could, she'd explained. She said she'd promised her sire she wouldn't kill me, but I'm reasonably sure I would have died in that first hour had Felix's blood not been in my system still. And, oh, how the taste of it had enraged her.

She screamed that she didn't want to taste my vampire lover in my veins; she was there for me. She hadn't bothered to heal any of her bites, but they had closed on their own, much to her dismay. She'd gone into a rage then, biting just to bite, letting the blood run down my chest and legs until the wounds closed and she had to tear at my skin all over again. Eventually, the bites closed more slowly, and then not at all, and she finally began to drink.

"What do you want, Margaux?" I growled out now as she kneeled beside me. I'd asked several times the night before, but she'd just shushed me and continued her slow torture.

"I would think it would be obvious by now," she said. "I want you to know your place." She bit out the last words. "I couldn't believe it when you turned me down, time and time again. But I was positively stunned when you ran off to join the low-ranking House of an infant." She shook her head, making her dark waves fall around her pale face. "How could you choose her over me? How could you pledge yourself to such an embarrassment instead of joining the most powerful House in the territory?"

She was breathing hard now, whipping herself up in her anger. Her red lipstick had long since worn off, and her bloodless lips were nearly blue against her washed-out complexion, her white fangs poking out from the corners of her mouth. I couldn't help but focus on those two sharp points as she snarled at me. "You were supposed to be mine," she said. And although her words were harsh, she ran a gentle finger over the tattoos that started at my chest, wrapping around each shoulder and covering my arms and neck. They'd been my protection once. My boundaries, my armor. She'd bitten through those tattoos hundreds of times the night before. "I discovered you," she breathed, her anger seeming to cool.

"I didn't want that," I said. "I wanted to choose."

"But you didn't choose me." Her voice was that of a disappointed child. Someone who'd never been told no in all their young life. But this was no child. She wasn't even a woman. She was a hundred-year-old vampire throwing a temper tantrum because she wasn't getting her way. It was disgusting and pitiful at the same time.

I looked into her cold, dark eyes. "No. And I never will," I said softly.

"Then you'll die," she hissed. "I might not be allowed to kill you outright, but my sire will make sure of it. You're not walking out of here."

She launched herself off the platform to stand before the door to my cell. She banged her fist against the solid metal. The cell's walls were made of the same thick metal, with no windows besides a small panel in the door, allowing someone in the hall to peek in or shield themselves if the lamps overhead were triggered. The panel slid back, and the face of the guard appeared. He unlocked the door and let Margaux out, and she left without looking back. Only when the door was shut and rebolted did I sit up and lean against the wall.

I had believed, when I arrived there, that I just needed to hold out until Felix returned. There was a part of me that still cried out that he could fix this, make it right, and save me. But there was a more practical side of me, the side that had been paying attention over the last twenty hours, that chuckled and shook its head at how naive I was, asking if I had learned nothing in all my time in the vampire world. I swallowed and leaned my forehead against my drawn-up knees, knowing that Margaux was right. I was never walking out of there.

42

KATE

Glancing at my phone for the hundredth time wasn't making the minutes pass any faster. It was nearly five, and the sun was set to go down not long after. I was grateful it was winter. Had it been summer, not only would we have had a longer wait, but also less time to get Bruce out of that place before it shut back down for the day.

"Kate, would you please sit down?" Sybil asked. "You're making us all a little jumpy with the fast pacing."

I stopped mid-stride on one of my many laps across the living room. She had a point. "Sorry," I winced and sat down on the other end of the sofa where she was knitting. Knitting. *How did a person knit at a time like this?* I wondered. But then I began to watch the rhythmic movement of the needles, and the way her hands moved as she wound the yarn between the needles and threw off each stitch. It was mesmerizing, and I could see where it might help to dispel some nervous energy. *Huh, who knew?*

I glanced at Sara and Silas, curled up on the smaller loveseat. The looks on their faces were serious. I knew they were worried about Bruce, but I'd also never seen those two so in sync, looking so at ease with each other, so right. Something had happened. I would have to quiz Sara when this was all over, and we had time to worry about other matters.

The last person in the room, Lucia, sat up straight with earbuds in and her eyes closed as if she were sleeping. She couldn't fool me, though. Her breathing was slow, but not the even, steady breaths of sleep, and her heart rate was erratic. It would be fairly normal for long stretches to be followed by a rapid increase lasting ten to fifteen minutes. I wondered if she had a heart condition. *Something else I would have to mention to Sara*, I thought.

Then I heard it.

"Marcus is awake!" I practically yelled as I jumped to my feet. I glanced at the baffled looks pointed my way. "His heart is beating again so that I can hear it," I explained.

I dashed out of the room, but not before I heard Lucia mutter, "That's particularly creepy."

Ignoring her, I ran down the stairs and pounded on Marcus's door. I cringed; I hadn't meant to bang so loudly, and momentarily worried for the integrity of the door itself. Marcus appeared a moment later, the door swinging smoothly on its hinges. "They've got him," I blurted before he'd had a chance to take a breath, or get dressed, I realized.

Marcus stood in the doorway, fully awake but wearing only a pair of boxer briefs that left little to the imagination. "Kate, slow down and explain," he said, turning from the door and disappearing back into his room.

I was confused at first, until I stepped forward and realized he was getting dressed, wasting no time. I appreciated that. While he busied himself around his room, pulling his uniform from the closet and lacing up a pair of boots, I explained everything that had happened. He nodded and asked a few questions here and there, and by the time he was ready to walk out the door, he knew all I did about Bruce's disappearance, Felix's planned return, and the Council's actions.

He had his cell phone out and was dialing as we went upstairs to gather the others. His first call didn't connect, but his second one did. He spoke for a few minutes before hanging up, explaining to all of us that Bruce was currently in a cell ... alone. The person on the other end of the line hadn't been willing to elaborate, but it seemed Bruce was still alive, for now.

"Are you all sure you want to come along?" he asked the assembled witches and one shifter. "I can get you in, but I don't know what complications could arise from all of us being there."

"We all go," Lucia said definitively. The rest of the group nodded. It was decided. We would go together.

Slias and Sara rode with Sybil and Lucia, while I rode along with Marcus. I was glad we would have a chance to talk along the way. I wanted to hear his thoughts on our chances. The rest of us could only guess, but he was the one who knew all the players.

Before I had a chance to ask, my phone rang. It was Felix. "Hello," I answered, putting it on speaker. "I'm here with Marcus, we're on our way."

"Good," came Felix's voice. There was noise in the background that told me he was at the airport already and outside. "I'm having them fuel up the Falcon, but the pilot tells me it's going to take almost eight hours to get there. What's the current situation?"

Marcus filled him in on the latest news. "What about on your end? Have you been able to find out anything new?" Marcus asked.

The phone was silent for a moment, and then Felix answered, "Yeah. They've charged him personally with the death of at least one of Margaux's men."

"But I thought they couldn't do that," I protested.

"They can't, but they did," Felix ground out. "I'm going to remind them of that when I get there. Apparently, the law doesn't matter to them anymore. I'm not suffering from the same affliction."

"Got it," Marcus responded. "I'll get to work on it. Hurry back."

"Will do," Felix said before hanging up.

"What will we do if the Council overrides Felix?" I asked. "He mentioned a higher authority, the International Council or whatever. Surely they would care that the Council here is flaunting the law to appease the leader's House member?"

Marcus winced. "I wish it were that easy. What you're talking about is The Three. There are only three of them, although any one of them can rule on a case. But the problem is locating them and getting their attention. They have representatives, like Felix, who travel and practice law, but it takes one of the three to overrule a Council's decision. As far as I understand, they only meet once or twice a century to review the current laws."

"Well, then, Felix must know how to contact them. Right?"

"He might, but I doubt the Council will wait long enough to get the attention of one of them."

"Well, what the hell good are they if you can't reach out to them when you need them?" I sat back and crossed my arms. "Vampire law is unfair and ineffective."

Marcus let out a sigh. "It's better than nothing, but you're right, it isn't perfect."

I stared out the window, watching the trees give way to lights and buildings, only to be swallowed by trees again as we passed. "How is this going to play out?" I finally asked.

"I don't know," he said, his voice soft and full of regret. "But remember, no matter what happens, we are in this together."

My stomach dropped at the reminder. I hadn't thought about what Felix had told me in the back of the car on the way to accept my seal, when I'd screwed up and caused a scene. Marcus had tied his fate to mine. My punishments would be his punishments. My failures, his failures. "I'm sorry," I said. "I'd forgotten."

He turned his head and glanced at me, his brows drawn together and his grey eyes full of confusion. "Forgotten?"

"That you vouched for me. That you agreed to take responsibility."

He shook his head. "That's not what I was referring to at all," he said. "What I meant was, I support you, I will follow you. I trust your instincts."

"How can you possibly say that?" I demanded. "After all the ways I've messed up over the past months. I still have no idea what I'm doing. I just react ... usually badly."

He shook his head again. "You're wrong. You're doing beautifully, and your instincts have always been good. Except when it came to how Felix felt about Bruce, maybe," he said, his voice full of teasing. "You were way off on that one." He chuckled.

"It would have helped if any one of you had clued me in," I grumbled, but I appreciated his attempt at humor and his support.

"And miss the fun of you finding out on your own?" he asked. "Not a chance."

I snorted at the memory, but then sobered. "We're going to get him right?"

"Yeah. He's going to be okay," Marcus replied.

I knew he was only trying to make me feel better, but I was thankful for the lie. I'd choose it over the uncertainty, holding onto it like something precious to protect, at least for now.

We parked in a garage downtown, near the Council building. The six of us walked through the glass front doors and were greeted by a receptionist next to a set of turnstiles that led to the elevators. Marcus showed his badge and explained that we were there as his guests. Each of us received a guest pass to clip to the front of our clothing. It all felt quite mundane for the headquarters of a vampire organization.

The last time I had been here, I arrived by appointment and was solely focused on not embarrassing myself or my House. The last time, I'd felt scared, unsure, and intimidated. This time was different. This time, I was pissed, but I knew I needed to swallow that anger and get the job done. I didn't want my temper or vampire instincts putting anyone at risk. I would follow Marcus's lead, make sure that Bruce was safe, and hopefully get him out of there without incident.

We piled onto the elevator that took us up to the floor where the Enforcement offices were located. Marcus stood at my side, not saying a word. He was tense, more so than I'd ever seen him. It couldn't be easy for him. This was where he worked; these people we were going to confront were his colleagues and friends. I thought of E. *Where was she in all of this? Would Marcus have to confront her, too?*

We stepped off the elevator, and the place looked exactly as I remembered it. It was still a bustling office building, with people going about their usual tasks, but this time, more than one person stopped to stare at us as we moved across the floor. We weren't greeted by E or anyone else as we turned left and walked down a long corridor that ended in a heavy metal door. A single vampire sat in a chair beside the door. He rose as we approached and whispered into the radio on the shoulder of his uniform. I distinctly heard Marcus's name in the communication.

"Stand aside," Marcus said by way of greeting.

"I can't let all of you back there," the man said, looking somewhat uncertain.

"Waiting for whoever you just called on your radio to back you up?" Marcus asked. "I have full authority to enter the detention area and bring with me whomever I please."

"I was told the prisoners were to have no visitors," the man said.

"Prisoners?" Marcus asked. "How many do you have in cells at the moment?"

"Two," the man replied. "One vampire and one human."

"We're here to see the human," Marcus said. "I need you to get out of our way."

"Marcus," a voice called from the other end of the hall.

We all turned to see a sharply dressed Étienne sauntering down the corridor, his very presence exuding his superiority complex. "This is a rather large show of force for one measly human," he said, immediately marking him as my enemy. He lifted his nose in the air and sniffed as he approached. "Could this be the Heartwoods I've heard so much about?" he asked, glancing at Lucia, Sybil, Sara, and then up at Silas standing behind her. "And their associate," he added with a quirked smile.

"Yes," Sybil spoke up, introducing herself, her sister, and

Sara. When she got to Silas, she said, "And this is my daughter's mate, Silas Hemming."

I raised my eyebrows at that, and so did Étienne. "Hemming?" he asked. "Are you here on official business then or …"

"No," Silas replied. "That's my uncle's place. I'm here to support Kate and Bruce, of course."

"Ah, of course," Étienne echoed. "The human, yes. Well, I assure you he's well."

"I want to see him," I said, pushing my way past Marcus.

"Kate, how lovely to see you again," Étienne said, not selling the sincerity very well. "I'm afraid no one gets in to see the prisoners besides the staff and lawyers, and I'm told your House lawyer is out of the country at the moment." He smiled in a way that made my stomach twist and my palm itch.

"I was told that Margaux was allowed access," I snapped.

The smile fell from Étienne's face, and he leveled his gaze at me. "It is not your place to question my decisions, but if you must know, I thought it would be best for everyone involved if the two of them could work things out."

"And did they?" Marcus asked from over my shoulder.

Étienne straightened his jacket and lifted his chin. "Unfortunately, no."

I'd had just about enough of this. I wanted to see Bruce for myself. I wasn't going to let this pompous ass stand in our way. I focused on him, on his emotions. He was mostly irritated and annoyed, but he was also scared, and that sent a thrill of alarm through me. Unfortunately, I could only influence his emotions, not his thoughts, but it would have to do. I concentrated on what I wanted him to feel: sympathy, acceptance, and generosity. I got his attention with a wave of my hand, and as I spoke, I pushed. "Étienne, please.

I must see Bruce. He's a member of my Household. It is my duty to ensure his safety and comfort."

Étienne sighed. "I understand the pressure of being responsible for one's House members and all their follies. Believe me," he said, sounding tired. "Very well, you may see him, but only you and Marcus are permitted in the holding area. The rest of your party will have to remain outside." He turned and called down the hallway. His call was quickly answered by a young woman vampire who rushed to see what he required. "Yes, please see that Kate's guests are kept comfortable in one of the Enforcement conference rooms while she's busy, would you?" The woman nodded and held her arm out to usher my "guests" away.

No one moved.

"It's okay," I said. "Marcus and I will go talk to him and then come find you." I nodded in encouragement, and reluctantly, the witches and Silas followed the vampire back down the corridor.

Étienne turned and started walking after the group. "You're not going in with us?" I called after him.

He turned, and his annoyance was back in full force. "No, I have better things to do than babysit prisoners." Then he locked eyes with the guard who remained between us and the door to the cells. "If they try to leave with him, you have my permission to shoot. Start with the human." With that, he waved a hand and continued back down the hall.

I glanced at Marcus. His face was set in hard lines of disapproval as he watched Étienne walk away. At least I wasn't the only one who thought this was going poorly. Marcus quickly turned his focus from Étienne to the guard. "Open it up," he said shortly. The man nodded and punched a code into the keypad on the wall. A long buzz followed, and Marcus reached for the handle, holding it open for me.

"It's the first one on the right," the guard said.

I don't know what I expected. But it wasn't a very normal-looking hallway with doors on either side. "This is the jail?" I asked Marcus as we entered.

"Yes, there are ten holding cells. Each is solid metal with a metal mesh ceiling. There are UV lights installed overhead that are activated if a prisoner tampers with the integrity of their cell in any way."

"That wouldn't affect Bruce."

"No, but he wouldn't be able to get through the metal like a vampire might," Marcus said.

The door shut behind us, and we moved to the first door on the right. It was a solid door with a window covered by a panel. Marcus slid the panel to the side and peered in. Whatever he saw made him curse and lunge for the handle, disengaging the lock and sliding it open.

I didn't have time to ask him what was wrong. It all happened in the blink of an eye. One second, I was staring at the whitewashed metal door, and the next, I was looking at Bruce's crumpled body lying on a slab of metal, bound, naked, and covered in streaks of blood.

43

SARA

We had been sitting in a glass-walled conference room for two hours. It felt like we were on display at a zoo. Vampires walked by every few minutes, many of them pausing to stare at the witches' and shifter exhibit. You would think they'd never seen one of us before. But, at least there were snacks.

The vampire who led us there raided the human break room and brought back all sorts of junk food goodies. I was polishing off my second bag of Skittles when Marcus showed up. He pulled open the glass door and dropped into one of the office chairs before looking up to meet our expectant stares.

"Where's Kate?" I demanded.

Marcus sighed. "She's with Bruce," he said. "She refused to leave him in there alone. I can't say as I blame her." He ran a hand through his short, dark hair. I thought this must be tough for him on many levels. These were his people after all.

"How bad is it?" Silas asked from the chair beside me.

"Well, he's not dead, and that's the best I can say. I had to call in a few favors and arrange a blood transfusion. Kate healed most of his open wounds. I don't think there will be any permanent damage. And we managed to find him some clothes."

Lucia hissed air between her teeth. "Vampires," she muttered.

Marcus shrugged. "It's not supposed to be like this," he said, sounding more exhausted than I'd ever heard him. "This place in particular is supposed to be a place of laws and justice, not retribution and torture. This is not what I signed up for." He bowed his head and stared down at the table.

My mom reached over and patted Marcus's clasped hands, which rested in front of him. "We understand. We don't blame you," she said. Frankly, I was surprised that she would offer the vampire comfort, but it was nice to see.

"Thank you," he said, lifting his head. "That's kind, but no matter whose fault this is, it's a mess and it's not right. Bruce shouldn't be here. He never should have been targeted in the first place."

"The question now is, what do we do about it?" Lucia said, sitting across the table, her arms crossed over her chest. She had been quiet until now, not even taking any of the offered snacks. "I assume they're not going to let us walk out of here with him."

"No," Marcus said. "There is going to be a hearing."

"When is that supposed to take place?" I asked, leaning forward. "Kate says it takes the Council ages to get anything done."

"I don't know," he said. "The plan now is to wait here until Felix arrives." He looked down at his watch. "He should be here in about four or five hours. You all don't need to stay if you don't want to. There isn't much we can do until he gets here."

"We're not going anywhere as long as they have Kate and your friend locked up back there," Lucia said.

Lucia's words chilled me. It was true, Bruce might be the one charged with a crime, but Kate was locked in a cell as well. I wondered how easy it would be for her to leave if she chose to do so. Would she be allowed to walk out if things went badly for Bruce?

Marcus must have felt something similar because his face grew even paler than usual, and he squeezed his hands together until his knuckles were white. When he spoke, his voice was steady, but sounded tired. "Okay then, we wait."

44

KATE

The bag hanging from the magnetic hook on the wall was so familiar, yet seemed out of place there, being used for its intended purpose. When we'd first gotten to Bruce, he'd been so pale he almost looked like a vampire himself. I feared he was dead. He lay so still, his bound hands were purple from lack of circulation, and there were bite marks all over his body. I'd been so angry I'd wanted to tear the place apart. It was only my concern for Bruce that focused my attention on what needed to be done.

He looked much better than he had then. I tore my eyes from the IV bag and glanced at him. He was sitting beside me, relaxed, with one leg hanging off the metal shelf we rested on. He was clean, dressed, and no longer bleeding. His cheeks even had a rosy glow again. "Feeling better?" I asked.

"Much." He cleared his raspy throat. "Thank you."

I handed him a cup of water with a straw that Marcus had insisted someone provide for him. "You don't have to thank me, Bruce."

He took a sip and shook his head. "This was my mess

long before you got involved. I should never have brought this to you. I'm sorry I got you mixed up in all this."

I held up my hand. "No. Don't. This is in no way your fault. And, frankly, vampires have been getting away with shit like this for far too long. I don't know how, but we'll get you out of here." I considered the wording of his apology. "Is that why you did this? Turn yourself over to the Council?"

He nodded. "I thought if I could seek protection here, you and the House wouldn't be in danger. I called and spoke to E. I thought she might help me."

I didn't have the heart to tell him that E was in a cell of her own at the end of the hall. Marcus heard her call out to him when we were arranging to get what Bruce needed. She was okay, but was being detained for trying to reach us, to tell us what was happening. Bruce didn't need that on his conscience, however.

Instead of talking about E, I asked, "That's why you sent Felix away, too?"

"Yeah. I knew he wouldn't be on board with my plan." He rested his head back against the wall, looking up toward the mesh ceiling. "I don't want him to get hurt either. He has so much faith in the law and the way things *should be*. I think he doesn't see what *is* sometimes."

"He's an idealist," I said.

"He is," Bruce said, his mouth turning up into a smile.

I glanced back at the IV bag and the tantalizing red liquid within.

"Hungry?" Bruce asked, drawing my attention back to him.

"Oh, no. Sorry, I ate. It's just ..."

Bruce chuckled, which turned into a cough. He took another sip of water before going on. "You don't have to apologize either, Kate. You are a vampire, you know?"

"I know, it's just not a comfortable thought sometimes." I paused and then asked, "Bruce, why did you get involved with vampires in the first place?"

He tilted his head. "At first, I didn't know what I was opting into. Not really. I needed cash, and a friend suggested I sell blood. It seemed a bit strange, selling my blood at a tat shop, but whatever. The money was good. Later, I was given a choice, and I chose to know the secret.

"I suppose that was it. It was the thrill of being a part of a secret most people didn't know about. And the vampires themselves were fascinating. Powerful, ageless, beautiful." He shrugged. "I was young. It was exciting."

"Well, it's still exciting," I mumbled.

"Yes, it is." He nodded. "I didn't think about what my life would be like when I was in my thirties or forties or beyond. I couldn't imagine a time when I would want a calm, peaceful existence." He smiled again, but it seemed sad and full of regret.

We sat in silence for a time until Bruce finally spoke. "You know, I could have hired someone to put together a better outfit for you if I'd known you were going to come after me."

I barked out a laugh. It wasn't what I'd expected, and he was right. "You don't like my jeans and sweater?" I asked, my tone teasing.

"It's not bad, it's just that this is a more formal sort of establishment."

"Says the guy wearing jail-house PJs."

"Point taken. But, in my defense, my clothes were much nicer when I first arrived," he said.

"I'm sure they were," I replied, trying to banish the painful memory of finding him stripped and bleeding only hours before.

Our conversation was interrupted by a noise from the hall. I assumed it was Marcus returning from checking on the others, but when the cell door slid aside, it wasn't Marcus who stood in the hall looking in.

It was Margaux.

She wore a burgundy wraparound dress and heels; her dark waves were pulled up on one side, and she was made up like a 1950s pinup girl. She was gorgeous. And monstrous.

"I heard you were here, but I had to come and see for myself," she said to me, as if she were greeting an old friend.

Seeing her was a shock. I jumped to my feet, positioning myself between her and Bruce.

I knew she'd been in here. I had seen the marks on his body, the way she'd trussed him up and left him to die. The idea that she would come back never occurred to me. She wasn't getting anywhere near him, not while I could do something about it.

She motioned to the IV. "Oh, look, you've been kind enough to fix poor Bruce up for another round. How nice of you," she drawled.

I felt my fangs slide from my gums and opened my mouth, a fierce growl rumbling up my chest. My body was reacting faster than my mind. If I had taken time to think, instead of acting, I might have approached it differently. But at that moment, I was going on pure instinct, and all I wanted to do was rip her apart.

"Oh, honey, you are a baby compared to me. You do not want to pick a fight." She leveled her gaze at me and stepped to the side, as if to circle me and move me farther from Bruce.

"Kate," Bruce said from behind me. "Kate, remember who you are, what you are. You don't have to do this."

Margaux snorted. "You think your little Katie is so much better than me? That she's above fighting? Is that it?" Margaux didn't take her eyes off me the whole time she addressed Bruce, but it gave me a moment to let his words sink in.

He was right. I didn't have to fight her like this. I had better defenses at my disposal. And she was right, too. I wasn't going to win in a fair fight, but this wouldn't be a fair fight.

Maybe it wasn't the better angels of my nature that suggested I not even try to play with her emotions at that point. Perhaps it was the devil on my shoulder that had me flexing my knees. It might have been the darker, more sinister part of me that didn't want her to lose interest and walk away like before. Or maybe it was my vampire nature that wanted her to suffer, suffer like Bruce had suffered. Whatever it was, instead of pushing on her emotions as I had Étienne, I jumped. I launched myself into the air, grabbed hold of the wire mesh overhead, and yanked.

The light from the fixtures above was blinding. It flashed once, twice, three times, and then went off. I let go of the ripped mesh and fell back to the floor as the screaming rose around me. Blinking, I scrambled to my feet and pressed myself back against Bruce, who remained on the platform, trying to protect him from the raging, smoking vampire flailing about the small cell.

And, oh, she was a sight. Her exposed skin was burned as if someone had lit her with a blowtorch, charred in some places and blistered in others. The edges of her dress were singed, smoke rose from the top of her head, and the scent of burned hair wafted through the air.

After a few seconds, her screams died down to ragged

panting, and she turned to lock her swollen eyes on me. "You bitch!" she shrieked.

She looked like she was about to come after me, burned skin or not, and I shook my head. "One more step and I'll do it again," I warned her.

She froze, her body shaking with what must have been incredible pain. "I don't know how you ... You are going to pay for this," she said, her words coming out somewhat slurred from the effort.

"You should go," I said, standing straight and lifting my chin.

Margaux hissed but backed toward the door. Once out in the hall, she slid the door closed with an earsplitting crash.

"I probably shouldn't have done that," I said, letting my body slide onto the platform beside Bruce.

"Oh, I don't know. I thought it was particularly satisfying," Bruce said. He glanced up at the IV and then yanked the needle out of his arm. He put pressure on the site for a moment before scooting closer to wrap his other arm around me, holding me tight. "At least I don't think she'll be back anytime soon."

His arm around my shoulders steadied me. I gave a dry laugh. "Yeah, but I fear she's right, I may have to pay for what I did. I don't suppose maiming another vampire will go unpunished."

"You never know these days what laws will stick and which ones won't," he said, pulling me closer.

We sat like that for a while before we heard noise from the hall again. This time, it was Marcus. And he looked pissed.

"Kate, we have a problem," Marcus said as soon as the door was open wide enough.

"I know. I know. I shouldn't have done it. But, Marcus, she wanted to fight. I couldn't fig—"

"That's not what I'm talking about," Marcus said, interrupting me. He glanced briefly at the torn mesh of the ceiling and edged farther into the hall as if it might light up at any moment. "Étienne has called a hearing for Bruce."

"We expected that," I said. "So, what's the problem?"

"It's in an hour."

45

KATE

"So what do we do? Felix is still hours away. Are there any other lawyers we could speak with? According to Felix, vampire law doesn't apply to humans. Surely any lawyer worth their salt could straighten this out," I said, not quite believing what Marcus was telling me.

"No. Not on this short notice," Marcus replied.

"Well, there's got to be some court-appointed attorney or something? Right?"

"You're thinking of human law. There's no right of representation in vampire law." Marcus looked as worried as I felt, and that alone made me feel worse.

Bruce patted my shoulder where his hand rested. "Don't worry. What will happen will happen, and then it will be over," he said.

"That's not very optimistic," I grumbled.

"No, but it's practical," Bruce replied. "Any words of advice from Felix?" he asked Marcus.

"I've been texting with him, but there isn't much he can do from where he's at. He's been trying to get through to Étienne, but his calls and messages have gone unanswered.

It looks like Étienne is making this move now because he knows that Felix won't be here to intervene."

Bruce nodded. "Sounds about right."

"How can you be so calm about this?" I asked him, twisting to look at his face.

"I don't think throwing a fit will change the outcome. Do you?" he asked.

"No, but it might make me feel better," I said. "I'm not going to stand by and let them impose some sort of punishment on you for acting in self-defense." I glanced at Marcus. It was essential that, whatever I did, he was on board. It was both our futures after all.

Marcus nodded. "We will do whatever's necessary."

Less than an hour later, Bruce and I were escorted out of the holding area and into an elevator I had never seen before. It was likely a service elevator, or one designated for the less desirable members of vampire society to travel between floors without being seen at the front of the building. It was large but dimly lit, utilitarian rather than sleek and modern.

The elevator ascended several floors before stopping and opening to reveal an equally dark hallway devoid of any character. The nicest thing I could say about it was that it was probably easy to clean due to its lack of decoration, carpeting, or even signage.

I walked beside Bruce, who had been left unshackled due to his humanity. He wasn't seen as a threat, apparently. I'd half expected to be shackled myself, given the roughness of the guards, but no one had made a move toward me other than to prod me along with the pointed ends of their long batons.

Marcus had gone to gather the others. He told me it had been surprisingly easy to convince Étienne that the witches and shifter should be present for the hearing. Étienne had been the one to point out that witnesses were welcome, and he hoped they would report back to their communities how the vampires were upholding the laws and ensuring everyone's safety. I'd choked when I heard he'd said that.

As we neared a guarded door ahead, I wished that Marcus were by my side. I had no idea what I would find on the other side of that doorway. I could have used his calming presence at that moment. I still wore the locket. I wore it all the time now, and had managed to keep my hands away from it. So far, that had been enough to keep me from changing it again unintentionally. And it still worked, but the emotions it gave off were only so powerful, and I needed something more to calm my nerves.

As we paused before the door, I reached out and touched the back of Bruce's arm. Calm resolution. That's what I felt when I touched him, and it made me go cold. He didn't think we were going to be able to help him, save him from whatever the vampires had in mind. At my touch, Bruce glanced my way and smiled. "Everything okay?" he asked.

I dropped my hand. "Yeah," I said. "It's going to be fine," I lied. It was just what you said when facing the unknown with someone you care about. But that was stupid. *Why should I lie?*

Bruce took a deep breath as the guard unlocked the door, and I reached for his arm again. "Bruce?" He looked back at me with raised eyebrows. "It's probably going to be awful, but I'll be there with you," I said.

He gave me a genuine smile that touched his bright blue eyes. "I know, Kate. And that's why it'll be okay. Whatever happens." Then he turned and stepped through the doorway, and I followed behind.

After the darkness of the hall, I had to blink a few times as I stepped into the brightly lit chamber. It took me a minute to make sense of what I was seeing, who I was seeing, and where I was located for the proceedings.

The room was nothing like the warm-toned conference room I'd been in before. There were no mosaics, no wood, no color, no life. Everything was made from concrete and stainless steel. The chamber was roughly fan-shaped and reminded me a bit of an old-fashioned lecture space. There was tiered metal seating that rose in front of us, divided into three sections.

The central section consisted of four tiers. At the very bottom, closest to us, in the center, was Étienne, along with three of the other five primary House leaders, including Alexander. Above them, in the three remaining tiers, were vampires whom I presumed were other lesser House leaders. Most of those seats were occupied. On either side of the central Council section were areas with plenty of open seats. It wasn't difficult to spot the witches and Silas, along with Marcus, off to the left. There was a scattering of other vampires here and there, but no one I recognized.

None of that was surprising. What caught my attention was where I stood. When Bruce and I stepped through the doorway into the space, we found ourselves on a small raised platform at the focal point of the room. It was only a few feet off the ground, but it had metal railings along each side with no way down. Guards were positioned on the floor around the perimeter of the platform, all focused inward toward Bruce and me, holding long batons.

The door closed behind us with a foreboding thunk, trapping Bruce and me on the platform with no place to go.

Upon seeing us, Étienne stood. He was no more than fifteen feet away from us. "Ah, Kate and the human. Now we can get started," he said.

"His name is Bruce Fitzgerald," I said, not caring if my annoyance showed through in my tone.

"Yes, we'll get to that," was Étienne's only response as he gathered a stack of papers from a narrow steel desk in front of him. I wondered if he was both prosecutor and judge. I wondered why he was involved at all, given that the dispute directly affected his House.

I glanced at Marcus; his face was lined with disapproval as he sat behind a railing that separated his section from the floor of the room. I noticed that the Council's section had no such barrier.

Étienne held up a document and cleared his throat, drawing everyone's attention to him. "Bruce Fitzgerald, you are accused of the murder of three men employed by House Brogan."

Three men? What was he trying to do? I knew Bruce had admitted to killing one in self-defense, but I couldn't stand by and let them accuse him of all three deaths.

"Wait," I said, not caring whether I was interrupting an official proceeding or not. "He did no such thing. As the leader of House Ward, I take full responsibility for the deaths. Not Bruce. I killed those men."

Étienne lowered the document, his gaze fixed on mine, and smiled. "I see," he said. "This brings me to my second point. Katherine Ward, evidence has been presented to the Council that you are, in fact, not a vampire. And therefore, you are not the leader of any House, and Mr. Fitzgerald is an out-of-contract human, subject to the Council until a new contract can be ratified."

There were more than a few gasps from those assembled. Marcus stood, gripping the railing with one hand. "This is outrageous," he said. "Of course, Kate is a vampire. Her sire is right there." He pointed to Alexander.

"Ah, yes," Étienne said, turning to address Alexander. "Please tell us, Alexander, were you there to witness the transformation for yourself? I believe you when you say you bit her and fed her from your wrist, but were you there to see her awaken? Or when she took her first vein and completed the transition?"

I observed Alexander's features as Étienne spoke. His usual smug indifference wavered ever so slightly as Étienne mentioned my transition and his absence. He hadn't known what Étienne had planned, and that part made me feel a little bit better. Not that I needed or wanted him on my side, but it was good to know that not everyone had come here plotting against me.

Alexander let out an audible sigh before answering. "You know, very well, Étienne, that I was not there for those things. She was kept from me, hidden by another."

"So you can not verify that her transformation was complete or that she was turned at all?" Étienne continued.

"She is a vampire. She has fangs. I've seen them. She is my child. She might be special," Alexander said, some of the smugness coming back into his tone. "But what would you expect from one of mine? If there is evidence, let's see this evidence."

There was a murmuring from the crowd, but Étienne's smile didn't waver. "Yes, of course. Margaux, would you please stand?"

There was some shuffling and movement from a cluster of people seated on the right side of the room, and a robed figure stood up. At first, it was hard to tell that it was Margaux. She wore a long, dark blue robe with the hood up.

But under the bright lights, it was her red, puffy, newly healing face that stared out at me from beneath.

"The hood, darling. If you don't mind?" Étienne encouraged.

With slow, reluctant movements, she lowered the hood, exposing her marred skin and silk-wrapped hair to the crowd. I knew her hair would grow back throughout the day, but I bet it bothered her, and I took pleasure in her discomfort.

The gathered vampires began to murmur again among themselves, and Étienne had to gesture for them to be quiet before he continued. "A member of my House, Margaux, was purposely attacked by Kate in one of our holding cells only hours ago," he said. "The manner of this attack was UV light. Kate activated the lights in the cell, knowing full well that she would not be harmed while Margaux would suffer severe burns."

"I was defending myself from an attack *by* Margaux," I said. "And yes, I triggered the lamps. But only to keep her from killing me and Bruce."

"And yet here you are unburned, unblemished, after a dose of light that burned a vampire dozens of years older than you," Étienne said. "How is that possible?"

"I don't know," I replied. "I guess I'm just different."

"Or not what you pretend to be," he said.

I swept my eyes over the assembled. Besides my friends, the faces all reflected the same expression. I opened my other senses. Most of the vampires were curious, shocked, or disbelieving. Sara, Silas, and the others were afraid, and Marcus was angry. Then I focused on the front row, on Alexander, on Étienne. They were both excited, anticipating, but I suspected for different reasons.

There was one exception. One individual whose

emotions screamed louder than the rest. Margaux. She'd sat back down and covered her face, but she silently bellowed her rage in my direction. If it were up to her, I'd be dead.

"I don't know how I could possibly convince you," I said. "If you won't take the word of my sire."

"I think a series of basic tests would suffice," Étienne said.

The suggestion chilled me. I didn't know where this was headed, but I feared it wasn't anywhere good. I heard the door click open behind me, and before I could turn, I felt something hard jab into the back of my neck. I cried out, and at the same time, my friends did too. I stumbled to the side from the blow, and as I righted myself, I saw that Sara, Silas, Marcus, Sybil, and Lucia were all on their feet. Lucia cradled a ball of fire in her palm.

There was a commotion then as the nearby vampires scurried away from the group. I raised my hand and called out, "No, it's okay. I'm not hurt."

Everyone froze, and Lucia extinguished her flame, but the look in her eyes belied her reluctance. Once everyone was once again calmly seated. Étienne regained the floor. "That was the first test," he said, shooting a glare in the direction of the witches. "That baton delivered a shot of UV light from its tip, and Kate was unharmed."

"I never denied I could withstand sunlight," I grumbled. "You could have just asked me to submit to the test."

Étienne shrugged. "I wanted us all to be sure. I wanted everyone to see how unnatural you are for themselves."

It took a considerable amount of willpower not to roll my eyes. "What's the next test?" I asked.

"Make her drink from him!" The screech came from the crowd. From where Margaux sat. But of course it did.

Étienne nodded. "Some of the oldest of us can indeed

withstand a certain amount of sunlight. But we are the only creatures I know of that drink blood and can heal their prey. It seems like it would be a fair test."

"Absolutely not," I ground out. "Bruce was nearly dead just hours ago and is alive now due only to a blood transfusion. I will not endanger his life to prove a point."

Bruce grabbed my arm. "It's alright," he said. "I trust you."

"No," I hissed. I turned to the Council. "There has to be another willing human in the building somewhere?"

Alexander leaned toward Étienne and mumbled something. Étienne straightened. "Very well," he said, waving a hand at an attendant near a side door. "Find someone, and hurry."

I breathed out heavily. This was ridiculous. "What is all this going to prove?" I asked. "I prove I'm a vampire, and then you let both Bruce and me go? Back to our valley, back to our house, with the assurance that neither you nor Margaux will come after us?"

"I think you're getting ahead of yourself," Étienne snapped at the same time the side door reopened. The attendant was back, trailed by a nervous and confused-looking man in a suit. "Ah, good. Yes, well, not down here. Take him up there, to the accused," Étienne said.

The poor man blanched and was marched out of the room by two guards, only to reappear moments later behind me as the door to the platform opened. He was unceremoniously shoved through the door only to have it shut and locked behind him. He stood staring at me, his back against the door, trembling.

Oh, for fuck's sake.

I turned back to Étienne. "Was there no one else?"

"Drink from him or admit you are no vampire," he declared, like it was a new law.

I glanced back at the man. "Bruce, do you want to ..." I began, thinking that maybe a human might be the best one to approach him first. But then I looked at Bruce. He seemed much better, but still appeared a bit unsteady. That wasn't what made me pause, though. Bruce was human, but he was also huge, with tattooed arms and neck on full display. I, on the other hand, was an average-looking woman. "On second thought, I'll handle it," I said. Bruce lifted a corner of his mouth but nodded.

The crowd behind me was forgotten for the moment. I focused on the man in front of me. He was terrified, and definitely not a willing participant, but he also stood between us walking out of there, and Bruce's probable death.

"Hey," I said softly. "I'm Kate. What's your name?" As I spoke, I focused on the man. I shut everything else out, pulled my walls in tight, and crafted a connection between the two of us. I pushed calm and safety. At least I tried to. It was made multitudes harder because it wasn't what I was feeling at the moment. I tried again. And failed again. I did not want to take from this man by force. I would make this as painless as I could. I knew what it was to be violated like that.

"Kevin," the man stammered.

Fuck. It wasn't working.

"Kevin, that's great. I have something I want to give you," I said, reaching up and unclasping the locket from around my neck. I felt the lack of it immediately, but this was more important.

As I reached forward to place it in his hand, I was interrupted by Étienne. "Hurry this up, please. We don't have all night." Ah yes. Étienne knew Felix, the representative of The Three, was on his way here, and he was afraid the man would spoil his game. If only stalling for a few minutes would make a difference. Felix was still hours away.

I held out the locket, letting it dangle from its chain. Kevin looked confused, which was better than terrified, but he didn't reach for it. I took a breath and grabbed his hand with my free hand and firmly placed the locket in his palm. "Hold it. I promise, it will make you feel better."

Kevin stared at me in disbelief, clutching the locket tightly. The connection between us remained open, allowing me to sense the new emotions as they registered. Simultaneously, his expression relaxed, and I managed to gather enough composure to push him the rest of the way with the little calm I had left.

"Better?" I asked.

He nodded. "Yeah, thanks."

"Kevin, have you ever fed a vampire before?"

He blinked, and I feared all the progress we'd just made would fly out the window, but he nodded again. "Yes, several times."

"Would you be willing to let me take just a mouthful to prove to those here tonight that I am a vampire? There appears to be some confusion, and I want to clarify it for them. I promise I will be gentle and heal you completely when I'm through."

"Oh, yeah. No problem," he said.

"You're a real team player, Kevin. Thank you. Do you have a preferred site?"

He looked me over, his emotions going from willing to anticipatory. "Um, my neck ..." he said.

Oh brother.

Perhaps I should snatch the locket back, I thought

briefly, but then I took a deep breath and smiled. "Sure." If one of us was going to be uncomfortable, it might as well be me. I stepped in close, and he tilted his head back and to the side obligingly. I reached forward. "Do you mind if I undo your collar?" I asked, looking at the starched white dress shirt.

"No, go right ahead," Kevin said, his voice sounding ... sultry.

Thanks, Kev. I undid the top button and pulled the collar of his shirt to the side.

My hesitation only lasted until I brought my face close to his exposed throat. Then instinct took over, and I greedily inhaled the scent of the blood just under his skin. I flicked my tongue out over the pulsing vessel, giving him the benefit of numbing before I began. I felt Kevin's body respond and tried to shut it out, but I was too far in to turn back even if I wanted to.

I struck then, and Keven gasped. And, oh, I'd forgotten how good fresh blood was. Just a mouthful, I tried to remind myself, but realized I'd already swallowed twice. God, he tasted good. I needed to stop.

I clamped my lips together and pressed them to his neck as I withdrew my fangs, trying not to let the blood spill out onto Kevin's nice white shirt. As quickly as I could, I pricked my finger and brought it to the wound, but it was too late. There was a blotch on the collar that would probably never come out.

"Oh, Kevin, I'm so sorry," I said, looking down at the mess.

"What?" he said, slapping his free hand over the spot. "Am I going to be okay?"

"Oh, yeah, you're fine. I stained your shirt, though."

"Okay, that's enough," Étienne said. "We'll compensate

him. Get him out of there, please," he said to one of the guards.

Kevin blinked at me.

"Can I have my locket back, Kevin?" I asked. I had zero expectations at this point.

"Oh, yeah. Thanks," he said, handing it over as the door behind him cracked open, forcing him to take a step.

"And sorry again about your shirt," I said as he disappeared back through the door. I stared at the closed door, wondering who would emerge next.

A sound made me turn around, and I was shocked back into the reality of where I was and what was happening. I'd been so lost in the feeding and Kevin's emotions that I'd momentarily forgotten I was on trial alongside Bruce. It felt good, though, knowing I'd passed Étienne's pointless test and hadn't traumatized a human in the process. I deliberately did not glance in the direction of my friends, and I kept my walls up tight. Having them see me feed, especially in that way, made me feel very exposed.

As I composed myself, the same vampire who had shoved Kevin through the door came rushing back into the room to report to Étienne. After a brief conference, he turned to the assembled group. "We all saw her drink from the human, and it seems that her blood healed him completely. There are no marks at all left on his skin."

There were a few more gasps and murmurs from around the room, but I couldn't understand what the issue was.

"Hey," I said, getting Bruce's attention. "What's the big deal?"

Bruce leaned in. "A vampire's ability to heal, both themselves and humans, increases with age. Someone as young as you should have left at least some scabbing behind."

"Huh. So, I'm acting like an old vampire, and it's freaking them out?"

"That seems to be the crux of it," he replied.

"Everyone," Étienne said, rapping his knuckles on the table beside him to gain the group's attention once more. "I think it's safe to say she's a vampire, but not a natural one. I believe it's best if she remains here in our custody until we can discern what danger she poses not only to us but to the rest of the community. She and Mr. Fitzgerald will both stay with us for the time being." With that, he sat down.

Conversation erupted among the vampires, and the Heartwoods jumped to their feet. Lucia had a palm raised and an expression in her eye that didn't bode well for the Council. Marcus ducked under the railing and headed toward Étienne. Even Alexander had his brows knitted together and was saying something to Étienne that had the leader shaking his head in response.

While all this was happening, the door on the side of the room burst open, and several vampires I had never seen before entered. The one at the front of the group went straight to Étienne, while the others approached the various House leaders. Then, quickly, the murmuring around the room shifted from argumentative to something entirely different.

Marcus stopped halfway across the floor, listening to the messages being delivered, then changed direction, speeding right toward the platform where Bruce and I still waited. The guards halted him just short of reaching us, but allowed him to talk. "One of The Three is in the building and has demanded to be brought up to this proceeding. He's nearly here," Marcus said. His eyes were as wide as anyone else's.

"What does this mean?" I asked.

"I have no idea. No one here has ever met one of The Three, let alone seen them," he replied.

"Well, great," I mumbled. There was nothing to do but wait and see what this uber vampire bureaucrat would do. I glanced at Bruce, who looked lost for words, and I reached out to take his hand. It was warm and would have been comforting if he hadn't been so afraid. I gave it a squeeze, and he squeezed back. At least we were all here together.

We didn't have to wait long. Just as the ripple of news had started, so did the silence spread. It began in the hall and soon filled the entire room. Those who had been standing on the floor slowly edged back and found seats. By the time we heard the click of footsteps approaching, everyone was seated and holding their breath, waiting.

The first people to darken the doorway were nervous-looking vampires, who had presumably been leading the way. As soon as they cleared the entrance, a tall figure stepped forward. He was dressed in a gray suit and a thick gray overcoat, but even in his modern attire, he looked fearsome, as if he had just come from a battlefield. He exuded the power and gravity one would expect of an ancient vampire. His hair was long and loose, and a full beard covered the lower half of his face, yet there was still no mistaking who he was underneath it all.

Felix had arrived early.

46

BRUCE

"**W**as there ever such a beautiful creature as that?" was my only thought as he walked into the room. Of course, I recognized him immediately. It was the same bearded visage I saw each afternoon when I woke up. However, I'd never witnessed him like this, truly allowing himself to be seen. It was exhilarating.

Kate leaned close to my ear. "Is that really him? Or is this some sort of ruse?" she whispered.

"Oh, it's really him all right," I said.

"Étienne," Felix boomed, directing his gaze to the man.

Étienne stood. "Felix, what deception is this?" His voice was strained, and I could tell he was trying to convince himself that this was a ruse as well, but deep down, he already knew better.

"Quiet," Felix said. "I'm done listening to you. Now you will listen to me. Felix Voss is how I'm known in my capacity as a lawyer, but I am not here tonight in that capacity. My true name is Stig Ulvsson, one of the founders of the Council system and a member of The Three." He reached for the inside pocket of his jacket and produced an ordinary-looking wallet. From it, he drew what appeared to be a metal card and held it out. "My ID, if you care to check. Although I understand you're no longer as strict about the rules."

When Étienne made no move, Felix—or Stig—waved to one of the guards who approached cautiously and took the card from him, ferrying it over to Étienne.

Étienne looked at the card with wide eyes and carefully handed it back to the guard with a mute nod.

Stig tucked the card back into his wallet. "I'm surprised you didn't already know who I was. When I signed on as Kathrine Ward's lawyer in the fall, I used my real name. I assume you didn't bother to read the document. Just as I assume you didn't look over the House Charter you signed carefully enough to notice that one of the founding members is Ms. Heartwood, there. A witch," he said, pointing to Sara.

A rumble of disbelief rose from the vampires, and Stig raised his hands to quiet them. "There is nothing in our laws that forbids it. I should know, I wrote them myself," he said calmly.

"But that is not why I've come. I've been keeping track of what's been happening here via text, from Marcus, and I am ashamed at what I've read," Stig went on. "You have taken a system I've spent centuries building, and twisted it to meet your own ends. A human has no place in a vampire hearing as anything but a witness. Our laws do not pertain to them, and we do not enforce human laws upon them. And to accuse a vampire of being "unnatural" because she possesses abilities you don't, smacks of insecurity and pride. There is nothing in our laws that says every vampire must be like another."

He stepped back and looked around the chamber. "We did not empower the Councils to settle petty scores or seek retribution. We established this system to keep vampires safe from the human world and to ensure that we all lived by a set of rules that would promote better harmony with others, both within our community and outside of it," Stig said, glancing at where Silas and the Heartwood sat. "I'm glad you allowed witnesses here today. It is important to include Others in our struggles and let them know we are striving for something better. I'm beginning to understand that this is not a road we can walk alone."

For a moment, his gaze flicked to me, and then he was once again addressing the assembled vampires. "I've revealed myself tonight because I've failed. The corruption of this body is a failure on my part, and I will take a more direct hand in matters from now on. I don't know yet what that will look like, but for now, I'm removing Étienne as leader. The remaining four primary House leaders will share responsibilities for the time being, and I expect each of them to familiarize themselves with the laws. All of them. I'm going to be asking for input as we move forward."

There was a ripple of grumbling and whispering at his declaration. I couldn't tell if it was support or dissent, but it didn't matter. What he said went, apparently.

"Now, I want Bruce Fitzgerald and Katheren Ward released immediately, as well as E Thompson, whom I believe is still in custody," Stig said and turned to face Kate and me where we stood. With the audience to his back, we were the only ones who could see his face, and he fixed his gaze on me, his expression turning playful, and winked. I was stifling a smile when a roar sounded from behind Stig.

"Kate! You will not get away with this," Margaux shrieked. There was a blur of motion and a flash of dark blue, moving too quickly for me to track. And then Stig spun and came to a stop, facing me once more. His playful expression was gone, his face stony and grim. A dark blue puddle of fabric lay just in front of him, and he gripped a silk-covered head in his hands. It was then that I noticed the blood. Margaux's blood pooled from the exposed stump of her neck and dripped from the cloth wrapped around her severed head. He dropped it to the side as the screaming started.

"What have you done?" Étienne shouted, bolting to his feet and staring down at the body of his fallen offspring.

"Enough," Stig bellowed, silencing everyone present. "I've defended my House leader from an attack. That's what I've done. And I'm well within my rights."

"But you have no House," Étienne murmured, seemingly to himself.

"Until now," Stig said. "I filed the paperwork on my way up." He turned and bowed to a stunned Kate, who returned it with a nod. He turned back to Étienne. "Don't bother reading it over. I approved it myself," he said dismissively.

After that, there was a flurry of activity as Kate and I were ushered, more gently this time, off the platform and back into the dark hallway. Instead of being taken back to my cell, however, we were led down an adjoining hallway and out into a large lobby where Marcus, Silas, the Heartwoods, and, of course, Stig waited.

As I followed Kate toward the group, the side of Stig's body faced me, offering a view of his profile. I paused, unsure how to approach this creature. I knew him as Felix, a charismatic dreamer, but the ancient vampire who stood before me wasn't completely unfamiliar either.

Kate joined the others, and Stig's head turned, searching. His eyes locked on mine, and he excused himself from the others with a squeeze of Kate's shoulder and a few hushed words. I watched as he covered the distance between us, unable to move forward myself.

He came to stand before me. It was him, and yet it wasn't. The same eyes, the same soft voice, the same chiseled lines of his face, yet his bearing was different. He was letting the magnitude of his years show through, the complexity of his power. There was no doubt this was who he truly was. "Hey," he said, and his hazel eyes took on a familiar glow.

"I thought you said it was going to take you hours longer to get here," I said.

"Well, there is normal flight time and there is maximum flight speed," he said with a smile. "I thought you said you'd stay behind the wards."

"Hmm. I do remember something about that," I said. "I thought I had a better idea. Turns out, I was wrong."

He shook his head. "No. I was wrong," he sighed. "I led you to put faith in an imperfect system. I put you at risk because of it. I'm sorry."

"Stig, I—"

"Please call me Felix," he said. "I want to be Felix with you, if that's okay? I spent many years as Stig, some of them good, some of them terrible. When we are together, I'd like to be the vampire you met in the beginning."

"You don't have to be someone else with me," I said. "You can be yourself."

"Yes," he nodded, a pink sheen to his beautiful eyes. "That is what I'm asking for. That is who I am when I'm with you."

I didn't have the words to accept what he was offering. I didn't know how to honor such a gift, so I opened my arms instead, and he stepped into them.

I held him then and was aware, after all I'd been

through, that the most healing thing was to hold and comfort this being. My body had been abused, I'd been scared I was going to die on more than one occasion, but there was nothing that didn't feel put back together when I held him in my arms. I was going to be okay. We were going to be okay.

He pulled back and wiped at his face with his already blood-stained overcoat. "I wish I could offer you a handkerchief, but there are no pockets in this getup," I said.

He chuckled. "You would think after two thousand years, I'd learn to carry my own," he said. My expression must have given away my shock because he laughed again. "Come on, you knew I was an older man," he said.

I breathed. "Sure, but not like '*the calendar* old'," I said.

"Technically, I was born sometime around fifty CE, so I'm not quite as old as the calendar. Thank you very much."

"How modern of you," I said.

His face then grew serious. "Bruce, do you still want to be together? Still want to live together? I would understand if you'd changed your—"

"Yes," I said. "More than ever. I mean, you're a member of the House now, right? Where else would you sleep?"

He leaned in then, slowly, giving me time to stop him if I wanted. His cool breath washed over my face, and I parted my lips to accept his kiss. I pulled him closer, welcoming the feel of his mouth on mine, the feel of him back in my arms, even the unfamiliar feel of his beard against my skin. It felt right. It felt good.

This time, it was I who pulled back. Breathless, I looked up at him. "Felix, I don't want this to end any time soon," I said, studying his face. "I'm not asking for two thousand years, and I'm not promising that I'll be ready to ... change tomorrow, but I'm more open to the possibility of something longer term if you still want that."

His expression remained frozen, staring down at me, but his eyes welled with fresh tears, and he pulled me roughly into a tight hug. His lips brushed my ear. "Thank you. Thank you, Bruce. You have no idea how short a human life-span is. I … thank you." He took a shuddering breath, and I could feel his reluctance as he stepped back. "I think they're waiting for us," he said.

Only then did I remember the group of people who were undoubtedly still waiting behind Felix. "Right," I said. "Ready to go home?"

"Absolutely," he said, reaching for my hand.

47

KATE

Back in Marcus's car on the way home, I glanced in the back seat at Felix for the tenth time. He sat there, completely relaxed, with one arm around Bruce and a small smile on his face. "Seriously? Two thousand years old?" I asked.

"I should never have told you," Felix said with a chuckle. "Now it's all you're going to think about when you see me."

"No. I'll be thinking about that ghastly beard," I shot back with a smirk.

Marcus cleared his throat from the driver's seat beside me. "Kate, you should probably show a little more res—"

"Don't even go there, Marcus," Felix said.

"I'm sorry, sire, I—"

"That, right there. I'm no one's sire, and I want you to treat me the same as always. You and I have known each other for over fifty years; let's not let a small thing like this change that. Okay? Just call me Felix and pretend that you never found out, if it makes it easier."

"A small thing?" Marcus said, staring straight ahead, watching the road. "Well, I can try."

"It's going to be easy for me," I said. "I just found out about The Three, and considering what happened to Bruce and me in the hands of one of your sanctioned Councils, I'm not super impressed."

Marcus tightened his jaw and his grip on the steering wheel, glancing in the rearview mirror, presumably at Felix, who laughed. "Yeah, we're not that impressive after all. Speaking of which, what I told Étienne was true," Felix said. "I have filed the necessary paperwork to join your House. I thought it might come in handy, and it did. I don't like breaking laws I wrote myself, and killing Margaux in defense of Bruce, or you, would only work if I were a House member. And she was not walking out of there alive."

His hazel eyes had darkened at the mention of Margaux, but cleared just as quickly. "I can just as easily unfile those papers if you like—knowing now that I'm not that impressive," he teased. "But seriously, I didn't ask beforehand, and I would completely understand if you disapproved of my admittance."

I sighed. "I saw how you kissed Bruce back there, and I figured you might be sticking around, so if it's okay with Sara and Marcus, and Bruce, of course, then it's fine with me," I said. "But what I don't get is why, after saving me— thank you by the way—you would want to be a member of a strange little House out in the middle of nowhere. You're a million years old—"

"Two thousand," he corrected.

"Right, two thousand years old," I continued. "Why not have your own House? Or stay unattached? Why hitch yourself to me?"

He smiled, and even with the awful beard, it was charming. "I simply could not pass up the chance to be a member of the House led by the only vampire-fae I've ever met," he said.

The car grew silent. I glanced at Marcus, whose brows were so furrowed that I could barely make out the confusion in his gray eyes. I turned, looking into the back seat. Even Bruce seemed to have no clue what Felix was talking about. Felix, on the other hand, was grinning from ear to ear, relishing his private joke.

After a long pause, I said, "Vampire-what? Did you just call me a fairy?"

"No, Kate. I called you a fae. And I suspect you are only half-fae or less."

"Fae don't exist, as far as anyone knows," Marcus said. "At least that's what the Council believes. You've been around a lot longer. I'd be interested to know what you remember from any encounters you've had."

"That's the problem right there," Felix said. "And how I'm almost positive that Kate is fae." Seeing our confusion, he continued, "I went to Norway, to the house I keep there. It is very old and very remote. Not many know of it. It is where I keep my journals, at least the oldest ones."

"You have journals that you wrote two thousand years ago?" I asked.

"Well, no. First, I couldn't read or write two thousand years ago. It wasn't until I was turned that I learned some Latin, and even then, I wasn't writing. And the journals I have now have been copied over many times, but that's not the important part. The important part is that I found many entries where I mentioned fae. Among my relationships with beings from the Other communities, like shifters, witches, and humans, I also talk about fae as if they were a well-known part of my life, with their own thriving communities."

"Okay, and how does that prove that I'm one of them?" I asked, not understanding.

He paused and took a breath. "Because scattered throughout my journals, I mention their abilities. And all of them are focused on the mind and one's perceptions, like emotions. However, what convinced me was ... I have no memory of writing those entries or meeting those people. It's as if they never existed. Just like you have no memories of your father," he said.

"So you think ..." I didn't know exactly what he thought.

"I think," he went on. "That at some point, the fae withdrew from the known world and took all memory of themselves with them when they went. I suspect they are the original makers of what the witches call Relics. And I believe your father was one."

"And he what? Just popped back in to marry my mom and then ran off?" I said, feeling defensive for some reason. Which was stupid, because I didn't know the man and had rarely thought of him since becoming an adult. But something there hurt, and Felix had put his finger directly on it.

Felix's tone softened. "I don't know, Kate. It's just a theory. But it's the best I have, and it's a place to start," he said.

I turned back around and stared out the passenger side window. "Thank you for looking, Felix," I said quietly, knowing he would hear.

"You're welcome," he said. "I brought my journals with me, and plan to read through them. Would you like me to let you know what I find?"

"Yeah, thanks," I replied.

Marcus reached over and placed a hand on my knee. I covered it with my own and rode the rest of the way, comforted by his touch and the soothing hum of his emotions.

When we reached our house, it was almost three in the morning. Lucia parked, and I was glad to see her and Sybil get out of their car and head up to the house with Sara and Silas. It felt right to have them here. As we parked, an unfamiliar, though not unexpected, car pulled up beside us. I got out and stretched. I was glad most of my bad mood had worn off, and I went over to greet the driver of the new car.

E got out of the driver's side of the small red sports car and shut the door. "Thanks for letting me crash here," she said, gratitude shining through in her soft green eyes.

"Not crashing, landing," I said. "You heard what Sara said; you are welcome here as long as you want. We are grateful for what you tried to do for Bruce and are happy to have you here with us."

She nodded as her blonde pixie cut ruffled in the wind.

"Let's all get inside, and we can get you fixed up," I said, throwing my arm around the slight woman as we walked up the steps and through the wards.

Back inside, the lights were on, the fireplace was lit, and warm chatter filled the downstairs. It felt good to be home. I led E to the living room, where everyone seemed to have gathered naturally. Sara and Silas were back on the loveseat, Sybil and Lucia were in matching chairs by the fire, and Felix and Marcus perched on either end of the leather couch. "Where's Bruce?" I asked Felix as E took a seat between the two vampires.

"Oh, he had to get out of the prison wear; he went upstairs to change," he said before turning back to what Silas was saying.

Quietly, so as not to disturb anyone, I slipped out of the living room, crossed the foyer, and climbed the stairs to

Bruce's room. I knocked softly on the door and waited. It was only a few seconds before Bruce opened it, fully dressed in a fresh black t-shirt, a pair of dark jeans, and complete with black leather shoes. "You look better," I said.

"It would be hard to look worse," he replied.

"True," I admitted. "Bruce, I wanted ..." I paused. I didn't know where to start, so I decided to begin at the beginning. "I wanted to tell you, I'm so glad you showed up on our doorstep when you did. I know you think you brought trouble with you, but you didn't. You brought direction and purpose, at least for me. You pushed me out of my ratty old pink chair and made me take a stand for something, and it was long past time for it. So, thank you. I have zero regrets, and I'm thankful that you're here," I said, feeling awkward all of a sudden. "So anyway,—"

Bruce stepped forward and wrapped me in a hug, lifting me off the ground in the process. It was a good thing I didn't need to breathe, I thought, just before he sat me back on my feet. I looked up at him through a haze of tears.

He pulled out a black handkerchief and handed it to me. "I'll always be here for whatever you need," he said, leaning in and placing a kiss on my forehead before putting his arm around me and leading me back downstairs to join the rest of the House, the rest of our family.

48

___

SILAS

I t was late afternoon, several days after the events at the Council office building. Things were beginning to resemble their new normal around the house. Sara and I hadn't discussed it in detail, but I was now living there with the rest of the House and E. Since telling Sara about the bond, all hesitation had fallen away for both of us. We were mated, and I felt at peace.

The fresh wound between my shoulder and neck tugged a bit as I bent to grab another dish from the sink, loading it into the dishwasher, and I smiled.

"Hey, Silas? I hear a delivery van out front. Could you go get it and bring it in here?" Bruce asked from where he was preparing some of the fresh groceries he'd bought earlier, chopping everything in advance so this week's dinner prep would be mostly complete.

"I barely heard that. You've been sipping from your boyfriend again?" I asked.

"No comment," Bruce said with a chuckle.

"Sure. No problem. Is it what I think it is?" I asked.

"Yup, vampire food. Fresh off the truck," he said.

"Got it." I dried my hands on a towel and headed to the door. Sure enough, the large chilled delivery van was parked out front, and the driver was already unlatching the back.

I accepted the very large, very heavy box and brought it into the kitchen. It was a good thing the fridge was enormous, I thought.

"Just put it down by the refrigerator. I'll unload it. I've got a new system since we're juggling three blood types now. Everyone's got a favorite," he said.

I set the box down as instructed. "Three, not four, huh? Felix still refusing to eat from a bag?" I asked.

"Felix has a favorite, too," Bruce smiled. "And he doesn't need much."

"Okay," I said, raising both hands. "I'll leave you to sort it out."

We were interrupted by the sound of claws clicking on wood, followed by an excited Arrow barging into the kitchen. This time, it was clear she wasn't tracking the smell of blood. She came directly to me, wagging, whining, and begging for acknowledgment. I leaned down, careful to keep my face out of her tongue's reach, and gave her a good scratch behind the ears. She sat happily and accepted my pets.

A moment later, Sara and Beth entered the kitchen, chatting merrily about shop business and looking for Arrow.

"I should have known we'd find her wherever you were," Sara said with an eyeroll.

"What can I say. I'm the Big Dog," I said, and gave the German Shepherd a final pat on the head.

"Hey, Beth. Before you go," Bruce said. "Felix has been missing Arrow lately. Any chance you can stick around another few minutes until the sun goes down a bit more, so he can get in a game of ball with your girl?"

"Of course, Arrow would love that," she said brightly. "I'll take her to the shop and wait for him there while I finish up a few things." She grabbed hold of a reluctant Arrow's collar and half-led, half-dragged her out of the kitchen and back through the passage to the shop.

Bruce stood up from loading the fridge and shut the door. "Silas, I was going to show Kate her surprise today. Do you want to be there when I do?" he asked.

I looked down at Sara, curled into my side. She smiled up at me. "I think you should. Do we have time?" she asked.

"Yeah. It should be fine," I said. "When do you want to do it?" I asked Bruce.

He glanced at his watch. "She's probably already up, and I'd love her to see it in the light for the first time," he said. "I'll knock on her door and meet you down there?"

"Sure, be right there," I replied as he left the kitchen.

I gazed back down at Sara, my eyes drawn to the white patch of gauze peeking out from under the neck of her top, just where her shoulder met her neck, where I'd marked her the night before. I couldn't help the swell of pride that she was mine, and I was hers.

My eyes wandered from her neck up to her gorgeous face, staring up at me. Her soft brown eyes were troubled, and her neat black brows were creased in the middle. "You nervous about tonight?" I asked.

She sighed. "Yeah, maybe a little."

I pulled her close. "Don't be worried. It's going to be fine. You'll see," I said. I took a half-step back and smiled down at her. "I hear Bruce is ready. Want to come with?"

She beamed up at me and nodded. "Yeah, I'd love to."

We made our way downstairs, the basement door

already open despite the early hour, where Kate and Bruce were waiting. As we stepped through, instead of the large sitting room that had been there, a wall on the left now stood, with a recessed doorway, currently covered by a blanket tacked in place.

"Good morning," Kate greeted us with a wave and a fangy smile. "I'm dying to see what you guys have done with the space," she said, clapping her hands in excitement.

I glanced at Bruce. He was typically fairly stoic, but even he was grinning broadly at Kate's anticipation. "You ready?" he asked, gripping the edge of the blanket. Kate nodded enthusiastically, her dark ponytail bobbing up and down.

Bruce gave a good tug, popping the tacks from the drywall, and pulled away the blanket to reveal a newly installed door that I had routed, carved, chiseled, and sanded into a relief. Kate gasped, covering her mouth with her hands as she took in the honey-colored wood that now featured designs from her artwork.

Bruce had given me a series of printouts from the designs Kate had created for the shop, and I cobbled together a pattern that would work nicely on the door. There were crawling vines, leaves, and flowers. And in the very center was a rabbit from a drawing that Sara said was one of Kate's favorites. The rabbit had been tricky, but I think I got it pretty close.

"Oh my. This is too much," Kate said, shaking her head. "I can't believe ..." She glanced back at me. "Silas, did you do this?" she asked, her voice small with wonder.

I smiled in response and nodded. "It was a pleasure—" I started to say as I was hit around the middle by the grateful vampire, who had locked me in a tight hug. "Oh, hey there," I said, a bit surprised, and then hugged her back. "You're very welcome, Kate."

She pulled back with a sniffle and gave Sara a small smile before Bruce called out to her. "You haven't even gone into the room yet," he said with a chuckle. "Would you like to see the rest?"

"Oh, yes!" she exclaimed and leaped back to the door.

Bruce twisted the antique brass knob and pushed the door wide open. Kate took a tentative step forward into the warm glow of the room. We all followed closely behind as she walked in and turned in a circle, her eyes wide, taking in everything there was to see. Along the wall opposite the door was a long, wooden workbench that spanned the entire width of the space. Underneath, there were dozens of cabinets, drawers, and shelves stocked with everything an artist or craftsperson might need. Above, on the wall itself, some areas held open shelving while others had pegboard, all waiting for projects and frequently used tools.

Along the left side were a series of large tables. The center table was set at an angle, like a drafting table, to catch the light from the large sliding glass doors. There were also cabinets and carts positioned throughout the room, all loaded with things Bruce thought Kate might need down here. I'd even installed a deep wash sink in the corner for washing hands, paint brushes, and supplies. And as a final touch, in the open spaces along the walls were professionally printed and framed versions of the art Kate had done for the shop. The colors were all shades of green, red, and gold, and looked beautiful in the setting.

"You made me an art studio," Kate said in awe.

"Well, yeah. You're an artist. I figured you needed one, and this seemed like a good place for it," Bruce replied. "And out here," he said, pulling back one of the thin cotton drapes to reveal where the back patio had been. "I made an outdoor space just for you."

We all walked over to the floor-to-ceiling windows and looked out. The previously bare patio had been transformed into a lush garden space. Instead of concrete, the ground was covered in moss and flagstone, with plants lining the area and thicker bushes and small trees planted for privacy. At the center of it all stood an arrangement of outdoor furniture, including a small table and a beautiful wooden easel.

"In the spring, there will be flowers, and there are strings of lighting that you can switch on at night," Bruce said, before being swept into his own hug by our vampire-in-charge.

I glanced at Sara, and she nodded. We both quietly backed out of the room, letting Kate thank Bruce and explore her new studio. Back in the hall, at the bottom of the steps, I pulled the door closed and offered Sara my hand. "You ready?" I asked.

She swallowed, looking down, and then placed her palm in mine. "Yeah. I am," she said.

An hour and a half later, Sara and I were pulling into my parents' driveway. I looked at the half-dozen cars and trucks packing the front of the house. I parked the truck between my dad's and my older brother's and looked over at Sara. "You can still back out if you want to," I said. "Just because you're my mate doesn't mean you have to meet my family all at once."

She grinned at me. "No. I want to meet them. All of them. I hope they like me," she said, her voice trembling slightly.

"Don't worry, they are going to love you," I said and gave her hand a squeeze before we got out.

I offered her my arm and we walked to the front door, but before I could reach for the knob, the door swung open. My mother stood in the doorway, an apron tied around her waist and her grey-threaded braid over one shoulder.

My wolf, who'd been blissfully quiet for most of the past few days, sat up straight, interested in how the two most important women in my life would react to one another.

My mother's blue eyes crinkled at the corners as she beamed at us. "This must be Sara," she said.

"Yes. It's nice to meet you," Sara began and held out her hand, but my mother stepped forward and wrapped her arms around Sara, hugging her close.

"We are so glad you are finally here," my mother breathed into Sara's dark curls. "Welcome to the pack, my dear."

49

KATE

The drawing was slowly taking shape. It resembled more of a plan for a future artwork than an actual piece of art. I aimed to create something large and meaningful to hang in the main room of the house, and I wanted a plan first.

The sun had set a few hours ago, and I adjusted the work lamp mounted on the side of the table. The new studio was a dream come true. Not since my year in art school had I had so much space and so many tools to create whatever I desired. I could spend years in there happily, I thought.

Spreading a fresh sheet of vellum over my current plan, I taped the top corners in place and smoothed it down, then fixed the bottom corners next. My pencil hovered just over the untouched surface as a knock sounded at the door. I lifted my head. "Yes, come in," I called out.

The door cracked open, and Marcus poked his head through. "May I come in?" he asked.

"Of course," I said, laying the pencil aside and turning my chair.

"I just wanted to stop in and see the new space," he said,

glancing around, taking in the detail. "I think it turned out great."

"It's amazing, the door alone was worth the wait," I said. "Are you on your way out?" I asked. He was dressed in jeans and a button-down shirt, rather than the all-black uniform I was accustomed to seeing him in.

"Um, no. I'm not sure what I'm going to do tonight, actually."

"Have you quit working for the Council?" I asked. We hadn't talked about it, but he hadn't returned to work since we'd gotten Bruce back.

He shook his head. "I don't know. I still believe in the core mission. I want to help our community and keep everyone safe. I'm just not sure I know the best way to do that anymore."

"I can understand that," I said.

"E quit," he said. "She said she can't go back after what happened. She feels betrayed."

"I can understand that, too," I said. "Maybe you both should sit down with Felix and talk about what he has planned. Maybe there is some way you can still be of service but not have to deal with the existing bureaucracy."

"Maybe," he said. His gaze found mine, and he smiled. "Well, I'll leave you to your work. Come find me if you need anything."

"Thanks, Marcus," I said as he left, shutting the door softly behind him. I felt for both him and E. I understood what it was like to have your life upended, to be betrayed. It would take time for them to work it all out, and I wasn't sure I could help them beyond providing the space they needed and the friendship and support they deserved. I hoped it would be enough to get them through.

I turned back to my work, repositioning the light and

picking up my pencil again. I studied the drawing beneath and made a stroke along the bottom left corner just as someone else knocked on my door.

Seriously?

"Yes, come in," I called again. This time, it was a tall, blond, proto-Norse vampire with a wicked grin on his face. "Hi, Felix," I said as he strolled in.

"Pretty great, right?" he said, indicating the room around us.

"Yes, beautiful. Bruce and Silas did a wonderful job."

"Of course, they did," he said. "And now, you can spend more time making art and less time reading dragon smut."

"Hey, I like my dragon smut," I protested. "Besides, you read it too."

"It's addictive," he admitted. "Have you gotten to the part where Irina finds out she's pregnant, but it isn't Larz's baby?"

"Oh, for fuck's sake, Felix. Did you have to spoil it for me?" I whined.

"Yes, yes, I did," he said and winked at me. "Now, get back to drawing. Don't let me interrupt you."

I sighed as he sped out of the room, closing the door behind him. I debated whether it was even worth trying to get back to work. It seemed that now the whole House was awake, and everyone wanted to stop by. And it was nice, really.

Sure enough, after just a couple of minutes, there was another soft knock, followed by Sara's voice. "Kate? Can I come in?"

This time, I sprang to my feet and hurried to the door myself. "Yes," I said to my best friend, who stood just outside. "Please, come in." I stepped back and held the door open. "I would invite you to sit, but there's only one chair in here. And I'd invite you into the garden, but it's freezing out there at the moment."

"It's fine," she said. "I just wanted to give you an update on the pocketwatch."

I'd done a small engraving on the old watch the day before, filling it with as much calm and serenity as I could, and Sara had reached out to a few places she thought might be interested. I nodded for her to go on.

"I heard back from one auction house in France. I sent the pictures and a description, and they're interested. They require that we send the piece to them, of course, so that they can assess it for themselves. But if it does what we say, they are prepared to bring it to auction for us."

"Did they happen to mention how much they thought they could get for it?" I asked. It wasn't that the House was collectively hurting for money, but so far, I'd refused to dip into Felix's vast wealth. What I'd reluctantly let Marcus, Bruce, and Sara contribute was nearly gone. This was my House, and I wanted to provide for it on my own, or with as little help as possible.

"Yes, they did," Sara said, her eyes sparkling with excitement. "They suggest an opening bid of twenty-five."

"Twenty-five thousand isn't bad," I said, feeling very satisfied. The locket took no more than a couple of hours to complete. I figured I could create many more if they were going to sell that well. Of course, we'd have to consider not flooding the market ...

"No," Sara said, drawing me out of my thoughts. "Not twenty-five thousand," she said, shaking her head, curls bouncing around her grinning face. "Twenty-five million."

The words hung in the air, thickening it so that I couldn't breathe.

Sara stared back at me, waiting for it to sink in.

When I could manage speech again, I reached out and gripped her arm. "Twenty-five million dollars?"

She nodded.

"That's incredible. I could ... I could ... buy a car," I said lamely.

Sara laughed. "Yeah, a few of them if you want," she said. "You could do whatever you wanted with money like that."

She was right. It was an enormous sum. The possibilities were overwhelming. But the more I thought about it, the more I was sure I knew what I wanted to do.

I took a deep breath. "What I want to do is provide for us, for the House. I want us to be stable and ready to help others like Bruce and E if they need it," I said, knowing that I was asking as much as I was telling her what I wanted.

Sara put her hand on mine. "I think that would be a great way to use the money," she said. "And you don't need my permission, but you have it nonetheless—the more the merrier as far as I'm concerned." She smiled then, tilting her head and looking at me shyly. "But if you don't mind, could you set aside a bit for this summer?" she asked.

"Sure, however much you want," I said. "What's it for?" I asked, although I was pretty sure I knew the answer.

"Well, I thought we might host a wedding," she said just before I scooped her into a hug.

When I sat her back down, she looked as radiant as I'd ever seen her. "I can't wait," I said.

She laughed and gave me one final squeeze. "I should go back upstairs. Silas is waiting for me," she said, a deep blush on her cheeks.

I nodded and walked her to the door. "And Sara, if you see Bruce, tell him I need a sofa in here for visitors and a do-not-disturb sign for the door when I want to keep them out," I said.

"Will do," she said before I closed the door behind her.

I returned to my desk and thought about all that had occurred over the past few weeks—the ups, the downs, the changes. I meant what I said to Bruce. I felt now that I had a direction, a purpose, and a way to support that purpose. There was still so much I didn't know about vampires, about running a House, and about myself. But I was confident I could do this. I could be the leader this House needed, and we would face whatever the future brought us, together, as—

The House of Ward.

If you would like to read The Marking, a free, spicy bonus scene from this book, sign up for my **newsletter** and download it now!

Don't let the story end here!
The next book in the series, 'Strengthened by Love and Fire', is scheduled for release in January 2026. Order or Pre-Order now and discover what is next for The House of Ward...

Join the **House** newsletter to get a preview of *'Strengthened by Love and Fire'* and *'The Marking'*, a bonus scene from *'Bonded by Friendship and Fate'*.

ACKNOWLEDGMENTS

Books may be made of words, but they are built on love, patience, and the people you surround yourself with.

To my husband—this book is dedicated to you, but let me say it again here: thank you for being my partner in all things. Your love and encouragement are the foundation beneath every page. This story, and the heart behind it, would not exist without you.

To my Alpha Reader—your early support gave this story wings. Thank you for seeing the spark before it had a shape and for your steadfast belief in me.

To my Beta Readers—your insights, careful reads, and generous feedback helped shape this book into something truer, deeper, and more complete. I'm grateful beyond words for your time and care.

To my children—thank you for being my joy and my inspiration. Your creativity and curiosity keep me dreaming. May you always follow your magic, wherever it leads.

And to my devoted Border Collie—thank you for keeping me on track with your relentless schedule enforcement and gentle nudges. Every writer should be lucky enough to have such a loyal assistant.

With all my love and gratitude,

A.R. Abbott

ABOUT THE AUTHOR

A.R. Abbott writes lush, character-driven paranormal fantasy filled with magic, danger, and desire. A longtime lover of vampire lore and stories of witchcraft, she explores the power struggles, romance, and found families that emerge in supernatural worlds. Based in Northern Virginia, she's also a designer, illustrator, and avid traveler who has lived around the globe with her diplomat husband and their two now-grown children. Her debut novel, *Founded on Blood and Magic*, launched *The House of Ward* series, where politics and passion collide in a hidden world of vampires, witches, shifters, and ancient secrets.

Join the House at arabbott.com

instagram.com/a.r.abbott
facebook.com/arabbott.2024
tiktok.com/@arabbottauthor
bsky.app/profile/arabbott.bsky.social

www.ingramcontent.com/pod-product-compliance
Lightning Source LLC
Chambersburg PA
CBHW061041310726
48969CB00004B/1036